THE GREEN MAN

ABOUT THE AUTHOR

Dan Jones is the Head of European Space Agency Policy at the U.K. Space Agency. He hosts *Chronscast*, the official podcast of Science Fiction and Horror Chronicles, the world's largest online science-fiction and fantasy community, with around 6,000 listeners. His debut novel, the tech thriller *Man O'War*, was published in 2018 and he has a third novel due out in 2025–26. He plays bass for the progressive metal band Sky Empire.

THE GREEN MAN

A NOVEL BY

DAN JONES

ENVELOPE BOOKS

Published 2025 in Great Britain and the USA
by EnvelopeBooks
A New Premises venture in association with Booklaunch

12 Wellfield Avenue, London N10 2EA, England
116 West 73rd Street, New York, NY 10023

www.envelopebooks.co.uk

© Dan Jones
Dan Jones asserts the right to be identified as the Author of the Work in accordance with the Copyright, Designs and Patents Act 1988

Stephen Games asserts the right to be identified as the Editor of the Work in accordance with the Copyright, Designs and Patents Act 1988

Cover design by Stephen Games | Booklaunch

All rights reserved. No part of this book may be reproduced, stored or transmitted in any form or by any means, electronic or mechanical, including photocopying, recording or by any information storage-and-retrieval system, without the written permission of the publisher, nor be otherwise circulated in any form of binding or cover other than that in which it is published and without a similar condition being imposed on the subsequent purchaser.

A CIP catalogue record for this title is available from the British Library

Edited and designed by Booklaunch
EnvelopeBooks 25
ISBN 9781915023544

CONTENTS

IN THE YEAR 1367

13th October	2
14th October	8
15th October	26
19th October	32
23rd October	38
1st November	62
14th November	72
15th November	84
17th November	94
19th November	106
20th November	118
21st November	134
22nd November	146
23rd November	182
24th November	200
1st December	210
2nd December	228
? December (*date uncertain*)	242
8th December	252
10th December	262
11th December	272
15th December	292
16th December	306
17th December	322
23rd December	330
25th December	360

30th December	370
31st December	378

IN THE YEAR 1368
1st January	390
8th March	394

ACKNOWLEDGEMENTS
401

A NOTE ON THE LITURGY OF THE HOURS

The Liturgy of the Hours, also known as the Divine Office, is a set of daily prayers prescribed by the Roman Catholic Church to be recited at specific times throughout the day to sanctify the different hours of the day and to mark the passing of time. The Liturgy of the Hours is divided into specific times of prayer, known as canonical hours. The main prayers of the day are observed at Lauds, Sext and Vespers, and ordinarily last longer than the other offices. Not every office would be mandatory for every monk. The times are not fixed but indicative, and wax and wane in accordance with the lengthening and shortening of the days with the seasons. As Jacobus's account moves from late Autumn through to Winter, the daytime offices would have become more closely clustered on account of the sun rising later and setting earlier.

Matins / Vigil	2:00–3:00am
Lauds (Dawn Prayer)	5:30–6:00am
Prime (Early Morning Prayer)	7.30am
Terce (Mid-Morning Prayer)	9:00am
Sext (Midday Prayer)	Noon
Nones (Mid-Afternoon Prayer)	2:00–3:00pm
Vespers (Evening Prayer: 'The Lighting of the Lamps')	5:00–6:00pm
Compline (Night Prayer: Examination of the conscience to prepare the soul for the eternal night)	7:30–8:30pm

Devotional readings are contained in a set of books also called the *Liturgy of the Hours* or the *Breviary*, in which are organised psalms, hymns, prayers and other material according to the liturgical calendar.

IN THE YEAR
1367

13th October

In which I learn of a forthcoming trial for heretical sorcery while I am staying in Northern Italy

VESPERS

The accused was a woman, and the trial was for sorcery. Her name was Samanta and she was a peasant from a backwater village called Bussana. I assisted in her trial, though whether by chance or by the hand of God, I cannot say.

I had been staying at the newly-constructed Abbazia di San Gerolamo al Monte di Portofino when news of Samanta's indictment came to my notice. Heresy was common throughout Italy and the Holy Roman Empire in those days, and our Holy Father Pope Urban V was constantly raising armies and dispatching holy inquisitors to root out those who challenged the authority of the Church, but the crimes of witchcraft and sorcery were more unusual, and attracted my attention.

The local bishopric had adopted the chapter house of the Abbazia as its new seat, and seeing as the bishop was in residence during my stay, I petitioned that I might attend the trial as an expert, or even preside over it if a judge had not already been appointed. I was an inquisitor myself then, and enjoyed the unique dispensations and privileges that were afforded to that office, including participating in trials and litigations that fell outside my own region.

The bishop, Apollonio Fidelo, seeing no reason to object, granted me his blessing and gave me access to the Abbazia's municipal library, where I spent a few days reviewing the literature and case history on heretical sorcery and witchcraft. I took charge of one of Fidelo's novices, a sober young man called Marco di Verscaccio, who was learning his craft as a notary, and set him the task of collating the cases and information I deemed to be relevant.

Bussana was only a day's travel north from the Abbazia, but Marco and I travelled a few days early to settle in and familiarise ourselves with the trial and its participants. The trial proceedings would take place in the chapter house of a small, rustic abbey dedicated to St Jerome a little way outside the village limits. The abbey was set into the higher ground that climbs away from the Ligurian coast, surrounded by woodland and grapevines. The monks here—Benedictines, as were the monks at the Abbazia di San Gerolamo—welcomed me with some ceremony, and were pleased to have my expertise to support the trial.

After we observed Vespers at the lighting of the evening lamps, my assistant Marco retreated to the cell that had been readied for us, and the abbot, Father Riche, invited me to his solar, where he poured me a cup of the local wine.

Riche explained his extreme nervousness about the charge of heretical sorcery.

'Samanta is frightened,' he said. 'She has a mother and father of good standing and the family has been in this village for generations. She has never hurt anyone, and this accusation is very grave.'

'And who has denounced her?'

'His name is Serge.' Riche frowned, and he crossed himself. 'A wanderer. He has been in Busanna for a matter of months but he is clever with his tongue, and knows how to manipulate people. Ever since the Black Death people have been frightened of the wrath of God, and are easily persuaded to find scapegoats for things they cannot explain. I suspect that this Serge is playing with people's fears, but I do not understand why he would want to.'

'The wrath of God rarely manifests itself on this earth,' I said, 'Whereas His love does so every day. The Black Death may have been an intervention by God, but we must also understand its mechanisms. In China, which was also riven by plague, a scholar named Tsao Yuan-Fung wrote of something called miasma theory, which states that such diseases are the result of the natural cycles and movements of the gases and dusts of the world. Whether he is correct or not, whatever caused the plague here in Europe must have done so under the limits of reality imposed by God, but also must be a natural phenomenon which we can learn to protect ourselves from. I suspect Serge's complaint has some other explanation.'

'Bless you, Brother Jacobus,' said the abbot, taking my hand. 'Those are wise words. I hope you are right. The community will be devastated if Samanta is found guilty. I shall give thanks to God for your efforts, in any case. You say you are an inquisitor? You are most unlike the other one.'

I raised my eyebrows. 'The other one? I read that the trial is being overseen by the local jurist, a secular man with little knowledge of ecclesiastical law. That is why I offered my services.'

'That would be Raffaelle Mavelo. Yes, he has nominal jurisdiction over the procedure, but we are a small parish, Brother Jacobus, and Raffaele has no knowledge of litigations relating to sorcery, so he requested assistance from the Palais in Avignon, and they sent a Dominican monk by the name of Nastagio di Balino to provide the necessary legal expertise.'

I sighed at the mention of that name, and muttered an oath under my breath. This did not go unnoticed.

'You know him?'

'I do. He and I have somewhat different methods. Brother Nastagio is certainly as godly in his intent as anyone you could meet, but almost sinful in his zeal for his work. He spent his early years flushing out the very last dregs of the wretched Waldensian heretics and burning them on pyres. He has recently been modifying and applying the work of the Spanish jurist Nicholas Eymeric to show that the practises of magic, alchemy, sorcery, and demonology are tantamount to heretical depravity, and must be prosecuted with the full authority of the Church.'

Riche crossed himself again in some agitation. 'Heresy? Surely not again!'

'Again?'

'At the end of the last century the followers of Fra Dolcino passed through Cuorgnè, a town not far from here, and they brought with them his penchant for challenging the authority of those such as myself, and his disdain for serfdom. The Dulcinians burned down a tithe belonging to Cuorgnè's prebender, proclaiming its earthly belongings, pitiful though they were, to be a mark of great sin and a symbol of the corruption of the Church, which they were committed on purging. The Ancient Serpent still wends his way to the Garden! The inquisitors, filled with fury, overcompensated. They responded by burning not just the Dulcinians, but everyone who wouldn't or couldn't testify to their whereabouts.' He looked at me very watchfully, all of a sudden on his guard. 'And what about you, Brother Jacobus? Will you seek to prosecute?'

'My position is that the unexplained is rarely as fantastic as it seems. Often mundane explanations can be found for things which have baffled the headstrong. An inquisitor is an instrument of the truth. Some inquisitors forget that. God is the one truth, and He charges us with shining it into the shadows. Let us see how things go tomorrow.'

The abbot's face relaxed for the first time. 'You are correct, Jacobus. The truth must be found, whatever it is. In that case, I shall pray for Samanta, and for the truth to emerge, whatever it may be.

14TH OCTOBER

THE FIRST TRIAL

TERCE

A solitary bell rang from the abbey's chapel to signal the beginning of the trial.

We gathered in the chapter house, which was modestly appointed and cooled by the breezes drifting up from the coast. The chapter house was round and filled with benches arranged into a horseshoe shape which faced a small dais at the centre. This is where the plaintiff and accused would take their questions.

Father Riche, tense and agitated despite our meeting yesterday, greeted me with a kiss on each cheek and a blessing, and introduced me to Raffaelle Mavelo, the secular jurist. Mavelo expressed his gratitude that God had sent not one but two eminent minds to his aid. He was a squat, well-tempered fellow, who wore a colourful but rather worn velvet hat, and hung an eye lens framed in copper wire on a leather thong around his neck. I never saw him put it on his nose, and suppose the trinket was there to show how in-keeping he was with the trends of the time.

I was invited to take one of the seats that had been reserved at the edge of the dais for the judge, legal experts, and notary. In front of us was a battered bureau covered with papers relating to the case, and a copy of the Latin Bible.

'Are you well versed in these matters, Brother Jacobus?" asked Mavelo as his hands flitted over the papers in a skittish tempo. "I have not seen any cases like this in our small parish.'

'Let us hope that this is an aberration, then,' I said. 'Ah, here's our colleague.'

Nastagio di Balino, dressed in the immaculate black cloak of his Dominican Order, approached Father Riche with a hawkish smile and greeted him with a kiss before sweeping to our table, extending his arms toward me.

'My dear Brother Jacobus,' he said, taking my hands and kissing me on each cheek before staring straight at me with shining black eyes. That look would have struck fear into several heretics over the years. 'It has been so long. You look very strong. God must make it so. Father Riche informed me that you arrived last night. What a pleasant surprise. I had no idea you would be interested in witchcraft and sorcery. Brother Severus at the Palais says you spend most of your days buried in books written by long-dead infidel scholars.'

'Not just the infidels, Nastagio. I read the news, too. By chance I was staying at the Abbazio di San Gerolamo when the notification of this trial reached me. I thought I would investigate it further.'

'This one is known for being inquisitive,' said Nastagio to the others, wagging his finger at me with a knowing smile.

'Being inquisitive seems like it ought to be a good quality in an inquisitor,' responded Mavelo. He was smiling, but a tad nervously.

'It can be,' said Nastagio.

Despite the presence of Nastagio and me, it was not an officially inquisitorial trial; it remained under the jurisdiction of the secular arm, so Mavelo was responsible for questioning the complainant Serge first, and then the accused. Samanta stood by the dais, accompanied by a local man-at-arms. She was young, perhaps of an age with the novice notary Marco who was now sitting to my left-hand side with quiet obedience, absorbing events like a sponge. In his lap he held a bundle of scrolls we had borrowed from his Abbazia's library. Yet, whenever his gaze was drawn towards Samanta, he flicked it away in shame.

'Don't be ashamed to look at her, Marco,' I whispered as Serge was brought before Mavelo. 'But do not be judgmental either. Half the things you have heard about women are untrue.'

'And what of the other half?' he said nervously.

'Merely unproven.' As he did not appreciate the joke, I continued. 'Some scholars have written that women are particularly susceptible to the workings of demons. What do you think?'

'She looks so fair,' said the boy in a half-daze. 'Do demons and sorceresses always look like that?'

'Hold your tongue, boy,' I snapped. 'She's just a girl. Leave her alone with your eyes. Father Riche says she is terrified by this wretched gathering, and I believe him. Just do as I say, when I say it.'

Serge, the accuser, a ragged, twitching tatterdemalion, was now swearing his oath of truth against the Holy Book and being addressed by Mavelo. The jurist shakily read from a sheet of paper he held at arm's length from his face. Nastagio would have provided the jurist with this paper containing the right questions to ask, but would not have instructed him how to respond to any cunning answers; Nastagio would doubtless be saving that pleasure for himself so that he could step in and secure the confession. The majority of inquisitors were driven solely by the desire to secure convictions to hammer home the authority of the Church. But conviction was not guaranteed. Stubborn bishops with knowledge of the law could put legal blocks and obstacles in the way of the inquisitor, though in rural communities like this, such instances were very rare. Nastagio no doubt would have been looking forward to pouncing on this lack of legal knowledge.

'Can you confirm your full name?' asked Mavelo.

'Serge di Imperiaza,' said the wretched man, not looking at Riche but staring with some animosity towards Samanta. The girl looked away timorously.

'Serge di Imperiaza, by making this formal accusation with total openness before this community, you accept that if your testimony is proven to be false, or if you retract it or refuse to cooperate, then you will suffer the penalty of retribution which is is to be administered at the discretion of the secular arm.'

'Yes, yes,' said Serge with some disdain.

'What's the penalty of retribution?' whispered Marco to me.

'Most likely a fine. If he cannot pay, which by the looks of him is probably the case, then a flogging. In extreme cases it could be excommunication.'

'Excommunication!' the novice gasped, and he looked at me in shock. 'That is too severe.'

'For bringing a false accusation to somebody? Some would say it is lenient. Have you read the poet Dante's *Divina Commedia*? In his Inferno, Dante journeys through the circles of Hell, with the poet Virgil as his guide. As they descend, each circle becomes more venal —representing lust, anger, violence, fraud and so on. Trapped in the lowest circle are the betrayers, who wander around the figure of Satan himself, who sits encased in a block of ice at its very centre, and with good reason.'

As we spoke, Mavelo continued his questioning of Serge. 'How long have you been a part of this community?'

Serge shrugged. 'Three months. Maybe longer.'

'And do you know this person, Samanta di Bussana?'

'Yes.' Again he answered through a feckless sneer directed towards Samanta, who looked away, repulsed. He must have sensed I was staring at him, for he flicked his eyes momentarily upon me and seemed cowed. It was not much—a twitch of the eye, a slight wane of his smile —but enough to tell me that all was not well within him. Like a dog, he could not hold my gaze for long.

'You have brought against her the charge of heretical sorcery which was used by her person to bring direct harm against you. Will you provide the reason for your knowledge of these charges?'

Serge smirked with ghoulish pride. 'She removed my male member, judge!'

Muted sniggers and prim gasps wafted across from the public benches. To hush the audience, Nastagio spoke up, his barking voice cutting through the chatter. 'Quiet! It is known that such perverse effects can be achieved through humans acting as consorts with demons.'

Mavelo continued, squinting as he read the next question. 'Are there witnesses who will bear out this accusation?'

'The medicine monk will tell you,' said Serge. 'The abbey's infirmarian, Brother Sextus. He knows. I came here with no food and nowhere to stay, and the village people were afraid of me. I don't know why, I did nothing to them. I tried to speak with Samanta, as she has a fair face, but she was disgusted by me and told me that I couldn't pass through this village. Then she touched me on the hip, which made my male member disappear!'

This caused more sniggering and gossiping among the monks and villagers who sat upon the rear benches.

Some of them cried, 'Witch!' and, 'Lies!' and, 'The Evil One is among us!' At my side, Marco looked rather pale at the nature of the charges.

Mavelo looked at Riche, then Nastagio, and lastly me, and opened his palms with a shrug. The jurist was wide-eyed and bereft, evidently lost.

'Is this true, Father?' barked Nastagio to Father Riche, trying to bring some control to proceedings.

The abbot, perhaps naïvely not expecting to be questioned, stuttered as he got himself to his feet. 'Well, I am not the infirmarian. That's Brother Sextus, who is ... but he's not being questioned right now.'

'Come now, under inquisitorial practice we can demand to see any witness,' said Nastagio. His speech was performative and well-rehearsed. In this court he was the king, and he enjoyed it. Even though the trial was being conducted under secular jurisdiction, the presence of two inquisitors meant there was little chance of the secular arm being able to control the proceedings. And Nastagio knew this when he took the lead and asked the crowd, 'Is Brother Sextus among us, then?'

A tall, thin monk sheepishly raised his hand from the rear stalls.

'Come then, Brother Sextus,' said Nastagio. 'If you are the Infirmarian of this place, tell us what you know of this charge.'

Sextus got to his feet unsteadily, and tripped over his words as he spoke. 'Well, I... Serge came to the infirmary in some distress, my Lord, and he told me the same story he has just told you. So I ... I asked him how he could prove such a slander, and he ...' He looked around, evidently embarrassed, but Nastagio's sharp gaze kept a hold of him, and he continued. 'He dropped his breeches and showed me his groin. And, well, yes… there was, as he says, a wound upon him.'

Of course, this testimony brought further gasps from the crowd. Samanta looked horrified by the infirmarian's testimony. Beside me, the colour drained from Marco's young face.

'A mark of sorcery!' cried Nastagio. 'A grave wound upon his *membrum virile*! It is well known that sorceresses have the ability to cooperate with demons to undercut the authority of man by mutilating his masculinity. Sit down, Brother Sextus. Quiet, all of you! Mavelo, there is one more question to ask before you can proceed to interrogating the accused.'

Mavelo, looking quite perturbed by this point, once more squinted at his paper, and read out loud, 'Serge di Imperiaza, do you make this accusation about these matters through any hatred, or grudge, or bias that you hold against the accused?'

Serge rolled his eyes contemptuously before muttering, 'No.'

It was at that point that I seized my opportunity. I called out, 'Are you quite sure about that?'

Nastagio, Mavelo and Serge all looked at me with some confusion, and a breeze of whispers blew through the benches.

'What do you mean?' said Serge, looking at me with some distaste. 'I said no.'

I rose to my feet and spoke very clearly, so there could be no doubt. 'I think you are lying. Did the wound upon your member occur after Samanta supposedly touched you upon the hip, or is it in fact an older wound?'

Nastagio scoffed. 'Jacobus, you are once again late.

We have established the fact of the wound from Brother Sextus, and the causality of the contact with the accused woman. It is clear!'

'Is it?' I replied. 'The charge of heretical sorcery in this part of the world is not very common, so when I heard of it during my stay at the Abbazia di San Gerolamo I was curious. Have you seen the library at the new Abbey, Nastagio? No? It's marvellous. The legal documents from the diocese are kept there now, including a lengthy record of public trials. Some of them date back to the tenth century! There is also an interesting compendium of trials for heresy and sorcery.'

Nastagio smiled a little sourly and waved away my tangent. 'The history lesson is appreciated, Jacobus, as is your enthusiasm for the new Abbey. I shall be sure to visit it when the trial is over.'

'There is no need, Brother Nastagio, for I have brought the relevant documentation with me. This young Novice with me is Marco of Verscaccio. He is learning the craft of scripting at San Gerolamo.' Marco blinked with surprise at being suddenly pulled from anonymity into everybody's focus. 'I tasked Marco with searching the parish records for trials involving conjuration, dismemberment, wounding and harm involving witchcraft and sorcery. Such cases are very rare in this region, but not non-existent. Marco, read the summary readings from those records. Read the most recent first, and work your way backwards, as we discussed.'

Marco coughed, and with trembling hands filed his papers to ensure they were in order.

'On this day,' he began, 'The twentieth of April, in the year of Our Lord 1367, the woman known as Salina Tomassia was convicted and sentenced to death by burning in the tithing of Baddolucco, for the wicked crimes of sorcery and heresy by conjuration which led to the removal of the male member of the plaintiff, Serge de Pescina.' The boy looked at me for affirmation, and I nodded. He continued. 'On this day, the fifteenth of November, in the year of Our Lord 1366, the woman known as Lippa di Alia was convicted and sentenced to death by burning in the town of Molano di Triori, for the wicked crimes of sorcery and heresy by conjuration which led to the removal of the male member of the complainant, Serge Giradius. On this day, the sixth of March, in the year of Our Lord 1366, the woman known as Angelica Rossi was imprisoned and flogged in the village of Cisana Sul Mennasa for the charge of invocation of a magical demon which led to the wounding of the male member of the plaintiff, Serge di Leca.'

Nastagio and I exchanged glances. I knew he was itching to lobby Mavelo to consider these three new Serges as entirely different people but something kept him silent. For all his zeal for fire and blood, Nastagio was no fool. The boy continued, more nervous now than when he'd started, as the murmurs and cackles of the audience began to rise.

'... 1365, the woman known as Riguardatta Santa was convicted and sentenced to death by burning in the grounds of the village church of San Aquila di Barghettia d'Arrenscia, for the wicked crimes of sorcery and heresy by conjuration which led to the removal of the penis of the plaintiff, Serge—'

'Enough!' cried Nastagio, throwing his hands up in exasperation, making young Marco jump and upset his papers. 'How many more crimes must we hear? What are we to draw from this sorrowful list of sin? It is clear that this poor man has been continually assailed by the vices of the female form, and has thus been cursed by the touch of sorceresses throughout the region, not once, nor twice, but many times, and now Brother Jacobus drags his history through the mud in public for the sake of his own intellectual vanity?'

Serge sneered at me, no doubt admiring the twist Nastagio had put on my evidence.

'It is a shameful display, Jacobus,' said Nastagio. 'All you do is condemn the woman by proving the wretched company she keeps. What is the point of all this, anyway?'

I looked down at Marco, who by this point looked positively traumatised. 'Read the last one, boy.'

He flicked through to the final paper, and read aloud once more. 'On this day, on the ninth of February, in the year of Our Lord 1363, the woman known as Elizabeth del Sorrono was convicted and sentenced to a fine of fifty florins by the local justice of the town of Ossiglia for the crime of armed assault resulting in the dismemberment and removal of the male member of the complainant, Serge di Sorrono.'

Among the general chattering in the audience, the jurist Mavelo looked at me with some confusion. 'I do not understand, Brother Jacobus.'

'My lord,' I said, and then I turned to Nastagio di Balino, opening my palms to him in conciliation. 'Brother Nastagio. You know the stipulation in *Decretum*, and *Simony*, and in Eymeric's *Directum Inquisitorum*, that says mortal enemies are not permitted to testify against the accused because of conflicts of interest, which would bring the trial into disrepute in the eyes of men and God.'

Nastagio frowned. 'That's the point of the previous question, Jacobus, which he has already answered. I fail to see how this sorry tale of woe is connected to the question of hatred, grudge, or bias.'

'I put it to you that these women have been tried, imprisoned, tortured, and put to death, on exactly that question! The testimony of this man, Serge di … di, wherever he happens to be, must be therefore disregarded completely in accordance with the authoritative texts. And before you say that it is impossible that a man and a woman could become mortal enemies upon their first meeting, I say that the plaintiff is the mortal enemy of all women.'

Jeers emanated from the benches and the standing audience, but they did not deter me. 'I relate the words of Cicero, who wrote that some diseases manifest through men's desires and passions for women. The Greeks called them *philogyneia*. But there are diseases which are contrary to that, which have fear as their root, and a hatred of women, as displayed in Atillus's Hater Of Women, and these are collectively called *misogyneia*. The court records show that this man Serge admitted to the attempt to rape Elizabeth del Sorrono in Ossiglia, whereupon she defended herself. Serge was not to know she had a knife hidden upon her person, and cut at his manhood as he attacked her. She was fined fifty florins, which she was able to pay on account of her father, a local landowner, and that was that. Enraged with what he saw as a miscarriage of justice, Serge used his new disability to condemn a string of innocent women to satisfy his own miserable grudge against them. And yes, I know what you will say about women being receptacles of vice, but are they not also the closest Earthly realisation of the

Divine, that we mere mortals recognise through the blessed sublimity of the Virgin Mother?' I looked at Samanta, who at this moment was wonderstruck at the unravelling of her accuser's own lies and bias.

'Samanta is guilty of nothing more than being a woman. In the eyes of her accuser that makes her fit to burn, irrespective of whether she is guilty in any legal sense. He, however, is guilty of perjury, and should pay the penalty of retribution in accordance with his oath.'

'What say you, Serge?' asked Mavelo. 'Well, what do you say?'

Serge looked at me with fear and shock. His sneering arrogance was gone, shattered like a window in a storm. He knew I had disrobed his fallacy and broken his spell over the women of the region.

'She was a whore,' he eventually hissed. 'A sack of dung. Elizabeth del Sorrono should have burned! Witch. She cut my cock off! A whore! A whore! All of them, whores!' And then he raised his voice, and repeated the oath, causing the monks in the audience to whimper with shock and the local commoners to guffaw. Nastagio stood with head bowed, pinching the bridge of his nose, knowing the chance of another prosecution had evaporated into the morning air.

The gallery, a mixture of local citizens who had supported the defendant Samanta, and a smaller clutch of nosy people who had probably hoped to see a *bona fide* sorceress, now rose. The scrapes and scratches of their feet signalled the end of proceedings, despite diffident calls to order from Mavelo.

I made my way to the jurist and addressed him. 'Raffaele, Serge must be made to suffer the penalty of retribution. I am sure Nastagio has an idea as to what that should entail, but in the end it is a matter for the secular arm to decide.'

Mavelo closed his eyes, gathered his resolve, and nodded. When he opened them he gestured for Nastagio to join us. By now the chapter house was almost empty, with only a handful of monks and the Abbot remaining. 'It is clear the accusations were false. He freely confesses to it. Samanta should be afforded an apology, and compensation. I think we will manage in dealing with this reprehensible individual by ourselves now. But thank you both for your support; I could not have managed this by myself. And now I shall go and fetch myself some wine.'

And with that, he stood up from his seat, a little bewildered by what had happened, and the trial was over.

VESPERS

Samanta's family greeted me with tears and blessings outside the chapter house after her acquittal. They offered me hospitality, but I had no wish to remain in the village after the trial. I accepted their thanks with grace, but had no inclination to fraternise with the common folk. The wretched Serge was detained by Raffaelle Mavelo's men-at-arms and awaited the penalty of retribution. I just wanted to return to my work.

Ora et labora.

The trial had ended in mid-afternoon, so I remained at the Abbey's chapel to privately observe Vespers with Nastagio and the local monks. We then retired to the refectory to share the Abbot's table for a meal of local wine, ham and bread. If any resentment lingered within the Dominican's breast at having lost the conviction, he was gracious enough not to show it as we broke bread.

The trial had been overseen by the secular authority because the accusation had been brought by a private individual to the secular judge. The Church, despite providing legal and Scriptural counsel, had no authority to appeal or overturn the decision. Nastagio knew this; he accepted that Samanta had indeed been no sorceress, and that my presentation of the alternative version of events had been proven to be correct.

'These sausages are called Hunter's Sausages,' said a smiling Father Riche, presenting us with a plate of ruby-red cured sausage encrusted with tiny diamonds of fat. 'An Etruscan delicacy that made its way to Liguria during Roman times. The boars are typical to the northern reaches and dig deep to feast on the Tartufo Blanco D'Alba. The meat is perfumed and sweet.'

'Those pigs sound like you,' said Nastagio to me, taking a slice of the meat with a sly smile. 'Snuffling the ground for morsels of evidence.'

'Much like the pigs, I would say it is worth it,' I replied, taking a bite. 'The meat is very fine, Father.'

'On that much, we can agree,' said Nastagio, reaching for another piece.

'In that case,' said Father Riche, 'please allow me to fetch a little more.' He scuttled from the kitchen to visit the larder outside.

Nastagio stared at me knowingly when the priest was gone.

'You play a dangerous game, Jacobus.'

I huffed at what I thought was an over-fussy accusation.

'By insisting upon defending those who display all the traits of heresy and sorcery you take huge risks. Sometimes I wonder whether you do it just to satisfy your own vanity.'

'I never defend heretics, Nastagio,' I said firmly. 'But the Church must be careful not to tar the innocent with these black accusations and wrongfully condemn bodies and souls. You know as well as I do the things that happened with the Bogomils, and the Dulcinians. If we proceed recklessly then we do the Devil's work for him. As for my vanity, I confess I do enjoy exercising the gifts granted unto me by God—after all, Christ told us that God admonished the man who buried his talent—but I do try to suppress the vulgarity of pride when the lives of others are at stake. Misplaced vanity would not merely be sinful but mortal for the wrongfully accused.'

Nastagio tore a hunk of bread and used it to mop up some olive oil. 'Your gifts are well regarded, but I fear one day you will be responsible for mistakenly acquitting a real heretic. There are more artful creatures than the poor female and cockless dullard that we saw today, and one day you could find yourself outsmarted by one of them. You talk of Fra Dolcino, but do not forget that he outfoxed the inquisitors so well he escaped condemnation for eight years!' That was a guarded insult, and Nastagio must have noticed my distaste at the second mention of Dolcino that day, for he raised his hands in immediate concession, and continued. 'We both know the destruction that wicked firebrand brought upon the Church. All I am saying is, sometimes I fear that one day you could do more harm than good with your constant recourse to logic.'

'Logic and reason,' I said, 'are the basis of the method of scientia and the advancement of knowledge. Learning improves the quality of man's Earthly life, and brings us closer to God. Aristotle wrote that we are uniquely cognitive creatures, and that we ought to use that uniqueness. Samanta's innocence was based upon a fact I showed to be irrefutable; therefore it was willed to be by God. The salvation of a human can be an echo of the Divine. Everything can be explained. There is no place where this fact is more important than at trial.'

Nastagio scoffed. 'A man cannot live by logic alone. *Hic est enim calix sanguinis mei novi et aeterni testamenti, mysterium fidei.*[1] There is mystery in the world, Jacobus, and sometimes it outflanks logic. You know, you would have made a fine Dominican, if only you had had the tenacity.'

'I don't have enough bark to be one of God's dogs,' I replied.

He smiled at the joke, and for the first time looked quite disarmed and genial. 'If that is so, why do you snuffle around the ground instead of looking to the heavens?'

At that moment Father Riche returned to the table with another plate of the delicious cured boar sausages, which acted as a more perfect mediator between us than any philosophical conclusion.

---

[1] 'This is the Chalice of My blood of the new and eternal testament, the mystery of faith.'

15TH OCTOBER

IN WHICH
I TAKE RECEIPT
OF
A LETTER
DURING MY
JOURNEY
HOME

LAUDS

Nastagio and I went our separate ways the next morning, after Lauds. He travelled immediately with a small company to France, but I travelled south with Marco back to the Abbazia di San Gerolamo. My plan was to stay there a little longer before returning to my home in France, the Abbey de Saint André in Villeneuve, a small town close to Avignon.

Along the route, Marco asked me if I had been worried that my theory at the trial might have been wrong.

'If you were to believe some of the inquisitors, you'd think the whole of the Holy Roman Empire was awash with heretics, sorcerers and succubus demons,' I said. 'It is not the case. As monks are keepers of the knowledge of God, we are tasked with protecting and improving the earthly lives of men and women, as well as preparing their souls for eternity. That is a great responsibility. It means we must be vigilant in telling the difference between the symptoms and signs of the Devil's work, and the symptoms and signs exhibited by diseases.'

'Which diseases do you mean? I would hate to mistake a sick person for a heretic. Or the other way around, for that matter.'

'Good! Have you heard of William Grisaunt, the Englishman? No? He was a student of Oxford and a great physician and astrologer. He developed a theory that the circular red mark upon the skin, which you will know is called the Witches' Teat and is frequently interpreted as proof of the Devil's work, is in fact caused by the bite of a tiny spider that waits upon blades of grass for a person or animal to walk past. Not only did Grisaunt show this, but he correctly predicted the longevity and severity of the disease through the study of the astral horoscope.'

'And what about the disease you talked about at the trial? Mis … mison … .'

'*Misogyneia*,' I said. 'A disease whose symptom is the hatred of women. It is almost too strange to be true! The ancient scholars may have been pagans but they were gifted with great brilliance. Imagine the genius required to decipher a sickness which has no physical symptoms at all, but reveals itself through the behaviour of the sufferer! And Serge did suffer, for all his wickedness. I think the hatred he had for women really did convince him into believing that some sort of sorcery had taken place. It is necessary to approach these things with doubt.'

'Forgive me Brother Jacobus, but I thought doubt was sinful?'

'It is complicated, I grant you. Do not doubt what is Divine, Marco, for God's path is demonstrated by what you see. God's hand is at work in both good and evil. It is well known that Satan, the Evil One, is permitted to perform his tricks only by the Grace of God. God is above all, not least above the Evil One. But we must also doubt what we see sometimes, so we may discern the Devilish from what is merely natural, however unfamiliar it might seem. The trick is knowing when to doubt it.'

Marco thought hard about this. 'I see,' he said, not altogether convincingly.

'If I did not doubt the accusation,' I continued, 'then Samanta—evidently a good Catholic—might have been interrogated through torture, and possibly burned to death, entirely needlessly.'

The novice looked down at the scruffy grey mane of his pony's neck, as if that might provide him some answers, and I smiled. 'My dear boy. What I mean to say is that things are not always as they seem.'

'But don't you fear that you might be mistaken one day? What if you set a heretic free?'

My smile faded just a little. 'Brother Nastagio said the very same thing to me yesterday. Yes, I confess I do fear it. But I also fear that the zeal of inquisitors like him will cause their own judgement to fail, and convict innocent people to death. Even William Grisaunt, the scholar I mentioned, was hounded by his own countrymen so badly he was forced to move to France before his death. I wish that more people would use their judgement rather than be so quick to judge. But the stain of heresy startled the Church so badly that we must remain vigilant. Some clerics see heretics everywhere. I see puzzles waiting to be figured out. It is a perilous line to walk, but walk it I must. Mercy as Christ taught it is the true path to salvation for wayward souls.'

The rest of the journey was unremarkable, until the gloom settling over the Alpine crests was prickled by the ghostly yellow lamplights of the town of Bardonecchia, nestling at the foot of the Monti di Portofino. The sight cheered us, for the Abbazia di San Gerolamo was just on the south side of the town. I stretched my cramping thighs on my tired mount, and with a click of my tongue ushered him on for the final push before nightfall.

COMPLINE

The Abbazia itself was a marvel, a vast P-shaped sprawl atop a Ligurian cliff that basked in the autumnal Italian sunshine during the day, and now sat sleepily as evening descended. The white brickwork still shone with the vigour of youth, and the Benedictines were happy and even proud to commit their lives to the Church in such an attractive setting. A generous tranche of grapevines swept up the north face of the hillside, and a beautifully manicured garden had been established at the front, with a large field of vegetable crops at the rear. Upon crossing the main gate Bishop Fidelo greeted us, and immediately invited me to supper. I said my goodbyes to Marco, whose superiors ordered him to attend Compline, and the Bishop stayed with me in my dorm as I ate the hearty local fare the kitchen had produced for me.

I related the result of the trial to Fidelo, professing neither delight nor despondency at that result, merely accepting it as God's will.

'It sounds like quite the drama. I imagine they were pleased to have you there,' he said, as he poured us a second cup of the excellent wine from his cellar. 'Oh, while you were away, a message came for you bearing the seal of your abbey in Villeneuve.' He picked up a scroll from his satchel and handed it to me. The scarlet wax seal shone brightly with my Abbot's emblem, an X-shaped cross borne by St André, whose name was given to my abbey.

'Thank you, Father,' I said, opening and scanning it. It was signed not by my superiors but my friend Magnus of Holstein, one of the Abbey scribes. Though the contents surprised me, I did not reveal anything to the abbot. 'I'm being summoned back to France. It seems my stay here is at a premature end. I will have to travel tomorrow.'

Bishop Fidelo nodded philosophically. 'Well, it has been … .' He frowned deeply, carefully seeking the correct expression, before smiling and placing his hands upon my own: 'It has been an interesting experience having you here, Brother Jacobus. We do not often have such forward-thinking individuals staying with us.'

I smiled at the double-edged compliment. 'And I am grateful for the opportunity to speak to your monks, to visit your library and to share our knowledge, Father.'

After the meal I settled down in my dorm for my final night in Italy, and read the missive again.

Jacobus,

A matter has arisen which may kindle your interest. Sorcerers have made their way to England. Or so it would seem.

The Cardinals at Avignon wish to pick your brains on this matter, and the Abbot has requested that I summon you back here. I await your return.

Ora et labora.

Magnus

19th October

In which
I return
to the
Abbaye de
Saint André
in
Villeneuve
and discuss
the
letter with
my friend,
Brother Magnus
of Holstein

TERCE

Magnus's short missive played on my mind as I travelled back to Avignon. Sorcery was not much of a known phenomenon in England, and it surprised and worried me that somebody at the papal palace had been so spooked by the mere rumour of it that the cardinals had sought my advice on the matter.

I returned to the bosom of Avignon as I would to an old friend. The relocation of the papacy from Rome to Provence had attracted every type of human activity to Avignon, already a wondrous and teeming city. Thoroughfares trilled with the lilt of lyres plucked by musicians while bards and thinkers conducted open-air debates, mobile theatres played vulgar comedies and street artists of every school demonstrated their skills for all to see, bringing cheer and excellence and light to every street, square and corner. The air was filled with an alchemist's brew of different fragrances—the herby scent of hot stewed game sold on street corners, the sweet Provençal lavender drifting across from the nearby fields and the animal stink of livestock driven through the streets.

My abbey, in Villeneuve, sits atop a hill a little way west of the city. As I left the sights, smells and sounds of the city to ascend the hill, the Palais des Papes hove into view across the Rhône. I shall always be moved by the sight of the Palais rising above the river in Provence. It remains man's greatest feat of engineering, a monument to the glory of God and an impregnable fortification that has preserved the holiness of His office on Earth.

I always viewed the Palais as man's greatest attempt to free himself of his earthly bonds and touch the hem of the Divine.

It was a fine October day and the two towers of the

Palais—Trouillas and Campane—caught the afternoon sun, their lustre all the more splendid against the austere Romanesque blocks of the Cathedral. My heart was lifted by the sight of them, those twin beacons of modernity and antiquity, the wondrous scholasticism of Aquinas realised in stone and clay, sweat and blood.

I found Magnus in the abbey chapel on bended knee, praying before the relief of the Virgin in a bath of light that cascaded in from the coloured glass windows. Standing behind him, I coughed politely and he turned with a start before gently smiling, rising to his feet and embracing me warmly.

'Jacobus.' He stepped back, holding the sleeves of my robe. 'Wonderful to see you. You received my letter?'

'Of course. I came as soon as I could. There was a trial in Italy. For sorcery, no less.'

'Sorcery! Lord save us. All of a sudden it is everywhere.'

'Not quite. An innocent woman was the victim of a false accusation and was saved from the fire. No sorcery, no sorceress, no demons. Just plain old human lies and deception. Too many people are obsessed with sorcery these days, Magnus. I worry about where it will end.'

Magnus and I were similar ages; we had been novices together in Vienna yet he carried his approaching middling years with a sort of willing weariness, as if he welcomed the onset of advanced age and all the infirmity and dotage it brought. He gripped my arm and frowned. 'I also fear where it is headed and I pray for you.'

I rolled my eyes. 'Don't you start, Magnus. I've already had Nastagio di Balino issuing veiled threats to prosecute me the moment I make a mistake. I don't need my friends saying the same thing. Whatever happens to me will be God's will and God has already shown that false accusations of heresy and sorcery can be overturned. We have seen it done. As long as I can apply logic and reason to what is illogical and unreasonable, I feel that I should. Pope Urban is a man of great learning and founded the place of our own education. Does that not persuade you that such avenues of understanding ought to be pursued?'

Magnus looked affronted. 'That's not what I meant. I meant that you cling with such enthusiasm to the doctrines of people like Grisaunt and Bacon and even—' (he hushed his voice at this point, even though we were alone in the chapel) '—the infidels that perhaps you are as single-minded as those you claim to oppose.'

'I do not oppose the Inquisition,' I said firmly. 'Far from it. I have worked in that office with pride. And I resent your insinuation.'

He waved away my protest, clearly thinking I was being pedantic. 'You know I don't doubt you, Jacobus. All I would say is, do not wander far from the scholastic wisdom of the good Doctor. The world has its truths, and they are not to be stretched by the whimsies of philosophers. In work we may find the truth. Work and devotion. That is our motto.'

'*Ora et labora*,' I said, acknowledging his concern, though in truth I thought he was being finicky. 'Come, it is almost Sext and afterwards I must eat. The road has been wearying. Tell me what you know about what is happening in England.'

'Well,' he said, in that gossipy manner that monks sometimes have. 'It is as I stated in my letter. There have been reports of sorcery in the northern regions of England.'

'That's a queer thing itself. England is not known to be infected by sorcery, is it?'

Magnus shrugged as we continued to walk through the chapel and out into the cloisters. 'The Holy Roman Empire is rife with it, or so the reports would have us believe. It wouldn't take much for it to cross the water and settle in England. Or at least, for word of sorcery to cross it.'

'So you have doubts already?'

'I refrain from making judgements.'

'Very wise, too, for now at least. Let us not build our house upon sand.'

'I simply know too little, Jacobus. Inquisition and heresy are not my fields. I received this notice second- or perhaps even third-hand, after the cardinals received a message from a minor nobleman of England, and the cardinals commanded the abbot to summon you back here, and he discharged that task to me. All I know is that children are involved. For children to be exposed to such corruption before they are absolved through the sacrament of baptism breaks my heart and I have prayed for whatever souls may be caught up in it. If it is so, then such depravity may indeed be the work of demons.'

'Or so they say.'

Magnus half-smiled, a common expression among the austere Benedictines of our Order. 'Or so they say, indeed.'

23RD OCTOBER

IN WHICH
I MEET
THE CARDINALS
AT
THE PALAIS DES
PAPES
IN AVIGNON
AND FORMULATE
A RIGHTEOUS
CONSPIRACY

PRIME

When the day of the cardinals' meeting to discuss the English problem arrived, Magnus and I rose early to cross the river to the Palais so we could spend time in the papal library. It hosted the largest and most glorious collection in Europe, an affirmation that the basis for good Catholicism is the pursuit of knowledge that might improve our earthly lives. Magnus, being not only a scribe but also a devotee of Francesco Petrarca, indulged himself by reading letters by the Italian that were publicly available to visiting scholars. I lost myself in the recent astronomical advances of the infidels and found a remarkable theorem by the esteemed scholar Ibn al-Banna demonstrating how fraud could be committed through the use of irregular measuring devices. Al-Banna's idea was that vessels might display lines of measurements—for measuring liquids, say—which were erroneous to an imperceptible amount to the defrauded but over time would add up to a significant embezzlement. Treachery by degree, one might call it. Even if a ewer was fraudulent to the count of a mere drop, over time it would pour out an ocean of sin. I supposed that even were a measurement only slightly incorrect, it would lose its meaning and become a symbol of perversity against God's laws—a stain on order itself. I thought the supposition rather tangential to the general tone of the infidels' work, yet intellectually stimulating. It was as I was considering this that I was summoned to the Consistory by one of the Palais monks and so left Magnus to flick through Pertrarca.

The Alley of the Consistory is high, bright and coloured with glorious rainbows of light streaming in through the stained glass, illuminating its magnificent frescoes. They depict every detail of the Gospels, as well as examples of the excellent charitable and holy works undertaken by the Church, while also acting as a visual history of the papacy outside Rome. The Consistory itself houses a number of smaller and more private conference rooms where the cardinals and their administrators, a collection of secular and monastic bookkeepers, lawyers and scribes, take care of the more mundane tasks of the Papal See. I was called into one of these smaller conference rooms.

While the great Gothic engineers designed and built the palace to mimic divine sublimity, its deeper recesses were given to more utilitarian expressions of devotion. The small conference room was sparsely appointed, giving the working monks there the space and tools to complete their theological paperwork. One large window, somewhat dulled by grime, afforded a view across the Rhône and allowed a modest stream of light to illuminate and inspire the papal administrators. At the centre of the room was a square oak table, upon which were stacked an unruly accumulation of scrolls, papers, books, contracts gathered into large folders, and all the messy paraphernalia of the scribe: ink and inkpot, a quiver of quills and brushes, some of which were neatly lined up anticipating work, while others were smudged with ink, their bristles stiff with recent use.

Abutting the table were three seats but only two figures: an elderly cardinal whom I did not recognise and a scruffy monk, bent over a pile of books, who looked up at me by way of greeting, before frowning, averting his gaze and continuing with his scribbling.

'Good morning, Brother Jacobus,' said the cardinal from his seat, extending his episcopal ring, which I duly knelt to kiss.

'Your Eminence,' I replied. I dared not say more; it was not for me to speak without being spoken to.

'I am Pierre de Banac, of Castres,' he nodded, 'newly-appointed to the College.' Soft in his features and rheumy in his eyes, the cardinal wobbled his head from side to side as he spoke, and gestured to the empty chair, which I gladly took. I had often thought that the College of Cardinals was more hospice than college, a cosy reward for a life of prayer, work and devotion to God and the Church, a few years of meagre earthly comfort before passing.

There was a pause as I sat down and then Banac nodded in that queer, lateral wobble again. 'Your recent endeavours in the field of heresy and sorcery have caught the eye of the palace.' Before I had time to take this as a compliment, he continued. 'So your interventions might prove useful in this particular instance. I hear you are a learned man, Brother Jacobus.'

I coughed and furrowed my brow, hoping that through his milky gaze he might not be able to see me, for I suspected he was trying to lure me into some sinfully proud boast. 'I do what I can with the gifts given to me, and try to broaden my knowledge of the world where I can. *Speculum mundi*.[2] We must shine light upon all things, drawing them from the shadows and into the field of understanding.'

'Quite so. *Adorote devote latens deitas*,[3] as sings the Doctor. I also understand that you particularly enjoy using your talents in the area of …'—he waved his arm around weakly, mulling over the correct phrasing—'…

---

[2] A looking-glass world, i.e. one to be observed and looked through.
[3] I am devoted to the Hidden God. Love that which is hidden, to be brought into the light.

the natural philosophies, to determine true heretics from those falsely accused.'

'Once or twice, Father.'

He scowled at me and waved away my false modesty. 'Bah! I may be at the end of my days but do not take me for a fool. I hope for better times, when the stink of heresy that has blighted so much of this age will be ended and the gifts of young followers of the natural philosophies such as yourself will be used to better ends. Personally, I fail to see how your distinctive application of scholastic knowledge will lead to the eradication of this plague upon the Holy Church, but right now, your scepticism may come in useful.'

I nodded in agreement, though in truth I wasn't sure what I was meant to be agreeing with. I wanted to ask why I had been summoned but Banac forestalled me by ordering the young monk to produce a letter. The monk sifted through his papers and produced two scrolls which he handed to the cardinal. Banac unrolled the first of them, trapping one end of it under a glass paperweight containing a feather, and laid down the other, still rolled up, beside it.

'This first letter was penned by Albertus of Aachen, a scholar and physician from the Empire who settled in England as a boy,' he said, gently touching the rolled-up missive. 'This second is from the blessed Archbishop of York, John of Thoresby.'

I shifted in my seat. John of Thoresby had earned the respect of the papacy after his diligent work as King Edward III's representative, first in the Court of Rome and latterly at Avignon. Pope Clement VI had ordained him Bishop of St. David's and he had built a reputation for deep spirituality, Solomon-like wisdom, devotion to the proper functioning of the Church and a robust knowledge of secular law. If Thoresby had seen fit to endorse the letter written by this Albertus of Aachen, it would be taken seriously by the cardinals.

Banac propped a pair of eyeglasses upon his crooked beak with a quivering hand and began to read.

> To my Blessed and most Holy Fathers,
>
> I write humbly requesting your assistance in a grievous matter that has blighted a constituency of our northern earldom of Northumberland. I write, in my capacity as Lord Chancellor, because the Teutonic epidemic for sorcery and pact-making with demons seems to have arrived on our fair shores from across the North Sea.
>
> I relate this sorry episode on behalf of House Hayeford, whose lord is Thomas de Hayeford. Lord Hayeford is a bannerman of House Percy, who you will know has the ear of our noble king Edward III. You will appreciate, then, that this matter has gained some local significance.
>
> In and around the Parish of Berwick there has recently been a spate of infant disappearances. The first happened two years ago, when two children by the names of Griselda and Henry went missing from the village of Thornton. Over the following eighteen months, fourteen more children were taken from their families. In some cases, and only after lengthy searches, bodies were recovered. The reports suggest that the bodies had been altered—in some unnatural and upsetting manner.
>
> You must know that this has set a panic in the hearts of mothers and fathers throughout that parish. Their vigilance has not availed them. Disappearances happen with an alarming regularity. Every three months two infants go missing. With no apparent explanation, there are whispers of sorcery, demons and wicked things lurking in the forests.
>
> While it is incumbent upon all of us as diligent Catholics

to ensure that heresy and sorcery are eradicated with all the Holy force of Saint Peter, I believe there is more here than meets the eye.

Berwick and its surrounding villages lie upon the borderlands of England and Scotland. It is a much disputed piece of land. The Scots and the English often encroach upon each others' terrains, and while we presently sit in a moment of blessed but uneasy truce, it will not take much to ignite this kindling.

In addition, rumours abound that there are Scots who, while part of our own Catholic confession, practise dark magic with demons, and that it is they who whisk away young children and murder them. In addition to this being a grievous sin, it undermines the authority of the Church that we do not intercede.

At the same time, it would be equally damaging to the Church if we did intercede, only to find that either the rumours or the suspicions of guilt proved false, for then we would have offended against the innocence of those we had falsely punished and thus furthered the ends of those heretics and liars who wish to make the Church appear foolish, hasty and errant.

My role has always been an envoy of peace and resolution. I wish to preserve the peace, and not let cross-border relations deteriorate. While crimes committed in these areas fall under the authority of the local judiciary, because of the geographical disputation of the region and the sensitive nature of the accusations, I believe a more neutral presence would be more conducive to arriving at a satisfactory resolution. I therefore humbly implore that Papal representatives armed with sufficient theological grounding are dispatched to uncover the mystery to the satisfaction of all those involved. We do not have the ecclesiastical or scholastic knowledge of sorcery here. I therefore lean on your own intellectual experience, and pray for your assistance.

I should add that news of these terrible events first reached me nearly a year ago. I then commanded the Head Master at St. Peter's School to dispatch his most skilled physician to investigate the matter. That man was Albertus of Aachen. He is German and came to England as a boy with his parents. His report contains the full and morbid details of everything that has blighted the stricken town of Berwick. I hope his report will inform your decision on the matter.

I look forward to your response. Until then, fare well, always, and pray for me, most honoured and holy masters.

John of Thoresby,
Lord Chancellor
Archbishop of York.

Banac rolled up the letter and placed it beside the second scroll. 'Well, Brother Jacobus? What is your opinion?'

I cleared my throat and frowned. 'My opinion, Father? Of whether the purported sorcery is genuine? Or whether we should send help to the parish of Berwick? I cannot say. May I hear what is said in the other letter to which he alluded, the one from the local physician?'

'I think not, at this time.' With that, he handed both scrolls to the scribe. 'Ensure these are filed in the library accordingly, boy.'

The novice nodded and removed the two scrolls from the desk, handling them as though they were made of glass. I tried not to show my disappointment at not being able to discover the content of the physician's scroll.

'Father—'

'Speak not, unless you are spoken to, Brother Jacobus,' snapped the cardinal, eyeing me distastefully. He then nodded, as though he had made an internal decision. 'Some of the cardinals are due to meet this afternoon to discuss administrative matters and this English allegation of sorcery will be one of the items we discuss.'

'With respect, Father, this is not an allegation but a rumour. Thoresby wrote that—'

Banac shot me an expression of horror that I had again spoken out of turn and I snapped my mouth shut.

'You will join us at the cardinals' meeting, Brother Jacobus.'

I shifted in my seat and the hairs on the back of my neck bristled. Why did they want me at their meeting? A chance to test me, and see whether I could help, or a chance for the more fervent of the inquisitors to unpick my methods and ensnare me? 'I will join you, Father.'

'Yes. You may observe prayers at Sext with the other monks of the palace. Guillaume here will escort you to the chapel. That will be all.'

The young scribe looked up from his scribbling and gave me a simple sort of look. I puffed out some air through my nostrils in resignation. I would have to tread with care, as ever.

SEXT

After Sext, Guillaume silently escorted me back to the Consistory, his brows rumpled. Whether this expression was due to the familiar, devotional solemnity that grew upon the faces of most monks over time or his discomfort at being around me, I could not say. The young man had taken his vows and would not unseal his lips.

He showed me the interior room where the cardinals would be holding their meeting. I was the first to arrive and took a seat at the edge of the room to wait. It was the same sort of room as the one in which I'd met Pierre de Banac but larger and messier, perhaps reflecting the cluttered thoughts of the monks themselves. A large, circular oak table and rustic chairs filled the centre of the room, while bookcases lined the walls, stuffed with books and papers. Upon the table were carafes of wine, loaves of bread, a dish of juicy olives, cloves of garlic macerated in oil and bowls of delicious fruits: quince, apples, winter berries, peaches and figs, all of which would have been grown on the grounds of the Abbey de Saint André in earth that I had probably tilled with my own hands.

A lump formed in my throat as I pictured the cardinals devouring the fruits of my labour while they quizzed me over my use of natural philosophy to defend people accused of making pacts with demons.

I did not have long to stew, for the four cardinals arrived a few minutes later. Pierre de Banac was first, walking with a stick, his head wobbling—with palsy, I now realised. Then came Cardinal Rinaldo Orsini, a Perugian; Cardinal Gilles Aycelin de Mantaigu, a veteran from the Battle of Poitiers; and Jean de Blauzac, the Cardinal-Bishop of Sabina. Like four ancient scarlet birds of prey, they filed in and took their seats with funereal patience. Behind this austere quartet scuttled another monk, a scribe, carrying the tools of his craft.

The Perugian Orsini was the only one to acknowledge me and gestured towards the food. I waited for my seniors to help themselves, then took a humble cup of wine for myself and a few scraps. After the introductions were made, the cardinals settled into their meeting, hardly casting a glance my way, as if I wasn't there at all. They discussed many problems, never seeming to reach any sort of solution, and turning the entire meeting into more of an elevated exchange of gripes and canards than a serious discussion of papal matters. Nevertheless, they covered a wide range of matters. They considered the Gascony nobles and their lobbying of King Charles V, a subject the cardinals found sore, presumably because of their own habitual inveigling of the French crown. They discussed Pope Urban V's long-established desire to return to Rome. They also grumbled at length about the chaos of the old Papal states around Rome, much of which was caused by the activities of an Englishman, one John Hawkwood, and the band of mercenaries he called the White Company. Hawkwood and his men had been merrily laying waste to Northern Italy and exploiting the turmoil. This last point provided a convenient segue into the problem which I had been called to investigate.

'Ah, yes,' said Pierre de Banac, rifling through the papers in front of him. 'Our young intellectual, Jacobus of Vienna, has already been briefed on John of Thoresby's correspondence about the allegations of sorcery in northern England.'

I had been feeling a little drowsy from the food and wine and the rambling discussions, but at the mention of my name, I sat up and blinked.

'Has he?' said Jean de Blauzac, a fierce, haggard-looking individual with dark, insomniac eyes. Blauzac scowled at me as he tore apart a hunk of black bread that released the scent of cumin into the air. 'Well, it is clear to me that the honourable John has the right of it and makes a reasonable request. We have jurisdiction over both England and Scotland, so our presence would ensure a neutral investigation. You realise, Brother Jacobus, that you have been summoned because you have demonstrated an aptitude for investigating difficult conundrums, and displayed a singularly intellectual objectivity of your own.'

I swallowed. The cardinals were masters of ambivalence and could as easily indicate satisfaction as admonition. 'I try to use intellectual rigour as Aquinas taught it,' I said. 'But never more so than when the lives of faithful Catholics are put at risk through the overzealousness of a small number of inquisitors.'

'And you have saved people from death by burning on at least one occasion?' Blauzac continued, chewing the cumin-scented bread.

'I have saved innocent people, yes, Father.'

'Please, relate an example.'

I settled myself, cleared my throat, took a sip of wine, and ordered my thoughts. Then I recounted the precise details of the recent trial in Bussana and proceeded to carefully relate the tale of Serge and Samanta. All the while Cardinal Blauzac chewed upon pieces of the black bread, inspecting me with his sleepless eyes.

After I finished my report the cardinals said nothing. A couple of them looked as though they had drifted off to sleep. A tightness stretched across my chest and neck, and I coughed to fill the silence, rousing Blauzac into speaking once more.

'Very good, Brother Jacobus. Well, I say that if those accused individuals were found to be innocent through the determinations of a faithful brother such as yourself, then it is truly God's will. I believe he would make an ideal papal representative in this English matter.'

I breathed out a long breath I hadn't realised I was holding. The cardinals had not summoned me here to grill me on my suspected assistance of accused heretics after all. I sat up, eagerly. The thought of travelling to England as an emissary of the palace excited me.

'Indeed, I'm sure he would be,' said Cardinal Gilles

Aycelin. 'But we would be mad to agree to it! The English are not to be trusted, and in any case we are at war with them!'

'"We, we, we",' said Blauzac, waving his hand dismissively. 'You will have to forgive the blessed Cardinal Aycelin, Brother Jacobus, for he frequently has trouble differentiating between the Mitre and the Crown. A few too many coups d'etât at Poitiers.'

Orsini made a grunting, grimacing sort of laugh at Blauzac's joke. This annoyed the old Frenchman Aycelin, who pummelled the table feebly. 'The English have always been a thorn in our side. Yes, they can produce good and godly men, and I hold no man in higher esteem than John of Thoresby, so do not mistake my attitude as a dismissal of his blessed self. But, as a race, the English are untrustworthy and uncooperative. Think of the multiple problems they present! Not only does the wicked White Company march across the northern states of Italy, humiliating and openly embezzling the Church at every turn, but their king arrogantly dismisses our Holy Father's very reasonable and legal request for ransom repatriation. I know you will say that King Edward is an upholder of the Church but if that were truly the case, he would have humbly recognised that the Church is in dire financial straits and acceded to our requests that he pay our fiscal debts. Instead the English Parliament asserts its wretched sovereignty' (he spat the word out with distaste) 'and makes decisions on behalf of the Crown while the godly Edward is obliged to maintain an embarrassed silence on the matter. It is an obscenity caused by that filthy Magna Carta of theirs. *Caudam movet canis*!'[4] He

---

[4] The tail wags the dog!

banged the table again, before calming himself. 'So I am inclined to refuse aid to the venerable John in this particular instance.'

'So you would take a chance on heresy establishing a root in England?' asked Orsini. The Perugian was slimmer and more aquiline than his peers, and had a habit of stroking his chin, even while speaking. 'Any spat with the English, however distasteful, does not warrant such a risk. Better to send young Brother Jacobus to root out heretics and put them to the sword.'

'But the point of this request is to uncover whether or not sorcery is in fact the root cause of these happenings at all,' said Blauzac.

'Which we cannot do unless we dispatch someone to do so!' finished Orsini.

The old Frenchman Aycelin nodded in reluctant agreement. 'Well then, Brother Jacobus, what do you say? Do you believe that these mysterious goings-on are the result of illicit magic?'

I cleared my throat once more. 'It is impossible to say, Father, without conducting an investigation. But I am certain that whatever is causing poor children to disappear and die will have left traces and clues behind, and from studying those clues I could determine whether the cause is magical or earthly.'

'So you believe that magic could indeed cause such things?'

My chest heaved as though an icy blade had been pressed to my throat. That was one of the first questions inquisitors usually asked the accused. Of course, I had not been formally accused of anything and this was no trial, but to an inquisitor, that question was an examination, an exploration of my character, and Aycelin's utterance of it put me on my guard. I chose my words carefully.

'As an inquisitor, I know this to be the case. And I have seen it. The question of whether sorcerers exist is fundamental to the paradigms of Catholicism itself. There is no reasoning that supports the heretic notion that sorcery does not exist, and my work is based upon this. I must differentiate true sorcery from things that simply look like it. For just as Matthew said to watch for wolves in sheep's clothing, I would add that we must beware of sheep in wolves' clothing, so that we do not unnecessarily smite the innocent because of the deceptive nature of physical form.'

I bit a fingernail nervously, hoping this breathless answer would satisfy Aycelin. If he had even an inkling of suspicion, he could call for a more stringent interrogation. Wolves in sheep's clothing, indeed.

'Yet Scripture states that only God can change the physical form of something,' said Aycelin eventually, waggling a finger didactically, 'whereas demonic conjuration only changes the appearance of that thing, being unable to counteract the stronger power of Divinity.'

'But,' I said, gaining courage in my convictions, 'cannot other, natural causes, such as diseases and poxes, which are also under the natural jurisdiction of the Lord and evidence of His work, also cause changes in physical form? An example would be the hideous symptoms of the Black Death. Sufferers are infected by buboes, and their humours are awry, changing their very appearance. This is not conjuration! Yet the Evil One would be pleased indeed if we were to jump at the shadows of his work where there are none. Would we not be doing his diabolical work for him, then?'

Aycelin bobbed his head and considered this argument. At last the old man relaxed and sank back into his chair, and the scowl seemed to melt a little from him. 'I believe your devotion. I believe in your heart and I believe that you believe in the teachings of the one true Church. There is no heretic's stain on you.'

'I told you, it was a preposterous proposition,' scoffed Orsini, sitting back and sipping from his cup of wine. 'I am glad you have come to your senses. It takes courage to adopt such a position as yours, Brother Jacobus. *Sustinere est difficilus quam aggredi*,[5] as Aquinas said. Yet you must be aware that pride of the intellect can open the door to its becoming a conduit of the Evil One. Watch the path you tread.'

I swallowed. 'Amen,' I said, a little hoarsely.

'So, now we have established the holy character of Brother Jacobus, shall we decide whether it would be appropriate to send him on this mission to England?' asked Blauzac. 'Would you like to take such a journey, Brother Jacobus?'

'I confess my intellect is aroused,' I said, cautiously, 'for it is important that the truth come to light and heresy be prevented from taking root. If it is deemed that I may be of some use, I will gladly take the journey.'

Cardinal Blauzac screwed his face into something approaching a smile. 'Very well, then. I suggest we vote upon the matter. Who is for sending Brother Jacobus as a papal emissary to investigate this serious matter, and lend aid to the good Catholics of England?'

Blauzac waited for a show of hands and I edged forward in my seat, anticipating the vote with more excite-

---

[5] It is difficult to withstand the assault.

ment than I had expected. The thought of flexing my wits on the far side of the English Channel and seeing the land of some of my intellectual heroes was invigorating. If murky business was afoot, I aspired to uncover it. The quill of the young scribe ceased its furious scratching as he looked up to see the result of the vote.

Aycelin and Banac kept their hands by their sides, and their gazes down. I looked at Orsini, who of the four seemed the most likely to advocate for me, but he too kept his arms by his side. Blauzac himself did not raise a digit. None of them voted for me to travel to England, nor did any one of them gave any hint of satisfaction or otherwise at the unanimity of the decision.

I wondered whether their bringing me here was in fact a cover for their investigation of me and my conduct. Or whether none of them wanted to be held responsible for my journey to England, were anything to go wrong. Or, worse still, whether the idea of investigating heresy in the English borderlands was simply an item on their checklist, to be raised and dismissed and thereby dealt with. My heart sank. I cursed not having a voice in this matter.

'It is decided, then,' said Banac. 'Brother Jacobus will remain in France. I will have a response drafted to John of Thoresby informing him of our decision. Do you have any comment for the minutes, Brother Jacobus?'

'What if we risk the lives of more children?' I asked. In hindsight this sounded a little melodramatic and I felt embarrassed as I heard the scrape of the scribe's quill. 'And what of the truth?'

Cardinal Banac shrugged. 'There is no truth but God.' He feebly shuffled the papers in front of him. 'My lords, we have to discuss the request from Kraków to appoint more professors.' Remembering I was still in the room, he casually indicated the door and I left in silence.

COMPLINE

'There is more going on than the cardinals let on in that meeting,' I said irritably to Magnus as we ate later that day at the palace refectory. 'They never intended to send me to England. The vote was a sham. They simply wanted an excuse to warn me about my activities in interfering with the lives of people charged with heresy. If I didn't know better, I'd say that that little meeting this afternoon was the result of my dear friend Brother Nastagio's report of what happened at the trial in Italy.'

'But why?' asked Magnus, sitting opposite me and hunching over his food. 'Why call you here? Why not have an inquisitor talk to you directly?'

I swatted away his silly question. 'Because nobody accused me of anything, not even that hound Nastagio. No, the cardinals were merely informing me that my actions are not going unnoticed.'

'So you're fine, then,' he said with a smirk, clearly enjoying my intimation of conspiracy.

'Not entirely. Being watched implies I have something to hide. One mistake, and the agents of the Inquisition really will be upon me.'

'So what now? You'll stay here for a while, I suppose?'

I hummed in response as I chewed upon some hard salty cheese, but it was a noise of consideration instead of agreement. 'John of Thoresby is highly respected, even by the cardinals. He would not have written to the palace had the need not been sincere.' I chewed more of the salty cheese. 'Or so I think.'

Magnus screwed up his eyes in confusion. 'Meaning?'

'There were things left unsaid. When Cardinal Banac met me for the first time and related John's letter to me, he mentioned a second letter from a local physician in Berwick, which contained details of what happened there. But the cardinals made no mention of it.'

'You think they invented the second letter?'

'No, I think they hadn't intended me to know about it. I think Banac blurted out John of Thoresby's reference to it by mistake and then regretted it.'

'But why?'

'Because they never meant to send me to England, and now they know I know about it, that adds force to my wish to go, which makes me that much more troublesome. Magnus, we need to see the second letter.'

'"We"?'

'You're a scribe. You can ask another of the scribes for the location of correspondences within the papal library. Don't you think that we ought to pull at this thread?'

'Brother Jacobus, forgive me but I cannot be part of this!' he said.

'You are a part of it. Cannot the Evil One work through inaction as well as action?'

He made a face at that, as though I'd flummoxed him, then twisted it into a sly smile. As I thought: the role of co-conspirator secretly appealed to him. I'd got him on my side.

After prayers we paid another visit to the library. Unlike my abbey, where life quietened down as the evening settled in, the papal palace was still a buzz of activity, with music, dancing, work and conversation filling the Court. Magnus's got chatty with the other scribes and quickly discovered where the correspondence section was, and we headed there with what was probably ill-disguised haste.

Letters were sorted by date, so there was no difficulty in detecting the most recent pile of correspondence, and we quickly found the letters we wanted from John of Thoresby and the physician. Together, in low candlelight, we huddled over our treasures, and I confess a prickle of excitement ran across my shoulders when I read what the physician had written. It was in English, a language I spoke and read well enough, but Magnus's fluency was even better, so I held up to his candle and he read it out, in an excited whisper.

> To the excellent persons of the House of Hayeford and his most excellent Thomas Lord de Hayeford:
>
> Concerning the matter of recent deaths and bizarre occurrences that have made themselves unwelcome in our community, I seek to relate to you details which I cannot fathom.
>
> Berwick is a holy town, but not feted for its learning. They have little and less understanding of such matters as astrology, advanced medicines and natural philosophy. It was with this in mind that my Master at St Peter's school in York consigned me, a physician of many years, to the northern town, to lend my understanding of medicines to the householders thereof, in the hope of revealing the cause of the disturbances and deaths. But alas, I have found events there beyond my depth.
>
> I will begin by reminding you of the disappearance of several children, which began in Thornton, two years back. Of the first to go missing, neither had seen six summers, according to their mother. A large search was undertaken for them, to no avail, until their little bodies were found in the

thick woodlands bordering the river Tweed, some miles west of Berwick. I have been a physician all the time that the Black Death has raged, and I can say with all honesty that I have not seen anything like the bodies of those poor wretches.

From every orifice, vines sprouted, as well as creepers and weeds. Shoots poked through their half-decomposed eye sockets. Roots grew out of their mouths. Long grasses emerged from their ear canals.

I cut them open to conduct an autopsy—and their bodies, Christ have mercy on them, were filled with earth, mud and leaves, and worms and creeping creatures of the soil: beetles and ants and other vermin.

When a body dies in the woods, it decays according to an established process. First it is eaten by large predators—wolves and foxes—and then the smaller scavengers. Then it fills with gases, then deflates and dispenses with its own bad air. What remains is eaten by maggots and last of all by the air and the earth.

When I looked inside those little bodies it was as if the wood had attempted to consume them first. As though the wood itself was the predator.

I have enclosed the dates and details of this awful set of events.

Between January last year and July of this, another fourteen children, all of about the same age, were spirited away to the forest. Some of the children managed to escape, though by what miracle I could not say. At other times, bodies were recovered. Each time a child's body was found, it was in the same unholy state, bloated not by natural gases but by the fruits of the forest. Whatever devilry is afoot here respects neither station nor title. Always a girl and a boy are taken: a pair—one child of each sex. It happens in what appears to be a pattern. January, April, July, October and so to January, and the cycle starts again.

There is no evidence of Plague, nor other pox I know.

But there is something else, almost too macabre to speak of. Each of the babes whose body was discovered possessed a strange mark upon its forehead. These marks varied in size and shape. Some were just the size of a penny; others covered almost the entire front of the head. I touched them: they felt like what I can only describe as the bark of a tree. I am at a loss to explain it.

I shall now relate the queerest and gravest detail of this gruesome tale. This April just past, a girl named Alice and a boy named Piers went missing from the village of Horncliffe. Both were presumed dead. And then, just a few days after they had disappeared, the girl wandered back into the middle of village and just stood there, alone. I did not see her but those who did say her flesh was as pale as glass, and her body as spindly as a starved dog. They said she spoke in a strange voice, and talked of monsters in the woods, and dark lights in the trees.

It was at this moment that the dark magic of Satan started to be mentioned by people. A crowd surrounded her, and someone accused her of being the offspring of a demon. Others muttered accusations, then stones were thrown and in the end she was torn to pieces.

When the mother heard the commotion, came out of her little hovel, recognised her daughter and tried to save her, she too was killed. I gather that what remained of the body was then denied a Christian burial and burned instead.

Several people now blame the Devil and his earthly followers for these infernal happenings. I have no idea about the legal consequences of this horror. As for the religious aspects of it all, here I am also lost, for I am just a secular man with some knowledge of medicines. But Berwick's friars are equally bereft of ideas! Or so they say.

Every person here fears the future. Panic grips the

parents of those young children who remain. Most rely on their faith to fortify them. Others have started leaving the district for fear that their children too will be cursed, and this is impoverishing the land, which needs its labourers.

I have come home to York, and attempted to discern whether these events are isolated, or more widespread. So far, I am defeated, but I shall consult my books in hope of some clue, so that I might return to Berwick with some new knowledge that might resolve this abominable mystery.

We await the assistance of the King's men and cry for aid in whatever form it can be obtained, as we cry also for the mercy of the Lord and his Son.

God save us!
Ever your devoted subject,
Albertus of Aachen
St. Peter's School
York

1st November

In which I leave Provence and travel north to England

PRIME

Reading the letter made us even more excited by our clandestine plot, but we knew we could not simply leave France and travel to England without raising unwanted questions. We needed time to plan, so we returned to our abbey in Villeneuve and carried on with our daily work and prayers. I found this hard, because I could not stop thinking about the poor people of Berwick, and the more I thought about them, the more obsessed I became.

Meanwhile, Magnus and I continued to read, study and transcribe the details contained in the addendum to the letter, and I shall relate them here for clarity and so that I do not forget.

The first two children to go missing were named Griselda and Henry, from Thornton, as John of Thoresby had related in the first scroll. Another couple, Beorn and Willa, disappeared from a tithing named Ord in April 1366. Their bodies were never found.

Three months later, in July, a pair called Geoffrey and Agnes went missing from Murton. These children somehow managed to find their way back to the village after three days, but there was no physician available to aid them, and so they became catatonic and died from weakness. Albertus noted that their bodies showed no signs of the ruination suffered by Griselda and Henry, but they still bore the strange bark-like mark upon their foreheads.

In October, Harold and Margaret were taken from the village of Allerdean. Their bodies were never found.

The following January two more children, Oswin and Alvena, were taken from East Ord. Their bodies were found in the parlous state that Albertus described, as if "eaten by the woods".

Then, in April, came the lurid tale of Piers and Alice, which Albertus had related in his main missive. I re-read the report about the girl Alice returning to her village of Horncliffe, and about her strange appearance and horrifying prognostications, and her terrible death at the hands of her own people. I wondered what state of mind they must have been in to be driven to such an atrocity.

Two further children, Alfred and Matilda, disappeared from Murton in July. Another curious quirk. These children made their way back to the village but were not attacked like Alice. Even more intriguingly, and in spite of their apparent weakness, both survived their ordeal and recovered.

Albertus speculated in the notes that perhaps the hot summer had aided their convalescence and enabled them to return to the village more easily than the children whose fate had been to disappear in the winter. I must admit, I was sceptical of this explanation. Nevertheless, Alfred and Matilda, despite the miracle and mercy of their survival, were not untouched by their experience, whatever it may have been. They too bore this mark, the bark-like blot upon their foreheads, and still do, and are given as wide a berth by the more fearful of their fellow villagers as was Cain in the Holy Bible. But Albertus, evidently a goodly man as well as an intelligent one, praises the Lord for their continued life, even while he speculates that instances such as those in the region of Berwick are likely to have occurred in other areas too.

That is where the report ended, and I spent a great deal of time thinking it through. In each instance a boy and a girl were taken. The time elapsing between each disappearance was a regular three months, though Albertus could not always determine the exact date, and such suggested that another disappearance may have blighted the locale this October, only a few weeks past, perhaps while the letter itself was in transit.

In my free time at Villeneuve I cautiously consulted a few books in the Abbey's library, not wanting to alert anyone to my growing interest, but nothing shed any light on the matter. I started to conclude that the only way to find out more was for Magnus and me to take our chance and travel to England, by whatever means we could find. Magnus was less impulsive and argued against doing so. To begin with he urged that it would not be wise for us to go against the authority of the cardinals, and that we should wait for them to come up with the idea of investigating in person, and then make ourselves available. When he would not back down, I threatened to go by myself if he would not join me. At that, he tried to persuade me of the risks I would be opening myself up to, especially if I was found out, captured and accused of disloyalty to the Church, but I kept parrying his objections and after a while he stopped trying to change my mind. I was like a dog with a bone, he told me, and he knew when to give up.

To my surprise, it only took me a few days to make the necessary preparations once I had made up my mind. I would leave Villeneuve under the pretence of returning to the Holy Roman Empire, but this time travelling north through the kingdom of France and thence to Alsace, and I would leave as soon as I could. I would take care not to be distracted on my journey, as I often had been in the past, knowing that any unwanted scrutiny would endanger my secret endeavours and arouse suspicion.

After I had worn him down, Magnus falsified a paper

declaring my inquisitorial authority to investigate the events in Berwick, and sealed it with the stamp of the Abbaye de Saint André de Villeneuve. With this seal it would be impossible to know that the letter was bogus. Falsifying a letter was a sin, perhaps, but only of a minor degree and committed in the pursuit of a higher truth. I wanted to visit the local nobleman, Lord Hayeford, and a sealed letter, apparently with papal authority, would be essential in gaining his trust.

When the day came I said my goodbyes to my fellow brothers and the abbot, who were well used to my frequent peregrinations around the Continent and had no reason to suspect my leaving. I had arranged for a horse-driven cart to take me down to the river Rhône and, before mounting it, I saved the warmest of farewells for Brother Magnus, who embraced me like a blood brother and wished me every luck in my endeavours.

'To tell you the truth, Jacobus,' he whispered, 'I am afraid of what you might find. That letter from the physician Albertus frightened me. "Dark lights in the trees," it said. What do you suppose that means?'

'Fear not, Magnus,' I replied breezily. 'Christ is the light and His light is knowledge and His knowledge illuminates the dark places of the world. He will bring me light in any dark hours I am destined to endure, and all shall be knowable.'

'Take care anyway,' Magnus replied quietly, adding more loudly so that he could now be overheard, 'and be sure to send word to the Abbey.'

'Goodbye, my blessed friend. Pray for me!'

'I will!'

And with the crack of the driver's whip, the little cart rolled out of the abbey.

At the rapidly flowing river, I paid for passage with a Provençal textile trader named Ohler, who was bound for Paris. From a Chalonnaise merchants' guild, Ohler had leased a narrow-draft barge which took us to Lyon, where the Rhône meets the Saône, and then via the Saône northwards to Chalon-Sur-Saône, where he moored the barge and, with the assistance of the town's guild, transferred his goods to a horse-driven retinue upon land, which bore us to Auxerre. There he commandeered another barge to take us downstream, along the Yonne and the Seine, to Paris, where I bid him farewell. I then bartered my way upon a larger draft barge headed for Harfleur. A few years earlier it would have been highly dangerous to travel from Harfleur to England but the recently signed treaty of Brétigny had brought hostilities with the English to an end, and I was therefore confident of safe passage. All told, the journey took two weeks.

It was after I had left French shores and was sailing to Dover that the full folly of the journey first struck me. In embarking on this singular adventure, I had committed several sins of dishonesty and encouraged Magnus to commit others. I was also guilty of pride, pretending that I alone was capable of solving in a mystery in a country I had never visited before and knew nothing about. England was itself a mystery, after all. All manner of devilish stories emanated from its shores. People said it was full of knavish people and that strange rites, ancient and pagan, were still observed in its woodlands and fens. On the other hand, I'd heard it said that many of the people were good, stout-hearted Christians who kept God's word as well as any.

I still recall the thumping of my heart and the powerful sense of doubt as England's white cliffs hove into view, as imposing and suggestive as a vast, unwritten parchment.

The timing of our arrival had seemed auspicious at first, for it had been a calm crossing and I enjoyed a good night's rest in a hostelry by the seafront, but when I fell in the next day with a band of men who were also travelling north, the weather suddenly turned violent and a winter storm blew up of prescient ferocity. Coils of icy rain whipped us like the lash of a slave master, and very soon we were all drenched and shivering. Such was the wrath of the wind that I wondered whether this journey to the northern reaches of the known world was not an act of hubris, especially if its main purpose was to satisfy my intellectual pride, but I then chastised myself for thinking that my fleshly discomfort was in any way comparable with the immeasurable suffering of those woebegone souls in Berwick.

After sheltering for a day and drying out at an ancient farmhouse that had survived from Roman times, we set out again on a road that took us to Canterbury, one of England's twenty-eight cities, still called Durovernum Cantiacorum by some. We stopped awhile to pay homage to the venerable saint Thomas à Becket in the wondrous new cathedral, and then went on to Londres or Lunden or London or Lundenburgh with its great tower. Somewhere in the streets leading down to the shallow port we picked up another traveller. He called himself Poole and appeared to be little more than a peasant yet must have possessed sufficient financial means to join us on our wagon. He was dirty-faced and skittish, but was well-humoured, smiled easily and was always ready with a kind word when one was needed. I did not normally like to fraternise with the common folk, nor enjoy their vulgar talk, but since an understanding of local knowledge was likely to be beneficial to my mission, I decided to engage him in small talk.

It didn't take long for Poole to take a shine to me and to express his curiosity. 'Where you from, then, Brother Jacobus?' he said, rubbing an apple on his filthy shirt. 'Can't place the accent proper. Scotland? Cornwall?'

His own accent was one of the local London dialects, a hacksaw rasp of harsh edges and salty humour, but not without a savage musicality, with its ill-matched collisions of French and Latin and Saxon.

'Vienna,' I told him. 'But I travelled up from Avignon.'

He creased his simple face into thought before taking a bite of the crunchy fruit. 'Where's that, then? Wales? Poole's never 'eard of it.'

It was well known among the Church community that the Holy Father Pope Urban V deeply desired to leave Avignon and return the papacy to its spiritual home on the River Tiber. The French city was not as well known as Rome, but was still the proper seat of the Holy See, and the man's ignorance of this irked me. 'Are you a good Christian, Mr Poole?'

'As and when,' he said solemnly, placing a hand over his heart. I did not know what he meant by that, and assumed it was some sort of colloquial affirmation rather than anything untoward. 'God keeps me in His way, I s'pose, and I Him.' He took another noisy bite of the apple and added, 'I'm off up north.'

'Ah, so am I. For what?'

'Off to Lindisfarne, Brother Jacco. See what's what. There's work there. I'm a builder, of sorts. That's what Poole is.'

I sat back and raised my eyebrows. Lindisfarne was a place of great renown throughout Christendom, and not very far from Berwick. Locals called it Holy Island.

'So you are a true Catholic, Mr Poole. Good, good. And what are you building?'

He responded with an innocent, simpleton's smile. 'See when we get there, eh?' He bit into his apple again.

'And what are you headed up north for?'

I smiled. 'Church business. There are people there in need of … .' I broke off, struck by my awareness of the dangers inherent in my visit, and of my need for caution. 'People in need of help,' I continued. 'I am something of a specialist.'

Poole looked impressed, or pretended to be. Simple folk often mock the things they cannot understand. I remember young novices in my home town of Vienna sniggering and making fun of those of us who were hard at study, as though striving for enlightenment was an affectation, deserving only derision.

'God judges poorly the man who buries his talent,' I said to Poole.

'Well, He ain't got to worry about us, then,' he replied with a laugh, taking a last bite of the apple and tossing the core over his left shoulder—for luck, he said—before settling down and closing his eyes for a snooze.

14th November

In which I make a stop at Oxford and encounter a face I do not recognise

VESPERS

If Avignon is the architectural jewel in the crown of Christendom, and Rome its fiercely beating heart, then Oxford is its brain—or so I was told by those we encountered who came from Oxenford and held themselves in mightier esteem than the magisters of the University of Paris. Not only had England's king, Edward III, paid tribute to the six colleges at the heart of the city but many of our popes had commended the intellectual activity taking place there.

After a few days our wagon approached the centre of the town, and I felt the same frisson of excitement that I had felt at Canterbury. There, I felt I was on a pilgrimage to piety; here I was making a pilgrimage to learning.

'I love Oxford too,' said Poole, when I remarked upon my enthusiasm for the place, and he picked at something in his teeth. 'I love its stink.'

'Stink? It is respected by the most esteemed scholars in the civilised world,' I said, not detecting anything malodorous in the air. 'Had I been blessed with more time, I would like to have visited the college libraries and examined their manuscripts. I miss the stimulation of the written word.' It sounded sanctimonious, I knew, and risked driving a wedge between the two of us but I did not want my true nature to be misrepresented.

As the sun set the wagon pulled up outside an inn called The Green Man.

'This is our stop, Brother Jacco,' said Poole. 'You ain't staying here, then?'

'No, Mr Poole. I shall stay at Abingdon, a little further on. There is a Benedictine abbey there of great character. I shall stay with the brothers.'

'It will take you a good few hours to get there,' said

Poole, 'and then the wagon driver will have to come back to collect the rest of us, and that will be an expense which you'll have to pay for. Why not stay here'—Poole looked this way and that—'and then you'll have time for a beer, no?'

I smiled. I was an Austrian and he had hit upon my greatest weakness! The very prospect of a beer made my mouth salivate and my mood brighten. As much as I enjoy the wonderful foods and wines of Provence and the southern reaches of the Empire, there is nothing like beer to fill the heart with joy. Whether Benedictine or otherwise, all Austrians concur that brewing is a noble science and one that contributes to the betterment of humankind. So, having discovered that Poole and I shared some common ground after all, I decided that it was indeed time to partake of a cup of cheer, and asked the wagon driver to join us. I'd not be long.

Inside, Poole found us some spaces at a trestle table near the fireplace. Sticky black floorboards sucked at the soles of my sandals and now I did indeed apprehend the thick stink of humanity that Poole had professed a love for, though I could not understand what explained his relish of it. Nor could I understand how, further along the table from us, a couple of roughshod women sat, beauties, both of them, talking loudly, guffawing and taking man-sized draughts from hot and steaming mugs. Why they and others like them were not at home, spinning or darning or looking after their husbands and babies, I could not conceive.

Poole quickly explained that the women of England were friendly, and preferred not to be veiled or shut away in purdah, as women were in foreign climes. 'They'll keep you company too, if it's entertainment you're after,' he added, giving me an impudent dig in the ribs. I wrinkled my brow at the very thought of communing with members of the world's sisterhood, and busily administered to myself the Sign of the Cross. Protecting common women from false accusations of heresy and witchcraft was one thing; engaging in social relations with them was quite another matter, and well beyond my vows as a member of a monastic Order.

The wagon driver sat and smirked into his beer but said nothing.

'You would do well to stay away from such women,' I said, knowing well my advice would not be heeded.

'Bit late for that, Jacco!' Poole said, leaning into me and snickering. 'Cor, look at the sight of them—hoo!'

I ignored his crude language, and focused instead on the need for asceticism and the renunciation of worldly pleasures. This was hard work in a place so full of feminine and alcoholic distractions but I took comfort from the fact that the inn itself was marred by a physical drabness which dulled the spirits. I also felt horribly conspicuous as the only man of God to be present on the premises and this forced me to act with exemplary decorum, so that those sitting and drinking and laughing around me might look to me as a role model for their own behaviour.

Having said all that, the beer was indeed very pleasing, and Poole and I happily chugged down several tankards as we passed the time in merry talk. Before long, my bladder was full and I had to go outside to empty it.

As I was pissing against the side of the building, a clattering noise came from the yard, followed by a strangled yelp. A shiver of alarm shot up my neck and stopped me in mid-flow. I tidied myself up and peered outside the outhouse. The gloom was punctuated by a few burning torches ensconced into the earth, revealing straw bales and muddy puddles. The sounds of mirth from the pub were muffled by the damp air and sounded further than they really were. I went to investigate, my feet aching with the cold and damp.

Over in the shadow of a rickety stable, I saw two indistinct shapes and heard another muffled cry, which froze me in my steps. Base sinner that I am, my first thought was for my own safety and I thought to flee. Then I remembered that, as a man of faith, I should not tarry in helping my neighbour, so I cried out, '*Pax vobiscum*,' and then, 'Is all well?'

There was a grunting sort of noise, and then another, so again I called out. A curt reply from a breathless voice fell upon the night, instructing me in no uncertain terms not to interfere, but the next moment another voice let out another groan of despair, followed by a squeal, and another clatter, and something dashing away in the darkness.

'Don't let it get away!' I heard a voice mutter, and then a volley of vulgar curse words, and then quiet.

It was evident that I had encroached upon a scene at which I would not be welcome, but the thought of a man's death or wounding on my conscience was unbearable, so I plucked one of the dull lamps from a sconce, clutched the crucifix hanging around my neck and, emboldened, strode unto the scene.

'What's the trouble?' I said, raising my voice. 'I say, what's—?'

My words were cut short by two men, in silhouette, striding towards me out of the darkness. One was large, and held in his right hand a length of rope, which had been fastened into a lasso. The other man was skinny and walked half-hunched by his large partner, and held a small and cheaply made knife. It was too dark to see their expressions but I think they must have been fearful.

I thrust my torch towards them and, at first, thought that they must both have been monks, for they were both dressed in long cloth cloaks with hoods covering their faces. Then I made out, in the scant light, that the cloaks were a deep, forest-green colour, not the colour of any Christian order I recognised. I saw also that the cloaks were tied at the throat and chest, and disguised their everyday clothing. Their faces were caked with mud and dirt. This alone would have been sufficient to disturb me but I was gripped by a base horror when I saw that the men had vines and grasses growing out of their faces.

'What in the Devil's name are you doing out here?' said the big man, standing in front of me and blocking my path. I believe that, had I not been wearing the attire of a man of God, he might have assaulted me. As it was, he pulled back his hood and glowered at me like a wild beast. I stepped back, clutching my crucifix.

Up close, I saw the truth. The men did not have plants protruding from their faces. They simply had a handful of creepers and other such greenery stuffed inside their hoods, and some of it now fell to the ground. The thought crossed my mind that perhaps I had simply stopped them from slaughtering some animal, a pig perhaps, for their dinner, and that they were dressed in this peculiar manner to keep their normal clothing free of blood.

'You let it get away,' hissed the smaller man.

When he said this the bigger man clouted him about the head with the rope, making him squeal and beg for forgiveness in a pathetic display of submission.

'Shut up you bastard fool!' said the big man again and hit his companion twice more with the rope, and then again. With each blow my thoughts turned to my own safety and so I stuttered a pathetic response and took a step backwards to leave but I was slow and stumbling and all I managed to do was drop the flaming torch onto the damp earth and trip upon my habit. The big man, seeing this, took a giant step and grasped the breast of my robe, pulling me toward him like a doll.

'Man of the Church, eh?' He sneered at my Crucifix and held the rope to my face. 'You think your Christian Lord frightens me?'

I wriggled instinctively but his grip was like iron. He stank of sweat, and his eyes, red with drink and sin, looked down into mine without shame or fear. Even in the midst of my fear, I experienced an unbidden and grinding contempt for one who would sneer at Our Father in such disgust. These were low men, indeed.

'Let's go, my Lord,' said the smaller one, pressing his hand upon the larger one's arm.

'Shut your mouth, you dribble-dribble,' spat his partner, not taking his eyes from me. 'He's a brother of the Church. And he's seen us.' Evidently he was deciding what to do with me, and I said not a word.

With his free arm the big man pulled a short, wide-bladed knife from a pocket sewn into his hose and held it up to my face. My heart fluttered and my mouth dried, and I wriggled uselessly again. 'What did you see, churchman, eh?' he said, and squeezed the front of my habit tighter, making it hard to breathe.

I have one chance, I thought, and uttered a few words in German that I thought might put him off his stroke.

'*Ich habe nichts gesehen! Nichts!*' I stammered and, as expected, drew a confused look from my assailant.

'What's that? Where you from?' he said. 'Abingdon?'

'*Nein, nein,*' I stammered in German again, '*Ich bin Österreicher, stehe im Dienst der Kirche und komme aus Avignon.*'

Although my words had caught him off guard, I had only bought myself a moment's reprieve. 'Talk English, you foreign dog,' said the man and slapped me across the face with the side of his fist.

'Eyup, wha's goin' on 'ere?' came another voice from the darkness, puncturing the tension.

Striding towards us was a figure with blessedly familiar gait. Poole! I resisted the temptation to cry out for help and only stared at him imploringly as he sidled up and grinned at the three of us, as if I was complicit in a wicked tryst.

'Who are you?' said the big man.

'Came out for a shit,' said Poole. He wore the insouciant smile of a man for whom the sight of a monk being threatened at knifepoint by deviants was a nightly event.

'You know this character?'

'Aye and nay. I saw him inside, drinking beer. Says he's from Austria.'

'Austrian?' said the smaller man, now running up and taking the opportunity to get back into the action. 'What's he doing here, then? Spying?'

Poole shrugged. 'He went out for a piss. Happens to us all. Even to you, friend, sometimes, I imagine!'

Poole had been smiling. Then he noticed the bits of greenery inside the men's clothing and littering the ground beside them and his expression changed. When he spoke next, it was in a tone of mounting anger—even accusation. 'A better question, friend, is what you were you doing here.'

It was the big man who now looked unsure. He gave me another snarl and then let go of me with a shove. 'The man will have his share.'

Poole's eyes widened and, when he spoke again, his voice sounded keened to the quick. 'Aye, he shall. Not tonight though, an' not from thee. Now get thee hence.'

Despite their advantage in size and number, Poole stared the others down with a ferocity that I could not explain and that quenched the two men's tempers.

'Let him who's without sin cast the first stone,' said the smaller man, tugging his mate's arm. 'Come, my lord, let's get away.'

I apologised and thanked the two brutes sheepishly in German as they trudged past me.

When they were gone, and the threat drained from the evening air, the slap on my face hurt and I suddenly felt very cold. I thanked Poole profusely and watched as his face relaxed into its familiar grin, as though his brief explosion of temper had all been my imagination.

'Why'd you interfere?' said Poole.

'I didn't mean to,' I said. 'I don't know what they were doing. Whatever it was, they obviously didn't want to be disturbed. But I did nothing wrong; I didn't challenge them.' In spite of that, shame washed over me. I had witnessed something, but didn't know what. 'Mr Poole, do you know what they were up to?'

Poole hesitated for a moment and then said, with a laugh, 'This is England!', before packing me back to the tavern as he went off to do what he had come out to do in the first place. I hid my face in my cowl as I walked.

It was as I approached the tavern doorway that my

heart suddenly leapt with fright again. Staring down down at me from the middle of the lintel was the hideous face of a demon, surrounded by plants. I crossed myself automatically, then looked again and saw that the face was in fact the wooden centrepiece of the arch. Recovering my wits, I examined it. Its mouth was stretched into an insane rictus and its eyes were creased in mirth, as if mocking me, though its expression might also have been one of discomfort—that of a tortured soul in Hell. But its face was not that of a man. Long, leafy creeping plants sprouted from its mouth and nostrils, entwining the wooden beam like a nest of serpents. The cheeks were covered in leaves, and the tongue emerged like a long, thick vine. The eyes were the most wicked sight of all—they were blank, and yet the expression hinted at some greater intelligence, something more than it was letting on.

I had seen foliate heads like this before in different parts of Europe and had never liked the pagan idolatry that their presence conjured up. Some monks had even added them to the architecture of their houses of God, which I always found distasteful and sinful. Here, though, the vulgarity and arrogance of the idol, grinning at me in my moment of humiliation, was almost overwhelming. I shuddered at the strange visage, and tried to shake off the odd feeling it gave me. Or the odd feeling that I had given myself, for are not our fears mere emanations of ourselves? It was surely just my shaken wits playing tricks on me. Once I'd taken a moment to consider it, I laughed.

'You find it funny?' asked Poole, who had caught up with me and now stood watching as I examined the face and mused.

'No, I … I was just looking at this carved creature

and trying to make sense of it.'

'Creature?,' retorted Poole. 'Hah! That there ain't no creature. That there is men. Men of all colours, an' all of 'em green.'

It was too late in the evening and I was too befuddled to try and decipher this bizarre English idiom, so I made my way back through the tavern to the wagon driver, and begged him to take me at once to Abingdon. But he said that Abingdon was nearly twenty miles north and that he did not want to spend the night driving there and back for no reason. I'd be better off staying here with the rest of our company.

'And cheaper for you,' Poole reminded me. So, against my wishes, I shared a dormitory with some of the other travellers, saying my nightly prayers with a fervour that they sniggered at, and wishing to the bottom of my heart that I might one day sleep again under the roof of God.

15TH NOVEMBER

IN WHICH POOLE REVEALS MORE DETAILS ABOUT THE MEN IN OXFORD AND THE ODDNESS OF THIS PLACE

TERCE

I did not sleep well that night. The echoes of danger lingered on after my prayers, as did the odd encounter with the two armed men draped in that gaudy *fac similus* of a disengorged foliate head. I wondered if I might have happened upon something sinister, and prevented a calamity of some sort through my intervention. If so, I offered my gratitude to God not only for my curiosity, which had urged me forth into that suspicious meeting, but also for Poole, whose wit and timeliness had brought me back from it. When morning came, therefore, I broke my fast greedily but without pleasure, and was quiet until we were back on the road.

As we journeyed onwards, Poole gave no indication of wanting to discuss the incident, and told me instead about the towns we passed, the people he had met there and the things he had seen. Occasionally he would trail off in the middle of a sentence and fall asleep, as though he had exhausted all his energy, despite not apparently having used any. Sometimes he would sing a line from what must originally have been a sacred motet, and in his more animated moments would try to teach me the words and melody.

Sadly, I was not for learning. I told him I did not like the propensity for dragging liturgical music into the secular realm and adulterating it into songs about love, whether courtly or—in Poole's case—very much the opposite. He looked a little disappointed but had the good grace not to display any other emotion, merely reverting to his simple smile. In spite of that, I felt bad for not allowing myself to be drawn into what was obviously an extension of friendship, and so tried to engage him on the topic of the previous evening.

'What were those men doing, Poole? You seemed to have some understanding of them.'

'Bad stuff, aw'reet. Bastard stuff.' He grimaced and looked away, across the hills.

I decided not to press further and allowed him to continue in his own time, which he eventually did. When he spoke next, he was more thoughtful.

'S'an old place, this country—reet old. England, I mean. Some say the children of Adam walked here and scattered his seeds in our earth. I dunno about that. But us English got old memories, and we have to. See, the country itself has memory; it remembers.'

'What does it remember?'

'The old times. Most people forget. What were his name what came here and spread the good word of Jesus and all his disciples?'

'St Augustine,' I responded. 'So far as I remember.'

'The land remembers a time before Augustine. And sometimes it wants to make sure we remembers, too.'

I was starting to become convinced that the man was speaking in rustic riddles—a crude peasant's attempt to emulate the cryptic metaphysics of our Mother Church's divine theologians.

I sighed and took in the view from our horse-drawn trap. The day was dry, crisp and bright. Seeing my discontent, Poole spoke more plainly.

'The forest is alive, Brother Jacobus. An' the forest is England. It's older'n churches, older'n books, older'n folk. That head, that foliate head you saw in Oxford—that's what they're called, aw'reet—that's the wood. Some folk call him the Green Man.'

'A folk story, then.'

'Naw! Hoo, thee's a funny one, Brother! Not a story.

Not for some. You believe that what's written in your Bible is just a story?'

I thinned my eyes. 'The Bible is a book of stories. It is also the Truth.'

He nodded at me and smiled. 'There are those who believe that the Green Man walks among us. That the forest wakes, from time to time, and becomes a man who roams the land, taking his share until he's sated at last. A man made of earth and soil and all the things of the woods. He changes, that's what they say. In the springtime he's playful, in summer abundant, in autumn wise and generous, in winter bitter and rotten. But he never dies, and he can take as well as give. See, we been taking from the woods fr'as long as folk ha' been here. But folk can't take from the forest wi'out the forest takin' back. 'Cos the man can get nasty. So a lot of folk still talk to him, make offerings to him, keep him sated.'

'What sort of offerings?'

He waved dismissively. 'Mostly fruits and harvests and whatnot. You know the old stories: they used to make sacrifices. Blood sacrifices. Maybe a squirrel or summat. Maybe livestock. Sometimes, in the bad stories, even … .' His voice trailed off and he gave a sour look, before forcing himself into his simple grin and giving me a hearty clap upon the shoulder. 'But they were bad old days, eh, Brother Jacco!

He did not have to finish his thought for me to discern where he had been heading. I mulled over whether to outline for him the mystery that had brought me there, but decided against it, for now.

'There is no man, Poole. It is a cipher. A symbolic device. Nevertheless, I understand the sentiment. You said people make offerings to this idol? Is that what those men were doing? Capturing an animal for some sort of offering? If such things caught the eye of the Church, it could be treated as heresy!'

Poole shrugged, and muttered quietly, 'I don't know owt about heresy, Brother Jaccy.'

The revelation that some corners of England still cleaved to primitive nature superstitions roused little surprise in me but it did still fill me with distaste. 'Baal, answer us!' I said, accompanying the utterance with a mocking wave of my hands. 'But there was no answer, and they danced around the altar they had made.'

When Poole looked confused, I relented a mite. 'It is from the story of Elijah: the prophet who drove away the minions of Jezebel. He challenged the prophets of Baal to call on their gods to bring down fire and accept their offering. The gods did not answer, of course. There is nothing new about people worshipping the natural world. But it will avail them nothing. The woods and the trees are not gods, and certainly not the one true God, Poole. The world around us can seem spiteful or plentiful or beautiful, but such seeming is all the illusion of perception. The world is filled with colours made possible by God and our eyes that see these things are also the work of God.' I paused. 'I hope you do not indulge in this false idolatry?'

Poole shook his head and made the Sign of the Cross upon himself.

'The old gods make way for the new. That's the story of England. That's the story of all men.'

'Men of all colours,' I murmured, more to myself than Poole, but he raised his eyebrows upon hearing it '"Men of all colours." That's what you said, did you not? "Men of all colours, and all of them are green."'

'Aye. You want to watch out you don't turn green thaself, Brother Jaccy.' And before I could question what he might mean by this, he lay back and closed his eyes for a snooze.

Rather than disturb him, I let the man rest. Despite the sour topic, I was grateful for Poole's intervention. What a sorry end my tale would have had, had it ended in bloody catastrophe by an outhouse in Oxford! And yet here I was, still eking my way north towards a mystery that baffled even my masters in Avignon. I decided to take a leaf out of Poole's book, and let my head droop for a rest.

VESPERS

We rested that evening at The Peauterpotte, a tavern on the western edge of the town of Rokeby. The tavern sat upon the edge of a plateau and afforded us a charming view over the river Avon. It was run by a jolly fat man and his jollier, fatter wife, both of whom looked as if they were being plumped up by the local farmer in time for Christmas.

'The trouble is, my funds are exhausted,' said Poole to the landlord as we arrived, explaining that they would remain so until he secured some income from his building work in Lindisfarne. 'I'm happy to sleep in the stye with the pigs, if it's all the same to you.'

When the landlord refused either to room him or let him bed down with the beasts, Poole shrugged in that stoic, good-humoured nature of his and said, 'Well, I'll take me chances elsewhere, then. Poole isn't proud.'

I couldn't allow that. It was not just that he'd come to my aid in Oxford but that he had shown me great friendliness ever since we had first set out, and I felt a strong affection for him. I clapped him upon the shoulder and said, 'Not so, Mr Poole. Tonight you will dine and stay with me. There are enough groats and nobles in my purse for two.'

At that, Poole's simple little face, all lined and creased with the effort of having worked in the worst of English weather over the years, lit up, and he shook me by the hand vigorously. 'Ye won't regret it, Brother Jacobus! We'll have a fine old evening, and that's a fact!'

So my unlikely travelling companion became my even more unlikely dining companion, and I treated us to a meal of honeyed pork, crusty pies filled to bursting with local birds and gravy, and fabulous dark breads, which we washed down with flagons of foamy beer and stout. As we consumed this feast against the warming flame of the hearth, I felt at last pleased to be in England, a feeling I had not felt until now.

'That's real grub,' smiled Poole, smearing butter onto a chunk of bread and mopping up the gravy from his pies. 'Thankin' you, Brother Jacco. I'll remember this, to be sure. And when Poole makes a promise, Poole holds by it.'

'You're more than welcome, Poole,' I replied. 'And now, if I may, I'd like to let you into a secret.'

'Mmm,' he said, shovelling a handful of winter berries into his mouth and letting the red juices run down his chin like streams of blood. It seemed I had not yet impressed upon him the gravity of the situation.

'Poole, my work in Berwick is sensitive but perhaps I can reveal some aspects of it. Something has happened there which the local people find hard to explain. There have been incidents, mostly relating to children. One child … .' I hesitated, uncertain whether he was paying my words any attention. 'I heard that one child went missing in the forests of Northumberland, only to return, quite unexpectedly, some time later, when many had thought her dead.'

I waited for a reaction. None came. Poole put back another draught of beer, belched, and helped himself to more berries.

I continued, regardless. 'The child spoke of dark lights in the trees. Part of my holy mission is to decipher the meaning of this cryptic message. Does dark lights in the trees mean anything to you?'

He nodded straightforwardly as he concentrated on the more important business of eating, his bristly jowls making the best of what remained on the table, as though preparing himself for hibernation. The puzzle I had put to him, by contrast, seemed to him but a trifle.

'Mr Poole?'

'Sorry, Jacco. Where are we talking about?'

I paused, deciding just how much to reveal. 'Near Alnwick.'

He nodded once more. 'That's wolf country, that is. Horrible creatures, wolves. Go for the legs, they does.'

I blinked in irritation at his evasion of my question. 'Yes, yes, but what of the dark lights? Do you know anything that might help me?'

'Who can say, eh?' he said, leaning back and helping himself to another long draught of beer. 'There was talk of this 'ere serpent what was washed up on a beach near Colchester a few years back. Big as ten men, they said. Never believed it m'self. Mind you, which men was it that told the story? Most likely it was men with the Devil in 'em. Like them two bastards in Oxford.'

'I see,' I said, trying not to appear confused. The mention of Oxford brought to my mind the strange face carved into the tavern lintel. 'What did you mean about the foliate head in the wooden beam being men?'

'Eh?'

'"Men of all colours," you said. "Men of all colours, but all of them green."'

'That's the way of it.' He paused to chew on a piece of cured sausage that I'd left on my plate, and waggled the remainder of it in the air to make his point. 'He were in them two lads, though.'

'What do you mean, in them?'

'That's what he does! He gets in 'em,' said Poole, speaking with his mouth full. 'Ye don't want to be messin' with such things. He saw 'em and he got into 'em.'

I took it from this that Poole believed that the face in the lintel had somehow possessed the two men to take part in a wicked act in the tavern yard, and I sighed in disappointment. 'It was merely wood, Poole.' I said. 'Plain, dead wood. Like this.' And I picked up a small log from the scuttle by my seat and tossed it onto the fire, which crackled and spat gleefully at the fresh fuel. 'There was nothing in the wood but a base, pagan carving. An image, nothing more. But what does the image mean? And why is it thought to have power?'

I gazed at the fire for a few moments, hypnotised by the dance of the yellow sprites that erupted from the heart of the timber, rising like sacrifices into the air before withering into spirals of smoke and becoming nothing. How brightly they burned, but how fleetingly, before twisting into death, leaving only ash as evidence that they were ever there.

'Can't have dark lights, anyhow,' said Poole, his voice settling into a soporific rumble. 'Light's light, not darkness. S'why we call it light. Can't be nothin' else.'

'That's why we call it light, indeed,' I said in a thin voice. 'What else could it be?'

Poole, by now, was leaning back in his chair with his hands interlaced across his paunch, fat and content, his eyes slowly closing. Somewhere in the back of my mind, a thought came to me, as if through the fire, about the young Berwick girl who had been torn to pieces by her own townsfolk, but before I could grasp the story, it was gone, like the wisps of smoke.

'Mr Poole, what else could it be?' I said again, unable to conceal my frustration. I was half-minded to rouse Poole from his sleep and express my dissatisfaction with his cryptic answers but once again thought back to the incident at Oxford and permitted him his simplicity. I owed him a great deal—perhaps my life. In any case, to spoil an evening of excellent beer, food and fireside warmth was a sin, so I let things be. I decided to rest, too, and enjoy a night of rare peace.

Next morning, Poole was gone.

17th November

In which I arrive in York and meet the physician Albertus of Aachen

nones

The roads from Rokeby to York were rough and uneven and our progress was held up by the poor weather, the threat of cut-throats and the frequent need to change horses. Twice, also, we missed our route as we headed to Leicester, which I knew of as Ledecestre, and from Leicester to Doncaster, which the Scots had obtained in the Treaty of Durham and which, to my knowledge, has remained Scottish ever since.

On arrival at York, after more than a week of travel, I experienced a mixture of anticipation and distress. York was the seat of John of Thoresby, the city's archbishop and the correspondent to the Palais in Avignon. There was nothing I wanted more than to meet the great man, and yet I knew that I could not. The risk of his revealing my illicit journey in correspondence with the cardinals was too great. It was therefore with a heavy heart that I sacrificed a great opportunity for the better part of valour.

Instead, I asked the coachman to take me to the school of St. Peter, the *alma mater* of the physician Albertus who had reported on the business at Berwick. The school was half-a-mile along the city's northern road from York Minster, one of the Christian world's most glorious monuments to Christ, whose story was reflected in every aspect of its building, down to the last window and stone.

I arrived at the gatehouse of the school, where a guard was in casual conversation with a black-habited monk. The monk was completely bald, with bright blue eyes and snow-white skin. As I approached, he greeted me with a smile and a nod.

'Welcome, Brother,' he said. 'Can I help you?'

'My name is Jacobus of Vienna. I am here to see the

physician Albertus of Aachen. I do not think he will be expecting me, but I am here to discuss matters pertinent to his work.'

'How very enigmatic!' said the monk. 'I am Brother Antony. Walk with me and I shall take you into the school.' He bid the guard farewell and led me through the courtyard and into the main school building. A candlelit corridor bisected rooms containing younger children being taught the trivium and minors being taught various aspects of the quadrivium.

'I teach music within the quadrivium,' Brother Antony told me. 'We have a well-regarded group of choristers that provides accompaniment during Trinity mass at York Minster. Do you teach, Brother Jacobus?'

'I am a scholar of the natural philosophies principally, but also of logic and the Classical texts.' I thought it prudent not to mention the office of Inquisitor. That word had the power of a torch, to illuminate a person or plunge them into darkness. 'Most of my work is done in field study.'

'I see. You and Albertus have much in common, in that case. He is not in his study at present. He teaches two local apprentices in the ways of medicine and is keen on acquiring knowledge of the philosophies to supplement his practical expertise. He lectures occasionally on Galen and Avicenna here at the school—in fact, it is approaching midday and he will be completing a lecture in the Hall right now. But here is his room. You may wait or, if you prefer to observe Sext prayers, I can take you to the chapel.'

I accepted the latter offer and observed the midday prayer in the school chapel before returning to Albertus's study, where I found the physician standing before his lectern, poring over a sheaf of notes. He turned his head towards me and regarded me with a beady scowl. His was a hard-bitten face, a face made dark by dark work, and his eyes—black and unyielding—were eyes that had seen horrors and not turned away. A podgy nose sat atop a wild beard, unfettered by the constraints of grooming. He was not dressed as a monk but in the lay fashion, with a colourful but dirty robe sitting over his ordinary clothes. In a thick and stony voice he addressed me, and I noticed that spoke in the local flat brogue of North-East England but with the undertone of Alemannic German that marked my speech.

'Brother Jacobus.'

I touched my chest. 'You know me?'

'Brother Antony told me I might expect you. I was not expecting a visiting scholar, mind—least of all from Vienna.'

I entered the room and closed the door behind me. 'I confess, I did not send correspondence of my arrival, because of the sensitivity of the matter. As for Vienna, I was born there and became a novice there but I live in Villeneuve, near Avignon.'

I drew closer to the lectern at which he stood. 'Albertus, I took receipt of the letter and report that you composed, relating the mystery and tragedy that has befallen Berwick and its people. I am here to help.'

His eyes sparkled with understanding but the expression around his mouth did not change. He slammed shut the book he was reading and turned to face me.

'You're here to help?'

'In so far as I can, yes.'

'Good, good.' He stepped away from his lectern, scratched his beard and started pacing the room, speaking as he did so. 'This is a blessed mystery, and quite beyond what my doctor's eyes can see. Please sit, Brother.'

He gestured to a bunch of scarlet cushions threaded with faded gold-dyed trim on the floor. They were old and flimsy, worn thin by the impressions of several dozens of young pupils' behinds as they sat and listened to their master. I accepted his invitation with grace, but my bones were not quite so grateful as I lowered myself painfully to the floor and arranged myself in the same cross-legged position as his young charges were wont to. As I did so, Albertus searched through a messy pile of papers and parchments upon a table in the corner until he clutched at one and brandished it at me.

'You read my letters, then?'

'Yes. They are archived in France but I copied the details into my own journal and have read them again and again along my journey.'

'Here. This is a copy of what I wrote. What do you think?'

'What do I think? Your letters whet the appetite of the curious mind but they provide only questions. You said you were scouring the region for similar reports of missing children and desecrated bodies. Did your search yield any fruit?'

'I have my suspicions but the records are haphazard, and incomplete. I sent a missive to several of the local reeves, asking this question. The Reeve of Sherburn, not too far from here, responded: he said the body of a child was found in Little Moss Hagg Wood. Another letter, from the Reeve of Thirsk, said some children had gone missing in the Moors. But life here is cheap, Jacobus. These do not add up to a pattern.'

'Then we have a great deal of work to do. I have come here because I am something of an investigator in France and in the Holy Roman Empire, and place faith in the workings of the world. We are blessed with such capacities that we can fathom the earth's mysteries and break them into countable number and readable word. Well, I agree with you that the matter requires investigation for there is something very strange here, but I am convinced that, illuminated by the Light of Christ, we can uncover the truth of the matter.'

Albertus grumbled something under his breath. 'So you have not yet permitted yourself any speculative explanation?'

'Of course not. Why, have you alighted on a theory?'

'No, Brother.'

'A pity. Your letter related that some of the children made their way home and two survived. The boy was named Alfred and the girl Matilda. Are they still alive?'

Albertus nodded. 'Aye, they did. We had a very warm summer this year. I wonder if that had some bearing on their *Überleben*. The weather gets awful bitter up here. In the winter, a wee bairn couldn't withstand it. I suppose they had some blessing of the Lord about them, or perhaps just good fortune. But the weather has now turned bad. Winter is on its way. If more bairns are taken … .'

His voice trailed off and he stared at me, his face grave and his eyes hard. 'Brother Jacobus … the local people are afraid. Afraid of what they might find. Not many people saw the bodies of Griselda and Henry but for those that did, it was enough to put the fear of devilry into them. At first they treated it as exceptional. Then, at the end of the year, it happened again. After that, some of the villeins began to move away from the manors in which they paid for land to farm. That's how the word got around in even the sleepiest villages: cultivated strips were suddenly being abandoned, as if the land was cursed, leaving the more prosperous serfs wondering whether some unholiness would injure them too if they took the strips over. At the same time, the cost of fuel rose because the people feared sending their children into the woods to gather tinder.

'In short, some will cooperate in a search—mainly the families who have already suffered the grievous loss of a child—but most prefer to carry on in ignorance and by hoping and praying that they will not be the next to be afflicted.'

'Prayer is not enough,' I muttered. 'And I say that as one who is devoted to liturgical practice. If these people cannot bring themselves to help their neighbours when they are in dire straits … .' I paused, about to cast aspersions upon these people but then stopped myself. Albertus was surely correct. The people were scared; nor were they armed with the powers of logic needed to cut through their dread. I realised that my coming might indeed shine a light upon the darkness that had taken them over. 'If they cannot be called on to aid their neighbours in such times,' I continued, 'then their terror must indeed be great, and they must consider the riddles that fox them fiendish indeed. I understand their behaviour. It is tempting to turn one's face from the predator, hoping to escape his notice. But the Prophet Daniel was known to be able to read riddles, and like him we must face down the lions!'

'There bain't no lions here, Brother Jacobus. Wolves, maybe … .'

'Nonetheless, there is a predator at work here,

Albertus. Something is doing strange things to these children, and we must find and regard whatever it is with an unflinching eye, regardless of its grotesque countenance. Albertus, you are evidently a man of learning. May I ask a troubling question?'

'I have been burned with nought but troubling questions this past year, Brother. By all means, throw your logs on my fire.'

'I saw ... or, at least, I came upon a scene which ... I mean, I did not see anything, strictly speaking, but the aftermath ... or what would have been the aftermath ... .'

'Spit it out, Brother Jacobus. You may speak plainly with me!'

I stared at him, mastered myself and related the story. 'Do you think there might have been foul play? Two men outside an inn in Oxford, with knifes, acting as though they were trying to capture ... something ... or perhaps someone ... . I do not know what I saw but might it have been what has happened here?'

'Of course we have considered human agency,' Albertus muttered as he carried on pacing his room. 'But there was no evidence of such things on the bodies of these wee'uns. No stab marks, no slices, no penetrating wounds. You think there may be a killer among us?'

'They have built the high places of Topheth in the Valley of Ben Hinnom to burn their sons and daughters in the fire,' I said, quoting the *Book of Jeremiah*.

Albertus stopped, eyeing me with suspicion. 'What's that?'

'The Canaanites used to burn their young as an offering to their gods.'

'No one's being burnt here, Brother Jacobus. From what I've seen, this is something else entirely.'

'I understand, my friend, but my point is that the sacrifice of little children is well established among those to whom the saving grace of Our Lord is not known or valued. Having seen those men in Oxford, I wonder what other barbarous practices might have survived in the darker corners of this country, where perverted offerings may continue to be made to detestable idols and where the heresy of paganism is still venerated.'

Albertus stopped what he was doing and looked at me. His face was stern, hard, grey. Heresy. Paganism. The words had a chilling quality, certain to douse the fire in any Christian's heart and bring an end to lively conversation. These were matters that invited the intervention of the Church and its Inquisition—and the Inquisition was known and feared.

Eventually, and with great care, he spoke. 'Brother Jacobus, the people here are good Christian folk. I see them at church; they practise their faith with solemnity and grace. These ideas, of heresy, of child sacrifice—they are ancient stories, myths. Please do not throw around accusations in this careless way. The people are scared precisely because they are good Catholics.'

'Albertus, do not be afraid. I only wish to help. And I *can* help with my knowledge, as I said, of the natural philosophies. Can I rely upon you to aid me in my investigation?

Albertus sighed, his shoulders sagged. 'I want to see these people right and so I'll help you, if you can shine some light on these strange happenings. I don't mind saying, it is all beyond my knowledge. I'm used to dealing with wounds and sickness, not the strange magicking away of children and the corruption of their flesh. And aye, I've seen sicknesses and poxes that might appear from mischief and bad work, but none such as this, which is taking child after child every quarter-year, and not just making 'em sick but spiriting them away into the black woods, and then … .'

He stopped, perhaps fearful that he had said enough, then looked me in the eye. 'Look, I'm a secular man and I pay homage to the Good Lord as well as I can through my work and prayer. But life here is hard enough without this strange enchantment. So I will ask you to watch yourself, Brother Jacobus. While your natural philosophies may be of some use in the fancy libraries in the great palaces, the folks up here will have little truck with it.'

'A warning, Albertus?'

'A friendly one. From one man of the Empire to another. I've heard stories about what the Church does to those it accuses of heresy and I advise you against seeing heresy where it doesn't exist, Brother. But if you know something I don't—well, I'll swallow my doubts, if you swallow yours.'

I was not about to swallow any doubts. Doubt and scepticism would be two of the sharpest weapons in my armoury—but diplomacy would also serve, and so I nodded.

'Very good. You are a man of principle. I will need you. If we are in agreement, I should like to begin as soon as possible. The first thing would be to visit the survivors, talk to them, and try to make sense of whatever testimony they can bring themselves to bear.'

He relaxed a little. I had bought a little loyalty by subordinating myself to him in this way. Satisfied, he started picking about his classroom, packing things away.

'Aye, as you see fit. Of course, all have been questioned already, and precious little sense could anyone get from them. But I will take you round the families of the children harmed over the last two years, and then to the family of the brother and sister taken most recently.'

'Good, very good,' I said. 'But there are issues of diplomacy that must also be respected. If I am undertaking Church business upon his land, I must talk to Lord Thomas de Hayeford and inform him of my presence.'

Albertus rolled his eyes and looked away, muttering under his breath at my mention of Hayeford's name. 'You disagree?'

'No. You are right: you must comply with your obligations, Brother Jacobus,' said Albertus, folding his papers and putting them away. 'I will take you there, but I will not stay with him. Hayeford is a difficult man. I have had only limited dealings with him, but those I had were quite enough. I would not want more.'

I noted what he said but would not let his words deter me. I would head for House Hayeford, and thence to Berwick.

19th November

In which I meet the local nobleman Lord Thomas de Hayeford

Nones

The northern reaches of England seemed bleaker, more blasted and in some strange way more beautiful the more I saw of them. I had assumed, in my naivety, that the far north of England would be subsumed by such frozen wastes that any life would struggle to survive but it was no colder than the foothills of the Pyrenees, and when the sun shone it was perfectly clement. God casts His good light in the most surprising places.

Along the journey Albertus told me everything he had observed about the events I had come to investigate, relating in horrific detail the state of degradation of those bodies that had been worst affected. He could not tell me what he considered the precise cause of death. I rattled off a catalogue of possibilities—exposure, venom, pestilence, plague, addle, scourge, ague, leprosy, palsy, flux, scrofula, dropsy, scurvy, lues, perhaps even some catastrophic wound—but Albertus had considered all of these things and far more.

What had mostly confounded him was the unnatural state of ruination of the worst affected bodies. As he had written, they did not display the typical signs of having been left in the wild for any long period of time. The insides were not there but the skin was, inexplicably, almost intact. The bodies ought to have weighed next to nothing after being consumed by the forces of decay. In fact, Albertus said, moving them was like trying to move large sacks filled with soil. It took two strong men to move each child. When he had cut open their insides, there were no insides! No organs, no muscle, no cartilage, only the bones were left intact. Instead, the bodies were stuffed with soil—ripe, moist, fertile soil—in which various plants had taken root. We went through the details of the plants he had identified as growing there, and the insects and tiny bestioles of the woodland floor he had observed operating in it, but they all were quite benign: not poisonous or toxic in any way. If the children had been slain by some injury—a broken neck or a blow to the head—then the remaining bones would have provided a clue, but this did not seem to be the case. And since the skin was already punctured so liberally by roots and shoots forcing their way out, any evidence of stab wounds would have been impossible to detect.

'Did you bury them?' I asked, after hearing of these details.

'Aye, but … .' He shook his head, not in refutation but in disbelief at the memory. 'Once the gravediggers had dug the earth out of their corpses, there was nought left.'

We both sat silent for a while then, I digesting them and Albertus reliving them, while our cart slowly rumbled on. To my surprise I missed Poole. He may not have solved the mystery but he would have added some telling story or piece of local knowledge that perhaps Albertus was not a party to. I was conscious that, even though he dressed and spoke very like the locals, Albertus was not one of them—not of their blood or history. If there was some pox or practice embedded in the antiquity of this place, it might well have be situated in some blind spot in Albertus's cognition.

With nothing more pressing to discuss, I was left to observe this strange landscape of leafless, wintry forests on my own. Their canopies looked like the interlocking fingers of elderly friends. At the point where they thinned out, the road continued northwards, ploughing through brooding stone valleys and purple-tinged moors until, at last, the endless desolation was broken by the modest thumb of a Norman castle sticking up in the distance, its motte or base fenced off by a high wall.

It was Hayeford Castle.

I alighted at a fork in the road. Albertus helped me down with my bags.

'If you intend on continuing to Berwick after paying your respects to Thomas de Hayeford, I will collect you tomorrow morning and take you to the town's Franciscan friary,' he said. 'It is welcoming, and offers good protection from winter storms, and they have an infirmary, which is where I treated the surviving children and conducted the autopsies of the dead. It will serve you best, I think. But I would ask for Hayeford's permission first. And be careful of him. He will offer you succour if he thinks your beliefs align with his, but he's a suspicious old fool.'

'What do you mean?'

'He has his … prejudices.'

'Well, we are all sinners. But I will heed your words, my friend Albertus. Farewell!

'Until tomorrow, Brother Jacobus.'

He climbed back onto the cart which, after a crack of the driver's lash on the flank of its drey, slowly trundled onwards, taking the right-hand fork to the very end of England.

Once the physician was on his way I turned and made my way up the left-hand path. It was little more than a muddy incline, and for a mile or so I squelched along it, becoming hot and sweaty in spite of the chill, until the way flattened out and the castle stood before me, small and squat: a grim sentinel for a grim landscape. From the western turret a flag flew, depicting a blue lion rampant on a yellow background. The lion insignia made me think of Albertus, who had said that there were no lions in England. *What else do you have here that you say you have not?* I thought to myself with a chuckle.

One of two armoured look-outs who had been watching me from a shabby barbican shouted down to me in an accent I had not yet got used to.

'His Lordship's got nar bi'ness wi' Father Denis's lot the'day, Holy Brother!' he hollered. By his side, the other fellow leaned against the stonework of a turret and peered down at me with half-hearted curiosity.

'*Venio in pace!*' I called in reply, looking up and shielding my eyes from the winter sun. 'I know of no Denis; I come alone.'

'Tha's not of the Franciscans of Berwick?'

'No, good fellow. I am Brother Jacobus of Vienna, of the Order of Benedict, and serve at the Abbey de Saint André in Villeneuve, France. I have travelled thence to speak with the Lord Master, Lord Hayeford, in response to a request made on his behalf by the great man of God, John of Thoresby. I am here to do God's will and put right a grievous matter that has beset Lord Hayeford's land and people, and which has caught the attention of His Holy Father.'

The two men exchanged a word or two between themselves.

'Is it aboot tha bairns, then?' called the first man.

I was not yet familiar with the word but he must have fathomed my witlessness, as he continued sharply, 'the bairns, the wee'uns. The children gone missing!'

'Yes, that's it, the children! A letter was sent by a physician named Albertus.' I produced Magnus's letter from my satchel and waved it above my head as proof, realising at the same time that this must have looked preposterous.

The two men conferred once more and then the one who had done the talking rang the visitor's bell. As I walked towards a pair of fortified gates, I noticed, with some shock, another foliate keystone staring down at me from the head of the archway over the entrance. This one was hewn from stone, but the long vines and creepers sprouting from its orifices, and the rictus of pain or pleasure on its face, were much the same as the head I had seen in Oxford. Carved ivy crept out from the nose and ears, enveloping other images cut from the stone: men, wolves, soldiers, dogs and babies. This time I smiled wryly at the grotesque face and gave it a nod of recognition as the gates were opened for me and I passed between them. The English clearly possessed a greater fondness for these strange pagan faces than people on the Continent. Perhaps they thought them benevolent guardians as well as threatening spectres. Is not our Lord Himself both forgiving Son and judgmental Father, healing by water and curing by fire?

VESPERS

Thomas de Hayeford eyed Magnus's letter cautiously. His castle, originally a donjon built of wood by the Conqueror but subsequently converted into a more substantial stone keep, was cramped but surprisingly cosy. Upon hearing me explain my journey and my interest in his situation, Hayeford made it his business to make me feel at home. He invited me into his solar, his private living quarters, and commanded his steward, a military man named Thirlwall, to spare no effort in bringing me comforts to stave off the effects of the long hardship in reaching him.

'Thank you for your welcome, Lord de Hayeford,' I said after one of Thirlwall's staff had brought me a plate of food and a pint of beer. I had been seated at a grand table by a handsome fire, the warmth of which soon soothed the creaking of my bones. A serving boy stood in the corner of the room, waiting upon us.

'You are most welcome, dear Brother,' Hayeford replied, stroking his top lip nervously, 'but beware: it may be one of the only welcomes you enjoy in this hellish time.'

'Hellish?' I repeated. 'Did you mean to invoke the Inferno, Lord de Hayeford, or did you speak casually?'

'Not casually at all, dear Brother,' he said, crossing himself. Though physical characteristics are fleeting and the Lord forbids us from fixating upon them, Hayeford's appearance seemed the very embodiment of fear. A man of advancing years, and heavy about the face, there was no colour in his cheeks, and one of his eyes twitched. He inched closer to me as I ate, and grasped my arm, as much to reassure himself that I was real as to assure me of the sincerity of his words.

'God has forsaken this land,' he went on. 'It is beset by witches, and by wicked men and women who fornicate with demons and infect us with their magic and pox and sorcery and … .' He gripped the arm of his chair quite ferociously, as though overcome by a spasm, before looking into the hearth and attempting to master himself anew. He crossed himself again and muttered, in a dry, hoarse voice, 'The Evil One walks among us!'

Sweat had started to cascade from his forehead and his eyes bulged, and I inferred that the horrors of which he spoke had suddenly appeared to him right there in his room.

I confess that I breathed a sigh of weariness at the pitiable old man's fright, but I did not reveal it. 'What do you mean by the Evil One, My Lord? Satan himself? I read the letter sent by the physician Albertus. He made no mention of Satan. He said that certain local people had talked about being visited by the Devil—may God smite him—but I think he used the term in a more metaphorical sense. He did not mention your own thoughts upon the matter.'

Hayeford twisted his face into a scowl and thumped the arm of his chair. 'By God's bones, it's the Scots, I tell you! They are after this land, my land, the king's land, God's land! The heathens among them, both men and women, run wild across our lands, wielding axes, hunting game, taunting us. And while the men bring all manner of noxious follies, the Devil plants his seed in their women, who in turn bear macabre fruits that live in the woods, and dangle from the trees, and seduce and tempt the stout hearts of our English. Did you know their mere touch causes illness? Or that they steal our babies by night and do things to them—wicked, unholy things—in the depths of the cold forest where nobody can hear the screams, and then, when they have had their way with them, they chop their bodies into a potage for incantations or set them loose as wild, perverted animals to return to us to commit unholy things among us! These heathens touch our children with their bedevilled fingers and give them the Mark! A pox on them! A pox, I say, by the fingernails of Christ, and a pox on all their breed!'

Hayeford had become more and more agitated as he spoke, and was now panting heavily, teeth bared. He flung his cup of wine into the fire, where it sent up an angry hiss, and then collapsed into his chair, looking neither at me nor the fire but at the wild Scots plaguing his fantasies.

I waited while he settled, and gave myself a moment to arrange my thoughts. How safe was I? The majority of Hayeford's men at the castle would be military, and while it would certainly be outrageous to slay a man who had been taken in as a guest, and even more so a man of God (even one who had come under false pretences), I had to take into account the volatility that he had just shown me. However hospitable he had been in the last hour or so, I could not predict how hospitable he might be an hour hence. As so often in my work, I needed to woo him from blind passion to calm reason.

'Forgive me, my Lord, but do the Scots not keep the faith of the Holy Father and the Catholic Church just as well as the stout-hearted English?' I suggested. 'Are their kirks not also bastions of the Faith?'

He looked at me in disgust. 'What would an Austrian living in France know about the Scots? They may keep the faith well enough in their churches and when dealing with the dandies in Burgundy and Aquitaine, but up here in the north, the real north, they are altogether different. They were smashed once by Edward the Hammer, and should have had the good grace to recognise that they had been brought to heel. Instead, they refuse to accept that Berwick now lies under the authority of the English crown, and since their swords have failed to win it back, they turn to sorcery to do what they could not.'

I breathed slowly. I knew from my dealings with religious zealots and the halfway mad that there was never any arguing that could make them see sense. Whatever solid evidence one might put in front of them, they would only interpret it as proof of their own superstitions, and be sent deeper and deeper into the snares of their own mania. In investigating the strange fate of the children of Berwick I would therefore have to appease Lord Hayeford to some degree, for he would be a deadly foe if I lost his trust by challenging him. I would of course keep an open mind with respect to the Scots, but my search for the real answer to the conundrum would have to be conducted at a safe distance from his hysteria, and on terms that would satisfy God and the local people rather his unseemly prejudices. In short, I would have to operate on my own and in secret—again.

'I will heed your words about the Scots, Lord Hayeford,' I said, 'and I thank you for your candour. I well understand the fears you harbour; they are truly upsetting. I think it best if I take one step at a time. First I think I should turn my attention to the town of Berwick and its tithings.'

'What good will that do?' Hayeford wailed. 'What's done is done. God give those poor bairns peace.'

'Nevertheless, I am disposed to abide by certain methodologies, including the gathering of various types of material which have elsewhere enabled me to solve mysteries that have eluded all other inquisitors. I would therefore, with your leave, like to make Berwick the base for my investigation.'

He grumbled and looked towards the serving boy. 'Bring me a cup of wine, boy!' He turned back to me, looking pitifully tired. 'You will rest here tonight and in the morning travel to Berwick. My seneschal, Thirlwall, will this evening dispatch one of my men on horseback to the Franciscan friary in Berwick and inform them of your imminent arrival. The guardian there is Dionysius of Alnwick. The locals know him as Father Denis. He will ward you well and aid you in your … inquiry.' He gave that final word the full weight of his contempt, certain there was nothing to investigate and the matter was already concluded.

I bowed humbly. 'Thank you, Lord de Hayeford. It would indeed be better for me to board with the local friars. Perhaps it would also be prudent for your man to request of Guardian Dionysius that Albertus of Aachen be invited to our discussions, for I value his knowledge.'

Hayeford nodded with some impatience. 'It shall be done.'

'Thank you again, My Lord. And now, I must observe compline to finish my daily liturgy. May I attend the castle chapel?'

'You may. Good night, Brother Jacobus.'

20th November

In which
I leave
Hayeford Castle
for Berwick
and meet
the
Franciscan
Guardian
Dionysius
and
a new
companion

PRIME

After I had observed prime at sunrise the next morning, I discovered that Hayeford Castle was already abuzz with activity. Men-at-arms practised weaponry drills, in constant expectation of being mustered to counter the Scots. The marshal oversaw the work of grooms and pages in the stables. Servants under the direction of the pantler and butler busied themselves preparing the day's rations of food, which included providing a few extra supplies for me. It was a grey, chilly day with fine, misty rain dancing in the air.

Not wanting to be a bother to anyone, I left the castle grounds and took a short walk to the beautiful old church of John the Baptist so that I could observe Terce in the open air. Upon my return, Hayeford greeted me in the courtyard. However grey and miserable the weather, he looked a lot better than he had done the night before, although his eyes still flickered this way and that, as though the very walls of his house were beset with tricksters and knaves.

'So then, Brother Jacobus,' he said, regarding me with watchful curiosity, 'I trust you will take to heart what we discussed last night.'

I gave him a look of great sincerity. 'I will place all you said at the very forefront of my considerations. The Scots will not escape my attention.'

'See that they do not. Father Denis, the Guardian at Berwick, awaits you. And I will await news of your findings. To help you on your way I make you a gift of this horse and the protection of one of my best knights, Sir Walesby of Otterburn.' Hayeford gestured to a lightly armoured knight already mounted on his own horse.

Sir Walesby was a gravelly man with long, dark hair

that fell about his broad shoulders and a thick black moustache flecked with grey. A buckler and bastard sword were fastened to his baldric, and knives were strapped to his outerwear. When he spoke, his voice was thick and deep and rough, like the Northumbrian landscape. He looked at me with hard, joyless eyes, and gave me the merest nod.

'Brother Jacobus. Well met.'

'Sir Walesby served the king well at Auberoche, Crécy and Calais, and will not let you down,' said Hayeford with a thin smile, before turning to the knight. 'See that Brother Jacobus comes to no harm as he conducts his important investigations, Sir Walesby.' The undercurrent of sarcasm in Hayeford's voice was unsettling. So was his instruction. While Sir Walesby of Otterburn was indeed appointed to offer me protection, it was a fair guess that he had also been ordered to watch me closely and ensure that my investigations would result in a conclusion that would satisfy his lord.

'Once again you have my sincere gratitude and the gratitude of the Church for aiding this inquest,' I said, before administering him a blessing. 'May the Lord bless you and your house. Go in peace, Thomas de Hayeford, Lord.'

'And you also, Brother. We will meet again, I am sure.'

The rest of the day was taken up with our ride north-northeast, crossing Berwick's moat and passing through its great gates just as the sun, muted by chainmail clouds, set over the Northumbrian hills. The outer walls were tall and strong for a town of its size, a reflection of how attractive it was to both the English and the Scots.

As the gates were secured behind us, Walesby turned and asked me if I wanted to go straight to the friary.

'In good time, Sir Walesby. I want first to familiarise myself with the place. Apparently the Franciscan friary is up at the northern tip of the town, right next door to the Dominicans, while the Carmelites are down at the very southern end. As a Benedictine, I should have to be on my best behaviour wherever I stay. But will the Carmelites be more welcoming than the Franciscans, since their founder was also a friend of our Order. I'll go and find out. I can be back in fifteen minutes. Will you wait?'

'I'm not to let you out of my sight, Brother. At least, not until you're safe in your lodgings.'

'And you will lodge in the town's garrison?'

'No. I'll stay at the friary's dormitory as well. Oh now, don't look so put out, Brother Jacobus! My Lord Hayeford will make sure that the Guardian is compensated; you will not need to bear any of my costs.' He said this with just a twinkle in his eye, revealing that we both knew his real purpose in attending me.

Since I was unable to get shot of him, I allowed Sir Walesby to take charge and he led us, still mounted, through the muddy streets of the town to the Franciscan friary, up by the gateway in the North Wall. I kept my eyes and wits about me as we trotted, aware that no one would pay much notice to a Benedictine monk riding through their town, for we dressed in no specific colour, whereas there were so many others—Grey Friars, Black Friars and White Friars—who attracted attention by their garb, sometimes in the colour of their Order and sometimes plain brown.

This highly contested town would be my home for the next few weeks, and I wished to get a good first sense of it, before it got coloured by local prejudices and hearsay. At its north-western entrance Berwick castle could be seen projecting proudly above the town's highest point, catching the fading sunlight and reflecting an austere majesty. The castle watched over this fragile town and its environs in all directions, with watchmen posted to keep their eyes firmly on the Scots' lands to the north, but also along the waters of the river Tweed to the west and south, and over the bitter murk of the North Sea to the east. I later noted that the town walls themselves wrapped all the way around the town like an embrace, joining hands over the mouth of the river, which was blocked by a thick iron gate to prevent undesirables from gaining entry from the coast.

On our short trip through the town's narrow thoroughfares it dawned on me that Lord de Hayeford was not the only person fearful of Scottish incursions. This was a place, Sir Walesby explained grimly, whose scars and wounds went back further than those freshly riven by the Scots. The Danes in their warships had plundered these shores from the east many hundreds of years ago, sacking also the Holy Island of Lindisfarne. The trauma of that onslaught was still keenly felt and Berwick's military had remained on permanent standby ever since. For this reason, much of the town's business was concerned with martial matters, from the preparation of weaponry and military drilling to the provision of quarters for men-at-arms.

Sir Walesby pointed out also a trio of taverns in the town square which served as the meeting point for all classes, from the merchants who emptied the night waste from their bed pans out of their upstairs windows and down onto the streets, to the lowly wretches who were charged next morning to clean it up. They and the military men and friars were all packed together in this smelly town, which may also have been why not a single citizen paid me the slightest attention. All seemed preoccupied with what was beyond the town's high walls. And all seemed on edge.

A few streets east of the castle was the friary that we sought. Its typically grubby stone chapel and its modest chapter house and dormitory were clumped together on the ridge of grounds that looked out over the sea. Its habitations and infirmary stood on its north side and I was relieved to find that I would be able to live one step removed from the town's muck and filth.

Tonsured friars tilling modest plots of vegetables looked up as I rode past, and surprised me by offering smiles and waves of welcome that were so unguarded as to appear desperate. Their robes were typically mendicant: shabby, moth-eaten, without embellishment and uncared for. I was shocked that, despite my long and arduous journey, I had been able to take greater care of my own black gown than the residents of this place took of their clothing. While I responded with a polite and sober nod, I confess I silently bemoaned the Franciscan wont for overfamiliarity and their fetishising of poverty. They were a messy lot.

I was delivered to the chapter house, where Guardian Dionysius was waiting for me, leaning upon his crosier with the same broad grin as his friars. He greeted me by placing his left hand upon my right cheek and granting the Kiss of Peace upon my lips.

'Welcome, welcome!' he said. 'You must be Brother Jacobus, from Avignon. One of Lord Hayeford's men informed us you were coming. I am Dionysius, Guardian of our mendicant house, but I go by the name of Father Denis.'

'Father Denis. It is good to meet you. I am indeed Jacobus of Vienna, of the Order of Benedict.'

'You'll be fine now, Brother,' said Sir Walesby, dismounting and tethering his horse to a hitching post. 'I shall head to the Green Man tavern in town to sup, and return at lamplights. Father Denis,' he said, bowing his head towards the Guardian in greeting, 'will there be a palliasse ready for me in the dorm? And will you take care of my mare?'

Guardian Dionysius nodded to the knight, and gestured behind him to the cloister. 'All has been arranged.'

The knight strolled off without another word and I turned to the Guardian. 'Thank you for your warm welcome, Father.'

'Not at all, not at all,' he said, turning and placing his hand upon my arm to guide me through the monastery. He was a heavy-set fellow, well buffered to resist the easterly winds that blasted this place, but ruddy in the face and with a look of well-worn Franciscan contentment. 'So you are the one who has been sent to solve the mysteries of the children? I am surprised that you have come all the way from Avignon. I expected that Hayeford would call for a man from York, or Oxford, or London.'

'You did not see the letter from Archbishop John of Thoresby, then? It was he who corresponded with the papal palace in France and alerted us to the situation.'

He stopped walking for a moment and looked at me with worried eyes. 'The Archbishop? I had no idea that the matter had travelled so high.' He looked away, towards the town. 'Perhaps the episode really is as demanding of the Lord's attention, as some folk say.'

'"As some folk say"? Father Denis, should I infer that you do not take this business seriously? I have already met Albertus of Aachen in York and he has told me the tale of your parish. There is something amiss in this town and in the wider region, Father. That is why I was …'—I considered my words judiciously—'… why I came here to investigate. Things are surely far from normal.'

The Guardian turned back towards the chapel, continuing to walk. '"Normal," you say? Normal! And what is normal, these days? There is plague, and devilry, and threat, and invasions. This town changes hands more often than a bad penny. The common folk pray and follow the Lord but they also have their own superstitions and whimsies.'

I frowned at that. 'What does that mean? They do not kneel at the feet of false idols, I hope?'

He waved away the suggestion fussily. 'No no no, but you are not from here. There are things you have to learn. Local beliefs have a certain … coloration that you may not have encountered.'

'Actually, I think that I have. I have seen several foliate heads upon the buildings, from low taverns to noble houses.'

'Ah, well, those—yes, they are part of that tradition. They even appear in aspects of this friary's architecture. It may strike you as odd but it is not at all uncommon.'

Father Denis considered this for a moment and then struck a more wary tone. 'You mentioned an investigation? In what sense? Are you … .' Father Denis narrowed his eyes and his jocular face appeared more weathered. When he spoke again, his voice was hushed and troubled. 'Are you an inquisitor?'

I smiled and he reciprocated, but nervously. 'You do

not have to worry on that account,' I said. 'I have participated in the Inquisition but I am not a zealot, and I do not heat up tongs in the brazier to elicit confessions. I employ instead the scholarly arts, applying natural philosophy and seeking that evidence that exists in the world and its persons, for God places his truth in all things, and with sufficient intellectual effort it can be brought out for all to see and understand. There is no riddle that cannot be solved by the ingenuity of man, and I believe that the Lord expects us to use our talents for observation and logic as best we can. I have in fact saved several innocent souls from the flame, using such methods to disprove accusations of sorcery laid against them. I would even say, in reference to the local colourful beliefs you mention, that there may well be a sound reason for their being as they are. So long as such customs do not lurch into the diabolical frenzies of heresy, then all will be well.'

He nodded and crossed himself, as if he valued my insight but I was well aware that my presence was not really wanted. For him, I took it, Berwick's folklore was endemic but had no real meaning and he did not warm to the idea that it could be explained and rationalised. It was not that he bore me any ill will, just that he was a simple Franciscan.

'Well, well, well,' he said, as if to confirm what I had grasped, but then brightened up. 'Albertus is awaiting us in the chapter house, so you can explain your methods to him. Please, allow one of my friars to take your possessions to the dormitory and then we can head there directly.'

I cast an eye at the setting sun and realised it was time for Vespers. '*Ora et labora*, Father,' I said, piously.

'Ah, yes, you must observe the Rule of your patron. Very well. I will ask Albertus to tarry a little longer. He is most eager to catch up with you, as are we all.'

I was likewise keen to reacquaint myself with him. But the Rule of my Order remains clear, and since the journey had interrupted my ability to observe the liturgical hours, the higher part of my soul called to me to pay homage to the Lord and pray.

VESPERS

I took care to devote myself to the full office at Vespers, savouring every word of the versicles and responses, the psalmody, the canticle of Mary and the other prayers. By the time I had concluded with the Our Father and Sarum version of the *Kyrie Eleison* I felt refreshed and humbled. I did not want to keep Albertus waiting, and regretted having to delay the start of my investigation by a further night but I was determined not to let my devotions suffer and sang praises to the Lord that He might arm my wits and grant me protection from whatever hostile entities might greet me in this strange land.

In any case, the physician had not disappeared for the evening. I found him sitting around in the chapter house when I arrived there, talking to the Guardian Dionysius (whom I now addressed as Father Denis, as he had asked) and another friar. They sat at a circular oak table of huge size, on which stood a candelabrum and a few plates of good dark bread and cheeses and honey. Their chairs were of heavy oak too, with decorative backs.

The chapter house was octagonal and in the English Gothic style, with stone arches soaring eightfold overhead and tapering to a point, and with a single central column plummeting down to the floor. Dusk had settled in, the evening lamps were lit and the view was very grand.

'There is an hour or so before Compline, where I hope you will join us,' said Father Denis warmly, standing and offering me a seat before returning to his own. 'Enough time to discuss the matters at hand. But first, introductions. Albertus of Aachen you already know. He assists our infirmarian, Friar Herry, and his apprentices, for they have only basic knowledge of medicines, and rely on Albertus for his expertise.'

'Brother Jacobus,' said Albertus in a terse greeting, and left it at that. I extended him a terse smile in return.

'And this,' said Denis, turning to the third man, 'is Friar William of Alnwick. He is here at my behest, and will serve as your guide and companion while you lodge with us, to help you become familiar with the town and its people.'

Friar William, a tall and winsome man a few years my junior, rose from his seat and smiled as he took my hands and we exchanged the Kiss of Peace. 'I look forward to assisting you in your work, Brother Jacobus. I am yours for the duration of your stay, in whichever way you see fit.'

'You are most gracious, Friar William, to give succour to this old sinner.'

Denis's brows rumpled into furrows of contentment as he nodded with some vigour. 'While you were at Vespers, Brother Jacobus, Albertus and I discussed the manner of your coming, via the letters of John of Thoresby and the wisdom of the cardinals at the palace. Albertus has also tried to explain something of your suppositions and methods.'

'What little I could profess to know after only a day, that is,' said Albertus.

'That is well, then,' I said. 'Then, will you now update me? What is the current situation in the town?'

'No worse,' said Father Denis, 'but also no better.'

'Albertus told me about the children who have been taken from the local region.'

'Then you will know how frightened the people are.'

I nodded. 'Can you tell me whether any searches have been conducted in the woods for the missing bodies?'

'Fleetingly—and reluctantly,' said William. 'People are unwilling to enter the wood.'

'Because of the Scots?'

William made a sour sort of face and half shook his head. 'We have the measure of the Scots.'

'But Lord Thoresby told me they are devilish and carry out raids.'

'The Scots are troublemakers, but little more,' said William. 'Most people aren't afraid of them. They're afraid of—'

'Careful, Friar William,' growled Albertus.

'You can speak plainly in front of me, friend,' I said.

He continued, a little anxiously. 'The terror cuts them like a knife, right enough. The terror that he will come and take yet more of their children.'

'He?'

'Yes, he. Him.'

He looked up at the others, uncertainly. They looked back at him, transfixed to hear how he would convey what needed to be said.

'Who, William?' I pressed.

He looked embarrassed for a moment, then gave way. 'The Green Man.'

'The Green Man?' I repeated, incredulously. 'What, the name that's given to so many inns in this country?' I looked to the Guardian and his charge but neither of them gave any sign that this was a trick or jape or madness.

'Aye, the Green Man. The monster that lives in the forests.'

'The monster? That lives in the forests?' I paused to take this in. Again the Guardian said nothing. Even accounting for the Franciscan tendency to disregard what could be uncovered through study, I could not understand why Father Denis would let such pagan fallacies run wild in the community. 'And do you believe in this Green Man, Albertus? You're not a Northumbrian.'

He looked torn. 'It's a story, one to frighten bairns. Stay quiet or the Green Man'll take you away. Say your prayers or the Green Man'll have you. But now that bairns really have been taken away … .' He shook his head. 'Ah, I don't know what to believe, and that's the truth. All I know is the children who died weren't demons, just innocent little bairns. And some who might have died came back.'

'Yes, Albertus's letter said that one of the other bodies disinterred itself from its ungodly burial pit and returned to the town, only to be torn apart by its former kin.'

Denis bowed his head and muttered, 'The Lord killeth and maketh alive; he bringeth down to the grave and bringeth up.'

'*Dominus mortificat et vivificat; deducit ad inferos et reducit*,' I repeated. '1 Samuel 2:6.'

'κύριος θανατοῖ καὶ ζωογονεῖ κατάγει εἰς ᾅδου καὶ ἀνάγει,' added Friar William briskly and, I thought, a little boastfully.

An awkward silence followed as the rest of us waited to see who would deliver the verse in the most ancient and holy language of the Classical tripos, before we all piled in with 'יְהֹ' מֵמִית וּמְחַיֶּה מוֹרִיד שְׁאוֹל וַיָּעַל' which I think I managed to finish just ahead of the others.

At this, the physician spat with anger and shook his head. 'This is not the time for religious one-upmanship!' he barked. 'Father Denis, we have other fish to fry.'

I blushed, for Albertus was right. 'It seems that this lay physician has better scriptural understanding than all the rest of us, Father. Brother Albertus, if I may call you that: I apologise.'

The Guardian had the grace to look embarrassed too, and I feared that I may have gone too far in being the first to render a translation and thereby setting the stage for the others. Raising my hand in an effort at expiation, I said 'Lord, forgive us, for we know not what we do. There is more here than we have recognised and we let ourselves be distracted. There must be something that explains why this woman would act in egregious contravention of the practices of our dear Mother Church. The Lord raises the dead from the grave, but not so that they can return to the living with unnatural markings on their skin, if your account is true, Albertus.'

Albertus turned his sour gaze on me. 'Oh, it's true alright. I mightn't know every passage of the Good Book, but I'm a physician, and I know this: once you're in the ground, you don't climb out again. And if you do, that's nought to do with the Lord.'

Denis huffed. 'I do not purport to know the truth of the matter and it is not in my gift to uncover it. That is why you are here, Brother Jacobus. I understand the world as my sainted patron Francis did before me and my Brothers here: that all the world is God's and all the world is therefore to be cherished and worshipped in all its strange mystery.'

'Even the works of the Evil One?' I chipped in. 'Oh, don't look so alarmed, Father. I do not accuse anyone of heresy or sorcery; in my experience such accusations are made too frivolously, and bearing false witness to sorcery and witchcraft only ensnares the accuser, ensuring that Satan's work is done without the evildoer even being aware of it.

'Nevertheless, the facts are plain: devilry and demonism do infect the Earth, and need to be uprooted. Should the evidence indicate to me beyond any doubt that events such as those in Berwick are in fact the work of the Evil One or his subjugates, and a culprit can be identified, I would be duty-bound to initiate a trial!'

The word 'trial' struck Father Denis like a weapon. His face paled and he struggled to find a suitable response. I then remembered the wise words of Archbishop John of Thoresby, who advised in his letter that the conclusion of the matter ought not to add more distress to a land already crying out with pain. I would have to temper my inquisitiveness with discretion.

'But,' I continued, in a gentler tone, 'my experience has taught me that what seem to be supernatural events are usually the product of entirely natural, underlying causes—and it will be my duty to establish if that is so in this case. In my estimation, it is most likely that a trial will not be necessary.'

Denis crossed himself solemnly and nodded, recovering himself. 'That is why we requested outside expertise, because I would not have my friars look into the terrified eyes of our people and tell them that the horrors they have seen have all been part of God's plan. That would not have soothed their souls when their children continue to be taken—and sometimes return. A town in the grip of panic succumbs easily to temptation and the squalor of evil. We need an answer that carries the full authority of the Church and of scholastic study.'

21st November

In which I begin my investigations in earnest

PRIME

I spent the next day visiting the two surviving children, Alfred and Matilda, from the tithing of Murton. It was a short gallop from Berwick, and I made my way there with Friar William and Sir Walesby. The village was animated with women preparing food at trestle tables in the street, and skinning animals hung on wooden frames, and children playing with hoops and dolls. There was nothing remotely out of the ordinary.

Friar William introduced me to the affected family. The mother and father were happy to see him, thanked him for his presence, and invited us to sit on stools outside their hut, with Sir Walesby standing by to deter eavesdroppers. Alfred and Matilda, nine and seven years of age respectively, seemed as hearty and hale as any peasant child could expect to be. They had been helping with the chores during the morning, milking the goats and pulling up turnips and parsnips from a vegetable patch, and my heart soared at the thought that whatever travails had befallen them, they had not been fatal. When Friar William introduced them to me, I thanked God to see how well they were, but I was also perplexed, given the condition their bodies were said to have been in when found in the woods. When I queried this, Friar William reminded me that Alfred and Matilda's recovery may have been helped by the unseasonably warm summer that Northumberland had enjoyed that year.

To look at the children, one did not register that they had been subjected to any kind of trauma, except in one respect: the strange bark-like mark upon their foreheads, which bothered me. I was confident that, although I could not identify it, it was obviously the result of an ailment or injury, but I could see how the common people might read it as a sign that they had been touched by something not of this Earth—or not entirely of this Earth.

The parents were gratifyingly open in response to the questions I put. I had hoped that my interrogation of the children would prove equally satisfactory, given how very robust they now looked. My aspirations were dashed, then, when I found the answers given by the children to be meaningless, to say the least.

'It was like the forest was waking up,' said the girl. 'Like it waked up and took us.'

'We was frightened,' said the boy, sheepishly. 'So we said our prayers, like mam always says, and hoped we'd be away.'

When I pressed them on how they had arrived in the wood in the first place, they became sullen and unsure. This in turn made the parents uneasy. I changed tack and asked them what made them leave the woods but their account was incoherent. Whatever had happened to them had blurred their sense of time. Their recollection was a group of images: unintelligible stuff about dark lights and trees and leaves, leaves, leaves.

I had taken the liberty of borrowing a foliate head that had hung from one of the lintels in the friary to see what reaction it produced in the common folk in the tithings, and now brought it out to show the children. To my surprise the boy took it from my hands and looked at it without fear.

'What does that remind you of, my boy?' I asked him.

'Bad things,' he said, frowning at it, before his expression became more ambiguous. 'And good things. The bad man was like this. An' so were the good man. It's jus', the leaves was ever'where.'

'Some of the men in the trees was good,' said the girl,

'and some was bad.' She looked at her brother and he nodded.

I pointed to the children's foreheads, in turn. 'Do you remember what gave you that mark?'

The two of them looked at each other in that obviously clandestine way that children have when they want to keep a secret.

'Does it hurt?' I asked. 'Did it hurt?'

They shook their heads.

'May I touch it?' I asked the parents, and they nodded their permission.

The marks felt indeed like the bark of a tree. After I had finished, Alfred looked again at the foliate head he was still holding.

'Don't want this no more,' he said, handing it back.

I sat in silence, thinking, at which point the father politely asked if the children could be excused.

I nodded and off they went, back to their tasks. Their mother and father, simple folk who did not understand what had happened but were overflowing with gratitude, were willing to help but had little to offer.

'We're just grateful they're both living,' said Annabel, the mother. 'It was Hell, Holy Brother, not havin' 'em at home, if only for a day or two.'

'You are good people,' I said. 'God will smile upon you for your grace and humility. Do you have any idea what they meant by the bad men?'

The mother shook her head, at a loss, but the father, a stocky, heavy-set man, frowned. 'We're a simple lot, up here, Holy Brother. An' by and by we take care of each other, an' do reet by oursels. We pray to the Lord.'

'The only bad lot up here's the Scots,' said Annabel.

'Aye, them—an' the Wise Man,' said her husband.

'Though there's nought so wise about him,' said Annabel, and she spat upon the ground.

'The Wise Man?' I asked, looking to William for clues, though he simply frowned and shook his head.

'His name is Odenellus,' said William. 'He's … he is not worthy of your time.'

'He came around here, early in the summer,' growled the husband, 'hollerin' and bawlin' about this an' that in the woods, askin' for sacrifices and sayin' as we'd pay if the Man didn't have his share—though share of what I don't know, an' don't want to know—and so our men ran him out of town.'

The topic obviously caused the parents some agitation and so I decided to press them no further on the matter for the moment. Instead I made a note to ask William of it later on, commended them on their good judgement, complimented them on their children and gave them all a blessing.

Accompanied by Sir Walesby, we then sought to glean information from others in the village but those we met seemed aloof and hesitant. While the parents of the stricken children were relieved to have had their precious charges returned, the rest wanted to forget the whole affair. I tried to tell them that that was easy to wish for but difficult to achieve, if the underlying cause for their disappearance was not revealed, but I made no headway.

nones

After a plate of food, we took our little company south, to the village of Allerdean, where Harold and Margaret had been taken just over twelve months ago. Their bodies had never been found.

To look at, Allerdean was a little larger than Murton, but otherwise much the same. It had a bare patch of tamped earth that acted as the village square where most of the communal activity was focused, around which sat a cluster of small dwellings fashioned from thatch, mud, drywall and occasionally stone. People went about their daily business with humour and diligence, and I saw no shred of trauma on any of their faces.

I asked William where I might find the parents of Harold and Margaret. 'We can try the chapel,' he said. 'It has been some time since I visited here. Henry—Father Armestrang—will know.'

Father Armestrang, a chatty young chaplain, greeted us eagerly when we arrived at the chapel. He was filled with joy to see Friar William, as I was discovering most folks were in this region. There were pleasant introductions and Armestrang seemed very interested when told the reason for my being there. But when William asked him about Harold and Margaret and their parents, his smile faded and he crossed himself.

'Oh, William, this is a sorry tale. Dear Ned and Lucia. They died not two months ago.'

'They died?' asked William, evidently taken aback by the news. 'That is sad indeed. The plague?'

Armestrang shook his head. He was a thin, boyish-looking fellow, clean-shaven and with a tonsure which, coupled with his expression of sadness, gave him a faintly angelic air.

'I am almost afraid to say it. I am no physician, for no doubt a physician would say different, but if you ask me, they died from a broken heart. That is to say, they never recovered from the loss of their children.'

'God bless them,' I muttered. 'I have known many

parents whose hearts were broken with grief. It is a terrible cross to bear. But, Father Armestrang, you said a physician would say different. What do you mean?'

The chaplain paused, uncertain whether to proceed. 'They sinned, Brother Jacobus,' he responded, after a moment's further consideration. 'They died by their own hand. Poison.'

'Suicide?' I frowned and crossed myself. I felt at once a mixture of disgust at the tragic and sinful waste of human life, and disappointment too that this lead would also yield us nothing. Then I scolded myself for my iniquitous cynicism.

'Yes,' he went on. 'They could not live with it. I prayed with them many times for the souls of their poor children. In their hearts they knew the two would never return—but I cannot say more. Brother, know that I would help you but I am bound by the Sacramental Seal to say no more. Their fate is with Lord God, our Father, now.'

'They confessed to you?'

Armestrang nodded slowly. I could not and would not unseal the man's lips. A priest who violated this confidence was liable to be excommunicated at once, and only the Holy Father in Avignon could issue a pardon on such a matter. I sighed in resignation and redirected my questioning elsewhere.

'Did the parents not search the woods for the bodies? When Harold and Margaret first disappeared, I mean.'

'They would not. They ... .'

The priest became fretful, and William placed a hand upon his friend's arm. 'Be calm, Henry. Jacobus is here to help. It is as I said at the friary, Jacobus. They are frightened of this Green Man.'

'Preposterous!' I huffed. 'How can you allow such feverish thoughts to become so widespread?'

'We do not allow it!' said Armestrang, surprisingly offended at the suggestion. 'Such ideas take root and grow like weeds. They do not require human hands to tend them.'

'Perhaps it requires human hands to rip them from the earth,' I muttered. 'Please, Father Armestrang: is there no more you can say? I fear that what happened to Harold and Margaret and the other children in this region may happen again. Have you nothing more for me? Can you not at least disclose whether the sin the parents confessed to was venial or mortal?'

I caught Henry giving William a slightly apprehensive look but William simply smiled back, and Armestrang appeared to be placated. I wondered if this silent but knowing exchange was an indication of William knowing something or whether he simply had a way of putting people at ease. With no evidence for the former, I had to assume it was the latter.

'I cannot break the seal. You know this,' said Armestrang, solemnly. 'All I can say is that they were filled with contrition and tried to repent. Beyond that, some of the facts will inevitably remain beyond your grasp. Nonetheless, hearsay, though not as solid, may yet be grabbed in a pinch.'

'Please do not whisper cryptic nonsense,' I said. 'I prefer to speak plainly.'

'Speak to Gertrude Villiers. She is a cook and she lives at the north end of the village.'

With nothing more to be gleaned from him, I thanked Armestrang for his time, and left to find the cook.

We found her with no difficulty. She was inside her

cottage, butchering a pig on a large oak table with a huge cleaver. She was a large, powerful woman with a round, doughy face and she handled the carcass with great skill. She did not stop working while we spoke but continued slamming the metal cleaver through the pig's tissue and bone until it collided with the wood. Her voice was like her work: coarse, loud and bloody.

'Good to see thee, Friar William, and God bless thee. Who's tha friend?'

William introduced me and told her that the chaplain had recommended that we speak to her.

'Aye. About what?' Another slam of the cleaver.

'It is about the children who went missing last year,' I said.

She slammed the cleaver into the carcass once more and this time left it there, the point of the blade buried in the wood so it stood on end. She looked up, her forehead dotted with sweat, and wiped her bloody hands across her bosom.

'Poor mites, aye. An' I know well enough what you're wanting to ask.'

'Oh?'

'I saw 'em. Young Harold an' Maggie, with their parents. I was out walking in the fields an' I saw 'em all, the afternoon 'afore the kids was said to be missin'. They were 'eading north, on the road out of town, t'wards Thornton.'

'A family going for a walk together is not so strange.'

'I called out to Annabel—we was friends—but she didn't say nowt, an' she were close enough to hear, right enough. In fact, when I called, she an' the bairns hurried away from me. Or at least, she gave 'em the hurry up.'

'She took them into the woods?' I said. 'So she—and

perhaps the father too—would have been overwhelmed with guilt because it was they who had taken them into the woods, where whatever happened to them happened. And so they took their own lives. Poor creatures.'

'That's not all, Brother,' said Gertrude. 'They was actin' weird the next few days. We all knew the bairns was missing, an' they was hysterical—cryin' and the like, as any parent would be, if their child had disappeared. But they wouldn't go into the woods. They wouldna go searchin', not even when we begged and shouted at 'em. They already knew something weren't right.'

There was little more that Gertrude had to tell us so, after a quick exchange of pleasantries, we thanked her a few moments later and left the little butcher's hut.

'The tongues of these people are as fallow as the lands they till,' I complained as I mounted my horse outside. Sir Walesby, our ever-present companion, came up alongside us. 'Did you know all of this, William?'

'It is as Father Armestrang says,' said William, mounting his own ride. 'Hearsay. Fragments of broken glass.'

'Your friend Henry would not have pointed us towards Gertrude for nothing. And the parents would not have confessed for nothing. They knew something!'

'Come, Brother,' he said in that mellifluous voice. He had a trick of softening his tone just enough that it melted some of the tension in the air around him. No wonder the people here regarded him so fondly. 'It'll soon be dark. Best be getting back.'

COMPLINE

As the evening came on, a mist of fine rain floated above the land, unlike anything I had ever come across in my travels across the empire. I remarked as such to William, who again simply smiled. I mused that it might even have been attractive had the cold not been so intolerably penetrating.

The promise of taking comfort beside a fire while I ruminated upon the scant clues we had unearthed was dashed, however. No sooner had we returned to the abbey than we were approached by a young, ruddy-faced novice, hitching his robe about his knees as he sloshed through the mud in the quadrangle, making him look like a maiden from a courtly tale.

'Brother Jacobus!' he called. His face was fearful and pink. 'Brother Jacobus! The Guardian must speak with you.' He was visibly upset.

'Can we not take some rest, Boy?' I harrumphed, shaking my arms with theatrical verve so that I flicked the rainwater from my sleeves. 'We have been out all day. What is it you want?'

'Two more bairns, Brother,' he said. 'Two more have gone.'

At that, all thoughts of earthly comfort could wait. William and I exchanged a single look and strode to the solar of Guardian Dionysius. He welcomed us inside with a watery sort of glance, as though the news had sucked something vital from him, and he spoke to us in a conspiratorial hush.

'Peter and Emeline,' he said, when I asked the news.

'Gwendolynn's children?' said William, his voice raised in alarm.

'You know them?' I asked.

'Of course. Dear God, those poor wee'uns. They were sick, Jacobus. Father, what do you know?'

'News came when you were out,' whispered Denis.

'They have been gone almost an entire day. The mother remains at her home, in Ord. That is a tithing, just west of here,' he added for my benefit.

'We must go and search for them!' I said, at once forgetting my cold and tired bones. 'If there is a chance they can be found and saved, we must take it—now. Come: let us go and round up some villagers.'

'The people will not search the woods at night,' said William, promptly.

'Then we must do so,' I said. 'A band of brothers from the abbey can assist us.'

'No,' insisted William again. 'It is dangerous.'

'I'm not afraid,' I said, a little pompously. 'And I'm sure you cannot be either.'

'Sir Walesby will not permit it,' said William, changing the focus, I felt, from the mysterious to the political. 'There may be raiders from across the border. And he is charged with your protection.'

I considered his words and concluded that he was right. There might be a threat from the Scots and Sir Walesby would certainly not let me put myself at risk.

'Then I shall visit the mother as soon as it is light, and afterwards organise a search,' I said. 'As I am forced to stay here, I shall pray, and then sleep, that my body and soul shall be refreshed for the dawn and whatever we might then encounter.'

When alone, sure enough, I prayed, but sleep did not come so easily.

22ND NOVEMBER

IN WHICH
WILLIAM
AND I
VISIT
THE TITHING
OF ORD
AND MEET
THE WOMAN
GWENDOLYNN
WHOSE CHILDREN
DISAPPEARED
IN
THE WOOD

PRIME

The next morning I resolved to leave for Ord as early as possible. If there was any chance to save the children who had disappeared, time was of the essence. While breaking my fast with Friar William in the refectory I told him what I had in mind and he concurred without comment. We then left for the friary gatehouse, where Sir Walesby was waiting for us.

The journey was little more than an hour on foot, and William and I were happy to walk, but Walesby insisted on riding and shadowed us from atop his slim mare. I was not happy about being escorted for the duration of the trip and having Lord Hayeford's mad conspiracies dripped into my ear by his lapdog. Sir Walesby, however, had the soundness of mind to stay quiet and give me space to think and talk with William. He himself stayed a few yards behind us, keeping his eye out and every so often crunching his way through an apple. A gentle easterly breeze dragged a thin fog over the landscape, softening its edges and keeping the horizon from our view.

'Do you know much about this Sir Walesby?" I asked William, under my voice.

William made a noncommittal face. 'He can be spotted from time to time in the town. He is loyal to his Lord Master, which means he is loyal to the King. And he has the right experience. If Lord Hayeford has tasked him with protecting you, he'll see that it's done. Are you uncomfortable with his being here?'

'Lord Hayeford suspects the Scots to be behind the disappearances. So may this knight. I can't complete my task with the necessary objectivity if he's perched on his steed, watching my every move.'

William smiled condescendingly, which bothered me.

'Do you actually believe this task can be completed with any objectivity?'

'Do you find it amusing that I do?' I said. 'Do you not think it a great sin to smile, when we could be walking towards the very altar of the Evil One?'

'If I were to walk into the very presence of the Evil One, I would smile at him for I fear no evil from him. It is known that The Evil One can only operate within the worldly confines and limits of that which is permitted by God Himself. His evil can never be greater than God's love. But who are we to know such limits, being such limited beings ourselves? We cannot know everything. The total of human knowledge amounts to a pinprick in a never-ending tapestry. God moves in the shadows just as He moves in the light, and it is right to praise Him even when His actions in our realm are beyond our own reasoning. And yes, Brother Jacobus, that thought gives me cause to smile.'

'I do not have cause to smile while so much is unknown. I confess, though, that I do find joy in the act of discovering a truth that lies hidden from all others. It may even be described as pride, for which I should do penitence.'

'Brother, do you think sin is a worthwhile price to pay for the act of discovery?'

'We are all sinners, Friar William. But if we should sin and learn nothing from it, that truly is monstrous.'

We arrived at Ord in good time. The patchy road that ran from Berwick to Ord skirted the River Tweed, which provided the natural border with Scotland. I peered across the water to see whether the Scottish land would display some clue as to why Lord Hayeford was so afraid of it, but it lay beneath the same tumbledown fog that gently buffeted our side of the river. Either side of us, flocks of fat, lazy sheep rested in the meadows, contentedly chewing the cud and watching the sun in its watery ascent, untroubled by evil. Now that the harvest was over, and the rye, oats and barley had all been gathered in, the farmlands prepared to sleep through the bleak winter's dark night.

The little tithe of Ord was distinguishable by a stone barn and a few dozen cruck cottages dotted around it. Some of the farmhands we passed stared at the handsome black of my gown, which stood out against the grey inertia of that slumbering land, but then smiled at Friar William, who greeted them in return with a smile, a hand upon their bowed forehead, and a blessing.

William led me to one of the houses, stopped by the open doorway and announced our arrival. After a few moments a wiry woman appeared out of the darkness, her eyes dark and tired and her skin pale and dry. 'Friar William,' she murmured in a voice that seemed to have been cracked by the cold. She wore a loose canvas bodice over a once-white gown, a canvas skirt splattered with mud around the hem, and a thick, rough shawl. Spying me, she pulled her shawl nervously around her shoulders and asked who I was.

'Gwendolynn, this is Brother Jacobus, a Benedictine monk of the Abbey de Saint-André in Villeneuve. He means you no harm. He is a learned scholar and has travelled all the way from France to find out what has been plaguing us these past months. We hope that, in his way, he will deliver you some peace for your own pain.'

By this point I noticed that a few other villagers were watching us from a distance. 'Perhaps we would be better off speaking privately,' I said to William, before turning to Sir Walesby, who understood my meaning and nodded. As we disappeared into Gwendolynn's hovel, Walesby stood by the doorway, broad and immoveable, with one hand resting upon his sword's pommel.

Inside, Gwendolynn shared the house with some children, chickens and a goat, which nibbled on a pile of straw in the first of three rooms. She led us to the far room, which had cracks in the dry stone walling that served as tiny windows and permitted the entry of a little morning light and draughts that vented the smell and helped to feed the peat fire in the centre of the building. Gwendolynn offered me one of the three-legged stools to sit on but I declined, politely.

'Brother Jacobus intends to find out the true nature of what happened to Emeline and Peter,' said William. His voice was soft and melodious, like a lullaby sung to a sleeping child. Whatever troubles she was experiencing, his presence was a balm for her.

'Emeline and Peter were your children?' I asked.

She nodded, and looked down at her lap. She fiddled with her shawl and peered over my shoulder, as if seeking some answer from beyond.

'And your husband?'

'The plague took Alfred last year,' said William on her behalf, as she composed herself.

'I am sorry to hear it. God is with you. But I would ask you to recall all you can about your children after they were afflicted by their ailment.' I gestured to the next room. 'Are those also your children? Perhaps if I can know more, then God will shine a light on Peter and Emeline, even in death, and that light will prevent your surviving children from succumbing to that same fate.'

'Can the Good Lord shine a light on 'em now?' she asked in a fretful mutter. 'They's gone. All I can do is protect the rest of my wee'uns.'

'And how do you propose to protect them?'

She looked awkward, like a child being chastised. 'By what I done,' she said, looking away.

'What did you do?' asked William.

She stared at us through red-ringed eyes. She looked as if she had not slept for days but she held her gaze on me. 'Who is he, this one? Why is he here?'

'Friar William speaks the truth, Gwendolynn. I am here to uncover the truth. You must know that Emeline and Peter are far from the only children to have been taken, but they may yet be saved.'

She creased her face up and shook her head like a child, 'No, no no no no. They can't be. No, no no no no.'

William gave me a troubled look. I took him by the arm and gestured that we should speak privately in the corner of the room.

'She seems very sure that the children will not be recovered,' I whispered.

William frowned, either not understanding what that implied—that they could not therefore be received into the arms of Heaven—or not wanting to understand.

'How hard did you press her for answers?' I asked.

'Hard? Brother Jacobus, she is not … . Why would I press her, when she is in distress?'

'She is in distress, I agree.' I broke our huddle and returned to Gwendolynn. I fixed her with a hard glare and firmed my voice. 'Woman, why are you so certain that you children will not be saved? I bear holy witness to you by the order of the One True Church!'

'I done it!' she cried. 'I done it!'

By now the other children were gathered at the doorway. The smallest of them, perhaps two years in age, began to sob. William, seeing their disturbance, knelt by them and offered them comfort with an embrace and a soft prayer.

'What did you do, Gwendolynn?' I asked, softly this time.

'They was already dead, Holy Brother. I swear it. An' so I took 'em, I took em to the wood, and I laid 'em to rest there.'

'Are you quite sure they were dead?' I asked. William turned to face me, disturbed by the implication of the question.

Through a pink face flushed with tears, she thrust her hands towards her little children and William let them run to her. She took them in her arms and squeezed them all, in an abject display of motherly protection.

'They was sick. William, you know this. You saw 'em. They was sick!'

I looked at William. He nodded. 'Aye, the wee'uns were poorly. But I did not see them die, Gwendolynn ... .'

'They was dead, they was dead!' she cried. 'The physician came and gave 'em herbs and wine but it made no difference. And so, in the end, when it was done, when they was gone, I took 'em to the wood and I laid 'em out there.'

I looked at her in horror, and then at William, whose face was darkened. He looked on the verge of tears himself.

'A heathen burial?' I hissed, shaking my head in anger. 'Woman, that is a—'

I stopped myself, suddenly imagining the absurd scene to which she was confessing, and remembered the testimony of Gertrude, the butcher woman, from the previous day. In that story, the fated mother, Annabel, had been spotted walking freely with her two charges, very much alive, towards their stretch of the woods.

'You carried the bodies of your children to the wood all by yourself?' I asked, not concealing the scepticism in my voice. It seemed barely feasible that a small woman could bear the dead weight of two young ones for more than a hundred yards or so. She looked down and said nothing, hiding behind her tears.

'Friar William,' I said. 'The children who disappeared. Did they all die? Were they all buried like this?'

'I do not think so, no. I think we would have known. To bury a body other than in consecrated ground is a wicked thing.'

'Woman, you cannot save anyone through heathen rituals!' I said. 'The burial you administered to your deceased children was an abhorrent and unnatural act.'

'Aye, aye, it was, I know!' she said in a whimper. 'And even as I done it, I begged for mercy from Him who was put on the Cross and suffered his own pain.'

I allowed myself a wry smile. Such utterances were typical of the defences used by those tried for heresy. But unlike the Church's inquisitors, I was not here to weed out heretics but to extract truth, and I let the thought go.

'Do not be afraid now, woman. God is with you. It is clear from your admission, and the circumstances that have blighted this community, that you did these things through fear, not wickedness. But you must look to God, and pray for the strength to take the righteous path. That burial in the woodland will not save your surviving children. But perhaps knowing a little more about the condition of Emeline and Peter will.'

A look that was both spiteful and fearful came over her face. 'And what would you know? I didn't seek to do wrong in the face of the Lord,' she said. 'But the Man will have his share. That's how we protect the ones who remain. As for the rest, I pray for 'em, I and hope that's enough.'

'The Man? You mean the Green Man? This supposed monster? Friar William, is this whole community scared of this pagan nonsense?'

William looked at me but said nothing.

As if to fill the silence, Gwendolynn once more said, very quietly, 'The Man will have his share.'

'The Man will have his share,' I repeated, bitterly. 'You keep saying this phrase; what does it mean?'

'It is what he tells us.'

'Who? Who tells you this? This Green Man?'

She fussed over her skirts and looked away guiltily. When William looked at her, she could not hold his gaze.

'Please, Gwendolynn: you are safe. Be truthful,' I said.

She made a desperate sort of face and looked towards the heavens before summoning the strength to talk. 'I went to see the Wise Man, Odenellus, on the outskirts of the forest. The medicines weren't working, see, and so I thought somethin' else might work. I went to see him, and Odenellus made a divination, saying the man—the Green Man—would have his share, and it would go better if an offering were to be made to him. Otherwise he would take more and more.'

I noticed that, as Gwendolynn said this, Friar William looked shocked—and failed to mask it. He got up and went to stand by the doorway, as if he suddenly needed to check on something. It was the first time I had seen him perturbed.

'You went and spoke with Odenellus?' he marvelled. 'Gwendolynn, you should have known better.'

'I know! And now there's more blood on this town.'

Slightly confused, I held up my hand. 'Exactly who is this Odenellus?

William shook his head, and spoke with ill-concealed derision. 'He calls himself the Wise Man of the Woods.'

I scoffed. 'So. A peddler of ungodly myths and long-dead stories."

Gwendolynn's face creased up in further distress. 'Forgive me, Friar William! It is all too much to bear.'

William looked to the heavens and muttered something inaudible. 'Holy God, what a mess,' he eventually said. 'Gwendolynn, how could you be so foolish, when you have … but no, you shall hear no condemnation from me. Not right now.'

'Friar William, I would like to know more about this so-called Wise Man of the Woods.'

'Now is not the time, Brother Jacobus. While we are here, let us concentrate on the children. When we return to the abbey, I will tell you about Odenellus.'

'He told me to give Emeline and Peter up to the Man!' sobbed Gwendolynn. 'An' God save me, I did what he asked! What kind of mother am I that would do such a thing? Didn't I love those ones like I love these?' And she grasped her children once again and wept. I confess that, in spite of her sin, I pitied her for wandering from God's path in pursuit of these iniquities. I also shuddered to think how Nastagio di Balino would have reacted to her public admission! I, however, knew that one woman's erring, however grievous, did not constitute heretical practice, and that it would be but one piece of a larger puzzle.

I thanked the woman, blessed her, and left her house with William at my side. Outside, Sir Walesby remained in the same watchful pose, like a relic from a forgotten age. Whatever curiosity the villagers had felt upon our arrival had dissipated, and nobody paid us much mind.

'What on earth can she mean, Friar William?'

'It is what the people say. They hold the forests and woodlands in high regard here. And you should know that the Green Man—well, it *is* the forest. It is the forest here in Northumberland and the forest in Oxfordshire and the forest in Essex and the forest all over England. The Green Man is the forest and the forest is the Green Man, and when the forest breathes, it is as if the whole country breathes, and so it has always been. The forests hold all time in their grasp, back to when God first placed trees on the Earth, and they hold all the secrets of the future. I believe that that is what people mean when they talk about the Green Man in this way.'

I huffed, half in amusement, half in indignation. 'Very poetic. Can you not see, William? This Green Man is a metaphor, nothing more: the poetry of the people—the pleasantry of the peasantry, if I may suggest it. They apply the figure of a mysterious and ambivalent man-creature to things they do not have the wit to understand. That's not so odd. As Catholics we do it ourselves: in the Basilica di San Paolo fuori le Mura in Rome, there are fresco cycles that depict God as an old man sitting in the sky. An old man sitting in the sky? Ridiculous! God takes on the *attributes* of an all-knowing and all-seeing father and so we portray Him as such. What we really want to portray is unknowable, so we borrow a form we can understand. We ought not, of course: any representation of the divine is idolatry, as the Bible tells us, because it may lead us to sinful worship, but if imagery can bridge the divide between our base world and God's holy paradise, then we may perhaps be forgiven. So I do not look down upon these people for imagining the mechanics of the universe in the form of a man, for is not man the highest and most noble form in all Creation? What I do not like is the anthropomorphism that clouds the people's judgement and muddies their paths towards God, encouraging them to look elsewhere for salvation: that is idolatry. That is why we must discover what has motivated the people to shape their fears in the form of a Green Man, and I assure you, William, when we have done so, we will find that this Green Man has a perfectly good explanation. But I assure you also that these children were no more taken by a Green Man in a forest than by the Man in the Moon.'

'And yet they were taken by something. Or someone.'

'So it seems.'

'And just because they were taken, it does not explain why—' He wavered momentarily. '—It does not tell us why the children whose bodies were found were desecrated in that strange manner.'

I looked to the southwest where the trees, stripped of their summer foliage, stood bare and desolate, nursing the darkness that lay further in the depth of the forest. The sight reminded me of the poor children, and the people's stories of their clawing their way out of their graves, and it made me shudder.

'Is that the forest where the children were given their heathen burials?' I asked William.

'Aye,' he muttered, looking at me with some concern. 'But you cannot be thinking of entering the woods and seeking the creature out?'

I clucked with frustration. 'Did you not listen to a word I said? Of course I will enter the woods—but to find evidence, not to seek a creature. We have to erase all thought of a creature from our minds, William. It will not lead us anywhere. Gwendolynn has told us she took the bodies of her children to the woods. I do not believe her. Look how distant the trees are. She could not have borne them so far, not unaided. And if these bodies are in the woods, they must be hidden in its depths, not on the periphery. What a terrible thing! I must speak with Albertus. He said—'

At that moment, a scream went up to the south of us. We looked round to see a young farmhand, holding out his hoe for protection, pointing to the pastures that flanked the dead forest.

'Someone, look!' he cried, in a panic-stricken voice. 'Look! It's them! The creature's done it again! They'm come back!'

I have to admit that, despite all I had said about renouncing the creature, the hairs on the back of my neck went up, and I was stirred to a panic myself, such are the temptations that our minds can fall prey to when taken by surprise. I ran over to the farmhand and asked him what he saw. 'They've come again,' he muttered in a kind of delirium. 'The devil's spawn. Look!' He pointed to a spot not far off and I froze. Two small figures were ambling clumsily through the dying grass and coming towards us. I looked back to William, who stood with his mouth open and eyebrows raised, crossing himself repeatedly and mumbling.

'That is they,' the farmhand hissed under his breath. 'The two children, Emeline and Peter. That is they!'

Others who had heard the farmhand's cry had started

gathering at the patch of earth outside the tithing barn at the village centre, and even though they stood some distance from me, I could hear their frantic muttering and wailing. Then came the shrill shriek of Gwendolynn, who was running through the fallow fields towards the long grass, clutching her skirts about her knees.

Even from here, the freakish nature of the childrens' gait was evident. They stumbled in a grotesque manner, as though their legs were shattered and could barely support their weight. Their eyes were ringed with black circles and their skin was the colour of bruises. Muck and debris from the forest covered them from head to toe, and their bodies were garlanded in stray grasses and dieback brambles, so that from a distance, in the gloomy fog, they looked like foliate heads.

'Stay back!' I called after Gwendolynn, but it was no use.

'Demon!' a tall man behind me cried out repeatedly as Gwendolynn got closer to her children. When she reached them, she flung her arms around them and pulled them to her, kissing them on their foreheads and calling their names, which made the crowd of onlookers gasp but had no effect on the children.

'Could they really be risen? From the grave?' asked William, who had hurried over to my side.

I tried to answer but when I opened my mouth no words spilled out into the chilly air.

By the tithing barn, two men holding ploughshares lobbied the other villagers to help them destroy the children. They were met with shouts, some of encouragement, some begging for calm, but the ringleaders were determined to rid their tithing of evil and were already attracting others as they made their way into the fields.

Imploring William to follow me, I also ran to the field to try and intercept them. If there was still life left in the children, I would do my best to spare them death, and thereby save the souls of the men who wanted to cut them down where they stood. Moreover, if I was ever to have a chance of uncovering this mystery, the opportunity to speak with the children was too great to relinquish.

So I stood in front of the woman and her children, facing the oncoming villagers, with my palms up, feeling as helpless as King Canute of the Three Kingdoms in the face of the oncoming tide. The look on the faces of men was at fearful but terrified. It was the look of people who had seen this wretched scenario before.

'Stop, all of you!' I implored loudly, summoning as much authority as I could find. 'The power of the Lord and his son Christ compels you to spare these children! Would you commit the infernal sin of murder against your fellow people?'

'Ye canna' do a murder on a demon!' cried one of the men, shaking his billhook and becoming increasingly agitated. 'They was buried, Monk—buried in the cold ground. Stand aside, for they carry a curse, and if we don't destroy them, the curse will fall on us—and you!'

The men approached warily, holding their farm tools in front of them like weapons: flails, axes, mattocks and sickles. Behind them stood other agitated villagers, eager to see the children cut down and be able to talk about what they'd seen in future years. But I would not relent. I stood before Gwendolynn and the two children, shielding them with my arms and petitioning Our Lord and Saviour for His protection.

Most looked cowed but one of the original rabble-rousers got close enough to raise a ploughshare above his head and threaten to bring it crashing down, though whether its target was me or the children or Gwendolynn, I could not tell. I cowered from the impending blow but before the man could wield his weapon, it was ripped from his hands by Sir Walesby, who had appeared, unnoticed, on his horse. The man looked furious at being disarmed and humiliated in front of the crowd, but had no time to respond before Walesby cast the ploughshare onto the ground, dismounted, and drew his sword partly out of its scabbard.

'Any man who harms Brother Jacobus and those in his care will be slain,' he barked, 'by order of Lord Hayeford, whose land keeps you.' His black eyes glowered at the men, each of whom seemed to weigh up the situation, then lower his weapon and back away—except for one man who, with unexpected speed, produced a short, stubby knife from his longstockings and came lunging at Gwendolynn. Walesby stepped forward and barged the man with his shoulder, unbalancing him and spinning him around, then drew his sword fully out of its scabbard as if to run the man through. There were screams and gasps, and I even heard the voice of Gwendolynn behind me pleading for no more violence, but instead of plunging the blade into the man's body, Walesby bunted its pommel into the man's face. There was a horrid crunch and the man whimpered, dropping the knife and grasping at his nose, from which poured a gout of blood.

'They're not of this world,' snarled the other of the ringleaders. 'Would you side with them—what's been brought to unholy life by the monster of the forest, and who walk upon your lord's lands?'

'That is not my concern,' said Sir Walesby flatly, eyeing the man as if admonishing an errant dog. 'I am here to protect my charges and to stop the rest of you getting into worse trouble.' Not wanting to make a fight of it, the man turned away and helped his friend get to his feet and the two of them withdrew into the rabble.

'Thank you, Sir Walesby,' I said, weakly. The colour had quite drained from William's cheeks, and probably from mine as well. Alongside us stood the two ruined children and their shocked mother. All of us must have looked closer to death than life.

'I cannot protect the woman and defend you against the mob at the same time,' said Sir Walesby. 'You'd best start back to Berwick with Friar William here while I shepherd the people back to the village. If you bide longer you'll only provoke them. The mother has made her choice and will have to fend for herself with these … children.' To emphasise his point, he slammed his sword back into its scabbard.

'Catch up with us on the road, then,' I called out as Sir Walesby trotted with the villagers back to their tithing. I prayed for them as they walked, telling myself that the truth would comfort them, once I was finally able to deliver it, but aware, also, that the hearts of the ignorant are not easily turned.

SEXT

'It will not go well if we simply trade one type of violence for another, Sir Walesby,' William complained as the knight caught up with us on horseback. 'What did you think you were doing, breaking the man's nose? Do you wish to despoil the favour of your liege lord?'

The knight, who had taken up the rear of our little group, looked at William with some weariness. 'I do what

I need to do, Friar William, and you have lived to tell the tale. A peasant has suffered a broken nose. He was about to dish up much worse. Don't tell me you are not inured to a little roughhousing in your lord's barony.'

'Just because violence sometimes settles disputes, it does not mean I have to like it,' said William, scowling. 'What about you, Brother Jacobus? In thanking the good knight for his service, are you so permissive of such acts?'

I frowned at the Franciscan's insensitivity, especially as I had insisted on bringing with us Gwendolynn and the two children, whose fate, had we left them to face it, would have condemned them, and us, to everlasting torment. 'Would these children and their mother have seen Sir Walesby's actions as uncalled-for? And would you sacrifice the opportunity for truth? They are with us now. We can learn much from them. As for the man, I did not order Sir Walesby to strike him.'

'Nor did you protest.'

I laughed, but without humour, while Sir Walesby trotted past us and jumped down from his horse. After we had left the tithe of Ord I had administered some rudimentary checks of the two children, and what I saw tallied with what Albertus had described. They possessed an icy pallor and their skin was bruised all over. Their bodies were as thin as sticks and they were cold and clammy to the touch. They had voices, which surprised me, but high and wheezy, as though a fever had its filthy hands around their tiny necks and was throttling them. Whatever they had been through, it was miraculous that they were alive at all.

What I had observed of their frailty—as well as of the volatility of the villagers—made me convinced that we had to bring the children back with us to the infirmary, away from the wild fantasies of Ord and the prying eyes of the town, so that Albertus could make a proper study of them and give them the care they needed. With their legs waning, however, the wretched waifs could not have managed the journey themselves so I had to persuade William, not without difficulty, to pick up the girl and carry her over his shoulder, as I did with the boy, until Sir Walesby should relieve us and seat them on the horse, which he did now. Like that the two children rode, Walesby leading the horse by its bridle, with William and me on either side, ensuring that they did not slip.

With much to think about from what we had seen and little that any of us wanted to put into words for the moment, our hearts propelled our legs with haste and the journey to the friary was soon over. William now went to the infirmary and brought four friars and two stretchers to carry the children. Gwendolynn, not being able to enter a community of monks, had to remain by the gatehouse, where she was watched over by Sir Walesby, to ensure that she did not try to escape or break in or do herself any kind of mischief.

The infirmary was north of the main dormitory, along the enclosure's seawall, and set apart from the main cloister by a thick hedgerow which had been planted to create a small corridor. It possessed its own modest cloister and had a small dormitory and chapel annexed to it. At the centre of the cloister was a patch of soil filled with sweet-smelling herbs and winter vegetables. As we passed by, I wished I could have stayed here in more felicitous circumstances and engaged in God's work at my leisure but on this occasion I had neither *ora* nor *labora*.

The infirmary's main hall was gently lit by torches in

wall sconces and lined with cots, some of which contained convalescing friars. The cots were positioned alongside stained windows depicting the Stations of the Cross, allowing daylight to bathe the infirm with the sumptuous light of His passion, death and rebirth.

Inside, Albertus was already waiting for us, wiping his bloodstained hands upon a leather chamois, having just completed some kind of surgical procedure which I confess I did not want to hear any details of, let alone see. He observed the two stricken children and the colour drained from his cheeks.

'Oh, by the Bones of Christ,' he called out, more loudly than would usually be tolerated in a sick bay. 'Not again! Lord save us. Come, quick then: this way. Friar Herry has a private room we can use, towards the back.'

The lamplit room, hidden away from the main hall, had only a single bed and no windows. Albertus brought the infirmarian Friar Herry to us while the other friars set the children upon the bed. Herry was a paunchy, wan friar, a few years older than me, yet spry and bright-eyed, with slender, delicate fingers.

'You must be Brother Jacobus,' he hissed from the back. 'Let me through, Albertus! This is most irregular, my Benedictine friend, most irregular. Could you not have forewarned us that you intended to bring these poor souls here? They may have the very Devil in them! Was it not these two who were interred in the profane grounds of the forest? Oh, bless me, bless me! And now they have risen!'

I looked Friar Herry in the eye. I have met many infirmarians over the years, while lodging and working at different monasteries, and have found that they could be divided into two categories: practitioners who were men of medicine in their own right and administrators who depended on the skills of others. As I watched Albertus, appalled but maintaining his professional decorum, it was obvious which camp Friar Herry was in.

'Friar Herry, first of all, I regret this abrupt intrusion on the peaceful running of your sanatorium,' I said, 'but you must realise that no forewarning was possible. We had not expected to be returning to Berwick with these pitiable children but since they are here, they need special care. This is your infirmary, of course, and I do not presume, but Guardian Dionysius has given me special dispensation to uncover certain truths and these children are the key to my inquiries.'

Herry looked affronted. 'And to what degree does this special dispensation run? Am I to remove my other invalids and stop looking after them while these children are here, for fear that we all may get contaminated by them—or worse?'

William placed a calming hand on Herry's shoulder and the infirmarian flinched. 'Come, Friar Herry. Did Christ not compel the little children to come unto him and not hinder them? I am certain Brother Jacobus has your welfare and the welfare of all at heart. He merely asks you to allow Albertus, who has been fair and open-minded about all of this, to aid him in his investigation.'

William had the sense to lead the infirmarian away to give Albertus and me some space to work, for which I was grateful. First the physician warmed the children with lamps, broth and blankets, then gave them a hot herbal drink of sage, rose and lavender to calm them and ease their pain. He also took a sample of the boy's urine in a phial, which he held to the faint lamplight to observe. It was the colour of amber.

'What will that tell you?' I asked him quietly.

'Little and less,' he said with some distaste. 'I will not drink it, because of the possibility of devilry, but it is unhealthily dark. Their humours are in chaos. They need rest. They are too weak to bleed and too skinny for hemlock. But henbane should help them. I will ask Friar Herry to request that some rose petals and leaves are brought here to burn. I don't know if they can be saved but they can be comforted.'

As Albertus left, I knelt by the bed. The children were tucked in together, huddled beneath the blankets, looking at me as though they had never seen a human face before.

'Dear lambs,' I said, placing cloths cooled with water upon their foreheads. 'God has good plans for you, so do not be frightened. You are safe here, with Albertus caring for you. I will pray and keep watch over you. Nothing will hurt you.'

I think they were calmed by what I said but said nothing in return. Then, with some hesitancy, I said, 'I do not want to trouble your minds, my children, and do not want you to say anything that upsets you, but I am interested in what was in the forest when you were there. Do you recall anything that you saw? Anything unusual?'

The girl, Emeline, said nothing, but the boy, Peter, suddenly looked at me, as if seeing me for the first time, and nodded.

I took his hand in mine. 'What? What did you see?'

His breath quickened and, when his little voice came, it was no more than a series of jagged breaths, but sharp and urgent, as if he was desperate to get the words out.

'I saw a man … there was a dark man … in the … trees.' He paused and let out a choked breath, and his chest, as thin and brittle as a bird's, heaved with the effort. 'He was ... dark ... light. The leaves ... the trees.' The boy closed his eyes, then jerked them open again, scared.

'Did the man have a name?' I pressed, sensing that the window of opportunity might be closing. 'Was there more than one man? Did the man talk to you or say anything? Can you recall anything more?'

The boy made an upset face, looked away and shook his head. Within moments his eyes were shut and he was overtaken by a feverish sleep. Albertus returned with the rose petals and henbane, which he set to burning and administering to the little girl.

I turned to her next. She was a little older and, I hoped, more articulate.

'Emeline,' I said, softly, 'did you see anything?'

She looked at me with great suspicion, and no little fear but she was so weak that she could do nothing by it. I took her hand and pressed it gently, saying another prayer for her. I then asked again, even more gently.

I could see some secret truth hidden behind her eyes, but I did not push her further—just waited by her side. After several moments, she said, 'He took us.'

'Who do you mean, my sweet child? Who took you? Someone from the town? Someone with your mother?' I looked at Albertus, but he was busy mixing another elixir.

She shook her head. Then something above the window caught her eye, and she gave a little scream, turned away, put her hands to her eyes and wept. I looked round to what she had been looking at and saw a small wooden foliate head carved into the apex of the window frame.

'Enough,' snapped Albertus, bustling past me roughly. He set down this new concoction, which filled the room with strong herbal aromas. In moments, Emeline too was asleep.

'What did she say?' he whispered, eyeing the children.

I shook my head. 'The boy, not much. Something about dark lights again, leaves and trees. The girl … .' I said nothing but looked again at the foliate head. Albertus followed my gaze and looked troubled when he saw what I was looking at.

'So are they … are they risen?'

Again I shook my head, this time wearily. It had been a tiring and frenetic morning, and this pause gave me a great yearning to wash the dirt from my soul. But there would be times for such things later. 'No. As you said in the chapter house yesterday, they have not risen and this is no holy resurrection for these children did not die, Albertus. They may never even have been buried. Something else has happened here.'

I leaned over the boy and rubbed his forehead. I could barely see it in the low light, but I could feel it. A small, rough patch of skin that felt a little like bark. 'The mark you described?'

'Aye,' said Albertus. 'But it doesn't end there. Look.' He pulled back the bedclothes gently and raised the boy's tunic to expose his chest and arms. On the malnourished frame, angry red swellings gathered at the boy's joints and his ribcage pressed sharply against the skin. The fingers were red and blotchy, the nails cracked.

I sighed. 'It is little wonder that the strange appearance of these poor wretches aroused local superstitions. But everything can be explained.'

'By what?' said Albertus in hushed, expectant tones. 'What is the explanation?'

I smiled at him. 'I do not have it yet, my friend. I

need to talk to their mother again. But today has already provided us with more information than I expected it to, and these two little children may yet live, so we must count it as a good morning's work. I shall consult my books and you might like to join me. I think you would find it enlightening.'

'Thank you, Brother, but I will keep watch over the bairns for now,' he said. His face was still hard and grim. 'They deserve that much.'

I left him to his vigil and, requiring some convalescence of my own, decided to observe Sext in the infirmary chapel. Only two other friars were there and I was thankful for the peace.

When I emerged into the cloister, William was marching from the chapter house back to the infirmary, no doubt to inform himself about the children. I told him what we had found and invited him to sit with me awhile in the herb garden, to enjoy the late afternoon sunlight, the warmth of which lifted a fragrance from the lavender and mint, and helped counter the chill of the air.

'The infirmary at the Abbey de Saint André must be a splendid thing,' he said, after a moment's thought.

'In my Order nothing is more important than the care of the sick,' I responded, matter-of-factly, 'for in caring for them we serve them truly as Christ. In Matthew, Christ said, "I was sick and you visited me."' I nodded towards the infirmary. '"Whatever you do for one of the least of these brothers of mine, you do for me." But it is more than that. Through medical care we also advance our knowledge and understanding of the body and its ailments, and thus learn how to treat them, and better understand the wonders of God's creation. Therefore through medicine we serve Christ threefold.'

William nodded and looked away, first towards the infirmary and then towards the sea. 'I pray that you find an answer to this in your books, Brother Jacobus.'

'And I must start to read. But as we have a moment, please tell me about this so-called Wise Man, Odenellus.'

William winced in distaste. 'There is little to tell, Jacobus. He may be a man, but he is not very wise.'

'He is a pagan?'

'Something like that.'

'Well, tell me what you know, and let me be the judge.'

He let out a long sigh and uttered a tiny prayer before beginning. 'Odenellus takes himself for a mystic of sorts. If he had greater learning, I suppose he might describe himself as a Gnostic. But he's not a Gnostic, he's simply mad, and prefers to live among the trees than among other men. He says he can converse with the demon of the forest and perform acts of divination.'

'And you permit this?'

'Not in the town, but are we to police the forests? His acts are unholy but are not illegal. We tolerate his behaviour in the forest, no more than that. True, his actions go against the Word of God, but they are harmless enough.'

'Harmless? What he said to Gwendolynn did her and her children great harm. His words persuaded her to offer up her children to placate an imaginary demon.'

'Is her crime any worse than Abraham's when he raised the knife against his son Isaac?'

'That is false equivalence! Abraham was prepared to make the greatest of sacrifices in the name of the highest ideal; what Gwendolynn did was a perverted, unclean ritual, and it brought her less than nothing.'

'And yet in a perverse way the ritual worked, for the

children returned to her, or were returned. Changed, perhaps, but—'

'You must do away with all this thinking! They were never dead, Friar William!'

'It's not my mind you need to change, Brother Jacobus,' he said, a little impatiently. 'When the infants began to disappear, Odenellus ventured closer to the tithings and would tell people it was the Green Man's doing, and that the demon had to be paid. When some of the children started dying, he came back, telling them they got what they deserved. "The Man will have his share." After that the villagers requested a knight from the garrison to chase him away. Well, you heard what happened. Gwendolynn must have spoken to Odenellus in secret, and he must have told her to make some sacrifice to the Green Man.'

'A heretic, then,' I muttered gravely.

'He is a madman, Brother Jacobus, a fool. The word "heretic" is thrown around too easily, as you well know. He simply prefers his own way to the way of the Church. I pity him, in all honesty.'

'Does he have followers, acolytes?'

William shrugged. 'I do not know. Even if he does, I do not suppose they love him. Those who do what he asks of them do so out of fear, not love. I suspect the poor man has no one, not even the Lord.'

'Everyone has the Lord, if they have the wit to look,' I said. 'And yet I wonder … I am sure I can show that the marks upon the children were caused by some natural event. But in attempting to consort with this alleged demon of the forest, Odenellus may very well have been indulging in heretical pursuits through sorcery. I ought to speak with him.'

'You will have some difficulty in doing that, Brother Jacobus. He lives in the woods because he does not want to be found. I do not think he would willingly give himself up, even to you.' Then William looked at me in alarm. 'You are not thinking of having Gwendolynn accused of such things?'

I grasped his hand to offer assurance.

'No. In my experience, women are too often scapegoated for goings-on that have not been understood. I have seen it before. There is no wickedness in her heart. She has suffered enough. She needs to be reunited with her children. Apart from anything else, if they return to lucidity, it may provide us with further clues as to what happened.'

At that point one of the novices approached us. 'Friar William, Brother Jacobus. Guardian Dionysius requests your attendance at Vespers.

VESPERS

I spent the intervening hours in the scriptorium poring over the monastery's manuscripts and looking for sources in my own. As the sun began to set, I adjourned to the chapter house and found Father Denis already present with Friar William, Friar Herry, Albertus and, to my surprise, Sir Walesby too, leaning languidly against the eastern chapter house wall, allowing the light from the stained window to stream over his head, leaving the rest of him in the shade. Upon the great oak table were plates of bread and mugs of beer, but I found enough space to lay out several books and papers. Father Denis began the meeting by asking me what I had found out so far. I described the leaf-shaped marks upon the children, the few words the boy had spoken, and my theory that there had been no burial at all.

'How can you be sure of that?' asked Father Denis. 'Gwendolynn said she took her children to the forest and performed the sacrilegious ritual by her own hands. You know this.'

'She claims she undertook the ritual, but I doubt it,' I said. 'The Pagan, Odenellus, told her that "the Man will have his share" and I think she confessed to a confected sin to hide a greater one: that she took her children to the forest while they were still alive, as an offering to this Green Man.'

'But she considered 'em to be dead,' Albertus said gruffly. 'And you said yourself that they had not died. No mother would offer up her own living bairns to anybody—man, beast or God.'

'She might,' I proffered, 'if she thought they were so damaged that they were doomed to die anyway, and if, by doing so, she might spare her other children. The list of youngsters affected by this episode is growing but I believe I am starting to have enough evidence to narrow down the possible answers.'

'Please go on, Brother Jacobus,' said Father Denis.

'Friar Herry, I trust you are familiar with the works of the great physician Rogerius Salernitanus—Roger of Salerno?'

The infirmarian nodded. 'To some extent. We have a copy of the *Chirurgiae Magistri Rogerii* in the infirmary library.'

'Indeed! And if you consult that book you will find a detailed description of facial lesions similar to those that have affected our young patients, as well as a series of remedies and treatments. Rogerius attributes these symptoms to what he calls lupus, or the bite of the wolf, though lupus does not have to be caused by wolves.'

Father Denis let out a long, stiff breath, and fussed with his rosary beads. 'And do you have a hypothesis as to what might be the cause, Jacobus?'

He and the others looked at me suspiciously, as though I were the one under scrutiny.

'It may be that it really is the work of wolves, Father, especially if one of the creatures has become rabid and lost its fear of people. I have heard tales like that in Italy. Another possibility is St Anthony's Fire. I have seen instances of that affliction during visits to the Order of Hospitallers in Grenoble, when sufferers displayed similar marks and symptoms: burning, lesions, swellings and, most pertinently, erratic behaviour, lunacy and other things that look like demonic possession to the common eye.

'On the other hand it may be the action of some toxic wild flower being harvested mistakenly by the villagers, or picked by the children and eaten. It may even be the sting of an insect, if a colony has established itself in an area that children frequent—though in this climate, and at this time of year, I think it unlikely.'

I studied the visages of my scrutineers for some clue as to how they were receiving my perfectly sound theories, but they gave nothing away.

'All of these things are random,' said Albertus. 'Wolves, insects, poisons. These wee'uns are being spirited away regularly, every quarter-year.'

'Exactly,' I said. 'Nature is chaotic. But man is orderly. I believe nature is being wielded in some way. There is some intent involved. Or,' I continued with a wry smile, 'it could be the effects of some type of witchcraft,' an explanation which I guessed would flush out the goats from the sheep. It did.

'You're saying that if it is none of these natural things, it could be sorcery?' asked William with agitation.

Father Denis fidgeted in his seat and gave William a withering look. 'Do not be foolish, Friar William. That is not what Brother Jacobus means. He spoke in dark jest, though I wish he would not. Brother Jacobus, I do not want accusations of sorcery defaming this community. It is fragile enough already.'

I gave the Guardian a stern look of my own. 'Father, look about yourself. You know such accusations abound. That is why Albertus wrote his letter. But the gossip and rumours have not yet been formalised into prosecutions, nor do they have to. Do you know the number of cases I have seen throughout Europe where demonic magic has been proved without question to be the cause of strange happenings? I shall tell you the answer: none. Sorcery is a vulgar accusation thrown around by those who are befuddled by their lack of knowledge. If the cause is none of the natural things I have mentioned, then it will be something I have not yet considered. But I will tell you, the cause is something entirely natural. Cause and effect. We know that a pagan man of the woods is spreading lies and participating in unholy idolatry of a false god. This Odenellus may be wicked but William tells me that he knows the woods better than any other. I suggest that he is aware of some natural elixir or compound, or has devised some concoction, that would produce the symptoms we have seen. Perhaps he has found a way to wield lupus or St. Anthony's fire like a weapon, or as a poison, that he can administer.'

'So what, then?' asked Denis. 'We suppose that this

Wise Man, Odenellus, has somehow taken the children and poisoned them? As a sacrifice? Holy Father, what great wickedness!'

'It is a hypothesis I must test, Father. I cannot say with any certainty without visiting the forest itself. I suggest that ought to be our next port of call.'

The friars clucked loudly at this, obviously disturbed by the suggestion. Albertus said nothing. Sir Walesby still stood by the wall with his arms folded, detached from the conversation but attentive to all that was being said, and offered me a half-smile and a shake of the head, as if he was enjoying the consternation.

It was the Guardian who eventually settled the hubbub and spoke up. 'Why enter the forest, Brother Jacobus? You have your diagnosis. What more is there to do?'

'It's not enough, though, is it?' muttered Albertus. 'It's not enough to tell the people that this lupus, or St Anthony's Fire, or whatever it may be, is the cause of their bane. That is just to exchange a mysterious word that they're familiar with for another that they've never heard of. You have to have evidence, don't you, Brother Jacobus, because evidence may offer a cure, and evidence can only come from deep inside the wood.'

'Correct, Albertus! Father,' I said, addressing the Guardian. 'Do you believe the town folk will be satisfied with an explanation without proof and remedy? No. We must venture into the forest to have my hypotheses tested.'

The Guardian shook his head. 'It cannot be done. It is too dangerous.'

'Excuse me, Father,' came the granite bark of Sir Walesby, stepping away from the shadowed walls and stepping into the sunlight. 'Brother Jacobus requires safe passage. If Lord Hayeford supports him in this, I would see my master's word is done. I can send word for armed men and horses to protect us against any unwanted business. No one needs to fear the forest.'

'Well!' scoffed Father Denis. 'I would not enter the forest in any case. My place is here. If Brother Jacobus wants to dally in the trees, that is his business.'

I nodded in affirmation. 'You can make the request today, Sir Walesby?'

'I can be at Hayeford Castle tonight. But I am sworn to stay by you, Brother Jacobus, and to ensure that the children's mother is watched over. She is presently under the protection of the abbess at St Leonard's Nunnery, while I attend here.'

'You do not need to stay with me, Sir Knight,' I said. 'I shall remain at the abbey and no harm shall come to me, I assure you. But if there are godless souls who are inflicting maladies through nefarious means, we must find out—especially if they are Scottish heathens from across the border.'

I had fed this nonsense to the knight to help him pander to his master's prejudices. It put me under pressure to play up to his foolish suspicions, but I banked on the fact that when I eventually exposed the irrefutable truth of the matter, even Lord Hayeford would have no choice but to accept it. The knight nodded half-heartedly, as if working out his story in advance, and left us to take up his errand.

I turned to the man designated to be my helper. 'And what about you, Friar William? Will you accompany me into the woods, as my guide?'

'I would prefer not to. I confess, I am afraid. The woods are unknowable and unpredictable, now more than ever. If there is even a chance that sorcery is to blame for this ... .' He trailed off for a moment, then gathered his thoughts and started again. 'What I mean to say is, if you have found an answer in your medical treatises, maybe it is unnecessary to seek any further.'

'It strikes me that you are reluctant to choose the path that leads to greater understanding. I had thought we both might bask in the glory of God's enlightenment. Would you really not walk that path with me?'

He still looked unsure and I realised that I needed to be more persuasive so I stood up, went over to his chair and knelt at his side. 'My friend,' I said, addressing him in a tone of great affection, 'superstition and fear are bred of ignorance. It is ignorance, therefore, that we have to challenge. Yes?' I got up again and addressed them all. 'The world is like a magnificent cathedral erected in praise of God. It possesses beauty and grace but it is only a man-made structure, made up of so many stones. Each stone performs its task, adding to a wall or an arch or a dome or a buttress, with every stone relating perfectly to the next stone and the next stone and the next stone, until the whole thing makes up a logical and perfect whole that could not be any other way. We can view the whole world in the same way. It is a marvellous whole but if we can study it brick by brick, we can discover why things are the way they are.'

'A cathedral, for all its splendour, is not the world,' countered Father Denis. 'Stones, even when they number in the hundreds of thousands, are still not beyond counting. Think of the Tower of Babel, Jacobus. It was the Lord who thwarted the plans of men, who conspired to build a tower that would rise to the very heavens. If, as one people speaking the same language, they have begun to do this, then nothing they plan to do will be impossible for them. So said our Maker, and He dispersed the people all over the Earth. He does not expect us to know everything. In fact, it may be dangerous. His world is immeasurable by sheer numbers alone.'

I scoffed. 'Father, the reason for the people's dispersal was God's wish that they speak in numerous tongues instead of just one. Genesis 11:7. Come, let us go down and confuse their language so they will not understand each other.'

'*Venite igitur, descendamus, et confundamus ibi linguam eorum, ut non audiat unusquisque vocem proximi sui*,' Father Denis recited.

'Precisely, Father. Our Lord wanted them not to learn falsehoods from each other but the truth of His revelation. That is our task too: to resist the follies that we tell each other and to learn instead the truths that God has inscribed in his Divine Works.'

I thought I had spoken convincingly but William still held out. 'There is a paradox at the heart of your homily,' he said. 'You say the world resembles a cathedral, and can be figured out as such, but you do not consider that the world actually is a cathedral. It is where we gather to worship, and where we find God's majesty—under every pebble, in every lowly centipede that crawls through the mud, in every bird that soars in the sky, in every rose petal that blooms and falls, and in every act that we do unto our neighbours. It is not our duty to understand the world but to recognise its sacredness. We are the custodians of the world and our job is to protect it, not to pick it apart. Suppose, by examining the world too closely, you find it unravels?'

'Then I shall realise I am on the wrong track, for

God's world does not come to pieces by our examination of it!'

'All I would say,' said William, calmly, 'is that you do not let yourself be blinded to the way God chooses that we see things—and to what He keeps unrevealed. Things can be messy, and chaotic, and unknowable, but they are God's mess and chaos and we should recognise the beauty in that.'

'Then, my friend,' I said. 'Let us go and explore that mess and chaos in the forests and find the beauty of God that the people have been unable to discover for themselves! What do you say?'

23rd November

In which I investigate the forests on the English-Scottish border and find that we are not alone

TERCE

Lord de Hayeford was clearly keen to help me get to the heart of the investigation and mustered a dozen armed and mounted men from his keep, including Sir Walesby. They arrived at the abbey shortly after Prime two days later. Twelve men, Walesby reported, were sufficient to provide a muscular armed guard if required but small enough to move swiftly and quietly where necessary. After we had breakfasted, William, Albertus and I mounted additional horses that had been brought to us and we set out to to the forest at my bidding, in a combined company of fifteen.

'Take care, Brother,' Sir Walesby said to me as we left Berwick by its main gate. 'This may be a holy investigation, but if it comes to fighting, the special dispensation you presently enjoy would mean nothing to me. The welfare of these men is my first responsibility. I care little for your holy learning.'

The knight's bluntness took me by surprise. He was accompanying me at the head of the group, with William and Albertus riding behind us, and the other knights and men-at-arms bringing up the rear. 'Why does holy learning not concern you, Sir Walesby?'

'You can call me a man of God, if you like, and I dare say I do as well as any other man. I pray to our Lord God and ask for His favour, but I've never given it much thought. And nor have most people. We look at those who claim to be zealots of God, and we wonder where it has got 'em. Not very far, I think.'

'I'm afraid I don't follow.'

He laughed out loud and shook his head. 'I fought at Auberoche in 1345, I fought at Crécy in 1346 and I took part in the siege of Calais at the end of the Crécy campaign. I survived those battles and I stuck my sword into the bellies of other men in order to do so. Did God help me do that?' He shrugged. 'Maybe. I fought in the name of my liege lord, and in the name of the king, God save him, but do you suppose those poor French bastards weren't fighting in the name of God and their king as well? What use is God-talk when another man of God is sticking five feet of steel into your guts, Brother Jacobus? If they are both on the side of God, they cannot both be right, can they? That is my point.'

'But good Sir Knight, the circumstances in which you found yourself at Calais and the rest were not orchestrated by the hand of the Lord but by men on thrones. King Edward III and King Philip the Fortunate both serve God, and both believed their claims and causes were just. That does not confound the idea of God. It is God's judgement what our fate shall be and it is our job to praise Him for His wisdom. If you live as a knight of England with all the trappings of that noble rank, it is not as a special favour to you but because that is how you best fit into His plan. Nor, if a French fighter had stuck you in the belly, would it have proved God's disfavour with you; it would simply have shown the purpose He wished you to serve. Whether you are English or French, the Lord is your guiding light, and contentment comes from learning to understand His purpose through earnest prayer at different hours of the day and through good works: *ora et labora*.'

He nodded, but it was somehow a sarcastic nod, as though he had no reason to take notice of my response, let alone consider its merits. 'When you have seen men— when you have seen friends—die in fire or boiling oil or mud, Brother, I could not smile and tell them that their pain comes by dint of the Lord's good grace. Nor could you, I think, in a way that they would thank you for. As for why I pray? Well now, I'd hate to be put to the torch for heresy. Especially with an inquisitor in our midst.'

This time it was my turn to give the surly knight a sour look. 'Do not joke about such things, Sir Walesby. I know what your master wants from these investigations, and why you're keeping an eye on me. You are not as opaque as you believe yourself to be.'

'I do not pretend there is anything idealistic about my master or about serving him. He may very well be an imbecile, and he is obviously moonstruck about Scottish sorcery, but I'm in his pay, and he keeps me and my family well. That's all there is to it.'

'I appreciate your candour, Sir Knight. And when we find no evidence of a heretical Scottish conspiracy?'

'Well that's the thing about conspiracies, Brother,' he said with a clever grin. 'If you believe in one, nothing will ever make you change your mind. On the other hand, whatever evidence you produce, my Lord Hayeford will always be able to turn it around so that it supports his obsessions, so you score both ways. And you never know, one day the conspiracy might turn out to be true. And then what happens, if we do find ourselves face to face with a horde of ravening Scots? Well, you can pray all you like, good Brother, but if I were you, I'd make sure you do it behind my steel.'

The morning was bright, which made a change from the gloom of the past few days. We passed by Ord without stopping but the sight of it acted as a mote in my eye and I crossed myself automatically, as did William, who now rode beside me, which made me hope, silently, that the mote was not a beam (Matthew 7:3–5) and that we were not failing to observe more heinous sins in ourselves.

A mile or two beyond Ord, the countryside became chaotic and messy, as the tilled fields surrendered to nettles and weeds, and the muddy path became choked with dying brambles that reached for us and snagged us as we invaded their terrain. Despite this inhospitable environment, however, I was excited to be exploring the place and learning its secrets. With our company made up of men who would bear witness to whatever proofs I might find, I was confident of doing God's work and of ending up with a solution to the region's awful mystery.

We saw no villagers as we entered the forest, just bare branches which waved around us in the breeze, as if trying to ward us away, and fallen leaves on the ground which the horses' hoofs kicked up. Because it was winter, more light penetrated than had it been summer, allowing the sun to shine with thin warmth at our backs.

'What are you thinking, Jacobus?' asked William.

'I am thinking that this path, such as it is, is the main route between Ord and these woodlands. It is the path the children would have used, if they had come or gone of their own free will.'

'And you think they moved freely?'

'That is the critical question. They must have left the woods intentionally. Whether they entered it the same way, I cannot say. But that is not important at this stage. If they chose to leave, however damaged their critical faculties may have been, we can trace the path to …'

'To what?'

'To the answer.'

'For a man who does not even know his way around, you seem very confident, Jacobus,' said William, smiling.

'The world is a text,' I said, returning the smile. 'You only need to know your letters and it will reveal itself.'

'A text?' he said, mulling over the idea. 'Really? I would have said that it's a palimpsest, written anew each autumn as trees and plants shed their golden canopies and are felled by age, disease and the axeman. In this cycle of change and death, the forest rewrites itself, erasing what it had been the year before, and the year before that, and hiding past secrets from the inquisitive—like us.'

I could not help but laugh. 'Very poetic—but even palimpsests retain traces of their histories.'

But soon enough William's metaphor proved fully justified. The path we had followed became obscured by a thick brown carpet of rotting leaves and by felled branches which reached across the woodland floor. Had we travelled further north, we could have used the River Tweed as our guide but the path from Ord did not reach that high. We would have to proceed by guesswork.

'How well do you know these forests, Friar William?' I asked as proceeded through a younger copse of trees.

'Not well enough that I could map it, but well enough to know I would not want to!'

I smiled at his glib answer, and we continued to ride.

Shortly afterwards we came to a meadow of modest size that resembled a forest clearing and was overgrown with ground cover. As it was a natural break in the topography, I decided it should herald a break in our journey, so I called on our company to stop while I called on Albertus and William to dismount with me and explore on foot. Six of the men, habitually attuned to military wariness, fanned out and kept watch. The others—two each—accompanied us as we went off to see what we could find.

'You don't think we ought to have stayed mounted?' asked Albertus, when we were on foot.

'I don't see why. In the summer we might be at risk of attack but the vegetation in this season is not so dense for ambushers to lurk in it. Besides, the knights will keep us safe.'

We spent some time exploring the area and, at my order, collecting different plants, some of which we smelled and tasted as we went. I concentrated on flowers, and harvested samples of hairy woodrush and oxeye daisy and heather and meadowsweet and autumn crocus, while William found a variety of fescues and other grasses such as wood melick and false-brome and tufted hair grass. Albertus ignored the common herbs like wood sorrel and yarrow and wild garlic and alehoof but took samples of different barks and various toxic fungi including fly agaric, with its red top and white spots, and the panther cap and false chanterelle and the very nasty death cap and destroying angel. All these things could produce unpleasant, even fatal, but quite recognisable reactions rather than the very strange but consistent symptoms suffered by the children.

'Is it possible?' William asked, as we caught up with Albertus examining spores on some rotting wood, 'that the culprit could be fungal?'

'It seems to be the category we should eliminate first from our inquiry,' Albertus responded. 'Look here.' He knelt down at the base of a damp hedge and picked a couple of decomposing fibrecaps which turned to sludge in his hand. 'Different species appear in the summer and autumn and look quite innocuous but you don't want to go eating 'em. Unless you're a slug, of course; slugs love 'em.'

'Are these the worst mushrooms that grow in these parts?' I asked.

'Ah, there are dozens,' he said matter-of-factly, 'but these are the most common. I'd be surprised if bairns would go picking and eating 'em, though. They're nothing special to look at and they give off a red stain, which ought to be a warning. If they did eat 'em though, they'd get a bad bellyache and a burning fever—or they'd die—but they wouldn't get the terrible things that we've seen. And if one bairn ate some for a dare, no-one else'd try it after watching 'em chuck their guts up.'

'We should take some away, in any case,' I said, 'just to look at them more closely. If you come across any others, let me know, even if they have no bearing on this case. I'd like to look into them for my own knowledge.'

As we meandered back to Sir Walesby and those of his men who had stayed back, dusk was starting to fall. I did not make a habit of travelling in the late afternoon in unknown forests, but with the company of soldiers at our backs I did not fear anything, and the safety of the open fields was less than half an hour's ride away, even if we did make the occasional stop to gather more samples.

It was on one such stop, when the horses' hoofs had stopped shushing up the leaves and Albertus and I were crouched over, gathering inky caps at the base of a rotten tree trunk, that we heard a low growl.

I met Albertus's stricken gaze with my own, and froze.

'Wolves,' he muttered under his breath, and gestured over my shoulder with his eyes.

I turned slowly, fearing what I might find, but in the fading light I saw nothing. A couple of the mounted men-at-arms turned about as their horses whickered in agitation. I frowned, not wanting to call out, but not wanting to stay in case I was being eyed up by some infernal beast with a taste for human flesh.

Another growl came, this time closer and more confident. Was the animal stalking us or had we come across it by accident? Wolves, I knew, did not normally make a noise before attacking, for fear of scaring off their prey. In the case of this one, we must have walked right into its lair. It may not have been looking for us but now we were in easy range, it might very well take its chance.

Even in the deepening chill, sweat slicked my forehead and, still crouched down, I crossed myself. I looked across at William and saw that his eyes were darting around, trying to locate the source of the sound.

I thought the easiest thing might be to make a loud noise in the hope of scaring it off but it was a risk—and others were having other thoughts. I watched as three of our mounted escorts silently nodded in agreement before one of them punctured the silence by rearing up his horse, shouting and drawing a sword. I heard an angry animal's howl and saw a flash of grey fur streaking behind a line of tree trunks. The two other guards pulled back their bowstrings and loosed off an arrow each. There was the brief sound of a whimper, and then all was still.

I found myself holding onto a tree, clutching at its bark as if it was my mother's gown. My heart was pounding and my throat was dry, but it seemed that the danger had passed. The three men who had brought the animal down chuckled triumphantly. One of them trotted towards the felled creature and ran it through with his sword, to ensure it was dead.

'Is it over? Are there any more?' I called out.

'No, monk,' one of the men called back with a condescending laugh. 'You're safe now.' And he pulled out a horn and sounded an alarm to call Sir Walesby and the others to join us.

'We should have left much earlier,' Albertus said, putting a hand on my shoulder to steady us both. 'Wolves are most active at dusk and dawn. We'd have been safer in daylight. But they also fear men. The fact that this one wasn't fearful tells us that it was probably rabid. You suspected as much. So, now you have your answer.'

I nodded, hesitantly. 'Perhaps, perhaps. As I said two days ago, Rogerius Salernitanus tells us that the bite of the wolf has many effects. It can transmit lesions and animal humours, such as lupus. If rabid, its bite may cause unpredictable behaviour in those who have been attacked. Such effects can even fool onlookers into thinking that the victims have been possessed or taken over by sorcery. And in the post-furious stage of the disease, death is certain. And yet …'

'And yet what?' asked Albertus. 'Did you not say that we'd find proof? Isn't this it?'

'We cannot be sure that this animal was rabid and would have attacked. Nor did it find us; we found it. The growling suggests it was being defensive, not aggressive: it may merely have been warning us not to get too close. Besides which, the body of one wolf does not constitute the proof we need. And there weren't any bite marks on the children. Perhaps the beast transferred its saliva to the children without breaking the skin or via some other puncture or wound. And let us not forget the most crucial evidence discounting the wolf: that Alfred and Matilda survived! They at least did not suffer any rabid wolves' bite. Either way, there are still many questions to answer. But we need to bring the creature back to the infirmary, so I can conduct a thorough examination on its body.'

'We don't need more questions,' muttered Albertus. 'We need to show people we've uncovered the mystery.'

I scoffed. 'You do not need a scholar to travel from the south of France to the north of England just to put the blame on a possibly rabid canine. Blaming all this on a dog would be lazy, anyway. What if we announce that this animal is the cause of the horror, only for another disappearance or death to happen? We would have betrayed the people *and* our sacred mission. What a sin that would be, Albertus.'

By this time William had walked across to where the dead animal lay. One arrow had pierced its ribcage, the other was in its right thigh. The frothing menace that had growled at us from behind the trees was now just a corpse. Its mouth lolled open, its long tongue hanging out grotesquely, as if it had been about to speak. The creature's body was large yet its limbs were spindly. It was a monstrous thing.

'The poor creature,' said William, looking at it almost mournfully.

Albertus gave him a sour look. 'It is an unworthy, diseased thing, and would have attacked us and poisoned us, as it poisoned the children, if the men's arrows had not reached it first. It is better off dead.'

William did not look at me but peered at the wolf, as if he could divine a lost nobility in the animal. Eventually he invoked Psalm 104, saying, 'Oh Lord, how manifold are your works! In wisdom you have made them all; the Earth is full of your creatures.' He then, to my astonishment, made the sign of the Cross over the dead animal, blessing it.

I felt this was inappropriate and wanted to upbraid

him for debasing the divinity of the Cross by using it for a wild and possibly deranged animal that might or might not have been causing whatever plague was affecting the children, but I held my peace. There would be time for remonstrations later, if necessary; right now, we needed unity and goodwill.

William gave me a strange look, as though reading my mind, and walked away, to be by himself for a moment. I watched him go, concerned that by blessing the creature, William was demonstrating his point about the secrets of the forest and their supposed divinity. It occurred to me that he and perhaps others knew more about the folklore of the woodlands they were letting on.

I thought at that moment that I now understood why so many people had accused the Fraticelli Franciscans in Italy of being unnecessarily rigid in criticising what they saw as the worldly compromises of the Church and urging a stricter observance of the Rule of St. Francis by their Order. Tensions with the Fraticelli—the little Brothers—led to divisions and schisms, with their accusations of heresy and their call for the lax to be suppressed and persecuted. The friary, and probably the secular powers too, probably saw me as a Fraticellus in miniature: over-pious, self-righteous and lacking in humour.

At that moment, Sir Walesby and his convoy galloped up, with our three extra horses. Walesby sprang down from his steed, was quickly briefed by our guards and went to inspect the wolf.

'We have work here that cannot go uncompleted,' he called, to the agreement from his men. 'If there's one rabid dog in this forest, there'll be others.'

'A rabid wolf is most often a lone wolf,' I answered.

'Then where did the creature get its malady, Brother?

There'll be a den somewhere. I say we come back tomorrow, find it, and slaughter them all. For now, let's go before we expose ourselves to more danger.'

I kept my own council as we started the return journey to Berwick and I mourned the fact that I had no trusty friend in whom I could confide. I wished that Magnus were present so we could exchange ideas openly and at greater length. A great secret, mocking and dangerous, was obviously hiding behind in the crevices of this borderland, and I had resolved to bring it to the light, not merely to satisfy any base pride in my own intellectual abilities, but in the name of God Himself.

But in all honesty only half of my mind was processing these thoughts for, in my fatigue, the greater part of me was yearning for bed and for sleep. It was a vain hope, for the evening had not finished with us yet.

VESPERS

The raiding party struck not thirty minutes later, as we were meandering through the copse. One of the men in Sir Walesby's company, a squire whose name I learned was Hepplewhite, fell from his horse with the dull thump of leather on earth. An arrow protruded from his neck, and I prayed that Our Lord had enabled him to expire before he'd hit the ground. As the squire's horse bolted, the others whinnied in fright and the men turned about, in search of this new invader.

'Scots!' Sir Walesby hollered, drawing his sword and barking orders. A torch was lit and tossed into the trees to illuminate the way and perhaps confuse our assailants. The knights configured themselves as well as they could in the confined space, and set about scouring the scene. As commands went out to our men to nock and loose their arrows, another arrow from the marauders whistled past by me, missing me by inches just as I ducked to tighten my stirrups. My heart hammered at my throat, and my eyes strained desperately into the darkness, and the words *Deus, Deus meus, respice in me: quare me dereliquisti?*—the Twenty-Second Psalm—issued unbidden from my lips.

'Get down, Brothers!' cried Sir Walesby to us. I obeyed without question, as did William. We slid from our horses and collapsed to the ground, where we crawled across the freezing earth into a bramble thicket that caught at our gowns and skin. I heard William's breath but could not see him, so dark was it now, and dared not utter a word that might disclose my location. There I remained, muttering desperate prayers, as thundering hoofs trampled the ground, raiders' voices mocked our own men's unpreparedness, swords rang from their scabbards, screams erupted and another man was thrown from his horse, burbling a stream of curses as he landed.

I could not leave him so I crawled towards him to see if he was one of ours, and in need of help. I found him lying on his back in the low brush, staring at the sky. One hand clasped a gushing wound in his abdomen and he was surrounded by his own blood and the stench of faeces. My stomach lurched as I encountered him and I covered my mouth to keep from retching. For a moment our eyes met and I saw he was not one of ours, though he was armoured rather similarly. He tried to mutter something to me but the word was lost on his lips, and he departed this life. I took his hand and uttered a silent prayer for him as he went on his final journey.

The screams died down soon after that, leaving the wind to blow away the smells. All that remained were the groans of the injured and the snorting of the horses as they were brought under control.

'You can come out from the briars now, Monks!' came Walesby's voice with a granite laugh, his breath still heaving with violence. I rose up gingerly and looked about me. William was nearby, but even in the gloom looked as white as milk. In that moment my recriminations about heresy could not have been farther from my mind, and I was overjoyed that he had come to no harm. Others had been less lucky. After a quick count it became apparent that Sir Walesby's company had lost three men in the melée and that, of the eight Scottish raiders who had attacked us, only two had survived. These two, battered and weary, had been dragged by Walesby's men to the trunk of an oak tree, where they were bound at knifepoint. The first of them was a mess of bruises, and cradled his side while one of Walesby's men trained a long knife on him. Beneath the blood and blotches he might have been handsome, and he was certainly defiant. Despite his injuries he regarded his captors with grim amusement, uttering foul maledictions at them in the roughest of Scots dialects.

The second of the injured parties sat limply, head slumped forward, breathing noisily. He was dark-skinned and wore a cascade of black hair that splayed untidily over one shoulder. Or so I thought, for when I stepped closer, I saw that it was a woman! Weary scorn was on her face and she shot me a wicked smile, as though possessed by a bad spirit. Despite her wounds, I saw that an undimmed blaze flickered in her eyes and she regarded me with the dull lasciviousness that typifies the sort of woman whom only the Lord Jesus had the strength to resist, when offered to him in the persona of the unknown anointer of his feet in Luke 7:36–50 and perhaps also the Magdalene and Mary of Bethany (Luke 10:39), all of whom the first Pope Gregory was pleased to teach were one and the same.

'Who are these people?' I asked, approaching them. The man looked up at me and tried to laugh, but wailed when he found it too painful. His pain was not abated when Walesby administered him a kick in the ribs.

'Well, answer the man, Gallus,' said Walesby, to a few jeers from his men.

'Gallus?' I repeated. 'That's his name?'

Walesby rolled his eyes at my ignorance. 'No. He's a Scot.'

'Ach, I've nae words for the likes of ye, Sir Knight,' said the Scotsman.

'Aye, that's right,' said the woman and spat into the air.

Walesby knelt down and ripped a portion off the man's tunic, causing him to growl and gnash his bloodied teeth like an animal. The knight then showed me the material under the torchlight. Stitched into it was a sigil of a black, wide-eyed horse in a circle. 'A horse's head wreathed in a bridle. That's the sigil of House Dunbar, Brother Jacobus. Which would make this low-browed bastard a member of that house. Isn't that so?' said Walesby, calling out to the man.

'Aye,' said the man, spitting out a thick gobbet of blood onto the grass. 'I'm Donal, son of Thane Gavin of Dunbar, the rightful lords of the royal town of Berwick, which was stolen by ye, ye *bassa mèirlich*.'

'And these heathen bastards will do anything to try

and wrest it back,' said Sir Walesby. 'The king, God save him, secured the border against the Scots only two years ago, and it sticks in your filthy craw, doesn't it, Gallus? And what you cannot take by fair means you will try to take so by foul. Isn't that right, young Donal?'

The young raider mustered a sneer but then let his head droop, his eyes heavily lidded now that the lust for violence had drained from his body.

'I know the conclusions your lord liege would draw with respect to these captives, Sir Walesby, but I prefer to reach my own answers,' I responded brusquely.

Donal raised his head upon hearing my accent, and cast a bruised, curious eye over me. 'And from where do ye hail, friend? You're no treacherous Saxon tuathanach.'

Before I could answer, Walesby ordered his men to hoist Donal over the back of a horse, which they did with rough abandon, causing the man to gasp in pain as his ribs were plopped down upon the haunches of his beast.

'You two will have plenty of time to talk in the days ahead, Brother,' said Walesby. He wore a look that was flush with vindication, and spoke with all the authority of a practised campaigner. 'Tonight, Brother, you will be escorted to Berwick but tomorrow I trust you will travel to see Lord Hayeford, where we're taking the captives.'

I balked at his plan. 'The prisoners cannot be taken to Hayeford Castle: they would not see the night through, not with your master's prejudices. Can they not be kept at the garrison in Berwick, for their own safety?'

Walesby responded with a fearsome, contemptuous look, and in my fatigue I quailed at the sight of him on horseback, still spattered with blood. 'Are you so stupid, Monk, for one so schooled? My liege lord will not risk a blood feud—or worse, the reopening of war with these vandals—so soon after the king has secured his northern borders. Remember why you are here, Brother. Legitimacy is the byword and the byword it shall remain. In spite of what they would have done to us, we'll keep 'em safe. You need have no fear.'

I nodded, having no option but to acquiesce. 'In that case, I will see them tomorrow, as soon as I have seen your lord.'

24th November

In which
I visit
the prison
beneath Haye-
ford Castle and
try
to invoke
reason
in order
to avoid
unnecessary
bloodshed

TERCE

It was with some trepidation that I journeyed to Hayeford Castle the next day, but was relieved to find that the prisoners had been kept as comfortably as could be hoped for. Lord Hayeford greeted me enthusiastically, and thanked me for suggesting that we take the investigation to the woods and lie in wait for the raiders.

'It was not quite my intention to return from the woods with captives,' I said, 'though I confess to having gone there to seek evidence.'

'Ah, well, the ways of the Lord surprise us all, do they not, dear Brother? Can you believe that one of the raiders was a woman! This, surely, is the root of the sorcery that has afflicted the area. I mean to take this to trial as soon as possible. That way we shall be able to settle the mystery, wipe out the raiding parties, and send you back to France with another feather in your cap.'

I nodded in appreciation but kept my concerns private. Hayeford worried me. His zealotry recalled that of Nastagio di Balino; he was less learned in theological and philosophical teachings but no less keen on persecution. The Scots had been tormenting him by encroaching on his lands and he was intent on destroying them. I found this reprehensible: the last thing I wanted was for the focus of my investigations to be diverted by prejudice and grudges. Yet I knew all too well how zeal can inflame the senses and pervert one's reason. Were I to challenge him too hard, there was every chance that he would implicate me in the conspiracy. As a stranger in a strange land, I was vulnerable and would need to be more artful than that.

'You are correct, Lord Hayeford, but we cannot start a trial without an interrogation. Guilt will always show itself. The skilful interrogator only has to know how to recognise it.'

The two surviving Scottish raiders had been put in separate cells in the castle dungeons. Each had a roll of damp, rotting straw for a bed and a pot to piss in, but nothing more. The stench of their bodily excretions— sweat, urine, faeces, blood and vomit—stank out the air. Rats came out to inspect them, then scuttled off elsewhere. I went to inspect them too, passing a guard whom Hayeford had positioned at the end of the short underground corridor, ostensibly to protect me but probably also to monitor my conversations with the prisoners. This was unfortunate because I had asked for privacy and Hayeford had repaid me with distrust.

The jailor, a hunchback who stank of stale piss, waddled along the corridor, cackling at some joke only he seemed aware of, and opened the lock. He then gestured for me to enter, and jangled the keys elaborately before waddling back up the corridor.

I found the prisoners both slumped against their cell walls and weak from wounds, fatigue and lack of food. The woman had been granted no special privileges or quarter and was locked in a cell that had probably only ever housed men. I stopped to talk to her first.

'Woman,' I muttered. She raised her head. One night in a cell had reduced her to a shadow of herself; her hair was a briar bush and her face, yesterday so colourful with paint and passion, was now a death-mask of resignation. 'My name is Jacobus,' I said. 'Tell me yours.'

She looked up at me but said nothing. A violet bruise had swollen over one eye and her lips were puffy and bloodied from where she had been hit. I offered her my canteen of water, which she scooped up and drank from so greedily that it brought tears to my eyes. When she had had her fill, I asked for it back, whispering that I did not want to deprive her fellow captive. Only now did she give voice to words, though these were slow and slurred. 'Donal said there was a monk from the Empire among the English. That must ha' been ye.'

'Yes, I am from Vienna,' I explained, 'but I came here from France.'

The woman paused, assessing me before giving away her identity. 'I am Anya. Black Anya of Dunbar.'

'I am surprised to find you alive, Black Anya of Dunbar,' I said. 'Lord Hayeford cares little for Scots. He will no doubt have plans for you.' I stared at the silhouetted guard at the end of the corridor and raised my voice for his benefit. 'You bear great sins, child. I have been sent here to determine them.'

'We are all sinners, Brother.' She paused, then sighed. 'Why are you really here?'

'To question you. Why were you riding through the English king's lands?'

She scoffed. 'To kill the English king's men, the wee Saxon *mèirlich*. Donal will say the same. And what's your interest, Brother?'

'I am on a mission from God, to discern an indiscernible truth and to shine a light where there is only shadow. Right now, Black Anya of Dunbar, you seem to be standing in the very heart of that shadow but it has nothing to do with your petty border disputes with the English. That at least is clear to me.'

'You're right,' she said. 'We are at least as good Christians as the English and our border dispute is with them, not with God. That does not make it worth abandoning.'

I let a silence hang between us, holding her gaze with

firmness rather than accusation. From experience I knew that silence can prove intolerable to those with something to say. And so it was with Black Anya.

'We were betrayed!' she blurted suddenly. 'The city of Berwick was stolen from us. It belongs to our house. It was the House of Dunbar that gave succour to the king's father and that hospitality was repaid with treachery. Berwick belongs to Scotland.'

'And how would a small band of Scottish reavers hope to win it back?'

She wrinkled her nose, looked at her latrine bucket and remained silent.

'If you could not achieve such an aim, then what is your purpose?'

More silence.

'Are you familiar with the incidents that have befallen some of the communities surrounding Berwick in recent times?'

She looked back at me. 'What incidents?'

'Incidents involving children? Disappearances?'

She rolled her eyes. 'No.'

As I proceeded to relate the tragedies that had befallen the region and the terrible things we had witnessed with our own eyes, the belligerence fell from her face. At some point—and I watched her like a hawk—I saw that the disputes that were troubling her had been displaced by my revelations and that she was enthralled by my tale. 'So you see,' I continued, 'what brought me here were not the testimonies of madmen and fools but of men of learning, and of God.' I let the weight of these matters settle on her mind, before pressing my advantage.

'We found certain ... effects upon your person and on

the bodies of your friends. Twig figures made from sticks and twine and leaves. One of the dead carried a leather-bound book decorated with strange markings. I have all the articles here.' I produced the foliate figures and the book from my satchel. Anya eyed them warily.

'What are these figures, Anya?'

'Just dolls, toys.'

'A little old for child's playthings, are you not?'

'They're not mine. They're for … the children. At Dunbar.'

'And you were carrying them because … ?'

She shifted uncomfortably. 'They're good luck charms. That's all. It's dangerous, you know. What we do.'

'And charms will help you, when you have all you need in the Cross?'

'As I said, it's dangerous.'

'Raiding in lands that are not yours? Yes, I should say so.' I fingered the book. It had a strange Celtic-looking glyph upon its front cover. 'And this book. Do you need books when raiding English land?'

'That's Kirk's journal,' she said in a hushed voice.

'Kirk is one of your companions who was slain?'

'Aye.'

'There are some interesting entries this Kirk seems to have written.' I licked my fingers and thumbed the book open to the relevant pages. 'His script is thin and elegant, and many of the entries are in verse. He was no mere brutish brigand. He had some learning about him.' Anya said nothing, so I proceeded to read.

> By valour a strange and mighty man
> Quicker to a world of wood than worship,
> Quicker to praise the ground than the Heavens

> Having no need of long-legged steed,
> Still spans the country wide and far
> A beloved friend of God's righteous men.
> When men move against him
> He shall have his way.
> Take from his spiralling branches,
> He shall have his share.
> Move against the law of the wood,
> And the wood shall move back.
> For surely as the trees grow anew from the rot
> The sapling defers to the oak.

When I finished I set the book down and looked at Anya. She shrugged.

'Move against the law of the wood, and the wood is sure to move back? The sapling defers to the oak?' I repeated. 'What does that mean, Anya?'

She let out a little sob and looked more like a child rather than a warrior woman. 'I'm no poet, Father.'

'Thou shalt have no other gods but Me,' I said, firmly. 'That is the law, gifted to man by God. Is there such a thing as the law of the wood? Do you believe instead in a law of the wood?'

Anya scowled at me. Her expression became baleful, and I was glad of the iron bars between us.

'I believe in retribution, Brother,' she said at last. 'It may be divine or it may be by the hand of man or it may be something else. But I've no hand in what happened to those wee'uns from that village and I'll take an oath to that. I'll say no more about it.'

I looked at her very hard this time. 'These things on their own may not be afforded great significance, Anya. But when put together and placed in the context of a band of brigands encroaching on foreign soil with vengeful intentions, and the terrible episodes that have befallen this place, the picture becomes very black indeed. In the eyes of many investigators this would be taken as compelling evidence of heresy and sorcery.'

These final three words finally pierced her defences. Fear swept away her contempt. Death by burning for heretics was not common among the English and Scots but I had no doubt that tales of executions had travelled north from France and Spain and horrified the locals.

'You must know,' I continued, 'that it would not be difficult to show that your violent band attempted to use these crude idols and spells to summon up a demon to entice and destroy the children of England as part of your border dispute.'

'I know of no sorcery, Father,' she said, coming forward to the bars and grasping them. "And I wouldnae harm a bairn, I swear! I've told ye, we are people of God, and the Holy Father has his word followed in our houses just as well as in any English friary or church.'

I had no desire to wear the sash of the Inquisition but even hinting at its existence was often sufficient to loosen tightly shut lips. And, in my experience, the ones whose lips were loosened were usually the most innocent—or at least, believed themselves to be.

'It is as I said. Lord Hayeford couldn't care less for the Scots. He's already convinced of your guilt. He wants you all dead. And he says that hanging, drawing and quartering is the favoured means of dispatching a convict in these isles.'

By this point the poor woman was trembling, shaking her head and issuing passionate denials. 'This was not … we didnae do anything … . There's no sorcery in us,

Father! I renounce the Devil and all his works and Donal would say the same thing.'

I sighed and bowed my head. 'Woman, let me confess a certain truth of my own. I believe there is something dark afoot here, but I think it will sooner be revealed by natural philosophy and scientific practice than inquisitorial procedures. Lord Hayeford, however, does not give a damn about my preferences and wants a trial, to show the common folk that he is in charge and has punished those who have brought tragedy upon his lands.

'Now, it is within my gift to administer a trial for heretical sorcery on his behalf. I do not want that but, in my capacity as investigator of these occurrences, I will be bound to participate, if he calls on me to do so. And know this: if you do not confess to the crime of heresy, as he wishes, you will be subjected to a protracted and unpleasant interrogation until a confession is extracted. And if a confession is not forthcoming, then you would be interred, which will bring about your death.'

Anya looked at me with tear-stained eyes and a mixture of fear, contempt and confusion tearing at her face. 'But ... we are no heretics!'

I waved away her protest as if I thought it silly. 'Such talk will bind you to the stake, woman! Have you heard nothing? The evidence is overwhelming. The testimonies of those who have been affected will be like nails driven into your hands and feet, and the items we found upon you will be like rope lashed round your chest. If you confess, with full remorse, your lives may be saved, in which case further bloodshed shall be prevented and you will be able to return to Scotland. If an innocent life is lost, owing to a false accusation, that is the very depths of the Devil's work and we must strike at him where we can!'

She laughed at that. 'And yet you are the one making this accusation, knowing it to be false!'

'I know the rules of the Papal Inquisition inside-out and I know how to manipulate them. God is pleased when his children have the intelligence to remake the world anew. So I implore you once more, plead guilty and walk away with your life.'

She shook her head, but something in her expression changed. I knew she was considering my proposal. It is a bitter pill to accept judgement for a crime one has not committed, but surely worse still to suffer death for it. Eventually she spoke. 'I shall think on it, Brother Jacobus. But Donal will not confess to any crime he did not commit. He is proud.'

I nodded. 'Ah, pride. It makes fools of us all. That is why it is sinful. Do not confer martyrdom upon yourself for this, Anya.' I got up to leave. 'Hayeford will push for the trial soon. When Donal is sufficiently revived to understand the accusations I shall visit again and talk to him. You should acquaint yourselves with remorse and the need for forgiveness, and think about what else you could do with your life. I shall see you soon.'

1st December

The Second Trial

TERCE

As was to be expected, Hayeford Castle lobbied directly and swiftly for the trial to be held. Two separate charges would be brought, the first concerned with encroachment and trespass, the second concerned with heresy. The charges were brought to me, as the present and designated papal official, and I received the lobby in my standing as acting judge. The full charge of heresy could not be brought lightly and so Hayeford brought me the accusation directly as a denunciation: an ostensible accusation based upon the testimony of Sir Walesby and those of his men who had captured the Scots.

Hayeford denounced the captives without offering evidence of his own or even participating directly in the trial (which, as judge, I would have prevented him from doing on account of his staunch enmity for the accused) but on the basis of his zeal for the Faith. Thus, it would be Sir Walesby's testimony, and not Lord Hayeford's, upon which the trial would hang. This was to my satisfaction as it took away the need for a full inquisition. A paper article, noting the general summons, was then fastened to the gates of the Berwick friary (that being my present place of residence as judge) and that was that. The game was set.

Word of the trial was sent to House Gavin, the seat of Donal's father, a thane of minor officialdom in East Lothian. I insisted upon writing the letter myself rather than leaving Hayeford to have one of his household do it, and risk its being packed with tactless gloating. In the letter I described the nature of the arrest, the accusation of encroachment and trespass, and the subsequent discoveries—the twig figures and the book with strange markings—that indicated pagan and heretical practices.

I supposed that the civil or feudal accusation would not have disturbed the thane (I guessed that he secretly approved of his son's raids or was wilfully blind to them) but the ecclesiastical charge of heresy surely would have done, as it carried a mark of disgrace that would stretch farther north than Dunbar and farther south than the Tweed, and would attract as much attention as the tallest treetops in the forest. Yet I stressed in the letter that there still remained an opportunity to arrive at an equitable solution, and firmly warned the thane in the name of the Papal See not to try recapturing his son by armed force.

The trial took place a week later. The two defendants had been kept well by Hayeford in the meantime. I cannot say whether my regular visits to the castle afforded them special protection, but my presence as a foreigner rather than an Englishman helped to keep things neutral and diplomatic and peaceful.

The hearing took place in the Franciscan chapter house in Berwick on a grey, scowling day. Both defendants, Black Anya and Donal of House Gavin, stood in manacles in front of curious onlookers. Most of those who had gathered to watch were gossip-hungry friars, ostensibly present to learn about the workings of the judicial system but really to catch up on the latest rumours with which to entertain the refectory hall. Guardian Dionysius sat in attendance, his expression offering no clue as to his thoughts, and surrounding him were his closest friars, including Friar William, Albertus and Friar Herry. Hayeford sat to one side, looking thoroughly pleased with himself, with a small clutch of household members.

I recognised a number of villagers from Ord, all bristling with derision. The man whose nose had been busted by Sir Walesby had come along and kept glowering at the knight through smouldering eyes, but did no more than that.

My letter across the border had encouraged a gaggle of Scots to turn up: various men of Roxburgh, led by Donal's father Douglas, and two of his men-at-arms. All carried weapons—swords or daggers—but all were also acutely aware of being in God's house, and although the bitterness between them and Hayeford knew no bounds, they knew also that violence would not be tolerated in this place and so civility presided—on the face of it.

With John of Thorseby's wise words to keep the peace at the front of my mind at all times, I prayed fervently that morning for God to be with me throughout, and help me walk that narrow path that would satisfy all parties: all parties except me, of course. Whatever the result of the trial, I was bound to be dissatisfied, for no true answers would be brought to light! But perhaps some false ones might be eradicated, and so I judged that the Lord was smoothing my way to the truth.

Finally, a local notary and two clerics from the friary were among those present, to ensure that the trial was undertaken according to the necessary protocols.

Once all present had settled down, I nodded to the scribe, who picked up his quill to take down my words, and addressed the onlookers.

'In the name of the Lord, Amen. In the year from the Birth of the Lord 1367, on the first day of December, in the presence of these notaries and the witnesses presently declared, the Lord Thomas De Hayeford from the Diocese of Durham appeared in person before me, an honourable judge, and offered to me a denunciation to the following effect: that Donal Gavin of Roxburgh, and Anya Dunne of Roxburgh, committed acts of harm against him and the persons of his lands through the medium of heretical sorcery.'

I paused. There were mutterings of dissent from the Scottish contingent but they were not disruptive. I then addressed Lord Hayeford and Sir Walesby in turn.

'Lord Hayeford, you have brought the denunciation to me on account of your zeal for the Faith. Sir Walesby of Otterburn, you are bringing the denunciation on behalf of Lord Hayeford on account of your witness to the acts in question. I ask you both to swear an oath upon the Holy Gospels of Matthew, Mark, Luke and John. Raise your right hand, both of you, then lower your last two fingers against the flesh of your palm, and repeat after me: by the testimony of The Holy Trinity and at the risk of the damnation of my soul and body, I shall tell the truth about the acts denounced here today.'

They both did as they were asked, and then Hayeford sat down to allow Sir Walesby to give his testimony. It was better that Walesby was the one to testify to the denunciation; he witnessed what had happened in the woods and was more professional than his liege lord. There were plenty of people present willing to believe that demons were in their midst, and Hayeford's sniggering, paranoid testimony in front of the Scots would have collapsed the trial completely.

As it was, Sir Walesby described the details plainly and without embellishment. He told of the presence of the Scots in the English woods with murderous intent; the idolatrous effects found upon the persons of the captives; the insidiousness of Kirk's journal; and, of course, the strange terror that had gripped the community surrounding Berwick.

Witnesses were then permitted to present their own

evidence; as an ecclesiastical judge I compelled each one of them to swear an oath to ensure the truthfulness of their utterances. Testimony was delivered by Albertus and Herry, who spoke about what they had seen of the two children; and the child's mother Gwendolynn also had her say. As an addendum to her testimony, the children were also presented to the gallery. The two, who had recovered significantly in the week since their arrest and internment at the infirmary, paraded their strange marks when called on to do so but I did not permit them to speak. This limited the number of witnesses to three, which meant that, in accordance with the alignment of their testimony, the act of condemnation laid solely with the conscience of the judge—which was me. Hayeford had no idea about the rules governing inquisitorial or ecclesiastical trials and everything played out as I planned.

The outcome of the trial hung not upon these initial testimonies, which I had orchestrated to my satisfaction, but on the questioning of the two defendants and the pleas they issued. After the witnesses had presented their facts, Black Anya and Donal were presented to the court together. I approached the two of them. They had kept silent throughout the trial so far but the fear on their faces was plain. In truth, I was at least as anxious as they were; here I was in England to discover an island of truth, and was swimming towards it in a sea of falsity.

After the initial general questions, I began.

'Donal Gavin, and Anya Dunne. Why did you leave the area of your birth, in Roxburgh, to encroach upon the area of Northumberland?'

Donal and Anya looked at one another, and then Donal proceeded to answer. 'To bring fear into the hearts of the English folk who lived there.'

There was barely concealed hissing from Hayeford's retinue at the admission and some brooding looks from the Scots in response. Nonetheless, this was the answer I had insisted they give!

I continued. 'Have either of you heard, in these areas or elsewhere, talk of witchcraft? Of children affected with sorcery, with specific reference to the accusations that have been brought against you both?'

Donal fixed me with a glare. 'Aye. We've heard such talk. Of bairns being … changed.'

'And are you aware of why the common people are so frightened of your behaviour?'

'Aye, for our raiding! Because we come to the woods with weapons and terrorise anyone who gets in our way.'

'And did you see these children, or any others, who come from the village of Ord and other tithes surrounding Berwick?'

This time Anya answered. 'We'd see bairns in the woods sometimes, aye, but we always let 'em be.'

'But you have heard the testimony of the witnesses! The unholy symptoms displayed by the children must have been brought about by the touch of a sorcerer or sorceress, so can you say with the utmost conviction that you never once touched any child, who could then have transmitted the demonic pox to others by their own touch, that touch having been made malignant by the actions of sorcery?'

Donal clenched his lower jaw and I sensed the slightest, almost imperceptible, shake of the head. During our conversations in Hayeford Castle's holding cells I had impressed upon both of them the strange, counter-intuitive manner in which the trial would proceed, and that an understanding and admission of their role in the proceedings would have to be acknowledged. However, it is one thing to have walked them through the act of self-denunciation in theory; at trial, with their reputations and lives at stake, I could see them weighing the risks and counter-risks in their mind. I had also to ask myself whether my own presence had all been an elaborate ruse to secure their guilt. Was I in fact a stooge for the English king? Or did I speak the truth and have their interests at heart? I prayed that they would see my good intentions.

'It might ha' been the case that we interacted with some of the bairns,' Anya muttered, sensing the possibility that Donal might issue a vehement denial, which would have made it more difficult for me to navigate a sure path. As she spoke, Donal looked at her with shock and fear, but kept quiet. He had the good sense to realise there was no sense in contradicting her. United they would have to stand, for divided they would certainly both fall.

'And do you abjure the heretical depravity with which you caused panic to the people of this shire?'

'Yes,' she said, again quickly. Then she got down on bended knee and looked up at Donal, imploring him with her eyes to follow suit. 'It was our great error to invoke such hideous malpractices! A catastrophic mistake! But I make the abjuration wholly, renounce the works of the Devil and submit myself to God.'

Donal sighed, sensing that, either way, the game was up. He got to his knees, provoking muttering on the benches and some choice oaths uttered by the Scots, and corroborated Anya's confession. 'I do also,' he said in a dull voice.

Before Donal's pride could intervene and offer a

counter-rebuttal, I addressed the room. 'The accused have spoken and all here present have heard them! These Scots admit not only the crime of encroachment and trespass, but heretical sorcery! Thus, by the witnesses who have testified today, evident deed has been established. Let it be so recorded.' And I nodded to the scribe.

'Let it also be noted that, the number of witnesses of good character being limited to three, this hearing cannot lead by law directly to the confirmation of a denunciation.

'But the defendants have stated their understanding of their complicity in the unholy acts that have plagued the region. This, as I search my own conscience in the sight of God, constitutes a confession, and in their abjuration of heresy they return wholly and without condition to the embrace of the Church of the Holy Father. As such, I seek to conclude this trial.'

I then called for a short break as I conferred with my laymen and laid out my proposed judgement and my rationale, and they offered no objections. Thus, after an hour we returned to the climax of the proceedings.

'I, being appointed ecclesiastical judge in these lands subject to the rule of the King Edward of England, and in conjunction with my fellow clerics, have noted that you, Donal Gavin and Anya Dunne, were denounced for heretical practices and accused of the crime of encroachment and trespass upon the lands of the king. In consideration of this latter charge, it is my determination that, since the defendants have suffered injury and been imprisoned at the hands of their denouncer, no further imprisonment shall be required.

'In consideration of the charge of heresy, I affirm that it is incumbent upon us to plant the Holy Catholic Faith in the hearts of men and women and root out the depravity of heresy wherever it takes root. Having convened a sensible scrutiny of the details of the case and weighed up the facts in consequence, it has been made clear by recent events and your own confession that you have been caught in the web of sorcery. But it is known that God, Granter of mercy and Lord of wisdom, sometimes permits certain people to lapse into heresy in order that they become more humble and roused in the works of God and in penitence. I have seen with my own eyes the keenness with which you have returned to the Church, publicly declaring not only your abjuration but your renunciation of the works of Satan. At the point of abjuration, you are absolved of the sentence of death, excommunication or exile, providing that you return to the Unit of the Church with a full heart, a true, unspoiled faith, and unfeigned devotion to God, as I believe that you have.

'In our sentence we therefore condemn you both to be banished from all lands south of the border dividing England and Scotland, and that a recompense ransom of thirty pounds be paid by the defendants or their houses to the Earl of Hayeford.'

There was some grumbling in the gallery at this, but I had calculated that the sum of thirty pounds would be a trifle to a landowner like the Thane of Gavin compared to the life of his son, and would be paid promptly and without fuss. Likewise, the fine and the banishment from English lands would keep Hayeford happy.

'The proceedings are over. Go now, all, in the name of the Lord. Amen.'

The two Scots were led away to the family of Gavin and the men from Hayeford's household gathered separately in a satisfied parlay. The trial was ended and I walked away from the central area of the chapter house, pleased that I had executed my plan to my own satisfaction and, I hoped, to that of my Maker. Turning my head for a moment, however, I saw Guardian Dionysius and Friar William looking at me. Their expressions were dark and bitter.

nones

The trial had exhausted me and I retired to the chapel to observe Nones in peace, praying with special intensity. The outcome of the trial had saved the lives of the defendants and satisfied the plaintiff but it had been manufactured out of fictions. I acknowledge had I had felt trapped, and had engineered the result to enable me to continue the investigation that had brought me here. I wanted to persuade myself that this was an example of God's work done well but the bitter gnawing in my stomach told me it was no such thing, of course. The truth—God's truth—still mocked me with its elusiveness and I prayed for His guidance to help my reasoning and observation unravel the real mystery before another calamity befell the area.

After the completion of my prayers I ran into Lord Hayeford at the gates of the chapel, on his way to meet me, apparently. He was in a jolly mood, laughing with his seneschal Thirlwall and gesticulating as he spoke. The sickly man even showed a touch of ruddy colour in his cheeks.

'Ah, Brother Jacobus! Well met! I was hoping that we might share a word—if you can grant me the time.'

I nodded, and walked with him to the vegetable gardens. He seemed oddly affable.

'You have some wiles about you, Brother,' he said at last. 'I knew you would confirm my suspicions! I knew those knaves were using the powers of demons in the forest to terrorise us. What leeches they are! I confess I would like to have seen them suffer more for their crimes, but what good would it do to open the wounds still wider? No, the Lord was right to send you to oversee everything. Quieter borders will allow the king to focus his attention on France. You may have done the English a fair favour, Brother! Perhaps, with France otherwise occupied, the papacy may be able to return to Rome after all! Wouldn't that be a fine thing?'

I smiled weakly. 'Amen.'

Hayeford looked me up and down with a thin smile. The day had been quite clement but now a chilly dusk approached, and the dogwood and viburnum that grew in clusters in the garden turned their faces downward in observance of the oncoming dusk. 'As a token of my appreciation for your efforts in ridding my lands of the heretics, I would like to offer alms for your own abbey. I suppose you have little need to remain any longer in the northern reaches of England. My treasurer has drawn up a bill of exchange, redeemable for the amount of a *livre tournois*. If you leave soon, you would be able to deliver my offering to Avignon in time for the Nativity Feast. Would that coincide with your plans, Brother?'

'I shall leave soon,' I said, watchfully. 'Perhaps as soon as the day after tomorrow. I want at least a day's devotion to my prayers and letters, and to rest a little."

He held out the scroll, waiting for me to take it, but I did not. 'Well? Won't you take this handsome payment?'

'I confess, I cannot.'

'Whyever not? Is the Church now so well funded that an abbey can say no to generous alms from those who wish to show their appreciation of its work?'

'I ... .' I stared at the scroll. I would have given it happily to my abbey to help with its good work but my work had been tainted with deceit and I could not have explained why I was arriving home with a generous gift from a northern English nobleman. 'I have no authority to take monetary donations,' I said weakly. 'There are others at my abbey who take care of such matters.'

With a curious look that bordered on contempt, Hayeford withdrew the scroll. He tried to resume his smile but it now looked crooked and disingenuous. 'Yes, of course.' He stepped back to regard me fully. 'You shall be fondly remembered in these parts, Brother Jacobus. I hope we will not have to call upon your expertise again.'

I smiled at the back-handed compliment, and the earl took his leave of me.

I returned to my cell and was in the middle of collecting my possessions together for the return journey when I was accosted a second time, this time by Friar William.

'You're planning on leaving so soon, Jacobus?' he said.

I stopped arranging my effects and stared at him. He looked unusually displeased, even close to being vexed.

'You look troubled, William.'

He stepped into my cell and spoke again in hushed, conspiratorial tones. 'You made a mockery of the process of the trial this morning.'

'Did not all parties depart with a degree of gratification? The trial process mocks itself at times.'

'That much is apparent, when it can so easily be subverted by the lies of an ecclesiastical judge.'

'Did I utter a lie, Friar William? What untruth passed

my lips?'

'The lie is inside you. It is as plain as the beam in your eye. You did not believe a word of that outcome, nor that the denunciation could possibly be true. The accusation runs contrary to everything you say you believe. And having watched you closely, I don't believe you would casually cast aside your presuppositions in favour of a convenient political settlement, which is what you seem to have done.' He stared at me, awaiting an answer. 'Well, what do you say to that?'

'What outcome were you hoping for, Friar? Would you have had me sentence that poor young man and woman to torture, imprisonment and the pyre?' I stuffed a book into my satchel.

'Poor young man and woman? They would have sliced us into mincemeat had Sir Walesby and his men not been with us.'

'That is irrelevant. Of course I did not take the Lord Hayeford's denunciation against the Scots seriously. It was an illusion, but a necessary one.' William looked at me sceptically, which did not suit him. I sat down upon the bench in my cell and gestured for him to sit down beside me, which he did.

'William, let me tell you about the Inquisition that works across the Holy Roman Empire. In its pursuit of heretic Cathars, the papal inquisitors swept away entire communes of perfecti and their credentes. But in their blind wrath for purification, they ensnared many innocent people. It became a crusade and the geometry of heresy became blurred; the inquisitors created a judicial process of such malevolent sophistication that guilt was not something to be determined but to be assumed—something intrinsic in which anything at all could constitute proof. In the Languedoc region, innocent Catholics, Cathars and Jews lived peacefully together as neighbours but were caught in the web of inquisitorial law. Many of the Church's most devout followers in the area came to hate the inquisitors, not because the inquisitors were blind to innocence but because in their wrath they were wilfully blind, and that is a horrible sin. The poet Alghieri himself stated that wrath sits above heresy in the hierarchy of the Inferno. That is why I must be inside the structure of the Inquisition in order to bend it to justice. Guilt had to be proven today. But the sentence … that is where I am free to apply some clemency.'

I thought I had spoken persuasively but William waved the point away. 'Do not lecture me with tales of the Cathars. I know full well how the Inquisition gathers lambs as well as wolves in its traps. The Cathars may have been scattered to the hills but the papal Inquisition continues to see their ghosts in every nook and corner. It's an obsession and legitimacy is its cloak: you can toss it over anything you like, but as men of God we should neither cast it over false devils nor false idols.'

'Pah!' I spat. 'You think legitimacy is only a cloak? In that case anything could be said to be cloaked. Would you say that about Aquinas? Or the Virgin Mother? Do they also hide their true nature? Such thoughts skirt the shores of illegitimacy itself!'

'You undo your own argument, Brother. The Virgin Mother is sublimity made flesh precisely because she is uncloaked. She requires no embellishment, no interpretation, no decoration. She is woman in all her perfection, just as Christ is man in his, and they transcend the wit of us poor, earthly sinners. Your desire to understand everything diminishes that sublimity.' He paused for a moment, rubbed his chin in thought and then quite unexpectedly gave me a broad smile.

'Did you hear about the two bishops from London? The teeth of the first bishop hung so loosely in his mouth that he was afraid they would fall out. "Oh, don't worry," said the second bishop. "My bollocks have been hanging loose for forty years and they haven't fallen out yet!"'

In spite of myself I let out a gay laugh, before mastering myself, slightly embarrassed at my loss of control.

'Let me explain why the joke is funny, Jacobus. The second bishop's testicles swung just as pendulously as the first bishop's teeth, and he was therefore able to compare the two phenomena, whereas of course there is no comparison.'

I gave William a sour look. 'I understand what you are trying to do. By explaining the joke you destroy the spark of divinity that gives it its humour. And you think that's a good way to illustrate my acceptance of what I do not understand? It is just as well that my Order, the Order of Saint Benedict, does not indulge in petty jokes about body parts. It is small wonder that the laxity of the Franciscan creed is so easily warped into the heretical philosophy of the gutter.'

By now the smile on William's face had dissolved. 'Perhaps you now understand why we were so nervous when we learned that a papal inquisitor was in our midst? Oh, do not look so appalled, Brother Jacobus; your motives are clear now and we mendicants do not fear you, but you must be able to appreciate what a nervous time it has been for us followers of St Francis, after the business with the Fraticellis.'

I sighed and retreated. It was easy to let one's prejudices overwhelm one's reason. But if I, a man who had chosen scholasticism, could not overcome that, then who could? 'You are right, William,' I replied. 'Forgive my stubbornness. Yes, I was not entirely honest during the trial. But the alternative might have brought more violence between Hayeford and the Scots, which could have escalated quickly. If I lied during that trial, then I can only hope that God will understand and that, by his Favour, I am permitted to return to Avignon safely.'

William's expression brightened a little, as if a weight had been lifted from him. 'But Brother, you were sent to uncover a great mystery and settle the matter for the people here. You may have settled the matter in Lord Hayeford's eyes, but you have solved no mystery. What if the phenomenon that brought you here recurs, even after the Scots have left? What if you return to the papal palace having fulfilled only half of the job you were sent to do? Would you lie to the cardinals?'

At the utterance of this last question the hairs on the back of my neck stood on end, and William—meek, mild William—seemed dangerous. Did he ask that question because he had learned something about my going against the cardinals' wishes, or had he stumbled by chance on a patch of ground that happened to contain my shameful truth? I declined to answer, forcing him to fill the ensuing silence.

'I am simply curious, Jacobus, because you yourself are a curious fellow, and you may take that as a compliment. I am interested to know what you will do. Will you really leave without solving what is going on? You do not seem the sort to leave without a satisfactory answer.'

I silently exhaled, and relaxed. 'I would like to stay, William—really I would. What little I have achieved by the trial will count for little if another child suffers as Emeline and Peter have done. The truth lies in the wood and still needs to be discovered. But how can I pursue the truth when my methods are so displeasing to all?—to the Guardian, to the other friars, even to you, whom I now count a friend. Hayeford has no interest in it any more, now that his prejudices have been confirmed and the Scots have been banished. No, it is time for me to leave and for you to conclude matters, should you wish.'

'Me? You see a place for me in this investigation?'

'Why not? You seemed eager to get to the bottom of it. However disappointed you were by the trial, these events will find their way into books, and books can outlast anything. Your efforts will be remembered.' As I said this, I waved one of my own books in front of me before tucking it into my satchel. 'What do you say?'

William sighed and offered me a weary smile. 'No Brother, I am not made for inquisitorial pursuits or philosophical questioning. We will have to manage as best we can, accepting the mysteries God has laid before us without prying into them deeply. But I shall pray for you.'

Then he kissed me upon both cheeks and departed my cell, leaving the door open.

2ND DECEMBER

IN WHICH
I RETURN
TO THE FOREST
SEEKING
A DEFINITIVE
ANSWER
BUT
ENCOUNTER
SOMETHING
QUITE
DIFFERENT

PRIME

The next morning I said farewell to Albertus and Friar Herry and made my way to the Chapter House to take my leave of Guardian Dionysius and thank him for his many kindnesses since my arrival. Like William, the Guardian was confused by my decision to depart, knowing that my settling of the trial had left the most burning questions still open. To my surprise, then, he told me I could stay as long as was required, but immediately watered down his offer by saying he could no longer furnish me with friars to help me, now that all were needed on other tasks within the friary and beyond its walls.

I thanked him and assured him that, having completed my duties as a papal representative, I no longer had any reason to remain in Berwick and therefore could not tarry but must return to Avignon, to be briefed on my next errand.

And indeed, I could not afford to stay with the friars. Every day I remained, I put myself at greater risk of word reaching Avignon on what I had been up to, or of Avignon learning of my unsanctioned mission to the north of England, and sending word to Berwick to have me sent back, perhaps accompanied by an armed escort.

In order not to raise unwanted suspicions by leaving too abruptly, however, I thanked the Guardian and said I would allow myself the luxury of one or two extra days during which I would continue my investigation into the forest phenomena on my own. I felt, after all, that it would all have been for nothing if I returned to Avignon with no extra knowledge in my satchel. And it was not unpleasant to think that, after saying farewell, I would be able to scratch around without being monitored by onlookers, whether religious or military.

I banked on there being enough time to find this Odenellus fellow, for I was determined to question him. The undulating English woods were thick and hushed and overgrown, and seemed able to squeeze an inordinate density of trees into a square mile but they were not enormous, not like the vast forests of Kalkalpen and Hagenbachklamm in my homeland. It would take a day, no more, to track down my quarry, I guessed. And then I would be able to return to Avignon with answers to share.

The next morning I left before sunrise, alone on one of the Abbey's ponies, Hayeford having taken back the horse he had lent me. I was even excited at the prospect of exploring the woods free of rabid wolves and marauders from north of the Tweed. I would have enjoyed the company of William but, without him, my mind was free to engage in exploration rather than having to keep putting up a philosophical defence of it.

The sun rose onto a day that was damp and miserable and the grasslands beyond Berwick were steeped in a low, dreary fog. The trees looked heavy with wetness, as if bowing in prayer. I made my way beyond the bramble thickets and moved under the canopy with my cowl up. Rain had fallen during the night, turning the path from the previous visit to freezing sludge.

My first thought was to return to the site of the Scottish attack to try and recover the body of the wolf that had been slain that evening. In the fury of the melee it had been forgotten and left. I had wanted to test it for signs of rabies but, following the chaos of the raid, the beast's carcass had been dropped and left. Despite the gloom I used the sun to navigate the woods and eventually, after an hour's wandering, reached the site of the attack. Thanks to the chilly weather, the cadaver lay exactly where it had fallen. The arrows that had felled it still protruded from its ribcage and thigh, the blood around them now a rusty stain.

I conducted a quick examination of the creature; its body had not yet been bloated by the air that sometimes collects in fresh bodies nor had it been invaded by blowflies, which I attributed to the cold and the season. The animal's spittle was still damp and its eyes still glassy. Its blood was thick and had congealed on the ground, not ideal to work with, behaving more like syrup than blood, but good enough for me to collect samples of and store in phials for later examination.

Once this was done, I wrapped the animal in a sheet and tying it with straps over the rear end of the pony, deciding not to spend more time on it here but to use my visit to the woods to look for other possible causes that might have led to the children's disappearance.

It was as I began leading the pony onwards that I saw it—a flash of something, or someone—through the trees. I peered into the dense mass of trunks and bushes but whatever it was had moved too quickly and there was nothing to see so I paused and listened, shushing my pony quietly when it whickered impatiently. Then a snapping sound echoed through the air, as if a large branch had been stepped on and cracked in half. The hairs all over my body stood on end. For the first time, I became physically aware of the forest and everything in it. It was an uneasy feeling and I did not like it.

As quietly as I could, I led the pony in the rough direction of the movement, and then stopped again, listening and watching. Suddenly, another dark flash appeared from behind a tree at the edge of my vision.

My heart was banging in my chest but I pushed the pony on, slowly—then tethered its bridle to a branch jutting up from a fallen log.

As I looked up from securing the bridle, I glanced across the trees and saw, in the middle of a dense thicket, a green face wreathed in leaves. I gasped, and almost stumbled back. It must have been fifty yards away, and staring straight at me. The figure was crouched slightly, one hand resting on the trunk of an adjacent tree. Its face was round and green and thickly bearded. A crown of rotten leaves sat upon its head and, in the middle of the greenery, eyes and a dark mouth. In that instant I was gripped by an evil fear, and memories of the talk I had heard about the Green Man.

For a moment my mind was overcome: this was the demon of the forest! But I scolded myself and reminded myself that such talk was foolishness. I determined to face the figure down but, as even as I watched it, it deftly slid away behind the bushes. Crossing myself, I decided I had to confront it, and so stepped into the scrub, wading clumsily towards what I had seen, through the briar and undergrowth.

'Stop!' I called out. 'Stop, I say!' My words struck me at once as incongruous, but what else does one say to a woodland creature with a green and bearded face and a corona of leaves?

When I reached the tree where the figure had rested, I stopped—because, of course, there was nothing there. I caught my breath and leaned against the tree trunk, as the creature had done, when a sharp blow caught me across the face. Off balance, and with the taste of blood in my mouth, I tumbled backwards—only to find the figure flinging itself upon on me, its face crunched into a baleful sneer. I held my arms to my face as it tried to hit me again, then grappled with it, and we rolled over in the thorns. The creature was lithe but, to my surprise, no more powerful than me. I had expected it to have all the dark energy of a devil.

'Get off me, you Christian monk!' it shouted, and struggled to release itself from my grip.

In my panic, and not knowing what else to do, I thumbed it in the eye, and it cried out, clasping at its face. I shoved myself away on my backside, panting in cold sweat. The man—and I was under no more illusions that this was anything other than a man—whimpered in pain, the fight having left him. His face was no longer green but smeared with mud, and his crown of leaves had toppled onto the forest floor, where it fell apart. The long beard, red at the tips and greying at the roots, was now matted and caked with soil, and I saw that the leaves, foliage and other detritus from the woods had all been stitched into his clothing.

'Odenellus,' I said, more to myself than him.

He sat up, and inspected his hands as he brought them away from his eye. 'You'm blinded us, you villain!'

His eye was a red blotch but I doubt very much that I had taken his sight.

'You'll live,' I muttered. The pain in my jaw where he had slogged me now became more apparent, and I wobbled it gingerly to check for any damage. I spat out some blood and stood up, rather unsteadily. In turn, Odenellus sat up, continuing to examine his hand for blood, as if it might prove my evil intent.

'You have answers for me,' I said. 'You have been spreading fear and lies throughout this community. That poor woman Gwendolynn, and her children—'

'She knows what had to be done. She knows that the Man will—'

'The man will have his share, yes, I know. And there is a man, isn't there? Not a demon Green Man of the Woods but *you*—isn't that right?'

'I'm no demon, monk,' he said. 'Just an agent of other powers, like you are.'

'Don't dare presume that we are somehow equal,' I scoffed. 'I follow the blessed Light of Jesus Christ. Whereas you … .' I scanned the sorry remnants of his disgusting costume laid in tatters across the forest floor. 'You are a showman. A performer of filthy deeds, a teller of empty tales.'

'Empty tales!' he said with a bitter laugh. 'Oh, I could tell you tales, monk. Old tales, like the one about the wicked king who was blinded in a fight with Chaos and who broke him into a thousand islands. I could tell you stories of Merlin, and the old gods, and how they made way for the new. And they did make way—they made way for your God, didn't they? And your God was supposed to lead us into the Light, wasn't he? And what have we got? Plague and war and death!'

As Odenellus continued muttering, I mastered myself and stood over him. I was an instrument of the truth and remembered that I had to act with the faith and responsibility of my office!

It was obvious that without the element of surprise, he would not be able to overpower me and he cowered like a beaten dog. A life spent scratching among the logs for a diet of beetles and larvae had left him wan and puny.

But I thought back to Emeline and Peter: even a runt like Odenellus could strongarm a child into the woods.

And grown men have words and manners as well that will entice the innocent into their snares.

'Tell me, Odenellus. Did you take the children from the villages?'

He murmured and looked away, flicking his gaze this way and that, looking everywhere around the forest floor except up at me.

'Well, did you?'

'He has to be placated. Has to have what he's owed. Sapling defers to the oak; that's the way it's always been.'

I grabbed him by his collar and asked him again. I had not noticed during the fight but he stank of rot and faeces, and I could not help but let him go again and wrinkle my nostrils in disgust. Nevertheless, my grabbing him seemed to put the fear back into him.

'Yes,' he said, covering his face. 'Took 'em, took 'em, I did. Be worse if I didn't! These woods is old, old, older'n time. Older than thou cans't imagine. And way older'n that.' He pointed at the Cross hanging around my neck.

'There are older things—older stories—than the story of Christ, of course,' I agreed. 'I have learned a little about the pagan stories of this land. And the Bible recounts stories of lost peoples sacrificing their children to unworthy deities. You are no more than a primitive, a creature of Baal, and you will be remembered as such.'

'You think you knows so much!' he snickered, and he winced and checked his eye again. 'You don't know all that much, little monk.' He blinked, and groaned, rolling his head this way and that.

'So what art did you use to tempt the children here? Gwendolynn, I know, you bewitched with your lies, and convinced her to bury her children, and they were mercifully awake enough to drag themselves from here, but the others? Did you drug them with poison? Or did you simply use sweet fearful words?'

The man shook his head like a simpleton, repeating 'No, no, no, no, no,' over and over.

'And what of your other abominations? The sacrifice of children, hateful as it is, I can understand the wicked pagan logic for. But why desecrate their bodies?'

He stopped babbling and looked at me. His nose was running, and a trickle of blood that streamed from his left eye where I had gouged it mixed with the mud and rot on his cheek.

'No,' he said.

'Tell me.'

'Not my place to touch the bodies. The Man does as he pleases.'

'What do you mean? Tell me, you wretch!'

'Look around you, you fool of a monk!' he said at last, his voice mottled with weary madness. 'Look at this cold, brutal place, and your unnatural world of bricks and mortar and windows and cathedrals. That ain't the real world. That's the tamed world of ritual and order. The real world ain't like that, it ain't something no man cooked up. It's nature and life and it can't be reasoned with, it can't be figured out. But it's hungry! It's been around longer'n we have. It has its own rules; its own needs. And it's got to eat.'

'When? Every three months?'

He looked at me, mouth open. 'When it wakes.'

Having at last tracked down the culprit responsible for the kidnappings, I was keen to find out how and why he might have desecrated the bodies in the way that Albertus had described, but we were both tired and I did not feel I was going to get much more from him of any value. I therefore turned my mind to more practical questions. Odenellus had no more fighting temper left in him, and I reckoned I could have frogmarched him to my pony and, without much resistance, led him back to Ord, where word could be sent to Berwick for assistance.

'Odenellus,' I said, wearily, ready to relate this plan to him, 'Here is what—'

A black, sharp crack of pain filled my head, choked my words and sent me to my knees. I groaned and felt for my crown, which made the pain bloom and spread to my neck. Spinning dots clouded my sight and my brain buzzed like a jar full of flies. I touched my head again, but the sensation made me cringe and caused a feeling of sickness. My guts heaved but nothing came up.

Fearing a second blow I held an arm above my head in a sorry attempt at self-defence but instead of further violence I heard only voices.

'Brother Odenellus! You're safe. It's Gibson!' called a first voice.

'Here, Gibson, my friend!'

'Are you hurt?' came a second voice.

'A little, but I shall survive,' I heard Odenellus say.

I got to my feet but my vision was blurred and my head ached. I touched the site of the blow again, and felt wetness there. My legs became unsteady and I fell to my knees a second time. I blinked, trying to focus on the men who were bustling around me.

'Shall we do him in?'

'No, leave him.'

'But he knows we led the bairns here!'

At that moment a third sound swept through the wood—'*AAAAAAAAAH!*'—like the sound of a fearful sigh or a note blown through a giant *Rauschpfeife*. The three men stopped talking and looked around. Their sudden silence indicated fear, and even though I could not see their faces, their emotions transferred at once to me.

'What was that?' I whispered.

'*AAAAAAAAAAH!!*' came the sound through the trees again, as though the very wind had a voice. It was not obviously human or animal, male or female, but a hiss that could have come from anyone or anything.

'We don't have to do him in ourselves now, anyhow,' said Odenellus, helped to his feet by his two assistants. He then stood over me, and booted me in the chest, sending me sprawling onto my back and blinking uselessly up at the spindly canopy. It wasn't the hardest of kicks but, in my state, it was enough to make me feel sick anew.

'Now, Brother monk,' he said, 'You'll see the power of the woods. The Man will have his share!'

And with that, the three ran off into the undergrowth, leaving me puzzling over what the source of the noise might be and what it meant. I had not imagined it, for the men had reacted to it, and it was no wolf's cry, and, if the Gavins knew what was good for them, it was no Scot, signalling from one to another.

'Is there … is there anything out there?' I said, and then realised that instead of calling out boldly, I was whispering—timidly and in fear. I started wondering afresh what that flash of movement had been that I seen. Had it been Odenellus, as the discovery of him had made me assume, or was it in fact another child, or somebody from the village, that Odenellus had been scouting for? In spite of my injuries and nausea, I managed to haul myself over to the pony and, reaching it, leaned against its left side, for comfort. Whatever I had seen, some inexplicable instinct told me that I had come across the answer to what I was looking for. I just needed to understand what it was.

I needed medical treatment from the infirmary at the friary but I had already said my farewells and it would cast further doubt on my credibility if it turned out that I was still at large. Where could I go, then, to receive the nursing that I needed? I reached for the pony's reins and led it onwards, the wolf still slung over its rear, until my way was interrupted by a narrow gully just a few yards deep and a few yards wide, out of which sprang a chaos of thorns, stumps, brambles, nettles, wildflowers and mushrooms. On the other side, the ground sloped steeply upwards.

I peered into the gully. A stream ought to be running through it—a small tributary of the River Tweed, perhaps—but there was nothing but a tiny trickle. As I wondered why a woodland gully would be dry in early December, after all the rain that we had had, I was shocked again by that ghostly voice: '*AAAAAAAAH!!!*'

Closer this time, something moved a few feet from me, and then, incredibly, from behind a tree some thirty feet away. I turned my head this way and that, trying to track what I was seeing, my hands now trembling, my voice cracked with fear.

'Show yourself!' I demanded, attempting to muster all my clerical authority but only managing a broken wail. 'In the name of the Lord, show yourself! I am here on holy duty!'

It was then that a dark figure flickered at the edge of my vision to my right-hand side. It appeared at the top of the gully, but whisked itself out of sight behind one of the myriad trees as soon as I looked. The apparition terrified my pony, which shrieked at the disturbance, turned and bolted, the reins tugging me off my feet. I tripped over, stood up too quickly and, in a great wave of dizziness, toppled into the gully, tumbling head over heels until I crashed into an upturned tree with roots in the air like great ossified serpents.

When I tried to sit up in the ditch, my back was wet and bruised and my mouth filled with damp, foul-tasting twigs and mould. My eyesight was blurry, too, and all I could see, in the ditch, were the thorns and brambles, and the carpet of fallen leaves that gave off a rhythm of squelching noises as it was disturbed.

Disturbed by whom?

I lifted my head once more, and saw it. A pair of giant feet—for they could be nothing else—approached me. They kicked through the undergrowth with such gentle ease, it seemed as though they were made of the same stuff as the forest itself. My first thought was that Odenellus must have come back—but these were not men's feet. I tried to blink away the fuzziness from my eyes and to spit the muck from my mouth. Not only the feet but, looking up, the figure's legs were covered in leaves, and leaves of all types: oak, rowan, laurel, honeysuckle, horse chestnut and a dozen more.

I worried that I had damaged myself in the fall but when I checked myself over, my faculties were intact, my mind was clear and my blurriness of vision had given way to clarity. I wished it hadn't! The giant figure was not just covered in leaves, it was made of leaves—and bark and sticks and twigs and mud and all the stuff of the forest, as though a tree had uprooted itself and become a roving spirit. Abject terror struck me. And in that moment, I knew, in spite of all the intellectual defences of my mind and my Faith, that I was looking at the Green Man.

The Green Man approached me, its branch-like arms covered with foliage and creepers, its torso a heaving trunk and its legs a writhing knot of roots, winding and grasping in every direction, dripping with mulch, and wriggling with worms and insects. Most fearful was its face, a living replica of those accursed foliate heads atop the archheads of England—as terrible and captivating as a demon, as bewitching as a sorcerer. A stink of rotting woodland hung from it and made me feel faint. Vines snaked out of its eye sockets and tendrils curled from its mouth and nostrils, winding themselves around its face and neck like veins. Over fifteen-foot tall it stood, the height of three men, exuding such a power that I felt puny by comparison.

As I looked upwards to peer into its face, the foliate creature crouched down, knelt on one knee, raised a knotty hand and brought it inches before my eyes. Twigs and creepers squirmed around its arm, and hundreds of tiny bugs streamed from the cracks in its woody flesh.

I tried to cry out, but the foliate head screamed the screech of the wind, and I could summon no strength. It touched my forehead with a long, spindly, wooden finger and everything turned black.

? December

In which I find myself in a strange place and have an unexpected reunion with an old acquaintance

DAYTIME

There was a sound of gulls squawking. Squawk squawk squawk. What a noise! Why do gulls squawk? What a question! Gulls squawk to communicate with other gulls, to fend off threats, to protect a food source. Maybe to establish their rule, to attract mates, to reassure their chicks. All good reasons. All very convincing, but there must be some other reason—some grand reason—why gulls squawk. I cannot grasp that reason. Why can I not grasp that reason? I am fearful. I panic. And in that panic, I remember, because of all the intellectual defences of my mind and my Faith, that gulls squawk to announce the glory of the Lord and to rejoice in His Grace in making them gulls and entrusting them with those duties which only gulls are blessed with … and I relax.

I awoke with a start and was immediately disorientated. I was in a small room I did not recognise, sparsely appointed but airy, with a large window letting in the rising sun. I lay on a mattress on the floor, dressed in my cowl and robe, and with a thick blanket spread over me. A snuffed-out candle sat in its holder on a small bedside cabinet. A crucifix hung on the wall opposite the window.

'What is this place, Lord?' I whispered hoarsely. The thought came to me that I had died.

I wondered why. Then my memory returned to me—the foliate man—and my heart began to drum rapidly in agitation once more.

But wait. Why would my heart beat so hard if I had already crossed the bridge to my final resting place? No, I told myself, this was not death—but what was it? And where? I needed to find out, but could not do that by remaining where I was.

When I rose from my mattress, my legs and neck were unpleasantly stiff and I had to stretch to get the blood circulating more strongly through my limbs. I was in pain and remembered the various knocks I had received in the woods: falling into the gully, the blow from Odenellus, the second blow from one of his crew. I shuffled to the window and shaded my eyes to look out.

My accommodation was evidently on a slightly elevated position below which the sea stretched out into the distance. The eastern sun shone brilliantly on the waves, which broke upon the shingle and made it purr as they ran back down the shore.

I tidied the blanket, crossed myself, prayed in front of the crucifix and stepped outside the door.

I was standing in a wooden cloister, with half-a-dozen rooms along one side and an open courtyard on the other. It looked like a small, exclusive dormitory, freshly built and very clean. As far as I could see, no one else was about. On the other side of the courtyard stood a common kitchen area. The other two ends of the courtyard were blocked off by simple palisades. At each end of the cloister was a door.

With confusion fogging my mind and prayers hanging upon my lips, I walked to one end of the cloister, opened the door and looked out towards the water. For no reason that I could think of, it seemed to attract me.

Walking down the slope to the sea, I quickly realised that it was still winter, for the sun was not very high, and I had to pull my cowl and robe tightly around my chest to keep out the chilly wind. Upon the shingle, little crabs sashayed, harassed by gulls and oystercatchers. The water was frigid cold but it felt good to step barefoot into the waves that nibbled round my toes.

As I stopped to take in the beauty of the place, I saw a man in the distance walking towards me. I squinted, and cast my hands over my eyes to see him better. Was I about to be attacked by another infernal creature?

No. It was nothing more than an ordinary man trudging along the shore, wreathed in watery light from the sun shining at his back. He waved at me, which seemed like a good sign, and I sighed with relief. There was something familiar about his lolloping gait.

'So, tha's up then?' called the man in a rough Northern accent. 'I were startin' to wonder if ee were gan te' wake at all.'

When the man was close enough, I made out his face, and my mouth opened in astonishment.

'It cannot be!' I exclaimed, running to him and clasping him about the shoulders. 'Poole!'

'Brother Jacobus,' he said with a grin, clapping me warmly on the shoulder.

Utter pleasure coursed through me at the unexpected appearance of this strangest of men, a familiar face in an unfamiliar landscape. But my delight was tempered for a moment as I realised that Poole's accent had changed. Where he had spoken in a southern demotic when we were travelling together, now he was speaking in the flat brogue common to this Northumbrian region. Of all the questions that flooded my mind, this was the one that I asked first.

'Me accent 'as'nae changed, Brother Jacco. Maybe ee's jus' listenin' better.'

'My friend,' I asked. 'I thought I was dreaming. Where are we?'

'This is Lindisfarne,' replied Poole. 'The Holy Island.'

Lindisfarne! The island was famed across the Holy

Roman Empire as the birthplace of Christianity in the British Isles centuries back. In Avignon I had seen a copy of the Lindisfarne Gospels, and marvelled at their exquisite beauty and craftsmanship.

'Why are we here?' I asked Poole.

'Well, I dunno about ee, but I'm helping to build yon nave for t'priory,' he said, pointing behind me. A castle sat on the crest of a dumpy hill at the southern tip of the island, while about five hundred yards further off, new buildings surrounding a magnificent priory were rising out of the ground, supported by wooden buttressing linked by scaffolds.

'Of course!' I exclaimed. 'When we first met, you said you were headed here for building work.'

'Oh aye,' said my companion, leading us further up the beach. 'I gan where I'm needed. There's a new section bein' built on the southern arcade. Ah, but there's time fer all tha' soon enough. Rest, scran and water, tha's what ee needs. Maybe then ee'll recall all that happened to thee.'

Poole led me away to Lindisfarne's priory and disappeared to fetch some food from the refectory. I still couldn't see anyone but I wanted not to be disturbed while I tried to make sense of everything, and found a stall to sit down on in the church. The church was a strange combination of bits. Stout columns in the English style stood like sentinels in formation along the side of the nave, while the east-facing apse had a more Roman feel, and the nave itself was a sombre Gothic, yet the chancel wall and its arch were old and dark—almost the colour of blood.

Christ, suspended from the cross over the altar, looked down on me from his place of ultimate suffering with forlorn eyes and I dropped to my knees and fell into such a deep prayer that my toes went numb against the stone floor.

I was roused by the clack of a metal platter on the stall as Poole sat down next to me. I was so deep in thought that it wasn't until I looked up and saw the bread, butter, cold cuts and cheese—as well as a frothing mug of beer—that I realised how ferociously hungry I was. I thanked Poole sincerely and attacked the plate.

'So,' said Poole. 'How'd ye get 'ere?'

I knew the question would be asked at some point, and now it had been, I had to face the truth—that I had no idea. The thought so troubled me that I felt I was on the verge of tears. 'I don't know,' I said simply. 'I've tried and tried and no amount of reasoning can explain it.'

'Where was ee before?'

'In the forests east of Berwick, near the Tweed, gathering … .' I had to think hard. What had I been gathering? It seemed so far away and so long ago. 'Looking for something, I think. And then I saw … .'

My mind summoned the image of the foliate creature and it struck me like a hammer. I trembled and put one hand to my mouth. Poole, sensing my disquiet, placed a gentle hand upon my own.

'Easy now. What did ee see?'

'A monster,' I said, staring at him with bafflement, for I could not quite believe what I was saying.

'A demon?' he whispered.

I put my food down and stared at the half-finished plate. 'Maybe. … I've never seen a demon before. I've seen people who've claimed to see them or claimed to be possessed by them. But demons are not … I mean, they do not … .' I winced. 'To be honest, I do not know what

I saw. And, after all, my head had been beaten—twice. It may all have been a fever of the brain.'

'Brother, ye seem confused.'

'I am. But it is so clear in my mind! Aquinas said that demons and angels can both do wonderful things but not miraculous things, because they use what is natural as their instruments. Who am I to contradict Aquinas? But this ... this was a thing, Poole, a thing, and it was real—as real as you and I are now.' I paused. 'Perhaps even more so. It was like a dream made flesh. It touched me ... .' I placed a finger hesitantly to my forehead, remembering where it had touched me. To my surprise, the skin felt very slightly rougher there, like a fresh scab. 'It was in the woods,' I muttered. 'A great giant of a thing, jumping like a spark from here to there so I couldn't catch it, and then looming over me and crouching down beside me and its whole body alive with the life of the forests. ... Perhaps if I had my books I could find an answer.'

'There's a library oop at th'abbey. It's modest but it may do thee.'

I nodded wearily. Normally the thought of visiting a library would fill me with gladness but now the thought left me bereft.

I did spend the day in the abbey's library and scriptorium, more out of habit than hope. Four monks briefly looked up at me when I entered, but otherwise they kept their eyes on their work. I was pleased to see they were clad in the thick winter black of my Order; to be back among my Benedictine brothers gave me some comfort.

The library was, as Poole had said, modest. The great treasures of literature that had once adorned the place had long since been moved away; what remained were more general texts, most of which I had encountered in

France and the Empire. Books of genuine interest were few. I found new Latin translations of Aristotle, Euclid, Ptolemy, Galen and Archimedes, and wonderful editions of the works of the great English philosophers Robert Grosseteste and Roger Bacon. I also found a book called Theatrum Chemicum bearing the name of the great Doctor of the Church, Albertus Magnus, which contained some entertaining but ultimately fruitless explorations of alchemy and the Philosopher's Stone. Like other monks involved in the rigours of scholasticism, I had heard stories about Magnus and his claims that the *lapis philosophorum* could transform base metals into gold, as well as reverse the ageing process and grant immortality to those who possessed its secret. However, nothing I had read by Christians or Muslims suggested that such claims were anything more than *stultus ineptias*. For myself, I was disappointed that so great a thinker as Albertus could be distracted by the vulgar and the greedy into such unsubstantiated claims.

After talking to one of Lindisfarne's Franciscans, I found a crumbling vellum roll containing records of the customs and behaviours of the English, from antiquity to the recent past. I even found a reference to the foliate heads, with a few rudimentary depictions of them, using inks and stains. There was even an image of a foliate man carrying the body of a person—though whether it was the body of a child or an adult, I could not tell. But since Odenellus and his wretched friends had already confessed that they had taken the children, I dismissed the image as metaphor. The text, written in bad Latin, observed that foliate heads were a left-over of the Old Religion as practised by English tribes before their conversion by Saint Aidan and his Christian followers.

Other than some lines about symbols of rebirth and fertility, however, I found nothing to explain what I was sure I had seen in the woods. Despite my disappointment, I took the book with me in the hope that it might reveal a clue upon further reading.

As for the other books, I could find nothing helpful in any of them. It was a waste of an afternoon and I left the library in a low mood.

8th December

In which I am subjected to a second unexpected visitation

COMPLINE

A few incident-free days followed but how many, exactly, I cannot recall. It was as if I was suspended not only on an island in the North Sea but on an island in time. My existence was spent variously in the library, the chapel, the refectory and the dormitory. Meanwhile, Poole was kept busy working on the priory's southern arcade, dressing stone blocks alongside just three other masons, whose constant chipping went on throughout the day, rather like the clucking of chickens.

One evening I spent some time with him over supper, and we exchanged news. On this constricted isle, away from the scandal and politics of the mainland, Poole's building work might have appeared small and insignificant, yet in its own way it was hugely important.

'Do you expect to see the completion of this priory before your death?' I asked him in the refectory after I got back from Compline.

He made a thoughtful face, then shrugged. 'Who can say, eh? Ah doubt it, though. An who's te say our work is ever really done?'

'What does that mean? When a job is finished, it's finished.'

He smiled at me. A less polite man might have scoffed at my naive remark. 'Lindisfarne. It's reet famous, aye. You knaw St Cuthbert?'

'Of course. He was one of God's greatest servants.'

'He founded this place. An' it were furnished reet well, wi' all the riches ee can imagine: gold, metals, fine cloth. Anyway, about five hunnerd year ago, maybe five an' fifty, the heathen Vikings came here for pillage. I s'pose they fancied landin' at Berwick and they found this place instead.' He shook his head and laughed bitterly. 'What must thay ha' thought, eh? They found all that loot, guarded only by a handful of priests an' monks, the followers of Cuthbert. The heathens killed 'em, cut out their eyes, cut out their tongues, cut off their hands and feet, cut out their stomachs, cut off their ballocks, took everthin' they could, took all the gold, took the stone, and pulled down Cuthbert's church and burnt it.'

He smiled, and swept his hand behind him, gesturing at the grandness of the hall, now populated with friars eating, talking and smiling. 'Still it stands. I ain't so good with me words, like, Brother Jacco, but I knaw this. The Vikings 'ad swords; the Christians 'ad words. And look who's still 'ere. If I finish this buildin', somebody could pull it down. That don't mean I built it for nowt. Nothin's e'er finished, Brother Jacco. Our work's ever undone.'

I smiled at his homespun wisdom. Here was a man with no books to his name, no letters and no learning, save what he had mastered with his hands, yet he showed me that even simple folk are capable of summoning great wisdom from deep within them.

'You are quite the mystery, Poole,' I said, smiling and taking another sip of beer. 'I wish we had spent more time together. Why did you leave our party that day in Rokeby? I was sorry to wake and not find you.'

He gave me a curious sort of look. 'I never left ee, Brother Jacco. I were always where I was s'posed te be.'

I considered countering this but could only manage a half-hearted hum of acceptance.

'And so where did ee end up, eh? Wi' them wee bairns ee were talking aboot? What happened wi'em?'

I fingered my beer mug awkwardly and shook my

head. 'Terrible things, Poole. That place is in the grip of something. I saw two of the children, sick, starved and filled with some sort of dread. It is not sorcery, it cannot be, but ... .' I tried to articulate the thought that was rattling around my head. 'The place is plagued by things that should not be, and yet are. The River Tweed is like a vein and the water its blood, and either side of its banks are great muscles, but the vein is corrupted and spreads a strange cancer across the land. It feels forsaken.'

Poole frowned, looking as though my remark had offended him. 'The land's not forsaken, Brother Jacobus.'

I ignored the comment and let out a petulant little laugh. 'If only Nastagio di Balino could see me now!'

'Wha's tha' now?'

'An associate from Italy. I always poke fun at him for seeing Godlessness everywhere, especially in those things just beyond his understanding.' Then the smile drained from my face. 'That nobleman, Thomas de Hayeford, was the same. He saw Godlessness, too. He saw it just beyond his borders. And so too the Scots, but from the across the river. It is as the Bible says in Deuteronomy. "They have corrupted themselves; their spot is not the spot of His children; they are a perverse and crooked generation."'

Poole's face remained stony. 'What are ye saying, Brother?'

I sighed and felt terribly weary. I had to tell him. I had to tell someone about what had happened, and so I breathlessly related the story of the children, the wolf, the Scottish raiders, the trial and my final trip into the forest where I encountered Odenellus and was left for dead.

'I saw it.'

'Ye mean this ... monster?' said Poole, warily.

'Yes. The ... the thing.' My words came out in a murmur and though what I said was true, it felt like a lie. 'The creature—a foliate ... not a foliate head but a foliate man. A man, Poole, a man! It was made from leaves and moss and vines, and it stood, eyeing me, its hair curling like snakes, sap bleeding from its flesh, its bark covered in worms ... . It was foul. But I know such things do not exist!'

Poole thought on this and, while doing so, I produced from my satchel the book I had borrowed from the abbey's library.

'When we were travelling from Oxford to York you told me about the myth of the Green Man. That he was the forest and that he could take as well as give.' I showed him the picture of the foliate creature bearing the body of a person, and he studied it with care. After a second he nodded. 'This picture shows the Green Man taking people—children, perhaps, into the wood.'

'Tha's nonsense,' he said, flatly.

'Precisely,' I said. 'I know the Green Man doesn't spirit people into the woods. Men do that, and they have confessed to it freely! But for me to see the Green Man, it must mean I was subjected to some drug, some poison which made me hallucinate—'

'No, you misunderstand me, Brother Jaccy,' he said, softly. 'It's nonsense that the Green Man would take people into the wood, as tha' says. But sometimes the old stories would tell of the Green Man becoming sated and fat—full, even generous. Then they'd tell of him taking people out of the wood, do you see? Of savin' 'em what was lost.'

I was preparing to continue my hypothesis about being drugged, but I stopped as he said this, and blinked. Questions raced into my mouth but could find no means of escape. In truth, they did not need to, for I then knew instinctively what he meant. Emeline and Peter, and the other two children, Alfred and Matilda—they had not escaped from the Green Man. They had been rescued by him.

I recalled what Alfred had said.

> There was good men in the trees. And bad.

That's why the children would not explain. The dark force that I had come to root out had, in their eyes, done them a favour. They were beholden to him. He hadn't taken their life; he had given life back to them. I felt the scabby mark on my forehead. A cold shiver bristled along the skin of my back.

'Poole, how did I arrive here?'

Poole looked pained, and said nothing.

'Poole, these are just stories, metaphors. What I saw, what I thought I saw … you cannot seriously expect me to believe them … . How did I arrive here, Poole?'

He looked away. 'What stories are ever only "just stories", Brother Jacco?'

I sat back and looked at him in shock. 'You believe too, don't you? You believe this chicanery is true!'

At that, Poole stood straight up, knocking his little wooden stool backwards as he did so, and slammed his chapped and calloused hands upon the table. His face was suddenly consumed by fire, as though a brazier had been lit in his heart, sending heat shooting upwards into his eyes and mouth, which glowed with a red-golden shimmer. His flaming head was horrifying to behold and I wanted to tear my gaze away, but he fixed me with a glassy stare that pinned me to my seat—and then spoke, in a voice as clear as a prophet's and as deep as if it been dragged up from the bowels of Hell:

Scio opera tua et laborem at patientiam tuam et quia non potes sustinere malos et temptasti eos qui se dicunt apostolos et non sunt et invenisti eos mendaces et patientiam habes et sustinuisti propter nomen meum et non defecisti. Sed habeo adversus te quod caritatem tuam primam reliquisti. Memor esto itaque unde exideris et age paenitentiam et prima opera fac sin autem venio tibi et movebo candelabrum tuum de loco suo nisi paenitentium egeris.[6]

The flash of Poole's fiery transformation made every hair on my body stand on end and my skin felt as though it was crawling with a million insects. The heat from his face was so hot I thought it might burn me, and had I been able to weep, the tears would have evaporated before they reached my cheek. The Poole creature—for he was now a creature, not a man—looked upwards at the heavens momentarily, as if engrossed by something else, and then turned to face me again. It pointed at me with a finger that was the finger of a man who had worked on the scaffolds all his life and yet of a creature born of fire:

---

[6] 'I know thy works and thy labour and thy patience and how thou canst not bear them that are evil. And thou hast tried them who say they are apostles and are not: and hast found them liars: And thou hast patience and hast endured for my name and hast not fainted. But I have somewhat against thee, because thou hast left thy first charity. Be mindful therefore from whence thou art fallen: and do penance and do the first works. Or else I come to thee and will move thy candlestick out of its place, except thou do penance.' *Apocalypse* 2:2–5.

Et bestiam quam vidi similis erat pardo et pedes eius sicut ursi et os eius sicut os leonis et dedit illi draco virtutem suam et potestatem magnam. Et unum de capitibus suis quasi occisum in mortem et plaga mortis eius curata est etadmirata est universa terra post bestiam. Et adoraverunt draconem quiadedit potestatem bestiae at adoraverunt bestiam dicentes quis similis bestiae et quis poterit pugnare cum ea. Et datum est ei os loquens magna et blasphemiae et data est illi potestas facere menses quadraginta duo. Et aperuit os suum in blasphemare nomen eius et tabenaculum eius et eos qui in caleo habitant. Et datum est illi bellum facere cum sanctis et vincere illos et data est ei potestas in omnem tribum et populum et linguam at gentem. Et adorabunt eum omnes qui inhabitant terram quorum non sant scripta nomina in libro vitae agni qui occisus est ab origine mundi.[7]

Then the Poole-creature held a finger to his mouth, and drew an imaginary line from it to my ear, and when he spoke next, it was not in a whisper. '*Si quis habet aurem audiat.*'[8]

I was so stunned by the Poole-thing's thunderous outpouring of Latin Scripture that it was not until he

---

[7] 'And the beast which I saw was like a leopard: and his feet were as the feet of a bear, and his mouth as the mouth of a lion. And the dragon gave him his own strength and great power. And I saw one of his heads as it were slain to death: and his death's wound was healed. And all the earth was in admiration after the beast. And they adored the dragon which gave power to the beast. And they adored the beast, saying: Who is like the beast? And who shall be able to fight with him? And there was given to him a mouth speaking great things and blasphemies: and power was given to him to do, two and forty months. And he opened his mouth unto blasphemies against God, to blaspheme his name and his tabernacle and them that dwell in heaven. And it was given unto him to make war with the saints and to overcome them. And power was given him over every tribe and people and tongue and nation. And all that dwell upon the earth adored him, whose names are not written in the book of life of the Lamb which was slain from the beginning of the world.' *Apocalypse* 13:2–8.

[8] 'If any man has an ear, let him hear.' *Apocalypse* 13:9.

stopped that I recognised the wall of speech as the Book of Revelation—the Apocalypse of St. John. I had heard the story of Christ's return to Earth many times but hearing it in this manner shook me to my bones. I tried to move but found myself bound to my chair, as this fragment of the apocalyptic vision was laid before me.

Then, just as suddenly as it had begun, the horror that gripped Poole subsided and he sank back into his chair with an expression of surprised exhaustion. He was sweating and breathing heavily, as though he had just sprinted around the perimeter of Holy Island. Bewildered, we looked at each other, neither knowing what to say. At last, he wiped the sweat from his brow with his sleeve. His arm was shaking. He blinked and tried to stand but so clumsily that I thought he would collapse. The forces trapping me suddenly vanished and I reached out to steady him but Poole held up a hand, declining my help. Where the apocalyptic fire had burned through his face there was only now ashen fatigue. He turned away and shuffled to the door.

A few of the friars and other monks watched Poole leave. None of them gave any impression that they had seen his transformation.

After he departed, my first thought was that a demon had taken possession of his body. But what sort of demon would dare utter the incantations of Saint John?

'No,' I muttered, shaking my head in an attempt at rationality. 'That cannot be the answer. But what is the answer? This north-eastern coast of England seems to me full of questions but empty of answers. *Quaestiones sine responsis.*'

My body was shaky but my mind was made up. I had found myself estranged on an oasis of convalescence where, with the Grace of Our Lord, my injured body had knitted itself back to together again—but, stranded from the mainland, I would learn nothing more here. Holy Island's role was to insulate me from the world, to swaddle me like a vulnerable babe, not to expose me to its worries, until I was strong enough to manage them.

I decided to leave Lindisfarne, return to Berwick to gather my things, settle this mystery once and for all, and then leave for the safety of France.

10TH DECEMBER

IN WHICH
I RETURN
TO BERWICK
WITH
A RENEWED
DETERMINATION
TO UNCOVER
THE TRUTH
AND
CONFRONT
THE GUARDIAN

MATINS

The library at Lindisfarne may not have held many useful books but it did have information about the tides that drowned the Lindisfarne causeway twice a day. The tide on that day would be at its lowest ebb in the mid-afternoon, just around the None hour, but I did not care. I was gripped by a fever. Shocked by Poole's demonic transformation, as it seemed to me, and his Ioannic conjuration, all I could think of was how to make sense of it. It was as though my mind had become an astrolabe and my thoughts were planets, which I had to bring back into alignment by the application of logic. I gathered what few possessions I had with me and walked from the priory dormitory down to the wind-lashed shore.

Darkness had fallen by the time I had crossed the causeway to the mainland and the first village I came to was Beal, which boasted a large and warm-looking inn at its crossroads. As I approached it, in the freezing cold of a Northumbrian winter evening, the golden glow of the fire danced invitingly through the windows and muffled music and laughter wafted on the chilly air to my ears. On another occasion I might have been tempted by the charms of the place, as I had been with Poole in Oxford, and would never have undertaken such a foolish journey by foot at night, for fear of highwaymen and predatory animals, but on this occasion I forced myself to plough on. I longed to savour the delicious aromas of whatever meats were roasting over the hearth but I could not allow myself to be seduced by earthly delights when God Himself had given me this divine duty.

I was in a fervour. I chattered to myself relentlessly, articulating arguments, counter-arguments and explanations for everything I had seen, and every argument led to a single conclusion: some sorcery had indeed wrapped its rotten hands around the heart of this place and was squeezing the holy life from it: of that I was convinced. I went over everything I had seen, again and again. Poole, a secular but holy man, had been possessed by some dark power. The Scots had abandoned their Church for pagan trickery in the woods. Lord de Hayeford had allowed his own prejudices to blind him to the clemency of God. Odenellus and his pagan acolytes had ensnared little children and led them to the woods. And the Franciscans, feebly accepting the unknown, had allowed metaphorical snakes to thrive in their garden.

And don't forget the Green Man, I told myself.

I laughed bitterly as I wondered what Nastagio di Balino would think of me now. I had always been able to show that the appearance of sorcery was a very different thing from being proof of it. Beneath any phenomenon, I would tell him, no matter how unlikely the truth seemed to be, its meaning stood waiting to be mapped by the willing and able observer—and I wanted to be that man! Now, overcome by confusion, I had to remind myself to return to the principle on which I based all my enquiries: that every earthly phenomenon was made possible by the Lord in His infinite wisdom. And that even Satan, who loves his own callous tricks and is predisposed to mislead us by them at every moment, could not perform any foul deed beyond the boundaries of the Lord's permissions. In short, there had to be a rational explanation for everything I had seen!

There seemed to me to be only one possibility, and I hardly dared to acknowledge it: that a sorcerer—most likely Odenellus—had either conjured the image of the Green Man or summoned it as a demon to outfox the intellectual and prey upon the innocent. I found it hard to admit I was thinking this. I had argued so many times against the possibilities of sorcery; now I was backed into the position of conceding that it was the only explanation that made sense.

Nastagio di Balino had been right all along: he knew that heresy existed, along with sorcery, and that both had to be destroyed. I considered how strange it was that Nastagio and I, two men with opposing views about the world, were both correct. We were both inquisitors, after all. I recalled the note Magnus had sent me while I was staying at the Abbazia di San Gerolamo in northern Italy.

'Sorcerers have made their way to England.'

I had thought that wholly unlikely at the time. Since then, with each step I took, the notion that dark forces were behind all of this, and that some dormant evil had awoken, became more realistic.

As I continued my progress through the dark night, I slowly pieced these thoughts into a coherent position. Until now, I had assumed that it was my egotistical disposition—the first of the cardinal sins—that had led me to journey to this strange place against the commands of the cardinals, but I could no longer ignore the probability that I had in fact been summoned by the Lord Himself to do His work as an inquisitor after all.

LAUDS

Rowan, one of the friary's novices, was the first person I happened upon as I walked through the courtyard. He was lighting the early-morning lamps and, upon seeing me, almost dropped his torch. I must have looked like a wild beast, for he recoiled when I approached him and demanded, a little too desperately for a sane person, to see the Guardian. Without any greeting, he pointed to the chapel, framed dimly by the lamps he had just lit, and left me to find my own way.

Inside the chapel, the friars were genuflecting in the stalls, their cowls quivering in the gentle candlelight. In this dimness I could not make out the Guardian and so I strode up the aisle, casting my gaze this way and that, calling, 'Guardian! Guardian! Dionysius! Father Denis!'

Dionysius was kneeling in the second row of the stalls and seemed not to have yet noticed me. I started to kneel beside him but something made me pause. The heady perfume of incense, coupled with my lack of sleep, caused my head to swim. The Son of God, suspended from the wall upon the Cross, stared sorrowfully downwards and away from me. Everyone knows that Christ looked down from the Cross because he was dying, in great physical pain, and felt forsaken by God. But at that moment I felt as though he was averting his gaze from me and that it was I who was forsaken.

'Jacobus?'

The Guardian's hiss started me from my thoughts, and I snapped my head towards him.

'Brother Jacobus, is that you? Where have you been?'

'I ... .' I looked around the chapel, grasping the pew to steady myself. Nosy friars peered out from beneath their hoods to see who had caused the commotion. I waited for them to return to their prayers, then said quietly, 'Father, I have to speak with you. Urgently.'

He looked at me with unusually stern eyes. 'I daresay.'

Instead of inviting me to kneel beside him, or berating me for interrupting him, Dionysius insisted that we retire to his solar. He rose, crossed himself and pushed past me in such an irritable hurry that I was taken aback.

Once we were in his private room, he poured himself a cup of wine without offering one to me. I was not offended at this lack of hospitality. I merely assumed that he was shaken by my sudden appearance or that he had prior knowledge of what deeds were truly afoot.

'So,' said the Guardian, beneath a shadowy frown. 'What have you been up to?'

'I have been at Lindisfarne,' I said in hushed tones. 'The Holy Isle.'

He responded with a suspicious glare and took a generous draught from his goblet.

'I was there for several night: three or four nights—or maybe more. I'm not entirely sure.'

Dionysius did not break his stare. His jocular and slightly giddy Franciscan countenance was completely gone. The man before me was an entirely different entity from the one I had got to know previously. He seemed the embodiment of doubt, gathered in his chair, watching me in the shadows of the early morning, his eyes full of accusation. Suspicions at once rushed into my head and I could not ignore the idea that the Franciscans were complicit—more likely out of feebleness than malevolence—in permitting heretical sorcery to take root in this strange corner of England.

'And why you were at Lindisfarne?' he asked.

'I cannot explain how I arrived there, Father. I have thought about it a great deal and cannot find an answer. Perhaps I ran there from the forest in a state of reverie—after all, it is a place of pilgrimage—or perhaps I was found asleep in the forest and taken there by a Good Samaritan, who passed by the Lindisfarne causeway and handed me to some churchmen who crossed his path.

Perhaps I was taken ... .' My words trailed off as the face of the Green Man appeared in my mind's eye. I composed myself, deciding not to reveal what I had seen in the forest, and continued. 'But how I got there is a small thing. There may be a thousand answers to the question. But why I found myself there, that is what matters.' I raised a shaking finger to the sky. 'I had a vision, Father.'

'A vision?'

'Of the Revelation of St John. I believe that the Beast described by John—the beast who was wounded but then healed—walks among us, parading its wounds as a badge of honour. Its vanity and pride sucks innocent souls into its orbit, making them do battle with the saints and God's followers, subjugating the path of righteousness. But John also said that those of us who have ears should listen! The Beast walks among us but has not the countenance of a leopard, nor the feet of a bear, nor the mouth of a lion. It is merely a man—a man who combines the leopard, the bear and the lion. Man is the dragon that gives the Beast its voice and this is sorcery, Father. I have seen it at work and it infects everyone who comes within range of it. Lord de Hayeford, the Scottish nobles, the people of the villages ... .' I stared intently at the Guardian, who had not shifted his gaze from me one inch. 'Even you, Father. It is my theological and philosophical duty to shed light upon these dark forces, expose them to God's light and ensure that the Church and the people are cleansed. I have to stay here and complete my work!'

The Guardian nodded slightly—almost imperceptibly—at my plea, and looked down at his chest, murmuring something I couldn't hear. After a long minute had passed, he rose from his chair and shuffled over to his desk, where he retrieved a scroll whose seal had been broken. Even in the dim light I could see that the seal depicted the crossed keys of the Palais des Papes. Upon seeing it, my heart faltered.

'Two days after you set off for the forest, this letter was delivered to the friary. You will permit me to read it.

> To our Blessed Brothers in the Abbey of Berwick-Upon-Tweed.
>
> It has become evident to the cardinals of the Holy Father within the Palais des Papes that a monk of Villeneuve, who belongs to the Order of Saint Benedict, has been in your midst these recent days and weeks.
> This monk, who is called Brother Jacobus of Vienna, has travelled to England to investigate the phenomena relating to infant disappearances about which we learned from a letter written to us by John of Thoresby, dated . . . . 1367.
> You should know that the journey made by Brother Jacobus was not authorised by the cardinals. Any business he has undertaken while in your lands is to be considered unofficial, illicit and not endorsed by the Palais.
> We are dispatching Palais representatives to apprehend Brother Jacobus and return him to France, where he will be punished for his misdemeanours accordingly.
> In the meantime, please instruct Brother Jacobus to remain at Berwick, should he still be there. There is no reason to assume that he is dangerous. He may even believe that his actions possess some theological or philosophical justification. But by interfering with this troubling episode without Papal authority, he has risked undermining the true authority of the Church.
> Do not send a response. We will await your hospitality in England.

In the name of the Lord Father, and the Christ, and the Spirit.'

'The missive is signed with the personal seal of Cardinal Pierre de Banac,' said Dionysius, rolling the scroll back up and clasping it upon his lap. He then stared at me with blue, watery eyes, his mouth closed tightly into a faint line. For my part, I could do nothing but stare, in turn, perplexed; Cardinal Banac's letter had thrown me into the abyss. In reaching a state of divine clarity upon my midnight walk back to Berwick, I had forgotten the web of deceits I had built to arrive here in the first place.

'Father, I—'

'We welcomed you, Jacobus!' he snarled, cutting me off. 'Into our abbey, into our house of God and into our lives.' He brandished the scroll. 'And you deceived us! Not once, not twice … which means that your judicial rulings involving Lord de Hayeford and the Scots!—they are worth no more than the wind in the trees … .'

'I came because Cardinal Banac said not to dispatch anybody to help your community,' I said, in a naive effort to defend myself. 'I alone advocated for a solution to this mystery. I alone wished to find out the truth!'

By now I was standing and jabbing my finger at the ground in defiance. 'The cardinals care little and less for the English. The Palais cannot separate itself from the influence of the French crown. Surely you understand why the cardinals chose not to aid the enemies of le Roi Charles? I alone cared nothing for the petty politicking of the Palais—I cared only for God's truth and wanted to help. So yes, for the sake of His mission, I deceived you.'

I exhaled and, to my surprise, my confession felt like a weight lifted from me. 'And I would do it again, Father.

I would disobey my cardinals if they stood in the way of the truth. I devoted myself to your need. Will you then obey their command to hold me here?'

The Guardian breathed out softly and let the silence sit between us for a moment before eventually responding slowly and carefully. '"For as by one man's disobedience many were made sinners, so by the obedience of one shall many be made righteous." I do believe you came here for good reasons, Jacobus, but the things you have done—'

'The things I did kept the peace in these lands when none else could! I satisfied that fool, Lord Hayeford, and I satisfied the Scots and I satisfied the people.'

'Did you satisfy yourself? Have you satisfied God? No, I did not think so. And you return here from your—whatever it was—with tales of visions and accusations; but perhaps you should be wary of your own behaviour. I am pleased you returned, Jacobus but you will not be permitted to leave the abbey again. We will not incur the wrath of the Palais. We have no means to withstand it.'

Aghast, I could find no recourse to any objection and simply stood with my mouth open.

'You may roam the friary as freely as before but no further. And now, this audience is over. Leave.'

'If that is your decision, Father, then so be it,' I said stiffly. 'I shall bid you good morning, and may God keep you.'

11th December

In which my attempt at formulating a conclusion to the mystery is interrupted by the appearance of unwanted visitors

MATINS

In spite of what had been an exhausting twenty-four hours, I could not sleep. After learning that the cardinals had sent a papal delegation to apprehend me, sleep was impossible. I paced the cell to which I had been assigned, trying unsuccessfully to organise my thoughts which raged within me like a storm. In my fevered state I flicked through my books in search of some sort of inspiration but found nothing among the mathematics, biologies and astrologies. At last I prayed and spoke to God. He told me to sleep.

I awoke to a sharp knock upon my cell.

'Enter,' I called in a voice as dry as chalk.

It was Friar William. I tried to rise to greet him but my efforts were clumsy and he gestured me not to stand. 'You look tired, Brother,' he said. 'You ought to rest.'

I did not have the energy to argue and slumped back down upon the palliasse. He stooped to kiss me on the cheeks and knelt down beside me. His brows were knitted sternly.

'You do not look your usual phlegmatic self, Friar William. Perhaps you should pay a visit to Friar Herry.'

'If I were not myself I would,' he responded. 'But I think you ought to remove the beam in your own eye first, Brother.'

'The beam in my own eye!' I blustered. 'That is the second time you have said as much to me, but I am not the one who is blind. In fact, only now can I truly see! I was so convinced that I could find an earthly explanation for these events that I discounted the possibility of sorcery. But the Evil One is like a plague; his work cannot immediately be seen—he can only be detected from observing the symptoms.'

'You see only what you want to see, Brother Jacobus. When I told the Guardian I intended to visit you he told me about the vision you claimed to have seen. Are you so convinced that evil is the only explanation?'

'That is a line I have heard from many heretics in my time.' I sighed deeply. 'I do not think you are a heretic, of course, but what other explanation can there be but evil? My beloved books are exhausted and the world has yielded horrors. What other explanation is there?'

'Whatever it is, it is the glory of God and requires no explanation. He is the Rock Eternal. We are nothing more than passing winds and cannot know all aspects of His mind. I have also spoken to God in my prayers about you, Jacobus, and He tells me that you must relinquish this epistemological fervour. It is not healthy. It is not giving you clarity of thought. The best you can do is to remember Noah, who took the best of the animals and the birds, and offered burnt-offerings of them to the Lord. Give to the Lord what is good, Jacobus; discard the rest which causes you such pain. The Lord has no wish for it.'

'I cannot do such a thing,' I said, tiredly. 'The desire to know is so pure, so sacred.'

'Noah selected only clean animals to sacrifice. And what sacrifice did the Lord ask of Abraham? One which had no equal: his son. And in that gesture of sacrifice he found that his son was returned to him. The fact that you see your philosophy as sacrosanct is the very reason why you should let it go. Offering up a sacrifice of the ideas that ensnare you would remake you; out of their ashes would step forth the new Jacobus, a man of even greater intellectual rigour.'

Deep down inside me I knew there was wisdom in

William's words, but in my exhaustion and pride I could not admit it. We prayed together a while and when he left I finally managed to sleep, only to dream about Cardinals Banac, Blauzac, Orsini and Ayecelin crowding into my cell in their scarlet robes to chastise me for my deception and have me arrested. When I awoke I recalled the dream vividly and fearfully.

With Guardian Dionysius effectively incarcerating me within his walls, and papal representatives bearing down upon me upon the North Roman Road, I had an almost irresistible urge to flee. A great hourglass had been placed over my head and I could feel the particles of time falling upon my shoulders, threatening to bury me. But I could not flee. I was a man of God and a member of a religious Order, and the only way to save myself from the justice of the Church was by using my intellect. Images from my adventure ran through my head and I desperately fought to turn them into a coherent story. Until now I had used philosophy for its own sake—and, of course, for the glory of God; now I had to use it for my sake.

The first thing I had to consider was the Franciscans, my captors. I was an inquisitor and yet I had not intervened in their toleration of pagan superstitions as they worked with the poor. In fact, now I thought about it, it was not impossible that they regarded the events in Berwick as unworthy of papal intervention. After all, it was not the Franciscans who had written to the Palais but Albertus, a curious and intelligent layman, and John of Thoresby, a great and holy man of the Church. On the face of it, the Franciscans had aided my investigation and yet, at every turn, they seemed reluctant to accept my methods and suppositions.

On top of all of this, the question kept returning to me: why would William wish me so readily to discard as a burnt offering that part of me granted by the Lord to so few others that had best enabled me to serve Him?

PRIME

I woke to the sound of the abbey's bells, which sounded light and reedy in the pre-dawn darkness. I chose to observe Prime alone in my cell, lighting a small candle that flickered in the gentle draught.

The hour was still dark and the air cold and damp. I ought to wait here for the Palais representatives to ferry me away, but the burden of isolation felt more than I could bear. Though fearful of attracting the ignominy of onlookers, I mustered my courage and went to the refectory to eat. A vicious, clawing sort of hunger had visited itself upon me. Hunger, it turns out, is an excellent inoculant against embarrassment; when you are more belly than brain, you can endure the inquisitive glances thrown in your direction. In fact I was grateful for the shyness of mendicant friars that morning; it allowed me to devour a plate of spiced sausages, bread and dried fruits, without much intrusion, and wash it all down with a mug of good beer. It was only after I had had my fill that the infirmarian Friar Herry unexpectedly came to my table, setting down his own mug of beer and sitting with me.

'Brother Jacobus,' he whispered after crossing himself. 'I have only just learned that you were back. I have spoken with the Guardian. I know that a papal delegation is heading this way and will soon arrive.'

I held up my hand dismissively. 'Friar Herry, I do not

want to respond to any scurrilous rumours that may have been scurrying through the abbey. Please—let me spend whatever time I have left here in as much peace as I can manage.'

He shook his head vigorously. 'Oh, Brother, you misunderstand me. I am painfully aware that your time is short and I certainly have no interest in gossip. But there are things you need to know!' With some agitation he tugged at the sleeve of my cloak with his pale, slender fingers.

'Things?'

He leaned in and whispered. 'The children! Emeline and Peter. They are lucid. They are awake.'

The children! In my recent reveries they had slipped my mind completely. And they were lucid? In that moment my self-indulgence vanished and I saw the light of Christ's possibilities flood before me. *Sinite pueros venire ad me et nolite eos vetare talium est enim regnum Dei!*[9]

Friar Herry continued prattling about the children's improved condition as we walked to the infirmary but I barely heard him. My mind was racing with the various theories that might explain these recent events and provide me with some justification for my trip, however slim, that I could provide to my masters from Avignon.

The infirmary was painted brightly by the morning sun shining through the coloured glass. The second and third Stations, situated at the easternmost point of the building, were illuminated beautifully. A few bed-ridden, convalescing friars cast weary eyes in my direction, but said nothing.

---

[9] But Jesus called them unto him, and said, "Suffer little children to come unto me, and forbid them not: for of such is the kingdom of God."

'When were you last here?' whispered Herry.

The question was hard to answer. Time had merged into one long, unbroken stream. 'A week, perhaps? Ten days? The children were still in a deep sleep when I left.'

'We feared they would not wake up,' said Herry as we passed from the nave into the corridor of small private cells at the rear, where he stopped and looked at me with some agitation. 'You should know, Jacobus, that I have brought the children's mother here.'

'A woman? Into the friary? Are you mad, Herry? Does the Guardian know about this?'

Friar Herry shook his head vigorously and drummed his finger-tips against each other. 'I'm not mad, Brother. She has been here since the children awoke, two days ago. She was raving in St Leonard's convent, threatening to tell Lord Hayeford that demons still roamed in the forest, and that we kept evidence of it in the form of her two children. I tried to appeal to her common sense by telling her that her children were still well and would be returned to her soon, but you know what women are like when their blood is hot. So I asked for permission from Father Denis that she might see her young ones, in the hope that it would quell her madness.'

'Her madness? At this very moment a delegation from Avignon is headed to this place. If they find a woman here, they will … why in Heaven's name would the Guardian be so reckless?'

'Why would they find her? She would be kept here in the infirmary. There is no reason for any papal delegate to visit here. But now you are here, perhaps you can speak with her. If you can get the children to say what happened to them, she will leave.'

The children were in the same room as before, still

scented with rose and green herbs, and calmed by the sound of the sea gently lapping at the walls outside. To my astonishment, Emeline and Peter were awake, sitting on the floor, laughing gaily and tossing woodenjacks. Gwendolynn sat on a stool with a look of such wonder and delight, and a smile so beneficent, that for a fleeting moment she almost reflected the image of the Virgin Mother herself. Then she looked at me and her smile dropped. The moment of sublimity had passed and she was merely a woman once more.

I bowed silently in greeting and she gave a curt reply. 'Brother,' she said in her common dialect. 'I cannot remember your name, you'll have to forgive us.'

'I am Brother Jacobus, Gwendolynn, and I remember you full well. I would like to speak with your children, if I may.'

She considered this for a moment, then nodded. Her face was firm and her mouth pulled into a hard, thin line. 'If it gets 'em out of this place, then so be it.'

I nodded, not wishing to let a single moment go to waste. I put my hand upon the shoulder of the boy and blessed him with the sign of the cross, then did so with the girl. They stopped laughing. The boy looked at me with large, sad eyes, and the girl took on that same suspicious face that she had worn when last I saw her.

'Hello, my boy,' I whispered. 'Do you remember me?'

He looked at his mother for permission to answer. She nodded, forcing herself to smile, and the little one looked back at me and shook his head.

'I brought you here after you came out of the forest, about three weeks ago. You were very poorly, and you said you saw a man in the forest, and dark lights in the trees. And you, Emeline. Do you remember what happened there? Remember, you are in a holy place, and that Christ is the Truth, and so the Truth is Christ, and so if you speak to me, you must speak the truth. To do otherwise would be sinful.'

I paused, allowing this to sink in. 'I simply want to know what happened. I think that what you both saw holds an important answer. And there are people coming here who will want answers. So speak! Tell me everything about what happened in the forest.'

The boy's face collapsed, his mouth hung open and his lips trembled. Seeing this, Gwendolynn gathered him in her arms and embraced him. 'Can you not see that it troubles him?'

'He is not the only one troubled by it! But God has returned these two cherished ones for a reason—perhaps, in His infinite wisdom, He knows that they hold the key to this puzzle. If you—'

I stopped, and remembered that Gwendolynn herself had confessed to the heathen burial. No wonder she was here, to watch over these children. I had no doubt she had been delighted to see her two youngest children alive, but they were also living evidence of her crime. She would prevent them from speaking if she could.

'Gwendolynn, I must speak with Peter and Emeline alone,' I said, quietly.

She reacted with predictable alarm, and refused outright. Expecting this, I asked Herry to bring a guard to escort her from the room. 'She does not need to leave the friary,' I explained. 'Simply the infirmary, for now.'

She fussed, and wailed, and protested, but I waited with the outward patience of Job—though inside I was burning with anxiety—until two burly friars arrived and took Gwendolynn away.

'She will be just fine,' I said to the children, trying not to project my anxieties onto them. They still looked at me with uncertainty.

'I know it makes you scared,' said Friar Herry to the children. 'But no harm can come to you now. God has you in His bosom, and we have you in our care.'

'Do you remember the story of Moses, children?' I began, and the two little heads nodded in tandem. 'After Moses freed the Israelites from slavery he led them into the desert, where they were bitten by poisonous snakes. In the Book of Numbers it says the Lord told the Israelites to craft a brass snake and put it upon a tall pole so that when those bitten looked at the snake, they would live! And so it came to pass. Little Peter, you must look at the thing which causes you harm, because averting your eyes will only allow the thing to keep biting you, and you will never be rid of it. That is God's word.'

Miraculously, the story, so beloved of little children, seemed to help Peter and Emeline to summon up the courage to speak. What they said was not always easy to understand and I had to ask them to clarify several times. Despite that, I was at last able to understand what had happened to the two of them in the woods.

'We was desperate poorly,' said Emeline. 'Sick. But mama told us we had to go to the forest to—'

'To fetch wood,' said Peter.

'We heard a fair voice in the trees,' said Emeline. 'I thought it was an angel.'

The children, beckoned by their mother, followed this voice into the woods. Then the sound changed to the harsh shouts of men, and they heard their mother crying and wailing—which upset them very much. According to Emeline, the shouting men were bad.

'Did any of them look like this?' I said, pointing to the foliate head on the wall.

Emeline ignored me and began to weep. 'I saw Peter get hit on the head! And then—'

It was difficult to determine what happened to them afterwards, but I took this story to mean that they had been led to the wood by their mother and attacked by Odenellus or his followers.

'What happened next?' I asked.

'We was woken up,' said Emeline.

'By the men?' I asked.

Peter shook his head and looked away. 'It weren't no men,' he said, quietly. 'It was the wood. The wood itself. I saw its eyes. It was like dark light.'

Emeline looked at me sincerely. 'There was leaves everywhere.'

As the children described it, I could not help but conjure my own memory of the baleful creature and the way it had lifted its arm and delivered its acrid touch to my forehead.

'No!' I spat out, swatting the memory away, as if it was trying to touch me again. They all stared at me with alarm. I tried to compose myself.

'I'm sorry! Your description was so vivid! Well done, well done, for speaking so clearly and bravely. But, my dear children, was there not somebody else present? The man of the forest, Odenellus? Somebody who conjured the image of this infernal beast?'

They looked back at me in silence, unnerved by my unguarded response. After that, I could get no more from them and, in my frustration, began to hector them, which only made them more wary of me.

'Well, boy?' I continued. 'Can you not recall anybody

else who was present? Or you, girl? You must remember! You must!'

By now I was so desperate to know who had conjured the image of the creature that I was shaking my fists in anger, to the extent that even the mild-mannered Friar Herry intervened.

'Brother Jacobus, what is the matter with you? Leave the children alone. They have told you what they saw.'

'They have told me nothing that I did not know,' I shouted. 'The Green Man they describe is just an apparition, a conjuration, the spectre of a demon magicked by somebody learned in heretical arts! As an infirmarian, you know something of how the natural sciences can be used to mislead the innocent, Herry: how reflective surfaces can be used to deceive the eye, how phials of intoxicants can debilitate one's critical faculties, how venoms can upset the physical disposition—'

'Of course,' exclaimed Herry. 'But what is the connection between those and heretical sorcery?'

'Because these are the tricks that cause demons to appear before the afflicted, making them believe they are wreathed in flames or covered in insects summoned by the Devil to consume their flesh. This is how these children came to imagine a Green Man but I need to know who fooled them and what tricks they used on them! The cardinals are coming and I need a name! I am an inquisitor: I need a sorcerer to accuse! That is my job!'

By this time I had become shamefully wild and Herry had to restrain me further. 'Jacobus, I insist you stop this madness!' said Herry, placing both hands on my shoulders and looking into my face threateningly. 'Calm down now. You are not yourself!'

I wish that Herry had been right! But in those mad

moments, I am ashamed to say that I revealed my true self. The stripping away of my surface rationality had revealed a vast emptiness below, where hovered my fears and fantasies, propped up by nothing, suspended before God like a body caught halfway between the surface of the ocean and its bottom. With a great effort I tried to pull myself together but it was too late; I had frightened the children off and I would glean nothing more from them. In a weak voice I told them all to pray, and I left the infirmary in a black mood.

Striding into the courtyard, I cursed my intemperance. A group of young novices was standing around jabbering and, when they saw me, a frisson of excitement came over them, making them whistle and titter like imbeciles. I approached one of them and asked what they were so excited about; he squeaked back that a delegation from France had arrived at the friary to collect me and had gone to the chapter house with the Guardian.

So—Cardinal Banac's group was here and I was to be dragged back to France without any of the answers I had charged myself to get. For a moment, I was tempted once again to flee but knew I could not without permanently injuring my reputation. Besides which, flight was the coward's way; I had to face my fate. I took a deep breath, steadied myself and walked to the chapter house.

At the oak table sat the Guardian, ashen-faced, alongside William, who looked similarly dour. When I saw the monk sitting opposite, I gasped. It was the Dominican inquisitor Nastagio di Balino, immaculate in his black cloak over a pearl-white habit, sipping a cup of wine and looking utterly unruffled. Beside him were three other monks from Avignon whom I didn't recognise. Surrounding them in a ring stood two dozen papal soldiers, dressed in the red-and-white stripes of Avignon, no doubt tired and irritable from having to leave Provence to visit this damp, miserable land. Half of the soldiers were armed with bows, arrows and knives, eight of them with swords and the remaining four with halberds. As I looked upon this ominous representation of papal might, a warm and familiar voice called out my name.

'Jacobus!'

I turned, and saw my dear friend Magnus seated at the rear of the table. Despite the heavy load pressing upon my shoulders, the sight of my old friend brought a smile to my face and the burden on me lifted. He in turn looked at me with an open smile and sparkling eyes.

Turning towards Nastagio, two seats away from him, Magnus requested permission to rise. Nastagio nodded and Magnus came to me, whereupon we embraced and kissed each other on the cheek. I thought it strange that he should ask permission from the visiting delegate and not from the friary guardian.

'It is good to see you, my friend,' he said, offering me a seraphic smile which then faded into a more melancholy expression. 'Though, not so good, also.'

'Brother Jacobus of Vienna,' said Nastagio, rising from his own seat but offering me neither a smile nor an embrace. 'I am glad to have found you.'

'Nastagio,' I replied, frostily. I felt icy cold at the thought that an inquisitor been sent with the delegation to apprehend me, and particularly this one. 'You have just arrived?'

'About an hour ago. The journey was long. This part of England seems never to end. The journey would have been more tolerable were not the landscape so horribly bleak, wouldn't you say?'

'Actually, I have come to admire its raw beauty,' I said. I wasn't sure if I believed the sentiment but it was an instinctive parry to Nastagio's opening joust. He sat back down and gestured for me to take a seat. I took the one next to Magnus.

'I concede that the bleakness of the climate has been offset by the warmth of the welcome we received from His Eminence,' continued Nastagio. 'The Guardian Dionysius confirmed that he received the correspondence sent from the office of Cardinal Banac in the Palais and that he has explained the situation to you. He was half-worried that you might try to escape but I informed him that I have known you for many years and that you would never shy away from defending yourself with the full might of your intellectual arsenal. And did I also not say, your Eminence,' he said, turning to address Father Denis directly, 'that only a guilty man flees from his accusers and that only a virtuous man willingly faces them. Virtuous in his own mind, that is. And if I know of nothing else about Brother Jacobus, I know he believes in his own virtue. So I am pleased that his appearance proves me right!

'But you also know, Your Eminence, that Brother Jacobus is an inquisitor, an instrument of the truth. He knows the clever ways in which the accused evade justice. He knows that artful criminals enter willingly into the court of judgement, thus assuming the appearance of the innocent.' He paused, and looked at me as though very concerned for me. 'Brother Jacobus, do you know why we have been sent here?'

'I do,' I said. 'I make no bones about it. I deceived the office of the cardinals and came here without any official authorisation. But I came here to do the Lord's holy work. People here were suffering. I could not let them go unaided. But I am a sinner and I have sinned.'

'We are all sinners, Jacobus. '

I gestured towards the military unit that stood behind Nastagio, sweeping my hand around the chapter house to emphasise the size of the retinue. 'But why all this, Nastagio? Are all these men and their armaments needed to escort one tired Benedictine monk back to France? You overestimate my strength.'

'I never overestimate, Jacobus. When the knowledge of your journey came to light, the cardinals requested my opinion because of our joint experience in inquisitorial matters. I knew that you would have some logical reason for doing what you did. I believe your disobedience was neither wicked nor unholy. I believe it derived from your desire to know the truth about things. And when I investigated the matter in hand and read the letters from John of Thoresby and the lay healer of this parish, I deduced that there might indeed be a very terrible sickness rampaging through this community: the sickness of heresy, which infects the one true Church and tempts its followers with devilish arguments designed to undermine its authority. Oh, do not look so worried, Jacobus. You have earned the displeasure of the cardinals' office and you will pay for that. But that is not the end of the matter. I do believe that you have been doing God's work. The cardinals have therefore commanded me to find out what you have uncovered, so that the body of this community may be purged and purified of all sickness.'

COMPLINE

'How many people have you told about the creature you saw?' asked Magnus after I had told him my improbable tale. We were safely tucked away in my cell now. It was the hour after Compline and the friary had mostly retired for the night. Two papal archers had been posted outside my door to prevent me from leaving but Magnus had been let in to see me. He looked bewildered at my report, unsure what to think. I was no less baffled.

'I told the Guardian here about the vision of St John's Revelation but not about the creature in the wood,' I said, keeping my voice down.

'Do you think there is the remotest possibility that the creature you saw was real?' asked Magnus, looking at me with a very serious expression.

'I did not think so at first,' I said, bitterly. 'Now I would say it depends on what is meant by real. I obviously saw something odd in the forest. I know I'm not mad or prone to delusions, nor was I dreaming. I was as wide awake as I am right now, although I admit I had been hit about the head—twice. I deduce from that that I saw something in the forest, something that seemed like a thing of Nature, for it had features that were both human and plant-like, and yet was wholly unnatural. If such a thing could exist, then it was real; if not real, then it must have been a vision caused by some disturbance in my sense of perception. It may have been the effect of some strange herb that had entered my system or that pricked my skin when I fell into the ditch, something chemical that stimulates one's eyes and ears and produces apparitions. Or it may have been something conjured, malevolently. In both cases, the vision would have possessed a sense of realness, would you not say? And when the vision manipulates individuals into performing unholy acts, then it becomes very real indeed. Real enough that the instigator of such madness, if instigator there was, must be identified and punished. There are such things as false visions, Magnus. The Book of Jeremiah tells us that people can have visions that come from their own minds and not from the mouth of the Lord, as experienced by the Prophets. I think I experienced two visions like that: one supernal and one infernal. And since I do not believe I consumed a poison or was pricked, I conclude that my vision was the result of heretical means or incantations or spells. A logical recitation of the choices drives me to think so.'

'So it was real in the sense that you perceived it was real. But how can you be sure it was not actually real?' Magnus said, tentatively. 'There are such things … .'

'I know,' I said with a sigh. 'I curse myself for not gathering enough evidence.'

Magnus didn't respond but looked concerned.

'I'm sorry,' I said with a weary smile, and placed a hand upon his. 'I have hardly asked about your own welfare. Despite everything—or perhaps because of it—I am more pleased to see you than I can say. Tell me everything that has gone on with you.'

Magnus then proceeded to tell me that very little had intruded upon his own routine of inking and scrivening. He had assisted with the abbey's vegetable and herb gardens and had been enjoying a warm and gentle Provençal autumn until summoned to the office of the cardinals. They disclosed that they had received the generous and quite unexpected donation of a *tournois livre* from a landed nobleman from the north of England named Thomas De Hayeford, along with a curious note that thanked the palace for its involvement in this parochial matter and had praised the intellectual rigour and fairness of the monk of the Order of Saint Benedict whom it had dispatched to do this very job.

'The *tournois livre*. So Hayeford sent it directly to the Palais. My own reward pays the ferryman,' I muttered with grim bemusement.

'What do you mean?'

'Oh, nothing. It just means I will have to pay my penance.'

Magnus then told me he had confessed to writing a false letter of instruction on my behalf to give to the English. Because of his own role in the affair, and because of his friendship with me, it was suggested by Nastagio that it may be useful to bring him to England to appeal to my sensibilities. As Magnus related the tale I recalled the day we had stolen into the Palais library and dreamed up our subterfuge. The thrill we felt—the thrill I felt—now seemed tawdry and childish.

'I know we sinned, Jacobus. But I also felt as though I sinned more in disclosing the truth about you, because I knew the purpose of our lies and that our intentions were good. But as sinners, what else can we do but sin?' And he turned his head down and prayed.

'You sinned, Magnus my friend, but it was under my persuasion. God sees all. It was my pride that dragged you into this affair and I shall testify to that. It is my pride and deception that must be punished. But despite all that, I still have a strong contention that I was right to come here.'

'Why?' said Magnus, lifting his head. 'What is to be gained from lingering here? The only thing to look forward to is that I be led away in chains by—' he gestured with his head to the door, indicating the archers standing outside.

I gave him a wry look. 'Nastagio has always been puffed up with the desire to show the Church's strength, but even he would not bring such a large guard merely for optics. Did you hear him in the chapter house just now? He said he believed my reasons for travelling here were justified, despite my disobedience. That was quite a concession—and a surprising one. But that will not save me. The fact that the papal soldiers could easily be overwhelmed by the local militia is irrelevant; they would not dare strike a papal inquisitor and his guard. We inquisitors are given special dispensation in so many ways—though I may well have exhausted my own privileges.'

The worry on Magnus's face did not go away. 'Are you afraid, Jacobus?'

'Yes. But not of being led away in humiliation.'

'Then of what?'

'I worry that, when the time comes, I will not have the strength to do what needs doing.'

15TH DECEMBER

IN WHICH
I RELATE
MY STRANGE
TALE
AND
AM GIVEN
AN ULTIMATUM

TERCE

Nastagio left it an entire day before he paid me a visit. In the intervening hours he made no attempt to hide himself as he roamed the friary. Flanked by papal guards and always in his pristine black cloak, he milked the attention he received from the Franciscan brotherhood, regardless of whether it represented reverence or fear. There had been few, if any, inquisitorial trials for heresy in England, but the notoriety of those that had taken place had spread at least as widely as the stink of heresy itself. If my intellectual pride had been the cause of this mischief, Nastagio's vanity was no less ostentatious.

While Nastagio overawed the Franciscans, their attitude towards me changed from amiable curiosity to quiet animosity. Whereas they had greeted me politely, now they kept a coy distance, as though I might combust at any moment like an oriental grenade. Rumours spread quickly, and I wondered which parts of my strange story had been mangled by the friary's well-established talent for tittle-tattle. I spent the morning in the library, where at least I could tolerate the suspicious glances in silence.

It did not take Nastagio long to track me down, standing at a lone lectern and reading a chained copy of Van Bidoo's *Plague Diary of the Low Country*. He joined me and we exchanged pleasantries.

'Did you know, Nastagio, that Van Bidoo possessed a pet raven and had twenty perches for it? Each perch was positioned in a different place in his study. He would sketch the bird every day, and every day would place the bird upon a different perch. But Van Bidoo's seat at his desk in the centre of his study would never move. He stated that at any one point we can only see half, or part, of the bird. We cannot see the half of it not in our line of sight. And yet, by looking at something even for a short time from several different angles, we can put together an image of the whole that is richer than if we had viewed it from one perspective for much longer. He then observes that we ought to do the same for the plague, so that we can gain a better understanding of it.'

'It is all very well to observe a raven from twenty different angles, Jacobus,' said Nastagio. 'To try it with a victim of the plague would be rather different. I daresay there would be few scribes willing to undertake that task. The people of my city, Milan, have solved the problem of plague by bricking up the houses—every wall and window—of anybody who displays symptoms.'

I grimaced in disgust. 'Is that how you stem the tide? With the immurement of the innocent?'

'We Italians are a practical sort. If the few must be lost to satisfy the bringer of plague and ensure the survival of the many, it is a sacrifice well made. That surely is simple mathematics that anyone can calculate.'

I closed Van Bidoo's diary and looked Nastagio in the eye. A couple of friars standing hunched over a manuscript a few yards away studied us warily. Although speaking in the library was not prohibited it was frowned upon, but I doubted that anyone would remonstrate with the Dominican.

'I wonder, Jacobus,' he continued, 'what you would consider a sacrifice well made.'

'Do you mean me? You're not here simply to make a show of dragging me away in chains, are you?'

He pretended to look offended. 'I know you, Jacobus. I know you think I deride your philosophies as horsefeathers, but I do not. I never have. I have huge respect for you and your ability to make sense of certain things.

What I have always said, however, is that you walk along a knife edge in defending those accused of malicious and unholy practices.'

'I only defend people whom I am convinced have been subjected to a wrongful trial, and where there is a watertight alternative explanation for the things of which they are accused.'

'I have to admit, so far you have walked that edge adroitly. And you are right, I am not interested in arresting you. You wandered away from the Abbey, led by your sense of intellectual curiosity. My Order is filled with scholars and teachers, so I could hardly chastise you on that account. The most likely punishment for disobeying the cardinals will be some form of penitentiary work back home, during which you will of course absolve your soul through the sacrament of confession. But these are trifles. Any small platoon of archers could have been dispatched with a papal decree to put you in shackles and take you back without my presence. On the other hand, you have undertaken judgmental duties without a papal order—indeed, you carried them out under the auspices of a falsified order!—and that could have resulted in a more severe punishment.'

I frowned slightly. 'Could have? Does that mean no punishment will occur?'

Nastagio inclined his head, and smiled wryly. 'Well, now. That depends a great deal on your own report. It seems that you carried out your fraudulent judicial appointment with both wit and aptitude. You satisfied an idiotic nobleman, got the Scots to keep their heads and persuaded the locals that the cause of their troubles had been identified and swept away. Your obsession with logic and reason may have dragged you into this mess but may also have dragged you out of it. But again, that does not interest me.'

'Do not tease me any longer, Nastagio. I know exactly what interests you. Heresy.'

Any good humour was wiped from Nastagio's face. 'The only thing that interests me is the good functioning, the safety and the security of the One True Church, Jacobus, and you have wrought terrible damage to it with your stupidity and recklessness.'

By now the library was empty save for us. It had become our own, private, but very echoey meeting room. The friars would have regarded this inquisitor in the way that sheep monitor a wolf that has entered their pen, and had prudently taken the opportunity to leave without his noticing.

He continued. 'The Guardian has told me about the trial you oversaw and I have seen reports of it. They interest me a great deal. What also interests me is that the Guardian says you returned to the forest to continue your investigation after the matter had been concluded at trial.' He eyed me from beneath a darkened brow, barely moving a muscle, like a hooded snake from the distant East. 'You knew, then, that the matter had not been resolved. What did you think would happen as soon as another incident was reported? As soon as another infant was slain, or snatched, or changed? There would be more correspondence with the Palais and with your own abbey. The truth would out, and all public judgements you made under the pretence of Church authority would have been exposed as fraudulent bunkum.'

'There have been no further incidents—'

'Not yet! I have seen no explanation that satisfies the questions posed by this situation, nor any evidence that your investigation has yielded any answers at all. You have undermined the authority of the Church—and to do it now, Jacobus, when Pope Urban has only just planted his holy feet upon the marble floor of St Peter's, after sixty years of exile! The nobles of England already question the Pope's neutrality as they fight the French crown, and when they find that they have been hoodwinked by a charlatan—and not merely hoodwinked but embezzled as well, to the tune of a tournois livre!—into a false resolution, their sense of obligation towards the Church will evaporate like your own theories. You may be no heretic, Jacobus, but you possess a vulgar sense of self-importance that vastly outweighs the deference you owe to your superiors. The Guardian Dionysius wants you to be taken away quietly and without fuss.'

I laughed bitterly at that final remark. 'If he knew you, Nastagio, he would not have wasted breath on such a request.'

Nastagio looked at me with those fiery black eyes. 'But you know me. And you know what I must do. You have undermined the authority of the Church, and at a terrible time. You will be led from this place to face charges in France. The best you can hope for is to be given the white sheet and to undergo forced abjuration from your position as an inquisitor.'

'Abjuration? You would not deprive me of the work that I do in the name of the Lord? Nastagio, in spite of my errors, which I openly confess, you must know that I did all that I did for the best reasons. Give me the white sheet: I will wear it with shame and hang my head, as befits a foolish sinner. I will stand barefoot outside my own chapel in full view of the people of Villeneuve. But do not remove me from the Inquisition.'

Nastagio ignored my plea and continued. 'That is the best you could hope for. The worst would be to be given the white sheet both here and in France, and to suffer a public flogging and then excommunication.'

A shock of cold ran through me, and when I spoke, it was as if my voice had been strangled by some frosty devil. 'Excommunication? You would not dismiss me from the Church, which I love so dearly? Where would I go? What would I do? I would be a lamb, lost, with no home to return to. Give me the whip, Nastagio! Indulge me in the mortification of the flesh so I might rip away the poisonous part of me and make of it a burnt offering to the Lord, that I might emerge anew from the flames. I will hand you the scourge myself.'

'This is not an inquisitor's trial, Jacobus. I have no more say over your fate than you do. I can merely report the facts to our superiors.'

My hands, now shaking, touched the books on the lectern before me and then recoiled to my face, as if the pages were fiery. I swallowed, yet my mouth was dry. The library was as silent as death, and Nastagio and I seemed locked in a struggle at the end of the world. In my mind's eye I saw a road in a desert that led to a dilapidated palace of my own making. The crumbling edifice was being mounted by the angel seen by St John, whose face was wreathed in flame. The Truth. In that moment I saw my future, one of humiliation and ruin, and I saw the importance of my work, both done and undone, and I saw the Truth mocking and beckoning me, pulling me to excommunication and exile.

No, I told myself. I resolved then and there that that would not be my fate.

'You do not know everything, Nastagio,' I said, slowly

and deliberately. 'There is a great deal you do not know about this place. Before you drag me off in disgrace, which I will face as best I can, I only ask that you let me tell you all that I have seen. If you listen, it might change your understanding of these strange events.'

Nastagio, who had been standing behind the lectern, confronting me as he delivered his damning verdict, at last relaxed and stepped back, leaning against the end of a bookcase. 'Very well. Wilful blindness is as good as a lie. I will not knowingly compile an incomplete report. If by omission there is miscomprehension, then I as an instrument of the Truth, like yourself, will have failed. Tell me what I do not know.'

I nodded. I remember giving a long pause to think about my response to Nastagio, and in those moments the library itself felt as awkward and alien as the forest, as if waiting for me to err so it could swallow me up.

'I have dedicated my life to philosophical study,' I said. 'God's grace is without limit; everything in the world and beyond it is, by definition, in the palm of His hand. But we, as men, can only see what is directly in front of us; what touches our skin, flickers before our eyes and rings in our ears. We are mortals. Moreover, we are sinners. Christ taught the world that we are fallible. Every single one of us makes mistakes, and we must bear the suffering they bring. The architecture of faith is not a sound foundation from which to consider the mechanics of the world. There is a gap between the language of logic and the language of faith and morality. So I set out to build upon the great work of the ancient philosophers, and the great doctors who have lived in our own time, to deduct a way of observing the mechanics of the world that is beyond the fallibility and prejudices of men. Testing, testing and testing again. One must try to break open one's own arguments to see if they are strong; fling iron pellets at them, not straws. Not to do so is to do as the man who built his house upon sand; it is to act disingenuously, and seek not truth but expediency.

'I have confidence in these presuppositions, Nastagio, because they work. I do not believe that it is sinful to uncover the secrets of the world. I believe that man can and should uncover those secrets. But just as faith provides no foundation for the architecture of natural philosophies, nor can the natural philosophies provide the proper architecture for a moral life.'

I stopped talking for a moment and looked at the hundreds of books and scrolls in the gloom of the library. I noticed a small foliate head carved into the frame of one of the bookshelves. Its face, with its tongue out, its eyes bulging like a demon, mocked me and caused a cold shudder to flit across my shoulders.

'I saw something, Nastagio. In the forest. Something my logic cannot explain.'

'What did you see?'

I lowered my voice. 'I think it must have been a demon. I'd say that it might have been a phantasm except that the people know of it. They call it the Green Man.'

Nastagio grinned. 'What is this, Jacobus? You, a man who doubts so strongly the existence of demons, and who has presented so much evidence showing that the phenomena caused by demonic forces always have more mundane explanations, are now claiming to have seen one?'

'I know how it sounds. But I have been over it again and again. I saw it.'

I described the monster I had seen. I took care not to omit a single detail about its fiendish appearance, and as I did so, the grin of contempt fell from Nastagio's face.

'You have no doubt? Was it not a hallucination?'

'I have considered that at length but what would have caused it? Madness? I am not mad although, I admit, one can be made to behave as if mad for a time, with the use of certain techniques, and to imagine oneself mad. There are flowers, plants and ceps—even the blood and secretions of animals—that can be used to induce fevers and malignancies that can cause visions. There is also St Anthony's Fire: it can be induced.'

'Have you found evidence of such elixirs being concocted and used against either you or the population?'

'No! Not a trace of evidence. Which leads me to one conclusion and one conclusion only: that I and my faculties were undermined by sorcery and the invocation of this forest demon. But it is worse than that. The creature in the forest is only the spider at the centre of the web; its arms are spread out throughout the community, causing its people to indulge in depraved practices. There is a pagan man called Odenellus who is said to use divination to consort with this demon. He makes vile predictions to the villagers, scaring and convincing them to undertake foul practices.'

'Then we must apprehend him at once.'

'Yes, we must!'

Nastagio nodded. 'Tell me, then, what foul practices has he inveigled the local people to undertake?'

'There are many in the area but the woman I have come to know best is called Gwendolynn, and she lives in one of the nearby villages. She took the advice of this Odenellus, and offered—or thought she offered—her children as sacrifices to the demon by taking them to the woods to be buried in a heathen grave.'

Nastagio contorted his face in disgust.

'But the children returned! I saw them with my own eyes. They live still. They did not die. They were afflicted, somehow, but they were brought back from wherever Odenellus had told their mother to leave them, and they recovered. I went to investigate the woods myself to try and confront Odenellus and find out more from him, but I was attacked by his followers and left for dead. I could have died there, Nastagio, but I was rescued and borne away.'

'By whom?'

'By the Green Man.'

Nastagio glowered at me, fixing me in a stare that hid a myriad of calculations.

'Then we must apprehend and destroy this Odenellus,' he said at last. 'It is known that once the Earthly familiar has been destroyed, the demon cannot linger.'

'No, indeed. But there is more, Nastagio. When a party of us was in the woods. we disturbed a rabid wolf. It was slain, and one of the Franciscan friars administered a blessing to the fallen creature and said the last rites over its carcass. I wonder now if it was not said as some kind of offering to the monster?'

Nastagio crossed himself in horror. 'They would administer blessings to dead dogs and not to the bodies of their own young? It is blasphemous!'

By now I could see in my mind's eye the slow unfolding of the terror I was unleashing, but I could not stop myself. 'The Scottish raiders carried miniature idols of their own fashioning, ugly homunculi made from sticks, twine and mud, to which they made offerings and prayers. A diary contained notes of worship towards the forest. I asked them to denounce these terrible things upon their trial, and the woman who was tried—Anya was her name—did so, but the nobleman's son who was tried alongside her proved reluctant.'

'And yet you did not move to extract a confession under torture!'

'I have no military might, Nastagio. I have merely my wits, feeble as they may be. I wanted a peaceful resolution and that I managed. '

'At great cost to the Church! And they will carry on doing these foul things because you solved nothing! I hope you are satisfied with your great adventure.'

'Of course I am not satisfied! All of these foul things are done to appease the monster in the woods. One of the friars here said something to me a little while ago. He said legitimacy is merely a cloak, a covering that can be draped over false idols and false devils. False idols and false devils, Nastagio! The people here are in the grip of a false idol in the forest, an idol they create using magics and spells, the likes of which I cannot fathom. It consumes them. It seduces them. And yet the friars seem unwilling to consider it a problem.'

Nastagio sat perfectly still in his chair, his tonsured head glistening gently in the candlelight, his eyes half-closed and his chin lowered. After some time spent thinking, he spoke in a slow and measured voice.

'It is clear to me. The local population is under the influence of a demon which is either the product or source of sorcery. Either way, some local people are in such thrall to this demon that they would consort with it to heretical ends. Satan's demons can operate like this, but they require human conduits. Those who feel that

Christ's teachings are not enough to dispel the evil in their midst often seek to appease the evil in the hope of slaking its thirst for perversion. But that only grants the evil thing a licence to grow and increase its power. And you say some of the Franciscans are now gripped by this idolatry? Christ's wounds, have they not learned from the Fraticelli debacle? Jacobus, your story is very interesting. Will other witnesses attest that unholy acts were committed in the way you say they were?'

By now my heart was hammering in my chest and my voice was as dry as dust. I knew where these events were now going to lead.

'Yes,' I said, miserably, for I knew I was unleashing the whirlwind—the very thing I had not wanted to bring upon these simple people. 'The blessing of the dog; the confession to the burial; the children … there are witnesses enough.'

'Then you will act as the witness who brings the accusation, under the threat of the full penalty of retribution. Do not think you can confound me, Jacobus: you know the law! We are both ecclesiastical judges; in disclosing this information to me you have already made the accusation. You cannot retract it, or fail to disclose it in public, now I have it. You will be required to act accordingly. You will not be permitted the shield of anonymity. Your own sins must be atoned for but we may present the trial on the basis that even you were misled by the chicanery of this place.'

'Nastagio, I beg you, these people do not succumb to evil through wickedness. They do so through fear, fear of the demon in the forest. A trial is too great an ordeal for them to bear.'

'Better to suffer an ordeal that brings them back to

the Light than live in sin and condemn their souls to Hell.'

'Nastagio, we must treat them with tenderness, with mercy. Remember, it was they who reached out for assistance in solving this foul mystery! Do not ask me to denounce them.'

He gave me a fierce look and then raised his hand and flicked it forwards in a strange gesture. From the shadows near the entrance two papal archers stepped out. 'It was John of Thoresby who requested help, alongside the secular physician, this man called Albertus. Not the Franciscans. I have heard your story, Jacobus. Would you reveal the presence of heretics and then refuse to cooperate in their condemnation, risking retribution yourself? Would you risk torture? The flame?'

For the first time I looked at him with real, animal fear. I had known Nastagio through various inquisitorial tasks and trials, and never once had his zeal been directed at me. But I had seen it directed at several others, and he lived up the name of his Order as one of God's dogs. 'Torture! Nastagio, come … ! We are old acquaintances!'

He was unmoved. 'We are instruments of Truth.'

And of course he was right. I had said it myself: inquisitors are in possession of special dispensations in matters of inquiry and the execution of judicial matters. I had lost those dispensations. Nastagio had the advantage over me, but I was seized by the terrible realisation that I had handed it to him. I let out a whimper, placed my head in my hands and muttered a wretched prayer of consolation.

16TH DECEMBER

IN WHICH INEXORABLE PROCEEDINGS ARE INITIATED AND I WRESTLE WITH GOD

PRIME

Nastagio made a great show of arresting Friar William of Alnwick within the walls of the friary. He had a scribe write up the trial summons and had one of the archers nail it loudly and unceremoniously to the chapel door, whereupon a crowd of monks and friars assembled to watch the commotion shortly after the observation of Prime. The summons issued the usual formalities and, because of the intimacy of the community and how close we were to the festive season of Christmas, the notice period given for the trial was only seven days. In addition to William, Gwendolynn of Ord also stood accused.

Nastagio and I stepped to one side as the archer finished knocking in the nail. I had begged to be put in manacles, or deprived of the cloak of my Order, if only for a short time, but of course the inquisitor would not allow it. He demanded that I stand next to him as an equal, to demonstrate the full validity of this notification, and the severity of its implications. 'The inquisitors must stand as one,' he had said to me. 'We are the bulwark against evil.'

The Guardian barreled into the courtyard with a great deal of indignation, demanding to know who was responsible for this obscenity. One by one the friars read the paper and began relating it to the others. As the meaning of the notice became clear there was a great deal of gasping, crossing and gossiping, and as they all took in its full significance, they stared at me momentarily before turning away, as if their doubts about me now proved to be true. In that moment my breast swelled with protest and despite the bitterness of the English winter, my brow dripped with sweat and my face flushed with shame. A great voice within me wanted to cry out and tell them all, This is not of my making! This is not of my design! And yet that voice stayed firmly within me, never once escaping my lips. When the Guardian had pushed his way to the front and read the notice for himself, his eyes bulged in shock and he spun to face me.

'You!' he hissed and bustled over to us but before he could get his hands on me, two of the Papal swordsmen stepped in front of me and barred his path.

'You would do this? You would do this to us, who welcomed and sheltered you and put our faith in you? This is how you repay us? By accusing one of our own? You are no man of God, you are the seed of Belial and Paimon made flesh, a sack of pig's dung given life, a sink of depravity and vice!'

'Watch your tongue, Guardian,' called Nastagio. 'There remains space for further names to be added to this charter. A blasphemer has been identified; would you denounce the Church that is attempting to remove this poison from your midst? I would have no choice but to act against you.'

The Guardian turned pale at Nastagio's threat. 'You would not. Not in this land, where you are so far from home.' The words were strong but in his quavering voice there was only doubt.

William himself was one of the last friars to appear in the courtyard and, upon his arrival, all eyes turned to him.

'Run, William!' cried a voice from the crowd.

'Blasphemer!' cried another.

'God save us!' cried a third.

The crowd parted as William moved towards the chapel and read the notice. As the horror on his face grew, Nastagio gave an order and two archers stepped forwards and arrested him. William struggled and looked with shock at Nastagio and then at me.

'Jacobus? Jacobus! Blasphemy? A denunciation? I do not understand! Let me go. What in the name of the Lord is this about? Jacobus, you cannot put your name to this. Jacobus! Tell me the meaning of this. What have I done but serve the Lord?'

'You see how he demonstrates to the world that he has no understanding of these charges?' said Nastagio to me as an aside. 'I wonder, for whose benefit does he act in this way? Surely not for mine? If the sickness runs deep in the veins of this old friary, then it is not for his brethren. Perhaps it is for you, Jacobus? Perhaps he feels he can deceive you in the same way that others have deceived him with their lures of heresy?'

I said nothing, preferring to stare at the mud and straw beneath my feet. I could not bear to look at William.

Nastagio stepped forward and in his well-practised bark read out the accusations for which William had been arrested. I knew the words—I had heard them a hundred times at a hundred different spots across the Holy Roman Empire—but in that moment I barely heard them at all. All I heard were William's terrible curses and cries as he was dragged from that place.

Afterwards, I caught up with Nastagio as he returned to the dormitory that had been prepared for him.

'Clemency, please, Nastagio,' I said. 'William has been a friend to me while I have been here. He is a great comfort to the people here and I have seen his good works among the poor. They love him.'

'All the more reason to reveal and purge the deception. The most wicked acts come cloaked in the veneer of compassion and kindness. Just as Christ rebuked the Pharisees, we must be on our guard for outward displays of virtue as opposed to the inner humility He taught.'

'He also taught mercy and peace. William is a good and knowledgeable man, and he loves the Church.'

'Of course. God in His infinite grace and wisdom is filled with the milk of forgiveness, and always welcomes the wayward sinner back to His flock. But sinners must atone and accept justice. I too love the Church, Jacobus, and will not tolerate any disruption to its proper functioning—not from you or anyone else. If his heart is pure he will have nothing to fear.'

My blood chilled at that phrase. Such things were always said of heretics before their trials. It did not often end well for them.

'And what about Odenellus? The pagan man? If you apprehend him then all will be well. You will see for yourself that he, and not William, is the crooked one.'

'Four of my archers were sent with a small retinue of soldiers from the local garrison. The mission is under our jurisdiction.'

I stopped in my tracks. 'Archers? They won't apprehend him: they'll shoot him. If they even find him. He knows the woods better than anyone.'

Nastagio turned to face me. 'They have been tasked with apprehending him. So long as he does nothing reckless, or summons this supposed demon, he too will have nothing to fear.'

I recalled Odenellus and his men attacking me in the wounds, and winced at the memory. The idea that a man like Odenellus could be relied upon to do nothing reckless did not fill me with confidence.

TERCE

Mid-morning prayers were not for another couple of hours but nonetheless I went immediately to the chapel and devoted myself to fervent supplication. The eyes of all the friars were upon me but none dared speak with me. Gone was the amiable pleasantry of earlier days when all—friars, apprentices and novices—would ask me casual questions on all manner of topics. Now I was a threat to them and not to be engaged with. I prayed furiously, my hands clasped together so tightly the flesh turned pink.

After Terce I stayed after the other friars had filed out. It would be lunchtime soon but I had no stomach for food. I was consumed by confusion; because I was sure that the community had permitted and even practised sorcery, I was obliged as an inquisitor and a man of God to bring it to the attention of Nastagio di Balino. On the other hand, I had spent a month in the hospitality of these people and could not shake the feeling that plunging them into the ordeal of judicial proceedings was in some way sinful in itself.

'Jacobus,' called a stern voice at the chapel doorway.

I looked up to see the Guardian, his face the colour of cold ashes, and Nastagio, as hard as wrought iron, standing behind him in the shadow. I got up and approached Dionysius, kneeling before him to take his hand, but he snatched it away before I could kiss it and said, 'Come with us' in the coldest voice possible.

The three of us convened in the solar, where the Guardian poured himself a large goblet of wine with a shaky hand, then poured one more for Nastagio. He did not invite us to sit.

'You cannot be serious, Jacobus,' he said at last with a

dry, exhausted voice. 'This is an abomination. I told you privately and in good faith that we do not have the resources to withstand the Palais, and you smelled blood.'

'That was not my intention!' I protested.

Dionysius held up a hand, quelling me. 'And you, Brother Nastagio? I would urge caution in implementing this charge. You too are a visitor. I would advise against finding blasphemers and heretics lurking behind every door and prosecuting them without my consent. This is my diocese and the gift of trial belongs to us as much as it does to you.' He took a long draught of wine and held the goblet to his lips as he let its warmth course through him. When he spoke again, he was calmer. 'I understand that it is a subtle and difficult subject. We must proceed properly, with caution and safety, and not do anything with excessive cruelty. Do you agree?'

'Of course, Father," said Nastagio with solemnity. 'But the papal bull *Super Illius Specula*, issued by Pope John XXII, dictates that inquisitors ought to proceed with investigations against sorcery and such practices when heresy is suspected. Grand inquisitor Eymeric is quite clear on this. And the secular arm is with me.'

'Nevertheless, you cannot proceed without my acquiescence. This is our diocese.'

'Did you not just say you have no strength to withstand us? Would you prefer it if we returned to the Palais and the Grand Inquisitor and informed him that you willingly harboured individuals who are not only suspected but formally accused of heretical practices?'

The Guardian's mouth fell open. He gave himself another long draught of wine before sitting down and placing an elbow upon the arm of his chair and resting his forehead upon his hand. 'And you, Jacobus?' he muttered at last. 'A man of books, reason and learning. Is this your conclusion also?'

'I am still searching my soul. I am fond of William immensely and wish him no harm. But, as you say, it is a subtle and difficult question.'

'You see, Guardian? The accusation is made from a place of love,' said Nastagio. 'If a successful conviction through confession enables a young friar to be returned to the loving arms of the flock, then it will have been an act of grace.'

SEXT

I returned to the chapel, drawn inexorably as though in a trance. I saw Albertus standing at the small recess by the entrance, lighting a small votive candle next to a small and humble bye-altar. When he saw me his countenance darkened but I decided to approach him anyway.

'For my mother,' he said softly, as he delicately placed the lit candle among its softly dancing brothers and sisters on the votive stand. He lit another. 'For my father.' He lit a final one and administered the Sign of the Cross. 'For my son.'

'You have a son, Albertus?'

'Aye.'

'May I ask where he lives?'

'You may, but what makes you think I would answer? Why are you here, Brother?'

'To pray.'

He smiled sourly at that. 'I'd be at prayer too, if I were in your shoes. I will pray also. We need light in this dark time. Come and kneel with me, please.'

He led us to the choir stalls at the northern wing of

the chapel. Part of me was hesitant about joining him as he seemed prone to an outburst of anger at any moment but the other part of me told me to stay. We genuflected. I took the lead and led us both through the *Sarum Kyrie*, and I held onto each word.

> O Lord, fountain of mercy and of sevenfold grace, have mercy on us.
> All things came to be at your command, have mercy on us.
> O Lord, *Adonai*, blot out our sins, have mercy on us.
> Kindling fire, proceeding from the Father and the Son, fountain of life, purifying force, have mercy on us.

Afterward we knelt in silence for some time, allowing the peace of the chapel to breathe upon us.

'I was not sure of you when I first saw you, Brother,' he eventually said, keeping his forehead on his intertwined fingers and peering at the ground. It looked for all the world as though he was still caught in the devotion of his prayer, but I suppose that he simply could not bear to look at me.

'You told me you would swallow your doubts if I would swallow mine.'

'Aye. I did not think you would understand the country, the people. I reached out to that fool Thomas de Hayeford in the hope that he would provide some sort of reasonable solution to our situation, but the mere whiff of sorcery confirmed his prejudices and he bent your investigation into something that would please his own jaundiced eye. You, however, knew that the Scots were innocent and you saved them from torture and death.'

I knew what was coming and a feeling of dread stirred within my bowels.

'And I thought, aye, here's a canny one. I became

quite fond of you after that, for your dedication to self-improvement through books and letters. I thought, here's a man I can look up to, someone I could learn from. A man who truly walks with God!'

'I know what you are about to say, and—'

'So do you walk with God now, in making these accusations against William? Do you believe he is a heretic? He is so beloved by the poor folk in this region, in Berwick and its villages. And that poor woman? She has been through enough, would you not say? For a man of reason, that would seem like a fair supposition.'

For a minute or so I said nothing. 'You may yet be called to act as a witness. Then you will have the chance to offer your understanding of events.'

'By heaven, you are a vain man, Jacobus. I think you have been flummoxed by this investigation of yours, and now seek to settle the matter through vexation of others rather than looking to yourself. Doesn't the Book talk about removing the beam from your own eye before pointing out the mote in your brother's?'

I laughed, though it was a thin and mournful laugh. 'That phrase seems popular in these parts. I no longer know what is lodged in my eyes, Albertus, and whether they show me the truth or not. I have seen things. But I do not know how what I have seen can be true.'

'Well, you had better figure out what's true and what's not, and fast,' he said, not bothering to disguise the contempt in his voice. 'I have been summoned to act as a layman of good standing for your inquisitor's trial, and I will oppose the reprehensible tariffs that are placed upon Friar William. You may know everything about the world and its nature but you seem to have you lost your ability to see what is right.' And before I could respond he got to his feet, brusquely made the Sign of the Cross in the direction of the altar, and left.

VESPERS

I stayed praying in the chapel for most of the day and barely noticed it getting dark in the late afternoon. Outside, an angry wind rattled the building, indicating that a storm was approaching from the sea. Just as the first blasts buffeted the chapel, hunger struck me, urging me to retreat to the refectory and feed, but I refused. I felt as though I ought to stay in that chapel all week, scourging my body by fasting while seeking consultation from the Lord. Other friars came and went. Papal archers patrolled the chapel door at Nastagio's insistence, no doubt to ensure that nothing untoward befell me while I was alone.

Dionysius did not disturb me; if he had wanted to, he was probably waiting until he could corner me in a place of his own choosing rather than under the watchful eyes of the inquisitor's guard.

It was Magnus who in fact disturbed me by staying behind after Vespers and kneeling a few yards from where I had knelt for much of that day. His calling of my name snapped me out of my trance, making me realise I had a full bladder.

'Jacobus,' he whispered. 'May we talk?'

The twinge in my bladder had suddenly become uncomfortable and, unlike the pain in my empty stomach, was a pain I could not ignore. 'Must we, right now?'

'Why, what's wrong?'

With a wince I got to my feet, barely able to move for fear of bursting. 'I need to relieve myself,' I said.

Magnus looked embarrassed, which irritated me. I

waddled up to him. 'Don't be so pious, Magnus. We all have bodily functions that need dealing with. Come on, you can accompany me to the garderobe.'

I was faint from having eaten nothing since the previous day, so I took his arm. The archers stopped us at the door and insisted that Nastagio had commanded them not to let me out of their sight, but I waved them away.

'You will not march me to the pisshole like a dunce,' I snapped at the taller of the guards, who clearly was not used to being spoken to in this way—and certainly not by a monk. 'Your job was to protect me while I was inside the chapel. When I am through this door I shall be outside the chapel and therefore no longer your concern. If I were you, I'd go into the town and put back some ale. It's good stuff. As for me, I'm tired and I need to relieve myself. Move!'

I knew they would not arrest me so I pushed past. At the north-eastern corner of the friary, a chunky outhouse overhung the eastern cliff edge by a mite, allowing the effluence from three garderobes to trickle down the abbey wall to the ocean. Magnus waited outside while I saw to myself.

'You do not seem well, Jacobus. I think this place disagrees with you.'

'I do not care whether the place disagrees with me or not. I did not come to win hearts. I came to make a sound observation of the state of things here, and to— oh, blessed Lord, that feels so much better!'

As I finished off, a stray trickle of urine ran down my leg and I let out a mild oath of annoyance, which made Magnus ask what the matter was.

'Nothing. I have just sprayed a little upon my leg.'

'Ha ha! You are like the son of man from Ezekiel.'

I emerged from the outhouse, puzzled at his strange remark. He continued by way of explanation. '*Quia venit et tabescet omne cor et dissolventur universae manus et infirmabitur omnis spiritus et per cuncta genua fluent aquae ecce venit et fiet ait Dominus Deus.*'[10]

By the time he had finished the line, the ribald amusement on his face had disappeared as he realised what he had said. 'I'm sorry. I didn't mean … . But maybe it's true. Maybe judgement is coming,' he said, looking away to the sea. A fierce rainstorm had begun beating down over us, driven by the wind, the drops lit up like showers of Italian stilettos in the evening lamps. I had quite forgotten about the stain upon my leg now.

'Earthly judgement and divine,' continued Magnus. 'The Lord will take his sword from its sheath and it will never be replaced. That is what Scripture says. The good flesh will be ripped out along with the bad, from north to south. Is that what happens when heretics are outed? It frightens me.'

His face was now quite pale and creased with worry. He crossed himself and gathered his hood around his head to keep the cold out. 'Jacobus, do you really think that Friar William is a heretic? I've never seen a heretic before. I don't know what they look like. Are they all the same? I've heard tales—that they are able to sprout horns and roll tongues as long as snakes out of their mouths, and stare at good holy Catholics with eyes as red as fire that drive them to dementia and—'

'And they have claws of adamant, and tails of leather

---

[10] Because Judgement cometh, and every heart shall melt, and all hands shall be made feeble, and every spirit shall faint, and urine shall run down every knee: behold it cometh, and it shall be done, saith the Lord God. Ezekiel 21:7.

which they crack like whips, like the devils with whom they consort. Yes, we all know the tales. I have seen a hundred heretics and a hundred more, and if those stories are true, each one has somehow escaped me. Heretics, for all their rancid perversion of Scripture, are merely men and women. They beg when they are convicted, they scream when they are tortured, and they die when they are burned.'

'I am scared, Jacobus. We have sinned so greatly, you and I. Neither of us should be here in this strange, awful place! You should never have come here.'

I sighed deeply. The distraction of my bladder had now subsided, giving way to griping esurience. 'I have been praying this whole miserable day, trying to unpick that sin. I lied—and worse, I coerced you—in order to satisfy my own vanity. That vanity has gone unrewarded, and is soon to be punished, and yet I have apparently uncovered some form of heretical depravity. I should feel pleased, but instead I feel like … .' I looked around at the swirling weather. 'I feel like I'm falling.'

'That is what distinguishes you from Nastagio. He enjoys it.'

'Yes, he does. He said as much to me, once. But that is not the reason I feel so wretched.'

Magnus thought about this. 'Maybe this sense of dissatisfaction is the Lord's way of talking to you, telling you not to succumb to the whims of this vanity. Not when it has led you to this dark place.'

'Magnus, I … .' I looked at my old friend, who was desperately trying to make sense of this on my behalf, and I felt a great and abiding fondness for him. 'There is something I must ask you.'

'Name it. Anything.'

'Would you administer to me the sacrament of confession?'

He looked at me as though I had lost my mind. 'Why? We both know what we did. And now Nastagio knows it, and the cardinals, and no doubt the entire Palais. There is nothing to confess. We shall work to make our amends. *Ora et labora*.'

'I wish time and labour would absolve me,' I said. 'But only the sacrament will do.'

'My friend, you are upset. But if you are in pain then let us return to the chapel.'

'No. Not while Nastagio has his men everywhere. Do it here.'

'Here! But we are outside and it is raining! And you have had no time to prepare—'

'I have had too much time, Magnus! It is time now!'

So Magnus, with the worsening rainstorm slicking down the lip of his hood to his forehead, held up his right hand to make the Sign of the Cross before me, and welcomed me into the sacramental confidence.

'When was the last time you came to confession, my son?' The rain was growing heavier all the time, and the wind was harsh and violent, hurrying in from the cold sea to swallow up Magnus's voice, forcing him to shout.

'Two months,' I replied, after a moment's thought. I had not received reconciliation even once during my time in England.

In my hunger and fatigue, I had to clutch the handle of the wooden privy door to save myself from collapsing to the ground.

'What is your sin, my son?' called Magnus through the wind.

'I went to the wood ...'

'And?'

'I went to the wood to find out what had caused the death of the infant. I saw ... I thought I saw ... .'

'What did you see, Jacobus?'

'The Green Man.'

'The what?'

Before I could speak again, a massive gust of wind came lunging at me, tearing my grip from the slippery privy handle, and dropping me into the mud.

'Jacobus, this is madness. Let us get inside.'

But once I was on the ground, I rolled upon my back and had no inclination to get up, even as the rain pummelled my face and drenched my eyes, blinding me. I vaguely heard Magnus calling for help, but the main sound in my ears was my own voice mouthing one particular line from the Twenty-Second Psalm: *'in loco pascuae ibi me collocavit* [11] *... in loco pascuae ibi me collocavit ... in loco pascuae ibi me collocavit ... .'*

---

[11] He hath set me down in green pastures.

17TH DECEMBER

IN WHICH
I AM ROUSED
FROM THE
INEVITABILITY
OF WHAT IS
TO FOLLOW
AND HAVE
TO DECIDE
ON MY
BEST COURSE OF
ACTION

LAUDS

I awoke to the sound of the friary bells ringing. My head clattered with pain as I tried to stand and found that I couldn't, so I fell back into a supine position, my eyes still shut. The sweet warmth of the infirmary hearth sent waves of comfort through the air, and the gentle crackles of the burning logs softened the ongoing whistle of the wind and rain outside.

'At last,' came Magnus's voice. My eyes were too sore to open, but I could tell by the echo of his voice that we were not in my cosy little cell. 'I have been awake since the end of Matins, worried for you,' he continued.

'What time is it, then?' I asked in a croaky whisper.

'Lauds.'

'And where am I?'

'In the infirmary. Friar Herry told the soldiers to bring you here rather than to your cell. You were shivering from the cold and wet but insensible. We tried to talk to you but you would not respond. The friar burned some lavender and herbs by your bedside to help you sleep but they are all consumed now.'

I placed a hand on my forehead. I was burning up. 'I'm feverish. What do you mean, I was insensible?'

'Don't you remember? You demanded the sacrament of reconciliation when we were outside, and then you began talking about the wood—'

'The wood!' I interrupted with a start. I sat up, ignoring my headache. 'What did I say?'

'Not much. You saw something. And then you kept repeating a line from the Twenty-Second Psalm: He hath laid me down in green pastures. What did you mean?'

I sighed and lay back down with a harrumph. 'I don't suppose it meant anything. It was the fever talking. I've become quite enervated these past few weeks, Magnus. The thought of another trial disturbs me.'

'I managed to bring some bread and beer from the refectory. Here it is, on a plate by your mattress.'

I rolled on my side to assess the small offering and felt my will capitulate to the cries of my stomach. I tore off a small crumb of bread and held it in my hands. 'Will you perform grace for me, Magnus?'

'Of course,' he said, before placing his hands together. 'We give Thee thanks, our Father, for the Resurrection which Thou hast manifested to us through Jesus, Thy Son; and even as this bread which is here on this table was formerly scattered abroad and has been made compact and one, so may Thy Church be reunited from the ends of the earth for Thy Kingdom, for Thine is the power and glory for ever and ever. Amen.'

I ate the morsel and drank a small sip of beer and felt a degree better.

'Something troubles you, Jacobus. No one asks for absolution without a reason. What does the wood have to do with anything? What did you see there?'

'Nothing. I must have been mistaken. I saw nothing. It must have been a dream.'

'Did you see something you cannot make sense of?'

'Yes.' I laughed weakly as I chewed another crumb of bread. 'But how can it be? I have been so careful, so sure.'

'We can all be undone, Jacobus. Maybe you ought to let yourself be undone a little. Remember Saint Paul's epistles: *scriptum est enim perdam sapientiam sapientium et prudentiam prudentium reprobabo—*'[12]

---

[12] For it is written: I will destroy the wisdom of the wise: and the prudence of the prudent I will reject. *Corinthians* 1:19.

'Yes, yes, of course, but it is precisely the prudence and received wisdom of the Old World that will be rejected and destroyed by observation and discovery. So, *ipso facto*, the act of observation and discovery—the pursuit of knowledge—must be godly.'

But Magnus continued the quotation. '*Ubi sapiens ubi scriba ubi conquisitor huius saeculi nonne stultam fecit Deus sapientiam huius mundi*.[13] What makes you think that your wisdom is immune to the infinite divinity of God?'

I gave Magnus an impatient look. 'It is not. But in the impending trial, how can I testify to something I know to be false?'

'False? What is false, Jacobus? If there is something about this trial that runs counter to your vanities, then you must abandon your vanities. If you are concerned about how your name will be regarded if you offer testimony that undermines your beliefs, then what of it? Your belief in the Lord and the teachings of Christ are all that matters.'

'I am not concerned about my name," I said. 'I care only for the name of God. But how can I testify to something that takes His name in vain?'

'You mean this Green Man. You mentioned him before you fell insensible by the garderobe.'

I looked at him briefly but said nothing. I had the strange feeling that if I chose not to utter it, the truth would remain untrue.

Magnus spoke again. 'There may be things in this world that run counter to our understanding of it. But if it is of this world, then God has permitted it, and you

---

[13] Where is the wise? Where is the scribe? Where is the disputer of this world? Hath not God made foolish the wisdom of this world? *Corinthians* 1:20.

should not be afraid of saying that you do not understand it. You saved many innocent souls wrongly accused of devilry, and you countered the evidence presented against them with empirical observations. A few days ago you said you feared that you might not have the strength to do what is just. In that case you must decide what is just. If you do not, it will not be your name that is in danger but your soul.'

That was not what I wanted to hear. The bread and beer lost what little taste it had had and I nestled back onto the mattress to sleep.

nones
After observing prayers at Nones, I caught up once more with Nastagio in his cell. The room that had been prepared for him was a deal more furnished than the one I had occupied during my stay. He had been given a bed, a wardrobe and a battered old writing desk, at which he now sat, scribbling notes with a droopy but glistening peacock's quill. Even his scrivening was intended as a show of superiority.

'Brother Nastagio,' I said, softly.

'Sit down, Jacobus,' he said, not looking up from his note-taking.

I sat upon the bed. It was comfortable and although I was merely visiting the room, I felt guilty for allowing myself even this degree of luxury. Nevertheless, I waited for Nastagio to engage with me. At last he put down his quill and looked at me.

'I imagine that preparations for the trial continue apace,' I asked.

'Well enough. How can I help?'

'I wondered if there had been news of the party that went to chase Odenellus the pagan?'

'Actually, there is news. The group that was sent to the wood happened upon a man who had the moronic idea that it would be a good idea to attack one of our archers with a stone sling.'

'I do not think the uniform of the papal archers is well recognised in these parts,' I said, drily.

'Apparently not. In any case, while the man was being tackled, the party was attacked by two other men.'

I sighed, and remembered the blow to the back of my head, which I rubbed. 'That is what happened to me. Unfortunately, I did not have a company of soldiers to come to my aid. But have the captured men been brought back here? Can they be interviewed?'

'Calm yourself, Jacobus. I know what motivates your interest. You think the apprehension of these conjurers will exonerate your friend William. But each will answer for his own crimes, without prejudice. As for the men, only one was detained.'

'Only one? Did the others escape?'

'The others were killed, and their bodies were left in the wood.'

'Killed? But your mission was to apprehend them, Nastagio. You said so.'

'Indeed. And had they had the wisdom to hand themselves in, they would have been.'

'What a loss of opportunity,' I moaned. 'We might have learned much from them. Have you at least identified them?'

'The man who was detained is Gibson of Wandylaw.'

'Gibson!' I exclaimed. I remembered the name being uttered by the attacker who had hit me over the head, and then again by Odenellus. 'Yes, he was the one who attacked me. And he is alive?'

'Neither the archers nor the local soldiers were particularly gentle with him, but his heart still beats and his lungs still breathe. He will stand trial.'

I clasped my hands together in hope and silently thanked God for this window of opportunity. 'Did he give up the names of the others?'

Nastagio consulted his notes. 'Sandy of Bavington was one of the ones slain. He was killed by a local soldier wielding a morning star. Messy, by all accounts. The other was your local bogeyman, Odenellus—punctured by several arrows as he tried to flee.'

I let out a heavy breath. Though I would not mourn the odious runt, I was sorry that Odenellus had died. It was not that I did not want him to answer for his crimes at a trial—I most certainly did—but that he would so obviously have been unable to do so, and Nastagio would have made him suffer for it. I had also wanted to ask him a second time what had drawn him to become the servant of a woodland devil, in defiance of the goodness of our Lord. Had he not once been an innocent child, and then a man, himself? I would never now know what had turned him into the base thing he had become.

'Well,' I said darkly, turning back to Nastagio, 'at least one scourge has been accounted for. You must be satisfied about that.'

AFTER COMPLINE

The knowledge that I would have to swear a Holy Oath at the trial weighed heavily upon me. Upon doing so, I would be forced to choose between my head and my heart.

If the Green Man of the wood were real, it made a mockery of all the natural laws to which I had devoted myself, and all my efforts to show that demons had no hold in the realm of men, and existed solely in that most unreliable chamber: the human imagination. Worse still, testifying to the existence of the monster would prove to Nastagio that heretical sorcery had been used to conjure it, and condemn Friar William and Gwendolynn to ignominy and retribution.

On the other hand, if I testified that I had not seen any creature, then my presuppositions would remain correct, and the world of Aristotelian logic would still make sense to me! The trouble was, I had seen it and had told Nastagio I had seen it. If I now failed to disclose its existence as a true fact, two heretics might go free—the very scenario Nastagio had always said I would foment through my steadfast adherence to the natural philosophies. I would also face a penalty of retribution, and very possibly excommunication, for undermining the authority of the Church, thereby destroying me, my reputation and everything I had worked for. Nastagio would also want to punish me in other ways for cheating him of his prize.

'Eyes!' I cried out to the walls of my cell, where the flickering shadows thrown by the candlelight made me feel like the craven trapped inside Plato's cave. 'What have you seen? Is it the truth? Or did you deceive me? Saint Paul, grant me the wisdom to see where this should be headed!'

But it was no good. I was entrapped in my own convictions. With the trial bearing down on me, I would be forced to deliver an answer that would either shatter my work or shatter my soul.

23RD DECEMBER

THE THIRD TRIAL

LAUDS

I spent the rest of the week in fevered prayer. The Franciscans avoided me and Nastagio had no need to visit me. Magnus spent some time with me but even he had given up trying to understand what had happened to me in the forest. Instead, we prayed for strength for the task that lay ahead.

William had been remanded in the magistrates' jail and on the day of the trial, shortly after the morning's prayers, was brought by Berwick's bailiff and a couple of men-at-arms to the town's square. A temporary stand had been erected there—in truth it was little more than a roughly constructed wooden dais with a bench and desk to the side to accommodate the legal officials. The men-at-arms stood a fair way back, to keep order if necessary, while Nastagio's two-dozen papal guards stood like peacocks, parading their colours and weapons for all to see. Anybody who wished to leave the stand would have to run the gauntlet of these Avignon heavies.

The English cold was now settling in for a bitter winter's sleep, bringing frost as its blanket and snow as its quilt. The sun hung sullenly just above the horizon, peering over the edge of the sea as though only half interested in this queer gathering. I was seated upon the bench, pulling my hood around my head and rubbing my hands together inside a fur muffler on my lap. Quite a few townspeople had gathered to watch the proceedings; none of them would have seen Holy inquisitors or papal guards before; the sight would have aroused respect, curiosity and, by the end of the day, no little fear. The other officially appointed governors for the trial were seated close by me: nearest was Albertus, who would be acting as a secular man of learning and good standing, and a local cleric, Father Arthuis, who earned a stipend from Lord de Hayeford in the chapel of St John the Baptist, close to Hayeford Castle. Lord Hayeford himself sat on a small chair flanked by his own household guards, doing his best to look aloof and phlegmatic.

As William was brought to the edge of the platform by two papal archers, I saw some commotion among the spectators at the edge of the stand. William's wrists were in chains; he looked scrawny, grey and weak, and had probably barely slept or eaten all week. I hoped that he had not been treated too harshly by the town's jailers, and that his position as a respected man of the parish who had provided alms for the poor and sick had earned him some leniency.

Moments after William's arrival, the second defendant was introduced, not with the dignified silence of Friar William but a torrent of miserable howls. Gwendolynn was dragged to the platform and manhandled by two papal swordsmen. Where William seemed to be steadying himself for the ordeal ahead, Gwendolynn was shrieking, fighting, swearing and spitting. No longer was she the image of the Holy Mother; now she was a wronged woman in all her fury: vitriolic and abject and rank. She managed to rip an arm free from one of the guards and launched herself at him, lashing out to scratch and gouge. The man cuffed her about the head with a gauntleted hand, knocking the resistance from her, and her scream became a whimper. She'd put on a good show; it wouldn't do her any good.

Lastly, Odenellus's acolyte Gibson of Wandylaw was brought to the platform. He was a large brute and, of the three accused, he alone was brought to the platform in iron fetters around his wrists and ankles. It was as Nastagio had said: the soldiers who had captured him had not been gentle. He had bruises and cuts and his thick, heavy beard was caked in dried blood. The papal archers pushed and dragged him roughly. Despite this, he had the self-possession to grin and even laugh at the absurdity of the situation—or perhaps he was just very simple and did not understand the dire situation he was in.

Nastagio watched the pathetic parade with a mixture of disgust and relish, then turned to me and said, 'It is time to get this wretched procedure over with,' as if he had no taste for these events.

As for me, I usually looked forward to heresy trials; they offered an opportunity to ensure that God's will on Earth was carried out faithfully and not abused. There is a sacred quality not just to innocence but to guilt; only in the acknowledgement and acceptance of their guilt can wrongdoers begin to correct their course and return to the path of righteousness and the Word of God. As instruments of truth, inquisitors therefore have an ecclesiastical obligation to identify the guilty. But I was not filled with enthusiasm now.

Nastagio stood in the centre of the stage and called for silence.

'In the name of the Lord, Amen. In the year from the Birth of the Lord 1367, on the twenty-third day of December, in the presence of these notaries and the witnesses presently declared, the visiting papal inquisitor Jacobus of the Sainted Order of Benedict, from the Bishopric of Vienna in the Holy Roman Empire, appeared in person before this honourable judge and offered to me an accusation to the following effect: that Friar William of Alnwick who resides in this parish of Berwick committed the unholy crimes of heretical idolatry and abetting heretical sorcery; and that this women called Gwendolynn of the tithing of Ord committed acts of heretical depravity and idolatry, and did willingly abet heretical sorcery; and that this man, Gibson of Wandylaw, committed acts of kidnap, murder, heretical idolatry, heretical depravity, and heretical sorcery.

'Before I begin, I will introduce myself to you. My name is Brother Nastagio di Balino, a holy inquisitor of the Church who has travelled from the Palais des Papes in Avignon, where until recently our Holy Father the Pope has resided. As the case before us is one of heresy, your honourable Bishop and Guardian Dionysius has recognised the special rights that I possess as a holy instrument of truth. I will therefore be acting with his full dispensation to conduct this trial as representative of the full authority of the Church and of God Himself on Earth.'

Nastagio waited for a response but there was only chilly silence. I half suspected that he was awaiting some form of dissent from the locals, so provocative had his introduction been, but apart from the soldiers stationed at the garrison, the vast majority of the common folk had no interest in matters of Church, state or war.

'Come, then, Jacobus. You must stand,' he said at last.

As I stood I caught sight of Magnus, standing at the opposite corner of the platform to me, alongside some of the Franciscans. He looked at me with great intensity, and I knew what he was silently imploring me to do.

> Do what is just.
> Save your soul.

'Brother Jacobus has, by making his accusation with total openness, accepted that if his testimony is proven to be false, or if he retracts it or refuses to cooperate in its delivery in any way, it will result in his suffering the penalty of retribution. Do you understand this, Jacobus?'

As I was about to speak, the strangest feeling came over me, as though God had reached down inside me and detached my spirit from my physical form. I felt somehow distanced from the proceedings, as if one part of me was a mere automaton responding to Nastagio while the other part was screaming out silently, trying to say what I wanted to think, trying to shout out that of course the demon was not real!—that how could it possibly be real? At the same time, I heard my automaton voice uttering the response that Nastagio wanted to hear—'I do'—which sounded sticky and unguent to my outraged self, as though covered in sap.

Nastagio pressed ahead with inquisitorial questions that were very familiar to me; but even though I knew the text word for word, they seemed stripped of the holy power they had when directed at others. Directed at me, they felt aggressive and alien.

Nastagio then called for the defendants to be brought to the stage, and to swear the Holy Oath upon the Gospels. Gwendolynn started to wriggle and struggle again, spitting and cursing and pleading, and singing forlorn lamentations, but in the end the papal archers forced her to swear upon the Book.

When Gibson was yanked to the stage and asked to swear, he swore—not the Holy Oath but foul obscenities—and when the crowd gasped and jeered at him, he laughed at them. At this, Nastagio had a quiet word with one of the archers, who promptly strode over to the man, grasped one of Gibson's fettered hands and yanked a finger into breaking. I heard the brittle crack from my seat and winced, and the crowd cheered as he howled in pain. Accepting his subjugation, he swore the Holy Oath but with such sourness of tongue and hatred in his eyes, it felt as though he had sworn nothing at all except vengeance upon Nastagio and all the players of this circus.

William did not stoop to such histrionics. He maintained his stubborn quiet, staring blankly ahead, and kept his responses brief. Even now I could not believe he was a heretic, an abettor and an idolator. My doubts about William had stuck at the back of my throat for the whole week.

As for my doubts about the Green Man, these were equally hard to swallow.

Nastagio's barking voice snapped me from my reverie. 'Brother Jacobus, do you know these persons?'

'I do.'

'And what is the reason for your knowledge of these charges?'

'I have been in this parish for two months and was at close quarters with Friar William in the course of an investigation I was undertaking. In that time we spoke at length on various subjects. As for the woman, I have met her on a few occasions and spoken with her, and she openly admitted to have committed acts of depravity that have caused harm to her children and desecrated the sanctity of certain holy sacraments.

'As for that man, he attacked me in the wood and left me for dead.'

'Tell us, then, what did you see and hear? Exclude no detail.'

I related once again the things I had witnessed: Gwendolynn's children, their burial, the wolf, the Scots, the trial, the encounter with Odenellus and his men, and finally the Green Man, the last of which elicited gasps and shrieks from some of the onlookers.

'Quiet!' snapped Nastagio to the crowd. 'In whose presence, Jacobus? Which witnesses will bear out your story?'

'There are several who saw the blessing of the wolf, including Sir Walesby and his men. The villagers of Ord saw the incident involving the heathen burial and its consequences. As for that man, there were two others with him as he attacked me in the wood, but I understand they are now dead.'

'And what about this Green Man?'

I wanted to be able to answer more fully but could only shake my head and murmur, 'I alone saw it.'

And that was it! He moved on, asking the usual procedural questions about relations with sorcerers and whether the actions of the defendants were made in jest or mimicry. I answered all of them truthfully. And then he came to the final question.

'Do you make your accusations about these matters through any hatred or grudge, or through love or bias?'

At this question I faltered. For a moment I was reminded of Serge, the tatterdemalion whose manhood had been sliced off back in Italy, and how I had undone him when this question had been asked of him. Now it was my turn to answer the question, I found to my great shock that I did not know the answer. Was I biased?

'I ...'

Nastagio gave me a look of sourness at my hesitation. 'Well, Brother Jacobus? How do you reply?'

'Nastagio, we have always done this work. How can we ascertain the question about bias? I carry it with me, though not in a satchel I can easily put down by the side of the road to lighten my load. My biases are in me, they are in everyone, and without them I might be lost.'

'The trial demands an answer, Jacobus! This is no place for philosophy.'

'I am biased both for and against this accusation, Nastagio! I wish, more than anything, that this demon I saw had not been real. I wish it with all my heart. If I follow my scholastic bias and deny what I saw, I sin, and heretics may go free! Yet if I follow the bias of my faith, and admit that the monster is real and the work of unholy conjuration, my work is undone and false, and innocent people may be punished.'

Nastagio let out a frustrated laugh and waggled his finger at me. 'You risk undoing yourself, Jacobus. You have accused these people of heresy, and now you are on the cusp of a retraction! Do you remember the penalty of retribution for a retraction?'

'I do; I have sworn the oath.'

'Then do you make this accusation through some bias or not?'

'Only God knows the truth.'

'And I am the instrument of truth in this place and you will give me an answer!'

'I cannot!'

'You will answer!'

'No!'

'Gah!' Nastagio turned away in disgust. William and Gwendolynn were looking at me with a mixture of horror and confusion. Doubtless both had concluded that I was just another inquisitor, hell-bent on proving heresy at any cost. And yet, in the throes of my doubts, perhaps even they did not know what to make of me. The crowd also looked at me with bemusement. I was as shaky and faint as any of them.

Nastagio turned round and drew near, looking at me with undisguised contempt. He ached for a conviction. He was doing God's work, and now he had his teeth into me, he wasn't going to let his victory be taken away by a Benedictine in an existential crisis. And I was hardly trying to obstruct him, merely trying to articulate the truth. But even as I saw his distaste for me written on his face, I could see that he was formulating another approach.

'You have already admitted that you saw the demon, is that correct?' he said.

'I did.'

'And you have also said that you wished that you had not seen it. And yet it appeared! The facts are plain; in making the demon appear before a man of God, God Himself willed it. Yes, it is true. For demons, despite their abilities to interfere in human affairs, are only permitted to interfere through the infinite grace of God. You saw it because you were meant to see it, despite all your misgivings! And so it is in spite of your biases that you bring this accusation. Because, even though you purport to be a man of natural philosophy, you are firstly a man of God. Are you biased against God?'

I winced at the very thought of it and, when I spoke, I sounded weak and defeated. 'Of course not.'

Murmurs cascaded through the gathering, though none of the defendants let their expressions slip.

'Then we shall break from these proceedings and continue with the questioning of the defendants.'

TERCE

Nastagio approached Gwendolynn first. She stood upon the platform, held tightly by papal guards who had bound both her arms behind her back. During my questioning she had gone quiet, hanging onto my words, unsure which way my testimony would fall. Now that it was her turn to be interrogated by Nastagio she wriggled and shrieked once more, calling for her children.

Nastagio gently shushed her, and held out a placating hand, though he took pains not to actually touch her. 'Take care, child,' he said in his gentlest voice. 'You must be calm and take control of yourself. It will not go well for you if you do not. The accusations are serious. God commands you to give a proper account of yourself. You have sworn to provide testimony before God!'

For a moment, she was indeed able to master herself. In fact she was even able to look at Nastagio with a sort of longing, even adoration. I knew the thought process of the accused: after a week or more of incarceration, perhaps in filthy conditions, the sight of a holy man dressed in a splendid gown and habit represented a chance of salvation and rescue. Under such duress the accused would fling themselves onto him and tell him exactly what he wanted to hear, even if it meant their own condemnation.

Gwendolynn, trembling but pliant, swore her oath upon the Gospels and answered the basic questions, confirming her name and her parents' names and dates of death. Then Nastagio began the main line of questioning.

'Do you believe that demons exist?'

She made a humming sound with a forlorn look upon her face, looked away and winced.

'Do you believe it, woman? What do you say? Answer with honesty!'

'What would you have me say, Father? I believe the forest will have its share. That's what Odenellus said. If you believe that the Green Man is a demon then I will say it is so. Is that what you need to hear?'

'You took what Odenellus said? A man who by his own admission was a pagan sorcerer and who sought to consort with this Green Man demon? You lived by this man's counsel?'

'I did.'

'Do you believe what this Odenellus said?'

'I did.' She began to wail quite loudly now.

'And what did he say? That the demon lived in the forest?'

'No, Father, he said that the Green Man *was* the forest—all of it, all the grass, the trees … .'

'So you made an idol of the forest?'

'I don't understand, Father–'

'You led your living children there, to the forest, to this demon god, as a gift, to be buried in a shallow grave?'

'I—'

'And there was no conveyance to a church or holy place, there was no administering of blessed waters, no reading of the Psalms, no Holy man present, no absolution of the dead or Sacrament of Extreme Unction, and no candles to burn away their sins and keep aflame a vigil? No recital of the *Dies Irae*?'

'No, how could I—'

'To deny a soul the chance to complete the ritual of absolution and return to the arms of our loving Father is obscene. But to do it to one's own children! Only a demon or its conjurer could twist a mother to do such a thing. I have seen many things over the years, but this is as wicked as anything I have ever heard. This is idolatry at its most monstrous! Did you do these things, Gwendolynn?'

By now Gwendolynn was losing the calm which Nastagio had induced into her at the start of the interrogation and relapsing into a state of feverish trauma. Her breath became quick and harsh and her face creased into an ugly, blotchy ache as she struggled to articulate the contradictions within her. 'But they came back, Father! How could I have condemned them to the earth when they still live?'

'You laid them down because you meant to appease this demon of the forest! You buried them intentionally! If they came back, that is a separate matter! I speak of what you intended. Confirm that this was your intent!'

'Yes, I did! In the hope that the Man would grant peace upon us and leave us be.' At last she had buckled. I let out a long sigh. There had been no hope for her to escape the interrogation or prove her innocence. She should never have listened to Odenellus. He had offered her an expedient solution rather than the right solution of walking with God, and now she had to pay. Even so, I felt sorry for her and prayed for her.

'So you admit it!' said Nastagio, with bitter triumph. 'Such is the power and influence of demons, especially over weak women, that it can persuade and seduce them to make offerings even of their own children—'

'I thought it would save us, Father! You must understand! After everything that happened here, the children being given the Mark on their foreheads, and all the bad luck that befell this place, we prayed and prayed but God seemed to take no heed, see, and when Odenellus said that it was the forest, I gave 'em up, my own flesh, Father

—my own flesh! Like Him who sent His Son to die for our sins on the Cross and in such horrible pain, as Friar William tells us, I gave 'em up and put their beautiful faces in the cold earth to save us! And then my babies, my lovely babies, they come back, they was risen, just like Him! They have come to save me …' and she fell into a wailing, incomprehensible lamentation, crying out to God, and to her children, and to anyone else who would listen.

'Woman, listen to me. Get up from your knees and answer me truly. Did you, for such time as is relevant, partake in the heresies of witches and sorceresses?'

Gwendolynn fell back down to her knees again and held out her hands as though in supplication, and wailed an almost incoherent 'Yes'.

'And did you commit the disgraceful acts that have been described here today in this procedure?'

Another wail of 'Yes.'

And it was over for her. Nastagio gestured to the swordsmen to take her from the platform and then he turned to William. William's pale face stared blankly into the distance but his jaw was clenched in an expression of miserable, trembling defiance. Occasionally I would see his lips flutter in the utterance of some desperate prayer.

'What is your name?' Nastagio asked him.

'William of Alnwick.' Still he did not cast a single glance to the inquisitor.

'Give me the name of your parents, living or dead.'

'My mother was Hilda, and she is dead, Inquisitor, and my father was Eadred, who also is dead.'

'Did they die a natural death?'

'My mother, aye, she did. My father died of plague, Brother, fifteen years ago.'

Nastagio paused, allowing the notary to write down the details, and sipped his wine.

'Do you believe that sorcerers exist and that such things as have been reported can happen?'

'That depends on your definition of sorcerer.'

'My definition is that which is accepted by the One True Catholic Church!'

That snapped William out of his empty stare, and he locked his eyes onto the inquisitor, at once present and awake. 'Is that where the definition ends, Inquisitor? Or is it left so vague that it is used to ensnare those you consider to be troublesome, eccentric, different or otherwise undesirable? Is that why I have been accused of sorcery by the Benedictine monk—?'

'You are accused of heretical idolatry and the abetting of sorcery. Do not conflate the two. Do not attempt to mislead me into the thorns of questioning the legal suppositions that the accusations are based on.'

'Then, being a faithful servant of that same Church, I accept the definition. And yes,' he continued, glancing at the egregious Gibson of Wandylaw. 'I do accept that such sorcerers may exist.'

'And do you believe, then, in the demons with which they consort?'

'I will say again, Inquisitor: that depends upon your definition of demon!'

'I have heard these defensive counter-questions from many heretics in my travels but never in England,' said Nastagio with a thin smile. 'But it shows that those who have strayed from the one true path of the Church and into the despoiled wilderness of corruption do, predictably, take cover behind the same defence: that of petty semantics and word stew. The definition of demon is clear: a lesser god or idol who indulges in and champions heathen practices. One who seeks to divide, as opposed to God, who seeks to unite.'

'Scripture offers no such definition. Christ our Saviour drove out many demons from the people—men, women, children—even driving them into swine so they would drown themselves in the river; he also gave the apostles the authority to do the same. And in John's vision of the end of all things he mentioned the spirits of demons able to perform miracles. But he didn't describe the demon itself. Is it a physical beast that you or I can see and touch, as real as a frog or a cat or a wolf? Or is it an invisible thing that we may sense, like the wind, but cannot see? Is it a dark, sinful aspect of human nature that cannot be fully extinguished but only tamed through following the Light of the Lord? Or is it a blank page on which we picture the things we do not understand: our deepest, most shameful urges, excusing ourselves from our own ignorance?'

William looked directly at me when uttering these last few words and a sick feeling of guilt grew within me. He accused me with his eyes and in spite of everything I knew and all that I had seen, the gaze punctured me like a knife stuck into a bladder. I felt hot enmity for these feelings: why should I feel useless, I who was doing Godly work by enlightening the world through the expansion of human knowledge? And yet the feeling of guilt was there nonetheless, wrapping its ivy tendrils around my insides, stabbing me with its thorns, and encasing my heart in a trunk of wood.

'I have evidently not answered the question to your satisfaction, Inquisitor,' William went on. 'The fact is, there is no such definition in Scripture.' Then he looked at me once more. 'But, yes, demons do exist. I find they are everywhere. And they are seductive.'

'And they can make men, even Holy Men, err from the path of the Church,' responded Nastagio. 'Do you deny your blessing of the wolf, an idolatrous act?'

'I do not deny administering a blessing of thanks to a creature of God, which was forced to give up its life, Inquisitor.'

'Hah! Do you see how he frames his response! He admits to the act itself, because its occurrence is irrefutable, but he calls it a blessing of thanks, and so implicitly denies that this was an idolatrous act.'

'It was not idolatry. The wolf was one of God's creatures, and as much a part of this world as you or I. It lived and it died—'

'Again you admit to the act, and such an act is plainly idolatrous! And why did you undertake this act?'

'Because it was forced to give up its life, as I have said.'

'No, no, no, no, no. You do not administer a blessing to every bee, leech and chicken that gives up its life because of human activity. Why, then, this wolf? Brother Jacobus told me of your opinion that you believe there is a form of divinity in the forests beyond the town, and in its creatures. And not just wolves but the demon whose presence Jacobus has already attested to under oath, and which you have just admitted must exist in one form or another.'

'The Green Man is an emblem, an ancient symbol of England's forests. It is a sign of fertility and of the great depths of our land. And, yes, it also symbolises the natural world's potential for chaos and malevolence.'

'One that is worthy of adoration, to the extent of

blessings, it seems. We have been told that you teach the poor folk to love the forest, to love everything in it, and to pay heed to it. The Man will have his share!'

At this, Gibson of Wandylaw began to laugh and shout. 'The Man will have his share! The Man will have his share,' he called; 'You'll see, you all will see!' He no doubt would have continued in this vein had not one of the papal archers thumped him in the stomach with a gauntleted fist. As Gibson bent double and retched, the crowd taunted him anew.

'Enough!' barked Nastagio. 'The imbecile merely proves my point. Many of your small folk say this. It does not sound like a blank page to me. It sounds like something malignant. But this is not the word of God. This is not the teaching of Christ. So I ask you: do you deny that all this depravity is done in the service of this demon of the forest?'

William shook his head disdainfully. 'You do not understand this place at all. I have done no wrong here. I have only ever followed the Light of Christ and the Lord Father.' Then William turned his gaze away from Nastagio and toward me, and I saw tears in his eyes. 'And you, Brother Jacobus, who came to help us, and came to understand: you leave as ignorant as we are. Will you confess also?'

I almost opened my mouth to answer him, but was cut off by Nastagio. 'He is not accused, Friar.'

'Maybe not by men,' replied William with a grimace. 'What of it then, Jacobus? Will you confess to your own ignorance?'

'Do not attempt to turn scrutiny from yourself!' cried Nastagio. 'Do you confess? It is you who are under accusation! Do you confess? Well, do you?'

'I confess to no sin other than being a sinner, as are all men!'

'Why do you persist with this sophistry when you have already seen the woman confess and when we know that your acts are confirmed because of the testimony of others?' Nastagio approached William, almost close enough to kiss him. 'In truth, Friar, I pity you. You delude only yourself with your simple deceits. I can see you are racked with guilt to a greater or lesser degree. But the creature that instructed you and holds you in its thrall is fully guilty. Do not take that creature's foul sin as your own, nor perpetuate the illusion of your freedom of will; you were no master of your fate but merely a disciple to this monster!' By now Nastagio's voice was cold, low and filled with cunning guile. 'Tell me the truth. You can see that I know everything about this episode. Everybody knows. Unburden yourself.'

A frozen silence hung in the air as we awaited the confession that would end this grotesque affair. Had William learned from the charade of the Scottish trial, where Anya had spared the lives and souls of herself and her clansman Donal by admitting to the accusation? All inquisitors used tricks in their zeal for persecution; could the accused not do the same for their defence?

Confess! I implored him silently. Confess, and save yourself!

William looked at Nastagio with watery, bloodshot eyes and opened his mouth to speak. But when he spoke, he looked at me and I could not look away, as though he had frozen me in place by some awful magic. He recited aloud those same lines from the One-Hundred-and-Fourth Psalm that he had uttered over the body of the wretched canine shot by two arrows in the forest. 'Oh

Lord, how manifold are your works! In wisdom you have made them all, the Earth is full of your creatures … .'

'Confess, man, and it will be easier for you!'

'… This great and wide sea, in which are innumerable things. There the ships sail about, and there is the Leviathan, which you have made … .'

'Do you see, everyone! The heretic often will make recourse to Scripture in the moment of his reckoning. But God will know his own. Friar William, I give you one last chance to confess!'

'… You open Your hand, they are filled with good. You hide Your face, they are troubled. You take away their breath, they die and return to dust … .'

I realised that William's prayer of soft rejoicing was not said in defiance but in resignation, and my heart crumbled. In that moment I could almost hear the voice of God answering the Psalm, calling out to William on the bitter English wind and saying, Foolish child, seek forgiveness for your transgressions, minor as they are, and realign yourself with the Light!

But was God was speaking to William or to me?

SEXT

William did not confess. How I wished I could go to him, confess my own foolishness and implore him to confess so that me might only invoke a minor punishment! But I could not. I was bound by procedural protocols and was not allowed to interfere with the accused, now that the denunciation had taken place. As it was, I remained, as I had done for much of that week, alone, and sat through the final questioning in a state of fevered anxiety.

Gibson of Wandylaw was hardly able to understand Nastagio's questions, let alone defend himself. The brute answered only the most basic procedural questions, and when it came to the meat of the examination, he lost all coherence.

'You will see!' he cried, when Nastagio asked him about summoning the demon of the forest. 'The Man will have his share! He is hungry, and he will eat your children and fill 'em with soil and flowers!'

The crowd jeered at him again, and threw stones at him, and he shouted back at them. More than once Nastagio shouted and had to rely on force to gather control of the farce. The more this went on, the lower my heart sank. I realised that not only would this testimony not save William, it could very well condemn him.

'Did you, with your deceased counterparts, summon this demon of the wood or make it appear?' asked Nastagio, losing his patience. 'And I recommend that you give me a clear answer.'

'No, no, no, no, no,' said Gibson. 'Oh no: never, never, never.'

'But we have seen testimony from a man of God—an inquisitor—that the demon has been seen in the wood. And yet you deny it! So I ask again, did you make this Green Man, this monster, appear?'

Gibson laughed, a crunching hack of a laugh, showing no more than a couple of jagged brown teeth in his open mouth. 'He was always there. He was there before Adam; he'll be there long after he's eaten us all up. Odenellus told us we had to give him what he wanted—we had to or the wood goes bad. That's why we took 'em, see, them bairns!'

This brought more screams and shouts from the

crowd. When they had been hushed once more, Nastagio resumed his questioning.

'So you admit it. You engaged in heretical depravities: the unholy sacrifice of innocent children.'

'Yes, we done it! We done 'em and we took 'em and we buried 'em, and some of 'em he brought back, as is his way!'

'So you admit that you did these things in the service of the demon of the wood.'

'It en't no demon, it is the wood!'

'Do you see, once more, the attempt to deflect the accusation on technical or linguistic discrepancies?' cried Nastagio. 'Either way it is idolatry! But we have heard an affirmation that this creature—this demon—of the wood has been appeased and serviced by this man—'

'He'll come and get you!' cried Gibson.

'Be quite, simpleton!'

The crowd became restive again.

'He'll come and get you and your bairns!'

'Gibson of Wandylaw—'

'He will! You'll see.'

'Gibson of Wandylaw, do you renounce the demon of the wood and take shelter from its wickedness in the bosom of the One True Church?'

'The Man will have his share!'

'Do you vow to turn your face back toward the light of the Lord and accept the just punishment for your crimes?'

'The Man will have his share!'

By now the crowd were once more agitated, and again threw missiles at him, as well as at the other defendants in the trial. A fresh gesture from Nastagio sent the papal archer over to Gibson again, socking him in the mouth so hard there was another brutal crunch. The man went limp, kept upright only by the guards.

'Quite so,' said Nastagio. 'Now let us bring an end to this unseemly charade.'

During the break in proceedings Nastagio called the men of learning together around their small table to discuss the matter in greater length. In the many inquisitorial trials I had supported I had always had the ear of the judge or been the judge myself. For the first time I was sidelined.

I sat alone and listened to the sibilant discussion across the way. Albertus made various points, jabbing the table with a thick forefinger as he muttered something about suffering which I could not quite catch. Occasionally he would fling a reproachful glance in my direction before returning to the debate.

The other cleric, Father Arthuis, looked pale and said little, preferring to finger through the papers in front of him and reading from the Vulgate. He did not have the stomach to challenge Nastagio—perhaps because, as a cleric, he had heard of the powers and reach of the Inquisition throughout the Empire. Albertus had no such qualms but I suspected that his advocacy for William and Gwendolynn would be in vain, however impassioned. Sure enough, he eventually banged the table, stood up and stomped away, shaking his head. The irony did not escape me that in any other trial like this, I would probably be acting like Albertus, arguing against Nastagio, especially on such charges as the worship of a demon in the forest.

The friary's lone bell by the sea tolled Sext and Nastagio called for a break of fifteen minutes to observe the hour. He allowed Father Arthuis to stand in front of the totem to Nehushtan and lead the prayer of *Deus in adjutorium*. I left the platform and knelt in the freezing mud and observed the ritual.

Ora et labora.

The prayer did not have its usual cleansing effect. I took up my spot upon the platform again, silent and ineffective, and waited. When Nastagio returned, the two defendants were brought once more before him.

'The time has come to pass judgement,' Nastagio said. 'Gwendolynn of Ord, you have confessed to committing grave and despicable crimes against the Lord and against your very own children—for the Lord, Granter of Mercy, gives His flock the freedom to err, and thus, on occasion, some do fall prey to the predatory and beguiling errors of heresy. But I have found, through an examination of these acts and their circumstances, that, in accordance with the advice given, you flew back into the embrace of the Mother Church and her Unity and confessed, in consequence of which you may receive the benefit of Absolution, to which end you will be brought before the local congregation on a Christian Feast Day and you will be addressed by the cleric of that parish, and where, before your community, you shall once more confess to the crimes and acts of heresy that you have committed. Only then shall you be abjured. Until such a feast day occur, you shall be handed to the secular arm to be imprisoned and given only bread and foul water for consumption, so that you may reflect upon your crimes against God. Once you are handed to the secular arm there shall be no impediment to their undertakings.'

Gwendolynn smiled with tears in her eyes and started to laugh, a wet sob of pure relief. 'Sir, but the next Feast

Day is for the Birth of Our Lord, only two days hence! I shall only be jailed for two days?'

'You are indeed fortunate, woman,' said Nastagio. 'Only two days, provided that you do not relapse into the foul ways of the heretic. I shall ensure that the secular arm is unimpeded in watching you for such actions.'

'I shall not! I shall not! I am a humble vessel of the Lord, and shall keep him in my heart always and kneel at His altar as the Church says! You are merciful! Thank you.'

Nastagio gestured to Hayeford, who in turn signalled to his men-at-arms to take Gwendolynn away.

Nastagio then turned to Gibson of Wandylaw. The idiot had been revived with strong herbal scents and made to stand to receive his judgement. 'We, the judge and jurists and men of good standing within this community, find that you are guilty of the charges brought about by the denunciation. You have undertaken the most foul heretical practices, abetted in the practice of heretical sorcery, and subjugated yourself to the service of a demon of your own conjuration, and wrought havoc among the local community, spreading fear and lies and implanting ideas about the false worship of this demon. You have shown no remorse, and no willingness to return to the bosom of the Church and the loving embrace of the Almighty Father for what time remains for you on this earth. It is my judgement that the only fitting punishment is to have you burned until you are ashes.'

For a moment Gibson's crude, mashed face showed little evidence of his comprehension of the sentence, but then his face slowly creased into what I thought would be a rictus of terror. I had seen it many times: just the mention of the flame cracks open the tightest of chests.

He opened his mouth but, to my horror, he did not let out a moan or a scream or a plea for clemency but began to laugh. Quietly at first, but soon it was a torrent, a vomit of hysteria rushing free from a soul that had been poisoned so long ago by wicked forces beyond his understanding.

'Take him away,' said Nastagio, bitterly.

The archers dragged the pitiful fool away and Nastagio at last turned to William. 'We, the judge and jurists and men of good standing within this community, after a careful examination of the proceedings, find that you are not satisfactorily consistent with your confession given that there are various indications of the deed. You will therefore be handed to Lord de Hayeford as this trial's representative of the local secular arm, and exposed to an interrogation, so that the truth will be derived from you and these lies will no longer sour the ears of this community. The day before the interrogation commences, you shall be shown the implements of torture. When you are not under interrogation you are to be held in harsh imprisonment, in fetters and an iron collar. If, during interrogation, you do not take the opportunity to revoke your silence and fly back to our embrace, things will continue to be dire for you. The secular arm must be reminded that the interrogation must not draw blood. If you invoke silence by sorcery, you will be given a special blessing to banish the demonic spirit and be delivered from the Ancient Serpent, and if even then you refuse to utter a confession, you shall be interred in prison for a full year, or until such time that you confess to your crimes. If even then you do not confess, there will be no remaining option for you but to be burned until you are ashes.'

Nastagio's pronouncement brought gasps and shouts of dissent. William emitted a guttural, inhuman roar. Whether it was of pain, terror or wrath I cannot say. Guardian Dionysius stood up and shouted sternly at the inquisitor, 'This is a scandal! We do not torture and burn people for such things in England! There is no law of this land that says we must comply.'

'This is an ecclesiastical, inquisitorial trial, Guardian,' countered Nastagio, 'And is being conducted under the jurisdiction of the Inquisition by order of the Papal See, which, I should not have to remind you, carries with it special dispensation to root out the stink of heresy wherever it should fester. As inquisitor any sentence I pass is thus legally binding under the statutes passed by Frederick II of the Holy Catholic Church under which you and your Order still apparently serve.'

Dionysius looked at me in utter dismay. One of the key tools in the inquisitor's arsenal was a comprehensive knowledge of the legal details relating to inquisitorial matters. In trials conducted throughout the Empire, particularly in backwater areas, such knowledge would usually extinguish any dissent, given that the local population was unlikely to have any corresponding expertise. In England, where the papal decree would have been at best subject to local interpretation, this seemed all the more effective a weapon. It was with some sourness that I acknowledged Nastagio's knowledge of holy law far outweighed his learning of the laws of nature.

'Lord de Hayeford,' cried the Guardian, fluttering to the gallery. 'What of the King's Law? The Law of the Land? Surely you cannot let this sentence stand.'

Hayeford grimaced. 'The King would not make an enemy of the Church.'

'The Church! We are the Church!' spluttered the Guardian. 'Are we not as one?'

'Yes!' cried Nastagio. 'We are. And one of our own has strayed from your flock. Believe me when I say I grieve for his soul, and I am sorry to impose such stringent terms to secure a confession, but it must be done. Ecumenical harmony must be maintained. Heresy must always be purged.'

'Lord de Hayeford, please,' said the Guardian. 'This is a man of your people. He has helped your common folk with alms and charity and prayer. Ask the inquisitor to excommunicate him if he must, but do not take this good man's life.'

Hayeford looked pained by the thought and gave a half-hearted response. 'You will understand, Guardian. I have men to supply to the king in the war against the French crown. It would not be prudent to open up new wounds.'

'And what of wounds caused by torture and burning?' cried the Guardian. 'What of them?'

'It is done, Guardian,' said Nastagio. 'Come, it is almost time to observe the mid-afternoon prayer. We should leave.'

By now several people in the crowd were heckling those involved in the trial. Some laughed and spat at William, hurling insults his way, while others implored him to confess and save himself. Others in the crowd acted likewise towards Dionysius, Nastagio and Hayeford, whose knights bristled with threat, their mailed fists tightening around their pikes and halberds.

Much of the crowd's vitriol was aimed at me. Like Nastagio I was an outsider, a foreigner who had come to solve a problem. To some, I had accomplished that feat but at a catastrophic cost, and resentment and hatred were written plainly on their faces. I stood at the edge of the dais, feeling no relief or deliverance, and possessing no desire to return to my books, which had always been a place of refuge for me. Instead, that part of my mind with the capacity for calculation was busily at work. Nastagio's sentence carried the potential for the full brutality of Holy retribution, but it also contained the potential for salvation and life. William still had the chance to confess. Nastagio had permitted a window of opportunity for, if not acquittal, then confession and clemency. I could still save him!

William, for his part, had heard the inquisitor pass sentence, which experience has taught me is often more terrifying than the interrogation itself, and designed to be so by the inquisitor, to induce a confession before even the first fetter is clamped around the prisoner's wrist. He now stood in forlorn and silent resignation. I knew then that, left to his own devices, he would never confess; he thought his acts had been harmless enough—and the human heart is surprisingly strong when it believes itself to be in the right, even when it has been shown to be utterly wrong. Indeed, I have seen people, upon having their views disproved by the facts, become even more certain in their beliefs.

How well I have learned that lesson now!

25th December

In which Haye-ford Castle celebrates the Nativity Feast and I break an agreement

TERCE

I left the trial feeling as though I was the one accused. The sense of shame and guilt—of sin—throbbed in my guts as I made my way to Hayeford Castle. I could have stayed at Berwick Friary and though part of me wanted to, both Hayeford and Nastagio advised me not to, saying I would be safer inside the castle's walls. Being unwilling to stay in Berwick, Magnus also journeyed there, though he was markedly frostier towards me in the days that followed, as if in mourning. Nastagio and I stayed at the discretion of Lord Hayeford—a situation that had doubtless been secured by Nastagio—and so it happened that the inquisitor, the accuser, the condemned, the incarcerated and the abjured all found themselves, perversely, housed under the same roof.

During the Eve of the Cristesmaesse festival, Hayeford's seneschal, Thirlwall, barked at the cooks to prepare for the feasting that would bring the austerity of Advent to an end, and yapped at the lackeys to lug the Yule Log to the hearth in the Great Hall and hang holly and ivy from the rafters but their efforts were grudging and the castle continued to seem dour and bleak and doom-laden. Usually, at this time of year, large houses would invite guests to share in the celebrations. Lord de Hayeford's few guests were as austere as he was, and his castle remained chilly and remote. I ventured round the place like a rodent, keeping to the shadows and avoiding the gaze of those who knew me. Thankfully, the miserable workload of the staff meant they had little time to fraternise with me, and so I was on the whole left alone. As well as being to my preference, this allowed me to visit the dungeons without being observed.

The jailor was the same grotesque hunchback I had

encountered when I had visited Black Anya of Dunbar. Down here, where the stone was beaded with cold sweat and the air was burned by the acid of fear and effluence, the world stopped, penning its occupants in an endless, hopeless knot of time, their only company the hideous jailor and their own distressed emotions. That seemed to be just the way he liked it, judging by the inane grin that spread across his spiteful little face when I asked to see the prisoners.

'I 'member 'ee,' he said in a voice that sounded as though it had been burned into ashes. 'Come 'a see the pets?'

'I wish to see Friar William.'

'Uh, uh, uh, uh,' said, shaking his head like an infant. 'Not allowed.'

I did not press the point. 'Will you be at the feast tomorrow?'

The jailor grinned and nodded. 'Even ol' Bastereau—that's me—gets a cup o' wine tomorrow. But t'other guards'll be here. So don't try nowt!' And with that, he nodded to his bell-pull, set into the wall in case he needed to ring for assistance.

That settled it. The following morning, when Bastereau the jailor was away from his post to enjoy what few scraps and crumbs Hayeford permitted him for the feast, I crept to the dungeon. Sure enough, there was a guard posted, one of more sound temperament, as I assumed. This was to my advantage, as I would not have been able to bribe or inveigle the usual dolt, who had but one job: to allow no one to pass who was not authorised, and to ring the bell like a demon if anyone tried. It would have been too risky to try bribing him.

The new guard possessed a more rational mind, and when I descended the stairs to the dungeon and walked up to him, he looked at me with weary resignation. 'The inquisitor, Brother Nastagio, said you were not supposed to be down here, Brother Jacobus.'

I produced a paper-wrapped package containing two bottles of beer, some strips of good, dried meat I had procured from the kitchens, and a small bag containing a gold noble and some silver pennies. He took the package from me with a look of disapproval and stuffed it into the leather pack by his footstool.

'Twenty minutes, Brother.'

'Bless you, my son,' I said, and bustled along the corridor, the guard at my rear, fumbling for the keys.

I peered into the first cell and saw the pathetic figure of Gwendolynn lying on her side on the floor. By her feet, black with muck, was a water bowl and a dish containing a crust of moulding bread. Her back was to me and I presumed she was asleep. I said a short and silent prayer for her, beseeching her not to say or do anything untoward, for she would be released tomorrow and, pending an abjuration before the community, would be back in the arms of her children before sundown. Perhaps she and they, poor lambs, would be able to heal.

The next cell was empty. I looked back at the guard. 'Gibson of Wandylaw is not being kept here?'

'He is in the interrogation chamber, further on. You don't want to go in there.'

I shuddered, and kept walking. There was no need to interrogate the idiot of a criminal, as he had uttered a remorseless confession at trial. However, in my experience, that did not always prevent the inquisitor from prolonging the guilty party's earthly retribution, even when condemned.

The third cell was my destination. I peered into the

gloom and saw Friar William, sitting with his back against one of the walls, quite awake. The jangle of the jailor's keys made him flick his eyes toward me, whether in fear or hope I do not know, but when he saw who it was, the look of anticipation faded and he resumed his focus on the opposite wall.

Thanking the guard with a nod, I stepped in and regarded him. He continued to stare straight ahead, not casting the merest glance at me. To my relief, he had not been treated roughly so far. He was naked save for a cloth around his hips, and was covered in sweat and dirt, but seemed uninjured save for the angry chafes around his wrists and ankles. His cup of water had been left untouched, and so had his crust of bread. Upon inspection, this may have been for the best, for it looked brown and of ill-omen.

'William,' I said, softly.

He remained silent, so I muttered under my breath and went over to the water bowl. 'You were wise not to touch this water. Here,' I said, tipping it away in the corner and setting the bowl back down. 'I have brought clean water from the spring.'

After I poured the clear water from the pouch that I had secreted beneath my robe, I saw him glance at it. Good, I thought. He will probably drink it. I left another packet of dried meat wrapped up next to the bowl. Then I paused, wondering what best I could say. When I finally said the only thing that could possibly mean anything to him, it sounded cold and stilted.

'William, about the denunciation. I am filled with remorse.'

Still he stared at the wall, saying nothing.

'William. Truly I am. I was threatened with the white

sheet, with excommunication! I was frightened, and in my fear I told Nastagio everything I knew. I did not think that he would push things so far.'

Still nothing.

'I understand if you will not talk with me. But if you will not unseal your lips, at least open your ears. Nastagio is no brute. The sentence may have carried the ring of flame and ashes but it also contained a window for absolution! He is, as he says, only interested in the well functioning of the Church. His great desire is for you to walk back into his tender embrace.'

Still no response. I sighed heavily, paused, then tried again.

'It looks as though you have suffered no ill-treatment so far. That is good: it shows Nastagio has instructed the guards to treat you well. I have no doubt no one will lay a hand upon you if you simply confess to the crime.'

At that moment he snapped his head towards me and spoke with unfettered contempt. 'I have committed no crime, brother.'

The sudden bark of words made me jump, but I settled myself and knelt upon the cold stone. With hands enjoined I implored him, 'Please, William. This is the endgame: confess, and it is over. You will return to the Church, Nastagio and I will leave for France, Gwendolynn will be reunited with her little ones and it will be done and finished. All you must do is confess!'

'Confess? To what? I have committed no crime!'

'William, you saw how it was with Donal and Black Anya of Dunbar: yes, there was a confection at play, but did not everyone walk away alive?'

'Is that how it has to be, Jacobus? That for all the world to function properly all we must do is pronounce our guilt for crimes that were never committed? You are the Inquisition, Jacobus—you are not God.

'Repent, not to me—I will do my penance—'

'You will do your penance in the far-off sunshine of France.'

'I will do my penance,' I said, irritably. 'Repent, save yourself.'

'I will not repent. It is as the Dominican said: God will know whose hearts are truly His.'

I stood up, crestfallen, on the verge of weeping.

'Will you at least drink the clean water and eat the food I have brought you?' I said in a broken voice.

He made a face, implying he was considering it. 'I will drink the clean water and eat the meat, not for your sake, but for the sake of the Cristesmaesse festival, and the friendship I thought we once had.'

I walked to the gate, feeling light-headed and defeated. 'I have not given up on you, William of Alnwick. I shall return.'

SEXT

'You really are a sanctimonious fool, Jacobus,' said Nastagio, accosting me as I left the castle chapel for Sext prayers. He walked with me across the courtyard and towards the dormitories, wearing a look that combined disgust with amusement.

'Me?'

'Would you really corrupt the integrity of the inquisitorial procedure to salve your own conscience? Oh, do not look so confused Jacobus. I know you visited the Franciscan this morning in his cell to convince him to confess.'

'That blessed guard!' I muttered quietly. 'He snitched.'

Nastagio let out an amused chuckle. 'No, the guard played his part well and did not betray your confidence. I even let him keep the beer and meat, it being Cristesmaesse. It was William of Alnwick who told me.'

I stopped walking. Around us castle staff fussed and hurried, bringing gifts, food and wine from this place to that. More than once we were pushed out of the way with a few choice English epithets. 'William told you?'

'Not long after you left he called for the guard, and asked to see me. I assumed he was going to confess. Instead he told me of your clandestine visit. Is there no incident you cannot turn into a conspiracy, Jacobus? You are forbidden from seeing him again while the interrogation proceedings are ongoing.'

'Interrogation? He looked unharmed to me.'

Nastagio rolled his eyes and began walking along the walkway that flanked the courtyard's south side. 'I will not heat the tongs over the Cristesmaesse hearth. Christ's birth is no time for the ugly business of extracting the truth from the convicted. The time will come.'

'It would be good to exact some clemency.'

'I know what you are thinking, Jacobus. But I do this in the spirit of the season, not to give you some chance at springing him away. Besides, you have no option. Hayeford wants the matter ended, which means we have only a few days left to finish up.'

'But it has ended. What else is there to do?'

'Lord Hayeford does not want to keep your friend William for a year, and since he has already shown his stubbornness, Hayeford proposes to have him burned.'

A cold knot struck at my throat and my stomach turned as though I had swallowed a mouth of ashes. I grasped Nastagio by the robe, and looked at him. His eyes were implacable discs of righteous order. I felt filled with the desire to assert my holy authority, but when my words came out they were cracked and hoarse. 'Burned? No! Why? The sentence was for a year's imprisonment.'

'Come, Jacobus, you know the inquisitorial law. The secular arm must not be impeded once the prisoner is handed to them. If that is Hayeford's desire, I can do nothing to persuade him otherwise.'

I pulled him towards me and thrust my face into his. 'You mean you do not want to persuade him to do otherwise, Inquisitor.'

'Let go of me, Jacobus. You embarrass yourself.' He snatched back his robe and as I stepped back, I saw that people were staring at us across the castle courtyard. My flesh shivered with the cold fire of horror. 'That is the end of the matter,' Nastagio continued, 'unless he confesses, of course. He still has time. But with Hayeford's mind made up, the matter has become somewhat more urgent, for his days are numbered. Do you think you can extract a confession from him?'

'Certainly,' I said with as much conviction as I could muster, though I could not say how much I believed it.

Nastagio glowered at me, as if trying to read how much I believed in what I had claimed. I knew he wanted a confession; I wasn't at all sure that I could deliver it.

'Fine,' he said at last. 'You may see him. But not today. Try to celebrate the day; clear your mind. I brought a bottle of Trebbiano with me, for I cannot stand the honey syrup they call wine here. Come to my cell later, that we may toast the birth of Christ together.'

30TH DECEMBER

IN WHICH
I MEET
A FRIEND
FOR
THE LAST
TIME

LAUDS

Several times over the following days, I attempted to revisit William but despite Nastagio's promise to me, I was not allowed to. Nastagio must have lobbied Hayeford for greater security, for Bastereau the jailor was joined by a second guard—the feasting season meant the guards were at a surplus, so an extra man could be afforded to patrol the dungeon—and thus my attempts were thwarted and my vexed protestations made little impression on the two turnkeys.

When I took my protestations to Nastagio, he told me my wish would be granted, and then waved me away. This foul charade continued for five days, during which time no combination of anger, bribery, summoning of my holy authority nor base pleading worked. I suspected that, given that his days were numbered and the urgency with which a confession was required had increased, William had been moved to the interrogation chamber. I also assumed that he had not yet uttered a confession, for each day the same report was given to the inquisitor. Over the years I had seen many people convicted of heresy or sorcery who had refused to talk, even when placed under extreme duress. In these cases the interrogator often became convinced that some new sorcery was at work that bound the tongue of the accused and prevent them from disclosing the sin of the demon that possessed them. This meant another crime had to be accounted for. I pleaded with Nastagio not to add a further charge to William's burden, and to my surprise he acquiesced.

In the ample time I had to myself, I dedicated myself to prayer and thinking through everything I had done. I was repulsed by what had happened but remained convinced that my way of working was sound and that I had arrived at the only logical conclusion. The great English scholar William of Ockham had fifty years earlier formulated a great logical supposition that dictated that my philosophical approach, based as it was on the employment of as few elements of supposition as possible, was the most likely to be correct. And yet Ockham himself was hounded for heresy and forced into exile. The story goes that he spent his final days with Franciscan friars who were also filled with doubt and dissent towards the powers of the Church. *Speculum mundi*. The world is filled with contradictions.

At last, on the morning of the penultimate day of the year, I was permitted to enter the interrogation chamber. Unlike the intricate and grotesquely ingenious dungeons of the Palais des Papes, Hayeford Castle was equipped with only a small corridor of detention suites, among which were the cells in which Donal and Black Anya had been kept. The torture chamber, hidden behind a thick oak door at the end of the corridor, housed only a small number of interrogation devices: a handful of branding irons in a wooden bucket; a buskin, used for squeezing the foot and leg; various rusty foot presses and thumbscrews; a collection of chains, manacles, collars and fetters; pliers for denailing; and a few whips, flogs, flails and ropes. These were nothing like the marvels of engineering that could be found in France and Austria, but a creative interrogator could work wonders with even this limited equipment. At one point during the festive week I overheard Nastagio ask Hayeford about the imaginative method of torture and execution known as hanging, drawing and quartering.

'The king introduced the Treason Act around fifteen

years ago, and hanging, drawing and quartering is now the typical punishment,' I heard Hayeford reply, in an off-hand manner. 'But I think the practice is a bit older than that,' he added. 'It's quite a spectacle.'

Most inquisitors will not dirty themselves with the messy business of torture but will ensure they are present if a confession is deemed to be imminent, and so Nastagio arranged for daily updates from William's interrogation to be brought to him by Hayeford's men, leaving him to pursue other activities. So far, these had yielded nothing. So it was that Nastagio finally allowed me in, judging that exposing William to a sympathetic face after a week spent only with the interrogator would loosen his tongue.

The torture chamber was small and possessed only of one window—in the shape of a Celtic Cross no more than a cubit in width—which let in a scant strip of light. William sat slumped against a wall, as before, iron fetters clamped around his neck and wrists. His entire body was filthy and the room stank of festering excrement and piss. His head lay forward upon his chest and his breathing was wheezy and shallow. He had been stripped of his clothes and his tonsured head had been roughly shorn. The flesh around his wrists and throat was chafed red raw from the fetters. The right side of his body beneath his ribcage had been branded with a hot iron in the shape of a Cross and there were various rope burns around his limbs. His legs were mangled and bruised, a sure sign of the use of the buskin, the leather straps of which, having been soaked in water and tied round the calves, tighten as they dry.

I had seen such sights—and worse—before, but this time it struck me like a hammer. With a trembling arm, I pulled a three-legged stool from one corner of the room to where William was, but the fetters were too short for him to sit on it and I doubted that his body could have supported his weight, so I sat on it myself. He showed no sign of having acknowledged that I was in the room.

'William,' I said, softly. 'It's Jacobus. I ... I wanted to see you.'

William slowly raised his head and turned it toward me. It was scarlet and puffed up. He gave a moan and tried to speak but the sound was garbled and meaningless. I later learned that one of the interrogation methods used on him was his being forced to drink boiling water. I had protested against this procedure many times—for how was a subject supposed to confess when his mouth had been scalded raw?—but interrogators liked it because it avoided the shedding of blood, which the Inquisition proscribed.

'I have brought you more clean water,' I said softly, at which his eyes opened widely and eagerly. I took that as a signal of acceptance, and from my cloak retrieved the flask which I had smuggled in. I then washed his face as gently as I could, and offered him sips to drink, taking care not to overwhelm him.

He then attempted to speak. 'Why ... Jacobus? Why? Why?'

I did not know what to say! I took his face in my hands while hot tears streamed down my face. 'I did not know it would come to this!' I finally said. 'Why will you not confess? All this would now be behind you.'

'You ... .' He shook his head and began weeping as well, and his face became a grotesque mask of injury and dismay. His chest heaved with the shock of grief, and I held his head against me with a sense of infernal dread.

'I know why you will not confess. But it would have eased your burden!'

We sat that way, with him sobbing weakly against my breast for many minutes, until I began to speak in a weak and hushed voice. 'What is this place, William? What is this strange place which has Green Men made of foliate matter in its woodlands, and men who turn into firebeasts and have apocalyptic visions, and where the people turn freely and happily away from Scripture to seek their own interpretations of the world?'

I paused. William, at the last, seemed to be listening. 'I thought I understood what Scripture was,' I continued. 'Some of it is history. Some of it is law. Some of it is metaphor, and as the Master attested in his *Poetics*, metaphor can be even more powerful than the truth, so much so that it can even seem the truth. When Scripture is married to an objective view of the world, William, it is hard not to arrive at that conclusion. I used to know that demons were not creatures that can be observed in the known world but the representation of human behaviours. The cherubim that guard Paradise are not beasts with the bodies of lions and hooves of goats, wielding a flaming sword, but men—and not special men, but each and every single one of us! Because, through our words we wield great power and guard the realm of holy sanctity in our short and brutal lives. This much I was sure of. And what is more, I had seen it. And then this place revealed to me things I never thought I could see, and I was plunged into a ditch, where everything was upside-down. And I turned you upside-down, too. I placed too much value on my certainties and now my work fills me with such disgust that I do not know whether I shall ever be able to return to it—which means that all has been for nought. Cardinal Banac was right; I ought never to have come. And now I am bereft. But one thing will lighten my burden, and that will be to see you save your own life and continue your good work here. So I ask you one last time: confess. When Nastagio comes to remove you from this accursed cell, tell him you wish to confess, just as I have confessed to you.'

He made a muffled noise and shuffled weakly, as if indicating that he wanted to speak. I cradled his chin upwards to look at me.

'... Did you ... truly see ... the Green ... an ... ?'

Even then, the doubt still gnawed but I nodded and he responded with a smile. 'God will know ... for sure. Water.' And he flicked his blistered eyes towards the flask.

I watered him once more and did what I could to comfort him with prayer and company until he fell into an exhausted but merciful sleep.

31st December

In which the final consequences materialise and leave accuser and accused to learn their fate

LAUDS

It was after the prayer of the dawn—the final dawn of that year of 1367—that Nastagio took me aside.

'It is all arranged, Jacobus. Our carriage is due to leave tomorrow, at the dawn of a new year. It is a time of rebirth. Let us move away from these accursed events.'

'Has William confessed?' I asked in forlorn hope rather than expectation.

'No. His mouth is sealed. He has not uttered anything save proclamations of his love for the Lord and Christ. Latterly he has not even uttered that. The interrogators here are not very skilled. I had to give them instructions on how to proceed. But even after acting on my advice they could not extract a confession. I saw him last night. His flesh is wounded but his defences remain strong.'

Gwendolynn had been released a few days prior. Despite the trial's having been an ordeal, she was fortunate in that it took place close to Cristesmaesse, which limited her incarceration and enabled her to be brought before the congregation at St. Cuthbert's Church in Berwick on the day following the Feast. Magnus attended the service on my behalf—I would not have been welcome—and he refused the protection of the papal guards or archers. When he got back, he told me that he had not imposed himself but had offered blessings and humility where he could. He related that Gwendolynn had once more confessed to her evil deed and, being penitent and not deemed to have relapsed into heresy while being incarcerated in Hayeford's dungeon, in spite of being kept on a diet of foul water and mouldy bread, she was granted the full benefit of abjuration and was welcomed back to the flock with great delight.

I was overjoyed to learn of the merciful swiftness and

resolution of her ordeal. Magnus said that Gwendolynn would spend the rest of the festive season with her five children, eating and enjoying what fruits from the winter harvest had been mustered.

'I heard the strangest thing, Jacobus,' said Nastagio as he led me into the castle's hall to eat. 'Hayeford told me that he sent his men to collect the bodies of the other two pagans from the woods and—oh, look! Mutton. Have you come to like it? Apparently the English love it. I hate it.' We made our choice of the morning's victuals and sat down, Nastagio breaking his fast eagerly on roast veal and parsnips, I picking forlornly at a hunk of rye bread and cheese.

All around us, Hayeford's few Cristesmaesse guests strode about grimly, paying us no heed, having grown quite accustomed to the strange monks from the Empire during the course of the festivities. 'Yes, Hayeford's men went into the woods and when they found the bodies, they couldn't move them. They were as heavy as stone. They cut them open and found the bodies filled with earth. Isn't that extraordinary!'

To Nastagio's astonishment, I laughed.

Hayeford ordered the burnings to take place in the castle grounds. Nastagio offered to conduct them in the stables, away from the festivities, so his guests would not have to look, but Hayeford would not hear of it and saw the burnings as an opportunity for some lively entertainment, and even to collect alms for the Church. He told his seneschal Thirlwall to get the castle's men to build two pyres in the castle's great courtyard at first light and Nastagio supervised the construction. For my part, having insisted on not attending the executions, I took the mid-morning air and watched the pyres being put together.

We came to learn that the English method of burning was to attach the condemned person to a tall stake, above the pyre and flames. In this manner the smoke could cause drowsiness and bring on a deep, merciful sleep before the fire consumed them. Nastagio instead ordered the Spanish method to be used, where the condemned was placed in the centre of a ring-shaped pyre, so he would be roasted alive rather than put to sleep. I had seen skilful Spanish and German executioners apply pitch of differing viscosity to the body of the condemned to prolong the burning, ensuring that the feet and legs would burn first, then the arms, then the torso, and the head and face last of all. But the castle men did not have the wherewithal to learn this—or at least, not in such quick time—so Nastagio settled on an untidy ring of timber to serve the intended purpose.

VESPERS

The English winter had brought a little snow over the feasting period and as the temperature dropped during the day, footsteps had crushed the snow into a dirty ice, making the ground treacherous. After it got dark, lamps lit up the great courtyard, reflecting on frozen puddles and on icicles hanging from the windows, making it a prettier scene than usual, and disguising its usual grubbiness and disorder.

Somewhere from the battlements, a slow drum beat began, and from the chapel came the measured toll of a single bell: the time for the executions had arrived. I remained in the chapel, praying for the soul of William, and even for that of Gibson, if he had a soul, to be returned to God. William deserved to be delivered into the embrace of his Father. He was a kind and gentle man, who loved the people of his community and was loved by them. As for Gibson, his crimes were horrific, but God is all-loving, and even the wicked can be saved after their failed physical vessels have been destroyed.

I observed Vespers in solitude and returned from the chapel to the upper walkways overlooking the courtyard at the heart of the keep. As I walked along a high rampart I slipped on a patch of ice and had to reach out to the frosty battlements to keep from falling. I cursed as I steadied myself and grimaced down at the timber rings and pyres that Nastagio's men had spent the day constructing and that now dominated the space below.

William was supported in his walk to the courtyard by two papal archers. His condition was the same as when I had seen him in the afternoon: dirty, dazed and red raw with injury.

As for Gibson, he had to be dragged into the courtyard because he was incapable of carrying himself. If William looked traumatised, Gibson looked butchered, his face marked by lacerations, cuts, burns and lesions, the rest of his naked body bleeding from open wounds, tears in the flesh and suppurations. His hands and feet were broken. Since the drawing of blood is prohibited during inquisitorial interrogations, I worked out that Nastagio had instructed the interrogator not to extract a confession—that had already come at trial—but to maximise the ogre's suffering, in which case it did not matter if blood was spilt.

My eyes were on William. He was led inside the ring of stakes through a gap and was dragged up a set of steps to the top of the execution stake. There he was tied, the rope being wrapped around his battered torso several times. If William was uttering a prayer, he was doing so in silence; his mangled, scalded mouth would not have been able to muster enough sound to carry to the upper walkways. As a breeze whirled around the bailey, the strong, earthy stench of pitch filled the yard; they were going to tar him after all.

When William had been bound and pitched, Nastagio approached the stricken friar and began to speak. 'Friar William of Alnwick, you are to be put to death by burning on account of your crimes and your failure to confess and repent. Gibson of Wandylaw, you are also to be put to death by burning, on account of your crimes, to which you have freely and without remorse confessed. The secular arm will oversee the proceedings but Lord de Hayeford has requested that we conduct a prayer for the condemned. Since you are soon to pass into an endless and unchangeable state, and your future happiness or misery depends upon the few moments which are left to you, I require you strictly to examine yourself one final time. Let no worldly consideration hinder you from making a true and full confession of your sins, or from repenting for the wrongs and injuries you have caused in your life; that you may find mercy at your heavenly Father's hand, for Christ's sake, and not be condemned in the dreadful day of judgement.'

Nastagio then recited the Articles of the Apostolic Creed, a typical convention in the process of execution, but one I often thought distasteful when the condemned had already been subject to an interrogation and was now unable to answer the questions being asked. William barely summoned the strength to issue a moan of assent when asked about his faith. Gibson did not even appear to be awake.

I was shaking. It had been cold during the day, and it was colder now that the sun had set, but the coldness I felt was in my heart and I could feel it freezing my soul. Aware of the patches of frost on the ground, I clutched at the stonework of the parapet to steady myself on the walkway. A still, silent voice was whispering deep within me that I ought to cry out, demand they halt the proceedings and rescue William before his pyre was lit. But the voice was small and I was small, and every force was ranged against me. Instead I stood and watched.

After the articles of the Apostolic Creed were completed an archer brought forward a torch and lit the pitch-smeared stakes.

Nastagio spoke once more. 'In the midst of life we are in death: of whom may we seek succour but of You, Lord, who for our sins are justly displeased? Yet, O Lord God most holy, O Lord most mighty, O holy and most merciful Saviour, deliver us not into the bitter pains of eternal death.'

The flames began to spread around the rings, at first tentatively but then eagerly, with a thirst for the job at hand. William raised his head but still said nothing. But even if he had somehow being able to confess to the crimes at that moment, it was now too late.

Nastagio continued, projecting his voice louder so that it would carry over the rising fire. 'God, you know the secrets of our hearts; do not turn your ear from our prayers; spare us, Lord most holy, O God most mighty, O holy and merciful Saviour, the most worthy eternal Judge, suffer us not, at our last hour, under any pain of death, to fall from You.'

It was Nastagio's words—*suffer us not, at our last hour, under any pain of death, to fall from You*—that woke me up out of my hellish passivity. In not standing up to the combined forces of Avignon, it was I who had fallen. Nastagio had abused his powers as an inquisitor but I had put my own interests before my holy duty to protect the innocent. I felt suddenly as if I had betrayed Jesus Christ himself, not interceding wholeheartedly to stop him being scourged during his trial and sentencing, then making no adequate complaint as the soldiers of Rome brutalised him into carrying his Cross and nailed him to it. Our Lord had at least received the help of Simon of Cyrene in dragging his burden to Calgary; I had stood by and done nothing. How had I not realised this until now?

In a second, the enormity of my guilt overwhelmed me and my voice at last found its way out from me.

'Stop!' I cried, waving my arms. 'Stop this abomination!'

But Nastagio's voice was booming, and the fire's hiss and crackle drowned out what cries I could make.

In a panic, and now desperate to intervene and prevent the flames from licking away William's flesh, I started to race along the rampart. All I could think of was reaching Nastagio and somehow rescuing my friend from his terrible fate but I'd got no more than ten yards or so as the light snow fell when my feet skidded sideways from under me, and I pitched over the edge of the wall and crashed onto the ground.

Ice.

I have heard storytellers prattle about how time stands still for those who fall through the air and how their brains flood with thoughts. It is but talk. One moment I was running along the top of the castle wall, the next I was flat on my back, twenty-foot down, on the cold, stony ground, trying to understand how I could so casually have lost my footing, and now perhaps my life. I couldn't move. I was overwhelmed by a pain in my upper body like nothing I had ever felt before and the realisation that I could not feel my legs or make them move. Blood pooled around me and great waves of sound pounded in my ears, but as I fought not to pass out, I kept hearing again the terrible sound of my back snapping.

I lay alone and immobile, staring blankly at the sky, bewildered and furious at my own incompetence and wondering what facilities were left to me and how long I would last. I wanted to call out for help but my jaw only quivered and no sound emerged.

I remember that at that very moment, just when my voice failed, William and Gibson found theirs, for there came one monstrous shriek after another, both made inhuman and perverse by what I assumed was the scorching of their mouths and throats. One, perhaps Gibson's, was an ancient, animal screech too terrible to bear hearing. The other may not even have been an intentional sound so much as the air being forced from their lungs by the heat.

And now, as the barbarity played out, its author, Nastagio, pronounced the ceremonial liturgy. 'Unto God's gracious mercy and protection you are now committed,' he incanted. 'The Lord bless you and keep you. The Lord make his face to shine upon you and be gracious unto you. The Lord lift up his countenance upon you and provide you with peace, both now and evermore. Amen.'

The shrieks of the two dying men vied with the crackle of the flames as the awful stink of burnt hair and flesh wafted into the air. I tried to turn my head to look at them, assuming that I would now join them in death, but I could not move. And then I passed out.

IN THE YEAR
1368

1st January

In which I awake and the full extent of my injuries is revealed

TERCE

I awoke. I had not expected that, and was somewhat dazed to find myself in a quiet, dark room instead of being surrounded by fire and the screaming of the damned. By my bed was Nastagio di Balino. The inquisitorial zeal that had carved itself into his face at the burning the day before had melted away, leaving behind a becalmed softness.

'So, you are alive,' he said.

Instinctively I gripped the side of the cot I was in and motioned to see if I could get out of bed, but while my arm moved, no part of the rest of me would follow. I tried to pull harder, but had neither strength nor energy, and could only lie on my back, staring at the ceiling and panting. The scent of rose petals and rosemary being burned somewhere in the room intoxicated me. Though I knew the herbs were to soothe me, the burning stench appalled me.

'Hush, Jacobus,' said Nastagio, taking my hand and placing it upon my chest. 'Rest.'

I looked at him. It seemed to require the strength of Samson just for me to turn my face towards Nastagio.

'I fell,' I said, my voice as dry as a whisper.

'Badly,' he said. 'It is over now.'

'What … ?'

'You took a blow to the spine. The infirmarian believes it to be cracked.'

I let out a weak moan and looked up again to the ceiling.

'Hayeford has said you can stay here until you are fit to return home. Not that he is happy about it. He wants us gone and I admit to sharing his sentiment. I can bear this miserable place no longer.'

I flicked my eyes toward him—even the thought of moving my head again left me nauseous—and looked at him imploringly.

'But I will not leave until you are ready. I do not trust Hayeford to give you the care you deserve, so I have decided to stay and ensure that you are not ill-treated. You are a man of God, Jacobus.'

Having barely any capacity for speech, I breathed out a long and baleful sigh, and wept—painfully.

I spent the next two months in a tortured convalescence, ensconced in the infirmarian's cell, with only Nastagio di Balino for comfort. The castle's physician, a man named Stagg, was made responsible for my treatment. He was a bullish, hard-faced man with a brusque manner yet he was skilful and knowledgeable. He spoke little. On those rare occasion when he loosened his tongue, he would tell me that he had learned his trade in Crécy in the service of the King, and had seen injuries like mine many times, when knights fell from horseback.

One day Nastagio told me that he and Stagg had discussed the teachings of Roland of Parma, a renowned physician from Nastagio's homeland. Roland had emphasised that spinal injuries needed early treatment. A course of manual extension of the spine, coupled with vigorous massaging of the extremities, was recommended and Stagg took it upon himself to administer these treatments with vigour.

I can safely say that there is a thin line between the tortures administered by the inquisitor and those administered by the physician. Perhaps the recovery of the body must, by design, be as terrible and agonising as the recovery of the soul. Or as the experience of birth for the mother.

A week into my stay Stagg declared he was going to try a radical French treatment called a laminectomy. I was not familiar with the procedure and when I asked for details, he replied that it would be better if I remained ignorant. It was with some grim irony that I realised that only a few days before, I would have scoffed at the idea of remaining ignorant.

Ahead of the procedure Stagg drugged me with opium and wine before getting to work. As it turned out, despite looking more like a blacksmith than a surgeon, Stagg was gifted with no little art, and later informed me that he had made a short incision at the top of the spine and removed a quantity of inflamed tissue. This was to relieve the pressure on the remainder of my spine. It left me in monstrous pain but, to my amazement, his remedy soon brought me some relief. I started to regain some feeling in my legs, and Stagg —a hard taskmaster as well as a deft surgeon—encouraged me to sit up, then stand, and eventually make baby steps, ignoring my agonised protestations.

8TH MARCH

IN WHICH
I TAKE
MY LEAVE
AND
CONSIDER
WHAT MY EPISODE
IN ENGLAND
HAS TAUGHT
ME

SEXT

Though my recovery was slow, Lord de Hayeford made it clear that I had long outstayed his hospitality and that he wanted us out of the castle just as soon as my physical condition allowed it. It was, in any case, that we wanted to leave just as much as he wanted us out. By contrast, Stagg did not want me to go; he expressed concern about the effects of the roads upon my back and thought I should stay longer, but his Hippocratic instinct was subordinated to the misanthropic whim of his master. So instead he supplied me with opium and said he would pray for me. In the meantime, whereas my unwelcome presence seemed to distract Hayeford from the horror of what he had allowed to happen on his demesne, the castle would not release me from the thought of my own sins and shortcomings, and nowhere more so than where marks of the long-since dismantled execution pyre could still be seen.

Among the many things I learned during my trip to England was that the English winter is spiteful, and bears a grudge. Unlike the southern part of our European continent, England does not loosen its frostbitten grip upon the land for many months. Even by March, the temperature was still intolerably frigid, and the amelioration of my injuries was stifled by this bitter, protracted cold.

When we eventually left, the wagon that took us south was rickety and open to the elements, and Nastagio and I had to sit in the rear. The papal archers and swordsmen travelled on foot either side of us; Magnus had long since departed the country. On the day of our departure, the procession left Hayeford Castle shortly after we broke our fast, as soon as Thirlwall and his men could load up our meagre things.

I had the feeling that Nastagio was embarrassed by

my becoming a cripple—disgusted, even—though he had the good grace never to say anything to offend me, and the fact that he had remained with me argued that, despite everything, he still felt some abiding loyalty towards me as a fellow Churchman.

I was not yet able to walk independently, and so was carried to the wagon by the papal archers in a makeshift carrycot—a final humiliation, but no less than I deserved. I had felt inclined to read the story of Job, and in the pit of my depression I drew some solace from it:

Usquequo affligitis animam meam, et atteritis me sermonibus? En decies confunditis me, et non erubescitis opprimentes me. Nempe etsi ignoravi, mecum erit ignorantia mea. At vos contra me erigimini, et arguitis me opprobriis meis. Saltem nunc intelligite quia Deus non aequo judicio afflixerit me, et flagellis suis me cinxerit.[14]

For my part, I did not feel God's net close around me. I only felt the English cold—lingering, lingering.

Lord de Hayeford had arranged transit for us as far south as Nottingham, where we would be able to pick up a convoy to London and then to the coast. Hayeford thanked us once again for our work, though he said it with no grace. From his perspective my performance in the region had done what was needed. I had got rid of the Scots, and Odenellus and his henchmen had been destroyed, but now he was focusing on the French, about

---

[14] How long will you torment me and crush me with words? Ten times now you have reproached me; shamelessly you attack me. If it is true that I have gone astray, my error remains my concern alone. If indeed you would exalt yourselves above me and use my humiliation against me, then know that God has wronged me and drawn his net around me.

whom I heard him muttering dark things even before we were through his gates.

Nastagio was pale and exhausted, and spent much of the journey with his head leaning against the wooden chassis of the vehicle, drifting in and out of a sleep. The execution and its aftermath—and I suppose the entire episode—had sucked the vigour from him. He did not look like a fire-breathing zealot any longer; he was more like an innocent child, cold and yearning for home. He had covered himself with layers of blankets to ward off the frost; I refused any such comfort. Hayeford may have thought I had achieved something; I knew I had not, and I sat in sullen silence.

It was shortly after noon, when the sun was at its brightest for the day and our procession stopped for a short rest, that Nastagio roused himself and produced from his satchel a stick of good bread, which he tore and ate. He offered me some, but I declined.

'You must eat, Jacobus,' he said, rubbing his arms for warmth. 'Surely you are not still at war with yourself over this whole episode?'

I had nothing to say and looked instead across the blasted English countryside.

'I understand, Jacobus. You think I do not but I do. It hurts, this work we do: it causes pain, and shock, and because we are weak creatures of flesh, it raises as many questions as it answers. But I think of the words of Eymeric: "The death of the sheep is the life of the lion; the destruction of the grass is the life of the sheep." Without these trials, there would be no need for us inquisitors and judges. Martyrs only become martyrs because tyrants exist. All is merely light and dark, opposing sides of a coin. I know you think I revel in the triumph of my work and it is true that I am not immune to the vulgarity of pride, but even I sometimes feel the hollow centre of our work, for the cost of triumph is that heresy must exist. So look to the Lord, Jacobus. He sees your true path.'

My true path! I lay prostrate in my silly little cot, but with my satchel upon my chest. Just as Stagg had predicted, the rough roads were tormenting my ruined back. With painful effort I opened the satchel and pulled out the books I had brought with me: *Summa Zoologica*, *Compendium de Almaheste*, *Summa Logicae*, *Summa Contra Gentiles*, *Quaestiones disputatae de Veritate*, *De perfectione vitae spiritualis*, and more. One by one I dropped them over the side of the wagon, each landing with a splat upon the muddy path. Nastagio eyed the episode with some bemusement.

'Do you think that will lighten your load?'

Again I did not answer. In all honesty I could not answer. I had expected that disposing of my books would produce some great eruption of traumatic emotion, just as I had expected a reaction when my friend had been burned, but it too produced nothing. Cold had taken a grip on my heart. I was encased in ice.

As the procession continued its journey southward, I saw ghosts by the side of the road, one by one, appearing and disappearing and appearing again. William walked alongside the wagon for short stretches, murmuring a quiet prayer as he trod through the mud. Every so often he looked up at me but his expression was unreadable. We drove past Gwendolynn, kneeling on the grass, Emeline and Peter playing beside her. She too looked up and eyed me with frosty dispassion. The pagan Odenellus and his two acolytes stood watching me in the mud, covered in leaves. Then Poole turned up, walking serenely, his face in flame, pointing at me accusingly. He opened his mouth and I could hear his voice in my head: *Si quis habet aurem audiat.* And they were not alone. Behind them, unbeknownst to them but shadowing their every step, was the Green Man. He placed a knotted, root-like hand upon Gwendolynn's shoulder and the vines sprouting from its limbs crept around her, investigating her, claiming her for his own. As he stood behind William, shoots and leaves grew with impossible alacrity out of his eyes and mouth, which became engorged into a grotesque foliate grin, and he extended his writhing fingers around William's waist, supporting and exploring him like the tentacles of an octopus. Then he was with Odenellus, and vines and creepers poured out of his eyes and mouth, and shoots grew from beneath his shattered fingernails. And at last he walked beside Poole, grasping him too, and was not burned by his apocalyptic flame.

I wailed upon seeing this, and Nastagio, who was falling back into a dull sleep, jumped awake.

'What is it, Jacobus?'

But there was nothing I could say. I knew there was no use in pointing out what he could not see. It was not just that I had broken my back; I was a broken man.

I returned to the Abbeye de Saint André but from then on I only sought forgiveness from the world, rather than knowledge. I continued my rehabilitation and eventually became able to walk again, first with the use of a frame and after much time with a stick. The stick was, of course, made of wood and each time I looked at it I wondered if it might sprout vines and creepers and come alive in my hand. It became, then, yet another reminder of my follies, the thought of which I could not free myself from. I therefore plunged myself into prayer and work, and removed myself from the rigours of judgement and Inquisition. In expiation of my poor soul I tilled the earth and learned how to tend the sick.

I am old now, and my end approaches, as does the end of the fourteenth century of Our Lord. In my twilight years I look back on my time in England as a watershed; what I learned there I still have not come to terms with, nor can I say whether what I encountered there was the practice of sorcery or a mysterious reality, an unholy power quite separate from the Glory of God, the like of which I had never given credence to before but which I now cannot let go. I think I saw demons during those weeks in England; but even if I didn't, the thought of them haunts me still.

How queer it is that as age bequeaths wisdom, the more does it come wrapped in the wonderment of the child. I am ever more mystified that a world that had seemed to make increasing sense as I got to know it suddenly turned out to have a secret nature, one that all my learning could not penetrate and which made a mockery of the great philosophers and what they had taught me.

My sin, then, is great. I cannot say for sure whether the world that I had previously been exposed to was that of Our Lord or of logic. I cannot say, either, with any certainty, whether I truly saw a Green Man in the forest, but I can say without any doubt that I see him now. I see him at night after I have closed my eyes, standing behind William, who still burns on the pyre in my mind, with cords wrapped around his face. I see him during the day. I see him, dragging the body of Odenellus beneath the cold earth, when I am at prayer. And I see him still in Poole, wreathed in fire, pointing his finger at me, telling me his warning: that if any man have an ear, let him hear. Only with age have I come to understand that.

I also feel the cold. Even on warm Provençal summer days when I am tending the vegetable plots of the Abbeye de Saint André, the English ice that tripped me and left my backbone shattered still lingers in me. I doubt I shall ever be rid of it.

So whether the Green Man was really ever there all those long years ago in that forest, he is with me now and is a part of me forever, to carry the pain until such time as the Lord calls me to His side at the moment of reckoning, or casts me into the Inferno. What else can a sinner do but bear it?

FINIS

ACKNOWLEDGE-
MENTS

Brother Jacobus may have journeyed to the outer reaches of the civilised world, but he didn't journey there alone. There were others who read, assisted and supported him and made *The Green Man* the book it is today.

First, I thank my publisher Stephen Games and his colleagues Maggie and Alice at EnvelopeBooks. Stephen took a chance on a rough diamond of a manuscript and deployed his vision and diligence to hone it to a high gleam. Stephen is something of an old-fashioned publisher (and I can think of no higher praise than that) as he really works with his authors, offering insights and suggestions, but also listening to them to understand what they are trying to achieve. That is rare these days, when so many books are treated simply as commercial products, and I valued it.

In addition I thank Christopher Bean, who more than anyone convinced me that *The Green Man* was something worth pursuing. His encouragement kept me going, and I am forever grateful. I wish also to record my indebtedness to Peat Long for his pragmatic feedback and views about the world. Never change.

Next, perhaps appropriately for a book featuring an Ioannic apparition, there comes a quartet of Johns to thank. First Jon Rogers and John Hayward, my beta readers, who sorted the mendicants from the monastics and helped me navigate the ins and outs of ecclesiastical law. And then the legends that are John Jarrold and John Langan, for being so charitable and generous with your time. Thank to them all.

Last I must thank Jo and Ava and Penelope, who once again allowed me to go off on an adventure, this time to the fourteenth century, and to return with a tale worth telling.

More Fiction from EnvelopeBooks

Secrets of the Four-Chambered Heart | Steven Jay Griffel
In 1994 a group of Americans and Rwandans meet in the Rwandan capital of Kigali. The Americans have been sent by *The New York Times* to cover the ethnic violence; the Rwandans are there to treat the wounded and prepare them for interview. They all need to collaborate, but the more they engage, the more their own conflicts surface, exposing unexpected secrets that get ever-harder to conceal. A very deft piece of authorial plotting that defies reader expectation.

Mrs Woodbine's Prejudices | Michael Ladner
Prof. Arthur Lash, born Artur Lasch in pre-war Austria, takes his American wife and their three sons back to Vienna, in 1960, to see how well his father is rebuilding the life that was interrupted by Nazi Germany's annexation of Austria in 1938. For Arthur, the journey helps him re-establish his links with the city he was brought up in; for the rest of his family, other emotions are awoken—all watched over by Mrs. Woodbine, the needy, disregarded but loyal family nanny.

Belle Nash and the Bath Soufflé | William Keeling Esq.
In the first volume of *The Gay Street Chronicles*, bachelor Belle Nash attempts to navigate bigotry and corruption in 1830s Bath without compromising his boyfriend, the nephew of Immanuel Kant, or his best friend, the widow of Bath's greatest lawyer. Intrigue and whimsy overflow after—horror!—a soufflé fails to rise.

The Train House on Lobengula Street | Fatima Kara
An anguished, folksy and life-affirming novel, set within the Indian community in Bulawayo, Rhodesia, from the 1940s to the 1960s, about the capacity of women to gain the same advantages as men in the modern world while remaining faithful to traditional Muslim values. Affectionate and passionate.

Mustard Seed Itinerary | Robert Mullen
Po Cheng falls into a dream and finds himself on the road to the imperial Chinese capital. Once there he rises to the heights of the civil service, then discovers that in addition to the ladders that helped him ascend, there are snakes facilitating his fall. Carrollian satire at its best.

Frances Creighton: Found and Lost | Kirby Porter
Love demands trust, but trust is a lot to ask for a victim of abuse. Having been bullied in Belfast as a boy, at his school and at his church, Michael Roberts suppresses his childhood pains until the death of a girlfriend years later forces him to revisit lost memories.

A Sin of Omission | Marguerite Poland
An emotionally intense novel, set in 1870s South Africa at a time of rising anti-colonial resistance. The book examines the tragedy of a promising black preacher, hand-picked for training in England as a missionary, only to be neglected by the Church he loves. Winner of the 2021 *Sunday Times* CNA 'Book of the Year' Award in South Africa.

A Girl's Own War | K.J. Kelly
Flt. Lieut. Oliver Carmichael and Baron Julius von Stulpnagel had been living together in Berlin, trying to sell forged paintings. Why are they now in run-down Ballingore, in wartime neutral Ireland in 1940, and how will ex-convent-girl Mary Collins and her devoted red-headed sidekick Niamh Slattery play into their hands? Hilarious Irish farce.

The Attraction of Cuba | Chris Hilton
Chris Hilton went to Cuba to escape the boredom of everyday life and to make money, only to be entranced by the beauty of the country and of Yamilia, a street girl who brought him love and laughter but who could not help him from falling into an inevitable downward spiral.

Lagos, Life and Sexual Distraction | Tunde Ososanya
Twelve short stories, mostly focused on the struggle to survive in Lagos, Nigeria's commercial capital, illustrate the tensions that exist between the generations, between the sexes and between the country's different social classes and ethnicities.

Belle Nash and the Bath Circus | William Keeling Esq.
In Volume Two of *The Gay Street Chronicles*, bachelor Belle Nash returns to Regency Bath from Grenada, inspired by a new love that leads him into various pretences that may compromise the ambitions of black circus impresario Pablo Fanque.

Princess Brainy | Stephen Games
Poor Princess Raine couldn't help being hated for being clever, but it didn't help that her mother was modern and made her father ban the fairies. So what should she do when disaster hit Rainland and the rivers dried up? Accept her fate or get sacrificed to the revolution?

The Hopeful Traveller | Janina David
A collection of short stories about—and told by—single women who have put the past behind them but are still looking for their anchor in the present. It includes bitter-sweet accounts of the freedoms of postwar life, of foreign travel, of the rekindling of old friendships and of the search for new ones.

Non-Fiction from EnvelopeBooks

A Question of Paternity | David Tereshchuk
TV reporter David Tereshchuk has traveled the world questioning the perpetrators of injustice and their victims, but could never prise one answer from his own mother: who his father was. Her evasion set him off on a life of insecurity and alcoholism. And a quest.

The West and the Rest | Ian Ross

Having worked in the oil and tobacco industries, Ian Ross argues that trade is objectively more creative than democracy in bridging cultural divisions. Where diplomats are held back by caution and principle, business executives are incentivised to be adaptable, forward-looking, unprejudiced and trusting. An eye-opener.

The Martyrdom of Ahmad Shawkat | Michael Goldfarb

When Gulf War II broke out in 2003, Ahmad Shawkat became guide and translator to NPR-reporter Michael Goldfarb. After the fall of Saddam, Ahmad set up a cultural magazine, published eleven issues and was killed for publicly decrying Islamic terror. This is his story.

From Bedales to the Boche | Robert Best

Bedales, the progressive boarding school founded by J.H. Badley in 1893, instilled values that sustained many of its pupils for the rest of their lives. Robert Best recalls its influence on him as an enthusiastic army recruit in 1914 and, from 1916, in the Royal Flying Corps.

Wembley Speaks: A Year in the Life of a London Suburb

How do people talk to each other, react to each other, give and ask for advice, conciliate, commiserate and laugh? In a modern reconstruction of Mayhew's landmark 19th-century social study, EnvelopeBooks turns to the *Nextdoor* social networking app to observe a community engaging with itself on day-to-day issues. A priceless archive.

A Road to Extinction | Jonathan Lawley

When Britain colonised the Andamans in 1857, the welfare of its African pygmy inhabitants was of no concern. Nine tribes died out. Dr Lawley now assesses the survival prospects for the three remaining tribes and weighs up the legacy of his grandfather, a former colonial administrator

Lost Levant: A Journey of Ideas | Rupert de Borchgrave
In the last millennium, cultural innovation has moved inexorably westwards, leaving us with too small a grasp of the turmoil out of which our own civilisation grew. In 2003 Rupert de Borchgrave set off on a journey of ideas that took him to the much-disputed grounds where many of the possibilities and problems that shape us now were formed.

Why My Wife Had To Die | Brian Verity
There is no known cure for Huntington's disease, a wasting condition that sufferers acquire from a parent. In this painful account, the author vents his rage at society, lawmakers, health services and the Church for not grasping the need, as he sees it, to legalise compulsory sterilisation and assisted dying.

Artist Spy Prisoner | George Tomaziu
Artist George Tomaziu was imprisoned and tortured for monitoring Nazi troop movements through Bucharest during the Second World War but imagined that his heroism would be recognised if Romania ever became free. He was terribly mistaken. Three years after the war ended he was imprisoned again—this time for thirteen years.

My Modern Movement | Robert Best
London's Festival of Britain in 1951 marked the belief that Modern design was visually, morally and commercially superior. Robert Best, the UK's leading lighting manufacturer, thinks the dice were loaded. This is his memoir.

Postmark Africa | Michael Holman
Made an Amnesty Prisoner of Conscience while he was under house arrest as a student in Rhodesia, the author went on to document Africa's emergence from colonialism as Africa Editor of the *Financial Times*. This book is a must-read introduction to Africa's dreams of independence.

Printed in Dunstable, United Kingdom